Always new. Often controversial . . .

This is what NEW DESTINIES is all about . . .

. . . reversing the death of millions in violent catastrophe as Charles Sheffield defuses nuclear winter.

. . . one small man disrupting the universe: "Time Bomb" by Timothy Zahn.

. . . losing your heart to a waif—and your head to "Wires," in the super sequel to F. Paul Wilson's award-winning "Dydeetown Girl."

. . . controlled experiments *proving* telekinesis. Author, pilot, raconteur Martin Caidin will challenge your preconceptions with "Fiction This Ain't."

Not enough? Then check into one of Baen's Coke Clinics, and "Just Say Yes—to Freedom."

EDITED BY
JIM BAEN

NEW DESTINIES

Summer Edition 1988

**EDITOR IN CHIEF**
Jim Baen

**SENIOR EDITOR**
Elizabeth Mitchell

**MANAGING EDITOR**
Toni Weisskopf

BAEN BOOKS

NEW DESTINIES, Summer 1988

Copyright © 1988 by Baen Publishing Enterprises

A Baen Books Original

Baen Publishing Enterprises
260 Fifth Avenue
New York, N.Y. 10001

First printing, May 1988

ISBN: 0-671-65408-X

Cover art by Gregory A. West

Printed in the United States of America

Distributed by
SIMON & SCHUSTER
1230 Avenue of the Americas
New York. N.Y. 10020

# CONTENTS

## Introduction

In the last issue of New Destinies I promised to present a "perversely Libertarian plan for dealing with the drug problem, the deficit, and organized crime, all in one swell foop." As with my previous modest proposal ("Let's Kill NASA Today!") all it would take is a teensy weensy bit of tax policy. . . .

That's the trouble with tax policy: it's like a recreational drug. The immediate effects feel wonderful, and the negative effects take so long to happen that you tend not to relate them to their cause. The first time, proposing the use of the power of taxation to coerce rather than to raise revenues is a serious philosophical decision. After that it's easy.

Take me, for example. Last issue I gave way to the urge to meddle in other people's affairs through the tax code in order to save the human race from eternal misery by commencing the Age of Space. This time my goal is relatively trivial: to save several nations from being destabilized by the drug trade; to end the drug wars; to rehabilitate a large proportion of the millions of drug-dependent persons in the USA and elsewhere; and to cure the national deficit. Next issue I will probably be willing to use tax policy to encourage people to wear solar-powered propeller beanies. So it goes.

Still, there is one benefit to this proposal that is not common to most tax policy: the net effect would be to lessen government intrusion in the affairs of its citizens, and enlarge the area of legitimate civil liberties.

Well, enough build-up.

# DRUGS AND THE LAW

## or, Just Say "Yes"—to Freedom

As my second proposal for making the world a better place, I propose that we remove all criminal restraints on the purchase and consumption of cocaine. If the effects are as salutary as there is every reason to expect, other currently illegal substances would be similarly decriminalized in quick succession.

Before you dismiss this proposal out of hand, consider the benefits. First and foremost: the entire illicit distribution infrastructure, complete with its modest but respectful quasi-military forces from the K-9 Corps (pit bulls), to troops armed with automatic rifles, to *gunships*, would collapse, and the nightly invasion of our southern shores by air, land, and sea would be instantly halted. (As with alcohol at the end of Prohibition, why smuggle what can be imported legally?) Thousands of murderous inner-city encounters per year would never happen. Thousands of our police and customs officers would never be faced with bribes of irresistible size. (What would *you* be willing to "not see" for a hundred thousand dollars?) Foreign governments would no longer be tempted to aid and abet their drug traffickers in violating us.

Yes, the negative benefits would be startlingly large,

but there is also a major *positive* benefit. Americans spend about fifty billion dollars a year on cocaine at retail. Maybe one billion of that is necessary cost of production and distribution. The other forty-nine billion or so goes to smuggling, bribery, suborning of government officials, legal costs, murder, truly obscene profits, and so forth. By interesting coincidence forty-nine billion is about the size of the current federal deficit, and at first blush it would seem that virtually the entire forty-nine billion would be available for taxation.

So exactly how do we go about it? Simple. Give it to the friendly folks of the Internal Revenue Service. They deal with firearms and alcohol already, so all it would take is a bit of scaling up of their normal enforcement activities. And I expect they would be happy to deal with the resulting revenue.

The basic operating principle would be quite simple: only state-authorized vendors can sell it, and anybody who can legally buy booze can use it—but only with a license. Penalties for unauthorized snorting or dealing would be commensurate with the penalities for counterfeiting, and the rate of taxation would be determined by the street price: i.e., the legitimate price would be the current black-market price less whatever discount is necessary to put the competition out of business. When the current highly organized worldwide drug conspiracy had become a nasty memory, the rate of taxation would be determined by the condition of non-regulated trade in cocaine; if an underground begins to build up even in the face of severe user penalties, then the state price is too high. If there is no underground trade at all, the state price is too low. This "market mechanism" would be as simple and efficient as a thermostat.

If you feel that any government regulation and control of cocaine would amount to condoning its use and all the consequent social evils, consider the social evils we—already—suffer from attempting to totally suppress the activity. Furthermore, at present it is largely innocent general society that bears those costs and not the incontinent and uncaring persons who reap whatever benefits there may be.

We now come to the one practical objection to this approach to minimizing the trade in cocaine: Dare we "put our faith in princes?" Can we trust the government to be resolute in setting the price at a level that will make the illicit trade a non-profit endeavor, but within that constraint to set the price so high as to minimize use?

What's to stop the state from becoming just another pusher? After all, alcohol and tobacco are generally regarded as being socially noxious and personally debilitating substances, and yet the tax policy governing them hardly tends to minimize their use.

Well, that's where regulation comes in. For once we can give the regulators their heads. Let them think up and implement every conceivable demeaning, deflating, embarrassing, time-consuming and otherwise obnoxious bureaucratic ritual that has ever haunted their wettest dreams of petty power—and implement them ALL. *Harness* their will to power!

The ambience of a "cocaine boutique" should be somewhere between that of a venereal disease clinic for indigent persons and a New York City neighborhood post office, with a touch of 3:00 A.M. at the station house thrown in. And it should take at least three hours to make a purchase, and the maximum amount of purchase should be a three-hour high . . . And of course you would need to have previously gotten yourself put on the User's List for your neighborhood (available for public perusal), and maybe renounced your right to vote for at least one year (regardless of age, cocaine-dependent persons are *ipso facto* non-adults), and . . . and . . . But there are Others (shudder) far more competent than I to think up debasing rituals for interacting with government agencies.

So there you have it. A modest proposal for a major social benefit. And all it would take is just a teensy bit of tax policy . . .

—BAEN

## Introduction

It wasn't so long ago that you couldn't pick up a newspaper without seeing numerous references to "Nuclear Winter." Now that the basic thesis has been revealed as errant nonsense quite willfully foisted on a trusting populace, The Year Without A Sun is in the process of sliding gracefully down the Memory Hole. It's perpetrators have never specifically disavowed the Nuclear Winter scam, mind you; they just don't talk about it much, anymore.

The one lasting legacy of this exercise of agitprop masquerading as science will be that a lot of people, including those in the highest reaches of government, will vaguely recall that a limited nuclear exchange wouldn't be so terrible as was once thought. Now that is scary.

# UNCLEAR WINTER

*Charles Sheffield*

**INTRODUCTION**

The scenario is almost too familiar.

War breaks out between the United States and the Soviet Union. The cause of the final conflict is not relevant, but both sides unleash the full force of their nuclear arsenals. Within hours, the energy of 25,000 one-megaton hydrogen bombs has been released. Most of the United States and the Soviet Union, including all the major cities, is a flaming wilderness of destruction and radioactive contamination.

And then the real trouble starts.

The initial explosions, together with the fires that they have created, carry gigantic amounts of dust and smoke high into the upper atmosphere. It lingers there, blocking out sunlight, for months or years. On the surface below, temperatures drop dramatically. The earth is darkened, crops are frozen or fail to mature, and starvation becomes a universal problem. The civilization of the world collapses, and the development of humanity is set back for hundreds or thousands of years.

This is "nuclear winter," a projected future that suggests that the Doomsday Machine of Dr. Strangelove is already in our possession. For it is not necessary that both sides release their bombs. If either one does, the subsequent winter will destroy the aggressor country along with the intended victim. A pre-emptive "first strike" does nothing to guarantee a nation's security.

The general concept of nuclear winter is not new. It goes back at least to 1974, when a paper by J. Hampson was published in *Nature*. A year later, the National Academy of Sciences issued a report covering the same theme: "Long-Term Worldwide Effects of Multiple Nuclear-Weapon Detonations." It assumed that 10,000 one-megaton hydrogen bombs would be used in an all-out nuclear war, and drew the conclusion that the effects on the whole ecosystem would be small. The report was somewhat criticized as encouraging military solutions to general political problems, but mostly it was ignored. The whole subject was apparently of minor interest until 1983, when the paper "Nuclear Winter: Global Consequences of Multiple Nuclear Explosions" by Turco, Toon, Ackerman, Pollack and Sagan, and subsequent press conferences, introduced the phrase "nuclear winter" and gave the idea wide circulation.

The subject quickly became a hot issue for debate. On the one hand, the proponents of nuclear winter felt that they had a new and irrefutable case against anyone who thought it might be possible to "win" a nuclear war. On the other hand, critics said the analysis was inadequate and misleading. The models were accused of being (literally) one-dimensional, of ignoring the heat reservoir capacity of the oceans, and of assuming that there would be too rapid atmospheric mixing, so that the southern hemisphere would suffer as badly as the northern one.

The Pentagon in particular didn't want to hear anything about nuclear winter. If the idea were valid, it made the point that our arsenals are just as dangerous to us as to any possible enemy.

The criticisms of the original models seem to be valid. However, none of them proves that there will be no nuclear winter effects. They merely reduce the estimated size of the effect.

Reduce it, by how much?

No one is sure. There has never been an atmospheric nuclear explosion providing more than a thousandth of the energy release of a full-scale nuclear war. Also, even the biggest atmospheric tests were not conducted in areas where forest or urban fires could result. Thus all the arguments rely a great deal on theoretical (and simplified) results, on analogy, and on preconceived ideas. And the key question, what would all-out nuclear war do on a long-term global scale, remains unanswered. So does a rather different, but equally important question: how do the risks of nuclear winter compare with other forms of disaster?

## THIS IS THE WAY THE WORLD ENDS

All-out war is not the only way to produce the possible collapse of civilization predicted by nuclear winter.

In this article we will examine some of the alternatives, and see how likely they are to serve as instruments of doom.

The production of nuclear winter effects, by any mechanism, calls for the release of a great deal of energy. The way that this energy is delivered to Earth's biosphere is important, but the easiest way to begin is by looking at the raw energy provided by different events.

Here are some prime candidates:

1) Nuclear war
2) Earthquakes
3) Volcanic eruptions
4) Meteorite impacts
5) Solar flares
6) Nearby supernovas

To provide a standard of comparison, we will first consider a natural energy source which is definitely not destructive to the biosphere: the tides.

# TIDAL ENERGY

Humans harness a negligible fraction of tidal energy, although the available energy is huge. Other species do rather better, and the intertidal zones are the most biologically productive regions of the world, more so than even the tropical rain forests. On the average, waves powered by the tides deliver to the shoreline 0.335 watts per square centimeter, several times as much energy as comes from the Sun. Even so, the coastal area is small compared with the open oceans, and almost all tidal energy remains untapped.

A ballpark figure for the total energy is easy to calculate (though not easy to find in the literature). Let's assume that the tides raise and lower the mean sealevel of Earth's oceans by two meters, twice a day. Since the oceans cover 70% of the globe, and the total surface area of Earth is about 500 million square kilometers, the total tidal energy proves to be about 2.8 E26 ergs.*

This value of available tidal energy is probably good to within a factor of two, and we will not be trying to obtain results better than that.

# NUCLEAR WAR

To compare tidal energy with the energy release of a full-scale nuclear war, we have to make some assumption about the number and size of the bombs that are available. We will employ the same figures as in the 1983 "Nuclear Winter" paper by Turco et al., 25,000 megatons of TNT equivalent. Since one million tons of TNT release 4.2 E22 ergs of energy, our nuclear war can produce a total of $10^{27}$ ergs (assuming all the mis-

*For ease of typesetting I will often use computer notation for floating-point numbers. Thus 2.8 E26 is exactly the same as $2.8 \times 10^{26}$, but avoids the use of superscripts. Also, the erg is a standard but very small unit. The daily energy output of a sizable (1,000 Megawatt) power station is 8.64 E20 ergs. A one-megaton hydrogen bomb produces 4.2 E22 ergs, or a month and a half production from a large power station.

siles are fired, and they all work—an assumption that anyone who has had dealings with the Defense Department will have a lot of trouble swallowing).

The available daily energy of tides is thus about one-quarter of that produced by a full-scale nuclear war. However, that tidal energy is available *every day*; nuclear war can never be a regular event.

## EARTHQUAKES

Earthquakes are interesting in their own right. However, I am going to give them short shrift. Although they do tremendous damage, they do it mainly at ground (and sea) level, and they do not send finely-divided material high into the atmosphere. Earthquakes are thus not going to be a major source of nuclear winter effects.

There are two different scales used to measure the intensity of earthquakes. The better-known one, called the Richter Scale, was developed by C.F. Richter in 1935, and is now routinely reported for most earthquakes around the world. It is actually an energy scale, and a *logarithmic* scale, at that, so a Richter rating of, say, 7.5, releases ten times as much energy as one with a rating of 6.5, and a hundred times as much energy as one of 5.5.

As a rule-of-thumb, property damage begins with about magnitude 5. The largest recorded earthquakes rated 8.6 on the Richter Scale. There have been four of them: Alaska, on September 10th, 1899; Colombia, on January 31st, 1906; India, August 15th, 1950; and Alaska, March 27th, 1964. Judging from the reported effects, the Lisbon earthquake of November 1st, 1755, probably had a magnitude between 8.7 and 9.0. The great Chinese earthquake of July 28, 1976, killed half a million people in Tangshan, and was 8.2 on the Richter Scale. The 1906 earthquake in San Francisco was rated at 8.3.

The other scale is called the Mercalli Scale, and it is less precise. It defines "degrees of intensity" between I and XII. An intensity II earthquake is barely percepti-

ble to humans; intensity IX damages buildings and cracks
the ground, and intensity XI shatters masonry buildings, bends railroad tracks, and destroys most free-
standing structures.

The location of a volcanic eruption is not usually in
any doubt. Locating an earthquake is trickier, and its
point of maximum intensity, or *epicenter*, is determined
by inference. However, it is useful to note that the total
amount of energy release in a large volcanic eruption
and a large earthquake seem to be very comparable.
This emphasizes that energy release is only one of the
significant variables, and probably not the most important one, when we look at the climatic effects of natural or man-made disasters.

## VOLCANIC ERUPTIONS

Volcanic eruptions have been fairly well studied, but
there is no equivalent of the Richter Scale for volcanoes.

Volcanic eruptions are often divided into two groups,
termed Type A and Type B. Type B eruptions are in
many ways more interesting and spectacular, since they
are accompanied by gigantic explosions and produce
large volumes of *ejecta*—lava, dust and ash thrown
high into the air. Krakatoa, in 1883, and Mount St.
Helens, in 1980, were both Type B events. Type B
eruptions, foreshadowing thoughts of nuclear winter,
send their dust high into the stratosphere, to produce
colorful sunsets all around the world for several months.

Krakatoa is one of the most famous eruptions of historical times, perhaps because of the movie, "Krakatoa,
East of Java" (a nice example of Hollywood's disregard
of anything like facts; Krakatoa is an island just *west* of
Java). The Krakatoa eruption released an estimated $10^{25}$
ergs of energy—equal to a couple of hundred one-
megaton hydrogen bombs. The sound of the explosion
was heard 3,000 miles away, and the atmospheric shock
wave circled the globe several times. At Batavia (now
Jakarta), a hundred miles from the volcano, the air was
so dark with dust that lamps had to be used at midday.

Fifty-foot tidal waves hit the coast of Java and killed 36,000 people.

Yet there have been much bigger explosions. Tambora, in 1815, on the Indonesian island of Sumbawa, is estimated to have been 80 times as energetic an eruption as Krakatoa. The following year, 1816, was known as "the year without a summer," when crops failed to ripen throughout Europe. The most likely cause was a stratospheric layer of reflective dust from Tambora.

Biggest of all blow-ups during historical times, but one for which no eye-witness or contemporary records exist, was the destruction of the island of Thira (formerly Santorini) in the Aegean Sea north of Crete. From archeological evidence and the examination of the shattered remnant of Thira, this eruption is estimated to have released $10^{27}$ ergs of energy—equal to the energy release of the world's whole stockpile of nuclear weapons. The eruption, occurring about 1,470 B.C., also produced a monstrous tidal wave, hundreds of feet high, which may have been the agent that destroyed the Cretan Minoan civilization.

The most famous volcanic eruption of all time was probably that of Vesuvius, in 79 A.D. It covered the towns of Pompeii, Herculaneum, and Stabiae in twenty-foot layers of ash (65 feet in some places) and preserved everything nicely until systematic excavation began in 1763.

(It also, as an incidental, killed the Roman naturalist and historian, Pliny the Elder, who had sailed across the bay of Naples to take a look at the eruption and try to help people. He couldn't leave, and suffocated on the beach. Volcanoes are seductive viewing, and they induce strange psychological effects. In 1980, driving from Portland to Seattle, a friend and I made a detour to take a good look at the recently-erupted Mount St. Helens. About five miles from the crater, the road had been closed off by the police. We were very annoyed at the time, but in retrospect they were doing the right thing—we would have kept going until we were far too close for safety. The next morning, talking at breakfast, we found that we had both dreamed about that de-formed, ash-covered peak, with the ominous grey smoke cloud sitting on top of it.)

On the largest scale of things, the famous eruption of Vesuvius was no big deal. It released only an estimated $10^{24}$ ergs, less than one-tenth of a Krakatoa. By contrast, the 1912 eruption of Katmai in Alaska was twenty times as energetic as Krakatoa, but since it was in a sparsely populated area at the northern end of the Alaskan Peninsula, it attracted little global attention.

Type A eruptions are often just as energetic, but they are less noisy and colorful and don't get the same publicity. They produce great quantities of thermal energy, often heating the environment but not causing major explosions. They may involve huge lava flows, and even the creation of whole new volcanic islands. The most famous modern example is the island of Surtsey, created by a volcanic eruption off south-west Iceland, in 1963. That event was estimated to have released 2 E24 ergs—one-tenth the energy of the Krakatoan eruption.

Table 1 shows values for some of the biggest and best-known (and some surprisingly little known) of the volcanic eruptions of both types.

## METEORITE AND COMET IMPACTS

First, let us see how much energy a meteorite or a comet fragment will generate when it hits the Earth. This sounds like something that needs to be looked up in a reference work, rather than calculated directly. However, I will do it from first principles, because it is a nice example of being able to derive a result we want with almost no knowledge of physical constants, and in addition the calculation provides a surprising piece of additional information.

The kinetic energy of a body hitting the Earth is $mv^2/2$, where m is the mass of the body, and v is the relative speed of the Earth and the object. We can put in any value we like for m—and we will look at various sizes of impacting object. But what about v?

## TABLE 1:
## VOLCANIC ERUPTIONS AND ASSOCIATED
## ENERGY RELEASED

| Volcano | Date | Type | Energy (ergs) | Megaton H-bombs |
|---|---|---|---|---|
| Thira, Aegean Sea | 1470 B.C. | B | 1    E27 | 24,000 |
| Laki, Iceland | 1783 | A,B | 8.6 E26 | 20,500 |
| Tambora, Indonesia | 1815 | B | 8.4 E26 | 20,000 |
| Katmai, Alaska | 1912 | B | 2    E26 | 4,800 |
| Mauna Loa, Hawaii | 1950 | A | 1.4 E25 | 333 |
| Krakatoa, Indonesia | 1883 | B | 1    E25 | 240 |
| Surtsey, Iceland | 1963 | A | 1.9 E24 | 45 |
| Vesuvius, Italy | 79 | B | 1    E24 | 24 |
| Mount St Helens | 1980 | B | 4.2 E23 | 10 |

For comparison purposes:

| | | | | |
|---|---|---|---|---|
| Global nuclear war | ? | B | 1.1 E27 | 25,000 |

Eruptions of Type A are mainly lava flows, whereas Type B eject large quantities of material with explosive force. The thermal energy of Type A eruptions is usually transferred slowly to the environment, through conduction and radiation.

Suppose that the body is falling in towards the Sun from far away—perhaps from the Oort Cloud, which is the original home of the comets. Then its initial speed out there would be close to zero, and it would be accelerated all the way in towards the Sun by the solar gravitational field. Suppose that its speed relative to the Sun, by the time it hits the Earth, is $v_c$. The object has picked up as kinetic energy what it lost as potential energy, so

$$mv_c^2/2 = GmM/r$$

where G is the universal gravitational constant, M is the mass of the Sun, m the mass of the comet, and r the distance of the Earth from the Sun at the time of the impact. Cancelling the mass of the comet from the equation, we have

$$v_c^2/2 = GM/r \quad —(1)$$

It looks from equation (1) as though we need to know G, M, and r in order to determine $v_c$. But for the Earth

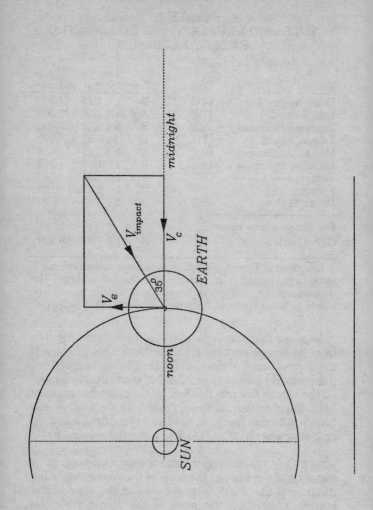

to be in orbit around the Sun, the gravitational force of the Sun on the Earth must balance the centrifugal force generated by the Earth's movement. This implies that if $v_e$ is the speed of the Earth,

$$v_e^2/r = GM/r^2$$

or

$$v_e^2 = GM/r \quad —(2)$$

Comparing (1) and (2), we have $v_c^2 = 2v_e^2$ —(3)

Thus all we need to know to determine the speed of the infalling comet is the speed of the Earth in its orbit around the Sun.

But this is easy to calculate. In one year, the Earth travels once around the Sun. The mean distance of the earth from the Sun is about 150 million kilometers (93 million miles) and the Earth moves roughly in a circle. Since there are 86,400 seconds in a day, the Earth moves $2\pi \times 150,000,000$ kilometers in $365 \times 86,400$ seconds, i.e., $v_e = 29.89$ kms/second—say, 30 kms a second, accurate enough for our purposes.

Thus from equation (3), we at once have $v_c = \sqrt{2}.v_e = 42.4$ kms/second.

The speed of the comet relative to the Earth is found by compounding these two velocities. The motion of the Earth and the comet are roughly at right angles to each other, so the final relative velocity is

$$\sqrt{v_c^2 + v_e^2} = 52 \text{ kms/second.}$$

This result is something of an upper limit to the impact speed of an object hitting the Earth. It is appropriate for comet impact, but since asteroids orbit the Sun in the same direction as the Earth, and are coming from much closer than the Oort Cloud, they will hit with less speed, usually between 15 and 30 kilometers a second. On the other hand, a metallic asteroid is of higher density, has more mass, and therefore delivers about as much energy as a faster-moving comet of the same size.

For cometary impact we are now in a position to deduce a second and very curious result: we can tell what *time of day* a comet is most likely to strike, provided that it is falling straight in towards the Sun.

Consider Figure 1. The Earth rotates on its axis in the same sense as it moves around the Sun. Further, midnight at any location occurs by definition when the Sun is on the opposite side of the Earth. The triangle of velocities of the figure shows that a body falling from far away to strike the Earth will hit soon after local midnight, at about 2:20 in the morning.

Is this the only solution? No, there is one other possibility. If the comet has already moved around the Sun, and is heading back out again to the outer Solar System, it will approach Earth from the sunward side. The triangle of velocities in this case tells us that the meteor will strike in the morning, 2:20 hours before noon, i.e. at 9:40 A.M.

Mornings are therefore more likely for comet impact than afternoons or evenings. This is *not* true for stony and metallic meteorites, which are small asteroids and have quite different orbit characteristics. They move in elliptical paths, almost always staying closer to the Sun than the orbit of Jupiter, and more hit in the afternoon than in the morning, by about a 3:2 ratio. But perhaps the computers of the missile defense systems should have a special test built into their code: If you detect a major impact, did it occur close to 2:20 A.M. or 9:40 A.M.? If so, take a closer look before you start World War III.

The comet fragment will be travelling at 52 kms a second. A fragment one kilometer in radius and with the density of water masses about 4 billion tons. Impact with Earth generates 5 E28 ergs of energy—5,000 Krakatoas, or 50 full-scale nuclear wars.

We need to know what size of fragment is reasonable, and how often such bodies are likely to hit the Earth. These are difficult questions, but we have at least a couple of available data points. First, a comet fragment* almost certainly did hit Earth, relatively re-

---

*Why a comet, and not an asteroidal meteorite? Because no metallic or stony fragments were found at the scene of the impact.*

cently. It happened early in the morning, on June 30th, 1908, at a remote area of Central Siberia called Tunguska. Although the fragment was estimated to be no more than a couple of hundred meters across, it flattened a thousand square miles of forest and left so much dust in the high atmosphere that colorful sunsets were produced in western Europe seven thousand miles away.

According to our formulas, the energy produced by the Tunguska meteorite was about 5.4 E25 ergs—five Krakatoas, or a thousand one-megaton hydrogen bombs.

However, a full-sized comet should be much bigger than the Tunguska meteorite. For example, Halley's comet has a nucleus about 10 kms across. Its impact with the Earth would release 7.1 E30 ergs of energy— equal to 170 million one-megaton hydrogen bombs, or 7,000 nuclear wars.

(One point needs to be made here. The world's most famous comets are *periodic* comets, like Halley's comet or Encke's comet. These objects do not "fall from infinity," but are in orbits that bring them close to the Sun at regular intervals of a century or less. However, they are the exceptions of the cometary world. They were once part of the Oort Cloud, and fell in from there a long time ago; then Jupiter or one of the other planets perturbed their motion by a gravitational interaction, and gave them a less elongated orbit. Now they travel in paths that are relatively close to the Sun, and their days in the Oort Cloud are over forever.)

There is evidence that major comet impacts have happened in the past, though fortunately not in historical times. Meteorite impact is the most popular theory to explain the disappearance of the dinosaurs in the late Cretaceous period, 65 million years ago, and also for an even more massive species extinction that occurred earlier, at the Permian/Triassic boundary 250 million years ago. The idea was proposed in 1980 by Alvarez and co-workers, originally to explain anomalous levels of iridium found in sedimentary deposits all around the world. It is holding up rather well, and is now supported by the discovery of so-called "shocked quartz" grains at widely dispersed locations.

Evidence of other large meteorite impacts can be found in many places: Manicouagan Lake in Quebec, a water-filled ring crater 40 miles across, is believed to be an impact crater; so is the mile-wide Meteor Crater, Arizona, which was created about 20,000 years ago. The Sudbury nickel deposit in Ontario is also probably an "astrobleme," or asteroid-impact structure, that created the world's largest nickel ore body. The asteroid that hit Sudbury is estimated to have been moving at 15 kilometers a second, and have been 4 kilometers in diameter. If so, its impact delivered 3 E29 ergs, 300 times as much as a full nuclear war. (Note that a comet, the same size but with the density of water, would produce very much the same energy, at 4.5 E29 ergs.)

These are North American evidence of what I like to call "close encounters of the fourth kind." The Earth must have seen many events like them in its long history. Only the weathering effects of the atmosphere, plate tectonics, and biological organisms save Earth from being as heavily cratered as the Moon.

Small meteors hit the Earth every day, and are burned up in their passage through the atmosphere. How often do meteorite impacts of a substantial size occur? This is an area where there are very few solid data to guide us, but we can make plausible estimates by putting together several apparently unrelated facts. First, the Earth and Moon are close neighbors in celestial terms, and they should encounter about the same number of meteorites, once we make allowance for the Moon's smaller size. We can count the Moon's craters, and their number suggests that an object big enough to make a crater a mile across will hit every hundred thousand years or so. A comet fragment twenty meters in radius would do it. Allowing for Earth's larger size, something that big should hit us about every ten thousand years.

Statistical analysis of bodies in the asteroid belt also provides a rule-of-thumb, saying that for any asteroid of a particular radius, there will be ten times as many with one-third that radius. We are going to assume that the same distribution law applies to comets, too. (We have to—data on comet nucleus sizes are too sparse to establish any frequency/nucleus-size relationship.) The rule-of-thumb can readily be converted to a general formula that tells the number, n, of bodies of any radius, r, thus:

$$n = N.(10)^{-\log(r/R)/\log 3} \quad —(4)$$

where N and R are any pair of *known* values.

Assuming the impact of an object twenty meters in radius every ten thousand years, the size/number relationship of equation (4) allows us to calculate the frequency of an impact of any size of body, and we already know how to compute the associated energy release. Table 2 shows the average time between impacts for different sizes of cometary bodies.

The table tells us that there should have been only four impacts of something the size of Halley's Comet since the Earth was formed. Given the huge energy release this implies, that's just as well. Conceivably, four such events correspond to major species extinctions in Earth's history. (A detached attitude to such calamities is hard to achieve, but possible. I was driving James Lovelock, originator of the "Gaia" concept (more about Gaia later), down to the Museum of Natural History in Washington. On the way we somehow got onto the subject of all-out nuclear war. Lovelock surprised me very much by remarking that it would have very little effect. I said, "But it could kill off every human!" He replied, "Well, yes, it might do *that*; but I was thinking of effects on the general biosphere.")

Even if we keep our missiles in their silos and submarines, the planet will have seen a "nuclear war" energy release from a comet or meteorite impact an average of every two million years; a one-megaton hydrogen bomb equivalent every two thousand years; and a Hiroshima-sized event every 130 years. Historical evidence suggests that these rates are on the high side—not surprising, considering the tenuous nature of some

## TABLE 2
### SIZE, FREQUENCY, AND EFFECTS OF COMET IMPACTS

| Size of body (radius in meters) | Frequency of occurrence (yrs) | Energy release (ergs) | Energy release (Megaton H-bombs) | Nuclear wars (1 nuclear war = 25,000 megatons) |
|---|---|---|---|---|
| 2.5 | 128 | 8.8 E20 | 0.02* | |
| 5 | 550 | 7.1 E21 | 0.17* | |
| 10 | 2,340 | 5.7 E22 | 1.4 | |
| 20 | 10,000 | 4.5 E23 | 11 | |
| 40 | 43,000 | 3.6 E24 | 86 | |
| 60 | 100,000 | 1.2 E25 | 286 | |
| 100 | 292,000 | 5.7 E25 | 1,350 | |
| 150 | 680,000 | 1.9 E26 | 4,520 | |
| 250 | 2,000,000 | 8.8 E26 | 21,000 | 0.84 |
| 500 | 8,500,000 | 7.1 E27 | 169,000 | 6.8 |
| 1,000 | 36,000,000 | 5.7 E28 | 1,360,000 | 54.3 |
| 2,500 | 250,000,000 | 8.8 E29 | 21,000,000 | 838 |
| 5,000 | 1,060,000,000 | 7.1 E30 | 169,000,000 | 6,760 |
| 10,000 | 4,500,000,000 | 5.66 E31 | 1,347,000,000 | 54,000 |

*The Hiroshima atomic bomb was about 20 kilotons TNT equivalent. The 2.5 meter comet fragment releases as much energy as one Hiroshima bomb, and the 5 meter fragment as much as 9 such bombs. A 2.5 meter fragment impact can be expected every 128 years. Objects of this size and smaller will produce a fireball as they burn up in the atmosphere, but normally will not reach the surface of the Earth.

of our assumptions. On the other hand, the reluctance of our ancestors to accept the idea of meteorites suggests that any fireball occurring, say, four hundred years ago, might have been misinterpreted*—or, in much of the world, not recorded.

It would be nice to think that explosions mimicking an atomic bomb in violence are rather rare. The response of a nervous nation to a Hiroshima-style fireball over one of its major cities is hard to predict.

## STELLAR EVENTS

The energies of a nuclear war or a cometary impact are huge on the everyday scale of Earthly events, but they are minute compared with the power production of even the smallest and dimmest stars.

The Sun, a rather average G2-type dwarf star, emits 3.9 E33 ergs of radiative energy per second—that's four million nuclear wars a second. Fortunately the Earth intercepts only a tiny fraction of the solar bounty, roughly one two-billionth.

The question now is, can this energy change enough to threaten the survival of life on Earth?

The obvious danger in this case might seem to be an excess of radiation—of frying, rather than freezing—since there are no signs that the Sun is likely to go out for many billions of years. But could the Sun become much brighter? The sunlight delivered to the Earth is known as the "solar constant," and it is about 0.14 watts per square centimeter. Can the solar constant change, because of, say, a very large solar flare?

Well, over very long periods the solar constant has certainly changed. Life has existed on Earth for about three and a half billion years; and in that time, the solar constant has increased by at least thirty percent. If Earth's temperature simply responded directly to the

---

*"I could more easily believe that two Yankee professors would lie than that stones would fall from heaven." —Thomas Jefferson

Sun's output, two billion years ago the whole Earth would have been frozen over.

But in fact, the response of Earth's biosphere to temperature changes is complex, apparently adapting to minimize the effects of change. This is part of the whole Gaia concept, of life on Earth as a giant mechanism that regulates its own environment in an optimum manner. For example, as temperatures go up, the rate of transpiration of plants increases, so the amount of atmospheric water vapor goes up. That means more clouds—and clouds reflect sunlight, and shield the surface. In addition, increased amounts of vegetation reduce the amount of carbon dioxide in the air, and that in turn reduces the greenhouse effect by which solar radiation is trapped within the atmosphere. There are many other processes, involving other atmospheric gases, and the net effect is to hold the status quo for the benefit of living organisms.

However, there is a big difference between a 30% change that takes place over three and a half billion years, and one that takes place overnight. We need to know if a rapid change is possible.

The picture is a little bit confusing. The Sun emits almost all of its light energy at ultraviolet, visible, and infrared wavelengths (99% of the total between 0.276 and 4.96 micrometers). Measurement of the solar constant over this range shows very little change. On the other hand, there is a definite cyclic variation in solar output at X-ray and radio wavelengths, corresponding to the eleven year cycle of sunspot activity and to other, longer periods. The fraction of energy emitted at these wavelengths is small, but the effects are certainly not negligible.

For example, although the Ice Ages took place before recorded history, there were two well-documented "Little Ice Ages," one from 1460 to 1550, the other from 1645 to 1715. These periods, known as the Spörer Minimum and the Maunder Minimum respectively, occurred at times when there were almost no sunspots on the Sun. Flamsteed, the first British Astronomer Royal,

never saw a sunspot in forty years of observations. Isaac
Newton, whose lifetime (1642–1727) neatly overlaps the
Maunder Minimum, was in a similar position.

Conversely, the so-called "Grand Maximum" from
1100 to 1250, when Greenland was settled, has been
studied by J.R. Eddy using carbon-14 dating of tree
rings. It proves to be a period of prolonged sunspot
activity and a warm Earth.

There is thus no doubt that quite small changes in
solar output can have significant effects on the Earth's
climate. The natural (but wrong) conclusion is that the
major Ice Ages were caused by correspondingly larger
changes to the solar constant. Actually, Milankovitch
has produced convincing evidence that the Ice Ages
correspond to changes in the Earth's orbit, rather than
to changes in solar output.

Theories of stellar evolution tell us that there have
been slow, steady increases in solar heat production,
over billions of years. But history offers no evidence of
large, sudden excursions of the solar constant from its
usual value. Sol is a remarkably stable furnace, having
less effect on Earth's climate than the eccentricity of
the Earth's orbit around the Sun.

As a competitor with meteors and nuclear wars to
effect an abrupt end to human affairs, solar energy
variation seems to be a non-starter.

## SUPERNOVAS

With supernovas, we move into the big league. If Sol
were to turn into a supernova, its light production
could increase by a factor of a hundred billion, to 4 E44
ergs a second.

This sounds like a lot—it *is* a lot—but it is only a tiny
part of the supernova's total energy production. Between ninety and ninety-nine percent of the energy in
the explosion is carried off by neutrinos. Of the remainder, ninety to ninety-nine percent is in an exploding
shell of matter, blasted outward at a twentieth of the
speed of light. Only between one percent and one

one-hundredth of a percent of the energy is emitted in the form of radiation.

The neutrinos appear at the moment of the explosion, whereas the emitted light and high-energy particles increase and then decrease in intensity over a period of weeks or months. The 1987 supernova in the Large Magellanic Cloud produced and emitted an estimated $10^{58}$ neutrinos in just a few seconds, and they carried off with them 3 E53 ergs—equivalent to one-tenth of the mass of the Sun.

Neutrinos interact with normal matter hardly at all, which is why they readily escape from the center of the supernova. A neutrino can pass through several lightyears of lead before being captured. However, the number emitted in a supernova explosion is so large that the neutrinos alone would kill a human a billion kilometers away. If Sol became a supernova, we would be wiped out by the neutrinos shortly before we were vaporized by the flux of radiation.

Before we worry about that event, we ought to note that today's theories (how much do you trust your theories?) tell us that Sol cannot become a supernova. There are two types of supernova. Type I occurs only in multiple-star systems, when a massive white dwarf star receives enough gaseous matter from a stellar companion to render it unstable. A Type II supernova happens when the core of a supergiant star, 15 or more times the mass of the Sun, collapses. Since Sol is neither a binary star nor a supergiant, we seem to be safe.

However, there are multiple star systems and supergiant star systems in the local stellar neighborhood of the Sun. It is possible that one of those could produce a supernova, and then conceivable that the event would be energetic enough to destroy life on Earth, or at least produce a huge perturbation comparable with a nuclear war or a large meteor impact.

The closest multiple star system to Earth is also the nearest star system, Alpha Centauri. It is not a likely candidate to become a supernova, but if it were to do so, would it harm the Earth? Alpha Centauri is 4.3

lightyears away, more than 270,000 times as far as the Sun, and distance is the best protection.

The best protection in this case is not enough. If one of the three stars in the Alpha Centauri system became a supernova and produced 4 E44 ergs per second in the form of light, it would appear brighter than the Sun by about a third for a few weeks. The increased heat alone might kill us, but the sleet of high-energy particles, carrying ten times as much energy as the light, would be even more destructive. However, we would have plenty of warning of the coming particle storm, since the radiation from Alpha Centauri would precede the particles by three-quarters of a century. Digging would become the new international pastime.

I can't help wondering how the world would reach to the idea that, following a terrible time of heat and chaos, the worst was still to come. Would people believe the scientists' statements? Would they be willing to begin preparation now, for an event so far in the future that most people would not be there to experience it? Or would they shrug and say, "Let them handle it when it happens—it's their problem."? We have seen a lot of that attitude towards environmental pollution.

Supernovas vary in the violence of their explosions, but anything closer than 50 lightyears might produce severe effects on the Earth, as much as if we had a sudden increase of ten percent in the solar constant.

Again, the *probability* of such an event is more important than the *possibility*. To determine this, we have to know the rate of occurrence of supernovas. The easiest place to look for supernovas is not in our own Galaxy, since much of that is obscured from us by interstellar dust clouds. It is better to look at neighboring galaxies, such as Andromeda, and count supernovas there. That exercise suggests that a supernova occurs maybe every century in a galaxy the size of ours, with an uncertainty on that number of at least a factor of two. Since the Galaxy contains about a hundred billion stars, and since there are about 1,000 star systems within 50 lightyears of us, we can expect a supernova within this distance only once every 10 billion years. This is a simplistic argument, neglecting the different types of stellar populations, and where they lie within the Galaxy, but again we are looking for ballpark figures.

The closest and brightest supernova in recorded history occurred in 1054 A.D., and the remnant of that explosion now forms the Crab Nebula. The Crab supernova was bright enough to be visible during the day, but it had no harmful effects on Earth. It lies about 6,000 lightyears away from us. We can expect a supernova this close or closer every 6,000 years. It is a little disturbing that the event actually occurred less than a thousand years ago, and it suggests that either supernovas are more frequent than we think, or more likely we are in a galactic region that favors supernovas. If a supernova as close as the Crab nebula occurs every thousand years in our galactic neighborhood, then we can expect a supernova within 50 lightyears every couple of billion years.

One final question is of interest: how often will a supernova deliver the energy equivalent of a nuclear war to the Earth, in radiation and particles? Taking the total radiation and particle energy of a supernova as $10^{50}$ ergs, it is easy to calculate how far away the exploding star can be if the Earth is to intercept the necessary $10^{27}$ ergs. The answer is a little over a hundred lightyears. Making the same assumption as before about the frequency of supernovas in our galactic neighborhood, this will happen every two and a half billion years. Apparently supernovas are not a major danger to the human race. (But of course, statistics being statistics, a nearby supernova could explode tomorrow.)

## DANGER SIGNAL

It is time to pull all this together. We have looked at a number of ways that the world can end, or at least become a very unpleasant place for human habitation.

Those disasters do not form a complete list. There are many other ways for the human species to become extinct, some of which would leave the rest of the world intact (some would say, improved). Disease is one excellent candidate. We can imagine, for example, a mutation of AIDS. Suppose that a form of the AIDS virus were to appear that could be transmitted, like the common cold, through a sneeze . . .

But that is a different article. The key question for each event considered in the earlier sections is not, can it happen, but rather, what is the *chance* that it will happen?

Some events serve as triggers, to produce final effects beyond the obvious ones. Nuclear war, meteor and comet impact, and volcanic eruptions all serve to charge the upper atmosphere with dust that cuts down sunlight and may produce results far more unpleasant than the original explosion. Similarly, a torrent of hard radiation and high-energy particles from a supernova may kill far more people in the long-term, from cancer, than die at once from burns.

Recognizing this, it is still instructive to compare the *direct* effects of each type of disaster. Table 3 shows the probable frequency of events equal in energy production to a full-scale nuclear war, derived from the discussion given earlier in this article.

### TABLE 3:
### FREQUENCY OF DISASTER OF
### "NUCLEAR WAR" DIMENSIONS

| Disaster | Estimated mean time between occurrences |
|---|---|
| Nuclear war | One hundred years* |
| Volcanic eruption | One thousand years |
| Meteorite/comet impact | Two million years |
| Supernova | Two and a half billion years |
| Solar instability | At least three billion years |

*Based on the assumption that there is a one percent chance of nuclear war in any particular year; many would consider this optimistic.

It is very clear that nothing in Nature presents such a danger to the human race as our own actions. We know we can survive a volcanic eruption of the size of Thira; for one thing, it is *localized* in effect; for another, we have already survived such eruptions, essentially unscathed. We are not at all sure how much of our civilization would survive a nuclear war.

The message: our future lies in our own hands.

Anyone who is at all reassured by this conclusion is a candidate for the Pollyanna award of 1988. As Pogo pointed out many years ago, "We has met the enemy, and it is us."

## Introduction

As is well known, Poul Anderson is one of the authors in the field whom I most admire, so naturally when asked to write an appreciation of the man and his works for a regional convention I was happy to comply.* I present it here in lieu of an introduction to "The Deserter."

### "Poul of Pook's Hill"

What with deadlines, mislaid manuscripts, undependable suppliers, fractious help, and my own weaknesses, the life of a publisher is not the easiest I can imagine. But it does have its compensations. Chief among them, I have become friends with some of the gods of my childhood, people I did not think I would ever meet and talk with till I had died and gone to Heaven. People like Robert Heinlein, Gordy Dickson—and Poul Anderson.

As for Poul the man, I appreciate him very much, but since he and I will doubtless break bread more than once during this convention, let me be nearly as brief in his personal praises as he would wish. As the ancient Persians might have put it, Poul Anderson is a writer who shoots straight and tells the truth, and what more is there to say about anyone? Not much, really, once you add instinctive kindliness. But for the record let me add that he's extraordinarily erudite, a fascinating conversationalist (once the conversation has grown beyond conventional trivialities), and that he has the gift of admiration, a gift much under-rated and sadly rare. (It is to that gift of his that I owe my current infatuation with Rudyard Kipling; I can highly recommend brandy with Poul and Karen on a cloudy autumn night as a way for burnishing one's education. But I verge on the personal . . .)

Poul the writer: Poul's virtues as a writer are innumerable, and since the act of listing them implies some

---

*Xanadu, held annually in Nashville, Tennessee in the month of October.

*precedence in their share of the Poulish makeup, as soon as I fix on one, several others jostle for attention as the primary virtue; indeed each one when fixed upon seems foremost—but when my mind twitches to another, that one does too. . . .*

*On reflection, for me Poul's greatest virtue as a writer is that no matter how high and action-packed the adventure, at base he is always profound. Not in some stuffy literary sense—a finned cylinder is just a rocket and a spinning torus is naught but a space station; you will find none of the clash of Freudian symbols that are de rigueur in Serious Writing—but in the way everything happens for a reason, and the way every reason has a deeper reason underlying it, and the way it all meshes so.*

*If you think, for example, that Flandry is trysting in the lounge of his incredibly decadent and very potent spaceship because he would have his less than honorable way with the beautiful damsel (and she with him), you're right of course. But you would also be right to think that he's there because as governments age they grow ever more externally impotent and internally oppressive—and you would be right on a deeper level. Look deeper still and you will come to see that for Poul Anderson history is little more than a howling nightmare spotted with brief episodes of relative peace and tranquility, and that those of us lucky enough to live in one of the quiet times should do something to extend and enrich it. Even though, in the end, no matter how hard we fight the good fight, night must come, and with it the howling peoples.*

*((You see? Writing so profound and affecting that it can even move such a creature as a publisher, with hair on his knuckles (except where he walks on them) and a cash register for a heart . . .))*

*But of course there is more to Poul's writing than mere profundity. He's witty too, with humor that ranges from the broad farce (so to speak) of believable space Amazons replete with swords and captive male . . . um, spear carriers . . . to rapier-sharp dialogue between* activist Flandry and the historian who has fallen so low on the scale of manhood as to think that because a cause is lost it's not worth fighting for. (On the debit side, he puns: "Our fault lies not in our stars but in our bars!" Indeed.)

Hmmm . . . I could spend many pages listing literary virtues—he owns them all—but this is no more a literary venue than I am a literary man, so let me close by measuring Poul's work against the one criterion that matters to me (other than sales!), the one that transcends and subsumes any other virtues a writer may possess, the one without which there is nothing: does the writer get you there? If not, are you just sitting in a chair, reading words.

Poul Anderson passes this test like nobody else . . . You are an angel sliding forever down a time and gravity gradient into a neutron star . . . a Roman Centurion become a pagan king just in time to witness the death of pagan gods as the saints of Christos triumph . . . a time traveler come to rescue the king of the Persians . . . and always you are yourself, on a voyage filled with wonder.

I have lived for a million words in the Polesotechnic League, watching the meteoric rise and glacial fall of a starspanning civilization. For near as long I was the King of Ys, striving to rescue my people as Rome died and the barbarians swarmed, failing nobly and fighting always to save what could be saved. I have sailed with the people of the Sea, and flown with the People of the Wind, and snarled with feline triumph as the human who thought himself a god fell beneath my sword—and I watched that sword descend . . .

Yes, I have been many places, done many things, and lived many lives beyond the dreams of mundane mortals, and for this I thank you, Poul Anderson. But even more I thank you for what I have brought back with me from those voyages: a sense of the infinite grandeur of reality, and the magic inherent with it.

# THE DESERTER

*Poul Anderson*

The sun was going down as I left the general's office. Clouds, tall beyond walls, hid that spark, but it kindled red and yellow in them, and the Lion Tower stood silhouetted with rays astream from its battlements. Otherwise the clouds were blue-black up to their tops, which Catseye tinged carmine. The sky was clear around it, deepening toward purple in the east, where the first stars blinked. A pair of moons stood near the planet. Their sickles looked burnished and whetted, for its own waxing crescent bore a storm that blurred it more than was common, distorted the bands across its ocherousness, and veiled the dull glow of the side still nighted. That storm could have swallowed all Haven, or any other world where men can walk. But here I felt only an evening breeze. It was cool, with smells of growth from the farmlands around Fort Kursk.

Out on the parade ground, day retreat had begun. Though I was crossing the compound some distance away, I came to attention. It was expected of any man outdoors who had no immediate business. I did, and could simply have saluted, but appearances mattered more than ever. Besides, those were men of my regi-

ment about to lower the flag they had watched through
these past fifteen changes of guard—no, these past four
centuries and more. How often again would a master
sergeant of Land Gators receive the Imperial standard
in his hands?

It fluttered slowly down the pole. From the front of
the rank a drum thuttered and the pipes wailed. "The
Marines' Farewell" sounded thin across empty paving,
underneath that hugeness of sky and primary planet. I
had never told anyone here that on Covenant we gave
different words to the tune, words from old Earth: "The
Flowers of the Forest." Already when I came to Haven,
twenty-three Terrestrial years ago, there was too much
mourning.

"Aloft and Away" sounded livelier, above the thud of
boots, as the relieving squad arrived. I recognized its
colors by a glint of light off the Phoenix image on the
staff. The marching was subtly wrong, not ragged but
too stiff. Pacifying the High Vales had cost the Third
Regiment heavily; new recruits were few, and veterans
didn't seem to take them in hand any longer. I waited
till the night banner had gone aloft, then continued on
my way.

Base hospital was not far off it. The visitors' ramp was
out of order and I had to walk down to reception.
Something always seemed to be out of order these days;
what technics we had must concentrate their efforts on
vital apparatus. My insignia startled the corporal at the
desk. He scrambled to his feet. "Yes, sir?"

"Lieutenant-Colonel Colin Raveloe, Second Infantry
Brigade," I identified myself, more to the scanner than
to him. "I'd like to call on Centurion Enrico Murakawa."

His eyes widened. He didn't need to punch the
register. "Sir, he . . . he's in the Plague ward."

"I know. How is he? Can he have visitors?"

"He's conscious, but— Sir, that's the *Red* Plague."
The man hesitated. "I can have the duty nurse convey a
message—greetings, best wishes?—but we are very
shorthanded and it may take a little time."

I shook my head. "Not absolute quarantine, is it?"

His face said it ought to be. "I'm going. What room?"
He didn't answer at once. "I told you to give me the
room number, Corporal."

He did, and stared after me when I left. Maybe I'd
been a tad hard on him. Terror was natural with a new
sickness that nobody understood, except that it seemed
to be airborne, and that was killing its thousands in the
Bolkhov and had now sought out the Marines themselves in their last stronghold on Haven. I would have
been afraid too, were it not for the news General Ashcroft
had given me.

I hope, though, I'd have walked those corridors and
ramps, on down into whispery antiseptic-smelling depths,
regardless. "Slaunch" Murakawa had been in my first
platoon when I was a new-minted second lieutenant.
Since, we'd campaigned together from pole to pole,
jungle to desert to mountains to towns full of wreckage
and snipers. He'd been involved in saving my life more
than once. Maybe what counted most was his good
humor that nothing could break, not hardship or boredom or the nastiness of those endless battles we fought
only to see the Empire let the outposts slip one by one
away from it.

Our last mission was decent. They hadn't remitted
their taxes from the Bolkhov for a long time, but still
they appealed to the Imperial garrison to help them
restore order when the Plague raised mass panic and
crime went rampant. However, soon after we returned,
Murakawa and a dozen more men came down with it. I
might have myself, if I'd been on patrol with them
instead of in camp. Adam Soltyk might have too—no
considerations of military doctrine, let alone prudence,
ever kept him out of action—but he had had a different
assignment and—

I dismissed memories. Enough that old Slaunch rated
a word from me, and not through any third party.

The medic in charge was less shocked by my inten-
tion than the deskman. After all, he'd been living with
the horror. "Avoid touching anything and you should
be safe," he said. "We wear sealsuits and go through a

chemical shower after every round, but we're right there in their breath." Awkwardly: "So good of you to come, sir. Not many people do, even immediate family."

Well, I thought, how many of us had families? Liaisons, yes, of course; understandings, perhaps; but few married till after their discharges, when it would be possible to stay settled. Once that had been different. The Pax prevailed, and the Marines were little more than a planetary police force. Now, why should a woman tie herself to a man who might ship out at any time, for years or forever?

No, who *would*. We were the last and were only waiting for our call. Nobody acknowledged it, everybody knew it. Leaves were for no longer than a hundred hours and the passes only for travel within a hundred kilometers of base. Just the same, more and more men never reported back; or they simply disappeared from barracks. I wondered if the Plague was stemming that leakage. Fort Kursk had the means to make death gentle. On the other hand, a deserter might hope that whatever country he sought would escape infection—not altogether an unreasonable hope, as sparse as traffic had become.

Again my mind had gone awol. The medic's voice called it back: "Morale's about all we've got to help us, you know. Otherwise supportive treatment, pain killers, and prayers. No antibiotic, no antiviral is any use. I'd think it was a native disease that's finally begun to feed on us, Haven itself getting rid of us—" He gulped. "Sorry. I realize that's impossible. Got to be some Terrestrial bug mutated, and the scientists will soon track the biochemistry down. Got to believe that, don't we? Please proceed."

The sickroom held twenty beds. Eight were occupied by those men still alive; the rest lay ready. It was dim, because normal light hurt eyes and worsened skin eruptions. I made my way through humming dusk till I found Murakawa. The mask that contained his labored, poisonous breath also hid much of the red patches and white blisters across his face. He'd shriveled. Fingers plucked the sheet. His vacant stare at a telescreen swung away and came alive when he grew aware of me. "Colonel Raveloe," he whispered. "Judas priest! Sir, what've you come for? You shouldn't've."

"Don't give orders to your superior officer," I answered. "How goes it?"

He sighed. "It goes. I wish it'd hurry up."

"That's not the kind of talk I'd expect from you," I snapped. "Straighten out, you hear me? I want you back on duty by Landing Day."

My words had more meaning than I admitted. General Ashcroft had explained the political and military situation to me in the sort of detail the high command was not releasing publicly, so I'd understand the importance of my mission. The war was now three-cornered, a score of wildfires consuming ships and men across half the Empire. Thus far none had reached this sector, and remnant garrisons like ours stayed in reserve; but the latest dispatches told of an engagement begun at Makassar between Secessionist and Claimant armadas, while Imperial forces marshalled to go there. Best estimate was that Haven would swing less than forty more times around Catseye before the troopships arrived and bore us off to do battle for His Majesty.

Which Majesty that would be, Ashcroft confessed he didn't know.

Murakawa attempted a grin. "Yes, sir," he got out of his throat.

I bent over him. "Listen, Slaunch," I said low. "If you can hang on for another fifty hours or so, and you can goddamn well do that much, you'll win. We'll win. It took a while, because medical research hasn't been done worth mentioning when people thought they knew all about everything that can hit the human body." Not much science of any kind had been done anywhere that I knew of, but never mind. "Now the answer has been found, and I'm on my way to pick up a batch of the medicine."

Life flickered through his tone. "You, sir? Yourself? Why, that's, uh, wonderful—"

"Sh! I'm supposed to keep it confidential. If I didn't trust you and need you, you old scoundrel, I wouldn't have stretched my orders like this."

Bewilderment: "Sir, I don't understand. The news—"

"Civilians mustn't hear yet. There could be hitches in production or distribution, or something else might go wrong." I wasn't quite lying. Word that the Marines had gotten priority could add to our problems with regions which no longer paid the Empire more than lip service, if that. The whole truth was worse, though. Something had in fact gone ghastly wrong. Adam Soltyk had never returned from Nowy Kraków.

"You're tough enough to outlive any small delays," I said.

"Yes, sir." Exhausted, Murakawa let his head sink back onto the pillow. "Okay if I act cheerful in front of the boys?"

"That's an order, Centurion."

I went on among the beds, pausing to greet whomever was conscious, let him know that the colonel remembered him. It was hasty. Nevertheless one lad mumbled, "Thank you, sir. This means so much. You're a Christian."

That took me aback. I left the Kirk before I left my birthworld. Surely no more of it remained with me than did any trace of Covenant burr on my tongue. Yet in dreams I still often heard my father speak or my mother sing. Maybe my heritage was more than a stubborn mind and a rawboned height. Maybe a spirit had quietly survived within me, and on Covenant would survive the Empire. I'd like to believe that.

Of course, I'd never know, and meanwhile there was a job to do.

Night was entire when I emerged topside. What with lamps and glowstrips on the ground, Catseye and companion moons overhead, I saw few stars. But somehow I felt them yonder, in overwhelming numbers agleam above the outback, through the thin air of Haven, stars crowding darkness itself out of heaven but filling it with their silence. How could it be that mortal men fared and warred among them?

Why, it simply didn't matter, I told myself. All our lives and histories, all our agonies and violences came to less than the infall of a single nebula or the blink of a single nova.

It was fast getting colder. My breath smoked white, my footfalls rang on pavement already hoarfrosted. Between two columns of buildings no longer used I looked down Shangri-La Valley toward the horizon skyglow that bespoke Castell. It too had dimmed over the years. Clearer and brighter were the windows of farmsteads, but they lay widely scattered. Most were ancient grants to veterans, whose descendants had supplied the Seventy-Seventh with sons for hundreds of years. I wondered how they would do after the division, the last Imperial Marines on Haven, pulled out. Maybe for another generation or two people would pretend Double Seven must someday come back home.

Before then, how would their daughters do? We'd take no wives along to war. Whoever won, if anybody did, would probably keep us busy for the rest of our useable lives, holding down his conquests and his frontiers. I was glad—I supposed—that Lois and I decided to wait for my retirement, even though that eventually caused her to marry a civilian. Saying goodbye to Corinne and Dee would be a great deal easier.

Bachelor officers' quarters were a block of multiplexes. I'd taken mine at the far end. It insulated me from most noise and most invitations to orgies of one sort or another. A few friends in, or simply a book or a disc, was my usual preference. A slim young fellow stood at my door. Planetlight reddened his blond hair. He snapped a salute. "Private Jezierski reporting, sir." He tried for military snap but couldn't quell the purring Polski accent.

"Ah, yes," I said. "Sorry to keep you waiting. Come in. We've things to talk about, you and I."

Mainly I had to size him up. He was nephew to Adam Soltyk; and Soltyk, whom I thought my amigo, had seemingly surprised us all.

We entered. Jezierski couldn't help himself, but stared around. The muted light made him look young indeed, almost girlish, though there were strong bones underneath. Guts, too. We didn't get many Haveners enlisting any more. They must often defy kinfolk who saw in the Empire as much of an enemy as was any outsider— even after the Lavacan raid. They must face the likelihood of exile, the chance of being killed in a strange land or beyond the sky. To be sure, the Soltyks were special. With them it was a tradition that every generation brought forth at least one Marine. And though now the White Eagle flew above Nowy Kraków in place of the Imperial standard, Cracovia was not hostile.

So I heard.

"At ease," I said. "I called from the general's office to have you meet me here because I need a trustworthy man who knows your people. Your uncle may be in trouble amongst them. For the honor of the blood, which I remember is a binding oath to him, will you stand true?"

Adam had brought the boy with him when he returned from furlough. That had been about one Earthyear ago, before leaves were restricted. He asked me to come over to his house and talk frankly. "Lech was orphaned early in his teens, by an accident," he explained. "I've become a father figure of sorts to him, in spite of us seldom seeing each other. We've kept in touch. He entered Copernican University, but wants to drop out and enlist. A good kid, though romantic. Not that that's necessarily bad." He laughed over the com. Gustiness ruffled his sweeping yellow mustache. "In fact, all proper Polaki are hopeless romantics. That's what's given us the hope to keep going, through the kind of history we've had shoved onto us. Very likely a career in the Marines will be right for him." He sobered. "However, if he does sign on, I want him to have both eyes open."

I was always glad to visit the Soltyks. He hadn't hung back like me, but married the girl he loved. Slowly I learned, never from her, that Jadwiga longed back to her island and lived for their return visits. Nonetheless she fashioned a home for them that was like an alcove of Cracovia, and met their troubles with a steel to match his, and to his dash and impulse added a quiet common sense. I never warmed myself at more happiness than when I sat in their place, under the crucifix and the country scenes, amidst the books and other well-worn little treasures. Nor did I ever eat better. What she knew about spiced fish, soup, pork cutlets, greens—

As was their custom, we remained around the dinner table when talk got serious afterward. The two children, Piotr and Franciszka, could have excused themselves but sat in polite wonder. The vodka glowed in me. I looked across at Lech Jezierski. Above broad shoulders he bore a male version of Jadwiga's face, which meant he was handsome indeed.

"I daresay your uncle has warned you about what to expect, starting with boot camp," I said. "He's probably also given you the ancient definition of war as long periods of boredom punctuated by moments of stark terror. I might add, if you will excuse me, *Pani*—" this respectfully to Jadwiga, well though we knew each other; Cracovians had an archaic concept of manners—"that girls aren't anywhere near as easy to come by as folklore claims. Once a uniform was glamorous; but that was when people considered us their protectors."

"We *are*, sir," Lech breathed.

I shrugged. "We try. We don't do too well these days. The Lavacans were just the splashiest case of that. It'd help mightily if Haveners in general felt enough loyalty to back us with their own efforts. But most of them don't. They see the Empire as a thing that takes and never gives."

Adam frowned. "Easy," he cautioned. An excitable boy might blurt out in public that we'd been talking subversion.

"I don't say that's right, I only say it is," I told them. "The bulk of our recruits on this planet are from territories that've gotten so miserable anything looks better. Cracovia is still fairly prosperous."

Lech flushed. "It won't be if the barbarians come!"

"And you want to help hold them off? Commendable."

"Uncle Adam—Major Soltyk knows how."

I nodded. Paradoxical it might be, but Adam Soltyk, fiery warrior, was as great a defensive leader as Fabius, Robert the Bruce, Alexander Nevsky, Washington, Sitting Bull—no, "responsive" is a better word, responsive to a superior foe, not merely huddling back in a fortress but actively exploiting every weak point. When his troops outflanked the Lavacans at Kimi, the nukes he put through may have been what turned the tide. Certainly he taught the Orfanians how to maintain themselves against the Tartarians, and so kept that small nation of friendlies alive on Haven. The jungle fighters he raised and trained would be holding Curaray for us yet if an Imperial legate hadn't come to "negotiate" with the Beneficents. The emplacements and specialist corps he advocated would make Shangri-La close to impregnable. But he'd never get them, and he might never make more than colonel. Too many feathers ruffled, too many established interests flouted.

"Well," I said, "we may not be doing that much longer. The Empire's in upheaval. Unless matters improve, we too may be called away."

"I know, sir." Lech spoke softly, but it blazed from him.

I saw his glance drawn helpless to the pictures, the keepsakes I had from worlds beyond this world. He had never so much as been in orbit, tumbled dreamlike through free fall, seen for himself the white-and-tawny glory of Haven and the undimmed majesty of Catseye. Besides, I'd had my missions elsewhere in this system, to Hecate's crags, dawn over the Rainbow Desert on Ayesha, the ice caves of Brynhild, an asteroid spinning across star-clouds, the multi-million-kilometer geyser as Comet Reyes plunged toward the sun. And earlier there had been Covenant, where villages nestle under snow-peaks aflicker with aurora; and I'd had the chance to travel as a lad, as far as the remnants and unforgotten graves on Earth; later, before assignment to the Seventy-Seventh, I'd served in the Roving Patrol, ridden with hawk and hound across a wind-rippled prairie on Table-top, walked with a golden-skinned girl where crystal spires lifted on Xanadu, lost myself as night fell over Tanith and the rings became clear—oh, more wonders than one room or one mind could hold memories of, and yet I had had just the barest glimpse. On some of those planets, hope itself survived.

"Yes," I said, "you'll get around in the Deep."

"Oh, sir—"

"It won't be any Grand Tour, you know. It'll be long hauls and long waits and then war. Still, you should see quite a bit, and have experiences you couldn't imagine on this back-eddy globe, and maybe, maybe end your days in a better place than here. But that's conditional. Sit down."

He hesitated. "Sit," I repeated. "I'd rather stay on my feet." He obeyed. I went to a table where I kept my pipes and started loading one. He stared. I laughed. "Don't worry, son. I've had my shots for this kind of cancer too. It's probably for the best, though, that nobody's found how to grow decent-tasting tobacco on Haven. I import mine, which costs enough to keep me moderate. The way it's going with the cost and reliability of freight, I may have to quit. The problem is incompatible biochemistries, you know. Our agriculture never has fitted comfortably into the Haven ecology."

Turning to him as I got the pipe lit, I went on: "This isn't idle chatter. I'm leading into the reason you are here. Listen.

"The Red Plague seemed like another mutation of some bug that the ancestors carried with them from Earth. I'm not an expert, but I know how the medics deal with such things. It's practically routine. Molecular scans find the peculiarity in the DNA or RNA, a computer program prescribes a cure and tells how to manufacture the stuff. But this disease wouldn't oblige.

And it's lethal, and has an unknown incubation period, and has now attacked some of our men. Do you see? It could kill off whole populations, bring down whole civilizations. The Empire's in plenty bad shape without letting something like that loose. It'd have to quarantine Haven, including its garrison. But they need us."

I passed by any questions of whether or not we'd really be doing humanity a service. We carry out our orders, that's all; semper fidelis. Anyhow, Private Lech Jezierski longed for the Deep as he had not yet longed for a woman. "Fortunately," I said, "Cracovia is still . . . associated with the Empire; and Copernican University is one of the few institutions left anyplace in the galaxy where science doesn't mean a set of cookbook formulas. They've cracked the Red Plague problem there, and have the medicine."

Breath whistled between the boy's teeth.

"The announcement was confidential," I said. "Politics. Once that wouldn't've been feasible, but when the only competent scientists for $x$ light-years around are concentrated in a single set of buildings. . . . Well, the stuff has tested out in the hands of a relief team sent to the Bolkhov. The first actual production batches were earmarked for us. A cure and an immunizer, seems like, so after we inoculate all personnel we can safely embark for the wars. Because he's a Cracovian and has high-placed connections in the country, Major Soltyk was dispatched to Nowy Kraków. His orders were to render official congratulations, make sure of preparations for a global eradication program, and ship us that first lot."

I planted myself before Jezierski, blew a stream of smoke at him, and finished: "The trouble is, Major Soltyk has not appeared. They claim in Nowy Kraków they know nothing. Accident? The TrafCon satellites record no transoceanic anomaly; he must have arrived.

"Everybody knows he and I are close friends. First the general grilled me, then he told me to go find out what the hell this means. I need a guide.

"You're the obvious choice. Can the Marines count on you? Think before you answer."

Within a couple of hours, we were on a suborbital trajectory. The flyer belonged to our regiment, as did the pilot and the three enlisted men with us two. The Land Gators look after their own.

In spite of his natural distress, Jezierski gasped when he first saw the globe beneath him, edged with sunrise and roofed with stars. He pressed his nose to the window. Sergeant Reinhardt, Corporals Rostov and Li didn't quite succeed in being sophisticated about the sight themselves. But then, they hadn't been told anything except what they barely needed to know, and . . . Lech was young. For my part, I held a poker face hard-clamped over my thoughts.

We curved over and thundered back into atmosphere, across dayside. At first Cracovia was a blue-green speck afloat in a bowl of mercury. It grew fast, until it filled the forward view with mountains, valleys, plains, rivers, lakes, many-hued woods, checkerboard pasture and cropland, under wan sunlight or towers of thunderhead. It is, after all, the biggest land mass in the Occidental Ocean, a million square kilometers. Nothing near that size shares those waters before they break on the shores of Tierra de la Muerte. I suppose isolation helped the colony in early days, gave a chance to lay firm foundations without being too much disturbed. It might stand the people in good stead again.

But any flourishing ranch draws wolves, once the watchdogs have departed. (Yes, I know what wolves are, I've read my share of classic books. Did you think military men care about nothing except their guns?)

We set down bumpily on the sole spacefield. I heard our pilot wonder aloud, with profanity, when the runways were last maintained. My guess was that that had been before my own time. Like a receding tide, the withdrawal of the Empire was slow and fitful. We rolled to a precise stop nonetheless, which cheered me somewhat. I led the way out.

Here the sun stood at midmorning and Catseye had not yet risen. So the air was chill, even at this low altitude. It smelled different from the air at Fort Kursk, spicy-acrid; that was native forest crowding in reddish masses around the rim, not fields long subdued to bear Terrestrial grain. The sky was clear, pale, a frost-ring about the tiny sun-disc, but mists eddied over the ground. They didn't always hide the cracks in paving, the relentless little herbs thrusting through. Buildings and control installations looked all right from this distance. However, I saw no sign of defenses.

Though a flag above the main terminal drooped in windlessness, I knew it displayed the White Eagle. Not that Cracovia had overtly seceded. The Województwo "assumed responsibility for the province, pending resolution of the present emergency." The Imperial Governor was happy enough to have this much amicability that he didn't insist on maintaining a proconsul and collecting taxes, nor protest the raising of a purely local armed service.

Half a dozen persons moved forward to meet me. Four were in the gray uniform of that service, helmets on heads and stutterguns slung at shoulders. A man in livery was obviously attendant on the middle-aged woman in the lead. She was big, her features strong but sightly under a grizzled bob, her frame erect in an almost aggressively native blouse, embroidered vest, and wide skirt. Did she bear a resemblance to Soltyk? Yes, I decided, she did, and this was to be expected. As often elsewhere, certain families had kept leadership for centuries, and generally intermarried. In Cracovia they had special pride, special tradition, rituals and coats of arms and so forth.

I'd had trouble understanding that when I paid my first furlough visit in company with Adam. On Covenant we discourage display, for only God may judge between one soul and another. Then he pointed out that in the Marines each regimental chapel keeps the old citations and battle banners.

The woman gave me a quick, hard handshake.

"Lieutenant-Colonel Raveloe, be welcome," she said in fluent if accented Anglic. "My name is Iwona Lis, associate to Wojewóde Kuzon. We wish to make everything as pleasant and expeditious for you as possible. With your permission, the squad will take baggage and we will convey you and your men to lodgings in the city."

"Thank you," I said, "but the key word is 'expeditious.' I must see his Excellency immediately, or whoever is in charge of this matter. Later we can settle in."

She stiffened. "Are you not being . . . swift?"

Anger jumped in me. "*Pani* Lis, I assume the message from Fort Kursk was clear. People are dying. We need that serum now."

The same feeling threw red across her high cheekbones. "Colonel Raveloe, the medicine is ready, together with physicians who know to administer it. They could be en route on an aircraft of ours, or already arrived. It is your high command requires an officer of its own be the carrier. We do not think this is so reasonable."

I curbed myself. A sigh passed voiceless through me. What answer dared I give? Well, how much did she herself know? Originally it had made sense for Major Soltyk to flit here in person, receive those precious vials, and arrange to have them sent in secrecy while he stayed behind a while to help plan the public distribution. But Soltyk had vanished and—

*"And what does it mean?" the general said to me. "No accident, that's for damn sure. Before you suggest he's taken the opportunity to desert, with friends at the other end to help him hide, I'll ask you not to tell your grandmother how to suck eggs." He leaned forward over his desk. The haggardness of him smoldered. "But why would he? Why would they? Furthermore, this isn't another case of some wretched rat of a trooper going over the hill. That problem's worse than we've admitted. In fact, desertions are draining us; and if you speak one word about it, Colonel, you'll be up before a court-martial. But this is Major Adam Soltyk, hero, brilliant combat leader, controversial policy advocate.*

*We can't hide his absence. We can't explain it away."*
The general's fist smote the desktop. *"What sort of
conspiracy is going? Or did Soltyk come to grief inno-
cently? Maybe by violence, for whatever dark reason?
We have to* know. *We have to have proof—and then
make an example of the guilty parties. Commandant
Santos told me this ranks with getting the Plague under
control; and he's right. Your record indicates you are
our best man to start the investigation."*

"I have my orders," I said. "They include a prompt
talk with your authorities."

I made no gesture at the flyer. She saw it behind me,
though, with guns and missile ports. "We were only
concerned for your well-being," she said stiffly. "Since
you insist— We have ground transportation to the city
arranged, because we wanted to let you relax. This
should give time for a meeting upon our arrival."

The upshot was that I'd be driven directly to the
Palace, together with my orderly Private Jezierski, while
the others were taken separately and provided for. I
wondered if this was some attempt at subtle intimida-
tion. Without my men at hand, would I be more pli-
able? Well, I thought, if they supposed that, they were
making a considerable mistake. Three infantrymen and
a spaceman gave me no added strength worth noting.
What backed me was Double Seven.

The cars that waited were aged but in good condition. Lis and I got in back of one, her adjutant took the
board and Jezierski sat in front beside him. We whirred
off along a road that was also well kept up. I remarked
on that.

"We take care of things we daily use," Lis answered.
"You will find it true of our airports and seaports too."

I refrained from telling about neglected public facili-
ties across most of Haven. Materials were in short and
erratic supply; money to pay skilled workers was worthless; and nobody in that jumble of quarrelsome statelets
looked to the future. Why should they?

"But we have no reason to spend resources on the

spaceport, do we?" Lis went on. "Rather, I think, we must destroy it before the invaders come and take it."

I sat straight. "Invaders? What do you mean?"

She shrugged. "You may have a better guess than we can. The Lavacans were the first. They will not be the last, nor the worst, if rumors that seep down from the stars have truth. We have neighbors on this planet too, restless and greedy. Oh, it is a story old and frequent. We remember the Land of Fields, which had no natural frontiers. Space has none."

"The Empire—" I fell silent.

We left the woods behind and came out into the Rzeka Valley. Broad and fair it stretched, cattle at graze in meadows fenced by stones the ancestors had taken out, grainfields ripening into goldenness. Buildings clustered in villages or stood not far apart on family-owned farms. They were mostly stuccoed, with bright tile roofs. Church spires soared among them. The weathers of centuries had softened all edges while nourishing lordly groves of oak and lanes of poplar. Northward the snowpeak of Góra Róg hung like a cloud in heaven.

"I wonder how a country like this can imagine anything except peace," slipped out of me.

"What we have, our forebears spent their lives to forge and hold," Lis replied. "They came as condemned political exiles, in the days of the CoDominium. Haven was a . . . dump for unwanted peoples, because it was meager and hostile. We would be ungrateful to forget what they did. And we would be unwise. Does God give us any special right to keep what *they* earned?"

Jezierski couldn't help himself. Something agonized broke from him. Lis responded in the same language. He settled back down. "Sorry, sir," he muttered.

I guessed he'd protested that he wasn't abandoning his kindred to their fate, and she'd given him a perfunctory reassurance. It seemed well for me to remind them both: "You've kept your inheritance thus far, thanks to the Empire. You'd be ungrateful and unwise to turn your backs on it."

"We have not," she said. "Let it return as it was, and we will strew flowers in its path. Meanwhile we must be prudent."

That hurt like a nerve-whip. Dead men don't rise again reborn, nor do dead hopes.

No one spoke through the remaining fifty-odd kilometers. That suited me well, gave me a chance to ease off, gather my thoughts, eventually even smile at recollections. Sights grew familiar, places I'd visited with Adam. In this little town there had been a fair, the marketplace full of booths and music and dancing feet. In that manor we had feasted, guests at the celebration of a son's confirmation. In yonder tavern we'd japed and yarned and matched beers with local men, till Adam arm-wrestled the blacksmith and won. He was briefly solemn on Dziewica Hill, because that was where the Freedom Commando made its stand and died; soon afterward, our whole party was merry, because a caravan of Cygani came jingling raggedy-rainbow down the road. And by one lake the whole family had picnicked, and I'd met his cousin Helena and come away all awhirl, but never managed to see her again. . . .

Houses moved closer together; industrial structures loomed between them. We crossed the bridge over the Rzeka and were in Nowy Kraków proper, winding along its narrow ancient streets. More and more I remembered—the fountain on whose bronze dragon graduating students rode; a winiarnia where an artisan, a philosopher, and I argued till Catseye sank behind the Sobieski Cross and everybody else was asleep; the flower stalls in Korzybski Square, where Frasyniuk first read aloud the Proclamation of Rights; whimsical façades in Booksellers' Alley; a cubbyhole cafe where Mama made the best pierogi in the universe; the Clock Museum; Chopin Hall; the roses and bowers of Czartorny Park—from such things a country is made.

The driver stopped at Stary Rynek and we passengers got out. I looked around. What with one thing and another, it had been several Earthyears, and surely this plaza was beautiful (is, still is beautiful, I pray to a God I do not believe in). Across the way, St. Mary's Cathedral lifted stone and stained glass up to the green copper cupolas; this happened to be a moment between hours, and the broken trumpet call sounded above us as it sounded for centuries on the mother world. Lesser walls glowed rose, amber, violet beneath steep roofs. Before us the Palace presented a rank of ogival windows. Vehicles were few in this time of scarcity, but foot traffic went dense over the paving, in and out of the Guildhall at the center of things. A young couple hand in hand; tea drinkers at outdoor tables; an itinerant musician; a gang of newly discharged Home Guardsmen, wildly decorated shawls across their shoulders, whooping it up; a priest in his cassock; a venerable man throwing bread to the pigeons; a painter at her easel, trying to capture the scene; homebound school children, books under their arms; ordinary folk on ordinary business—from such things a country is made.

"Follow me, please," said Iwona Lis, and led Jezierski and me up the stairs of the Palace.

The rotunda bustled and echoed with people, underneath its dark dome where the translucent image of our galaxy spiraled. The halls beyond were likewise busy, the rooms opening onto them crowded with desks and workers. I'd remarked on that, the last time Adam and I had dropped in: "You seem to have bred your share of bureaucrats."

He had answered wryly, "This is the only place we can house our public affairs, records, law courts, administrations, and the rest. Originally it was for ceremonies and cultural events, you know. But that was when computers and communications made most offices unnecessary. As they break down and can't always be fixed, while the Empire has stopped handling things for us, we need more and more government of our own." He paused. "We need it if Cracovia is to hang together. Farms are going under for lack of markets, fertilizers, biocontrols. Desperate men are taking to banditry. The big landholders are starting, each of them, to become a law unto himself." He rattled a laugh. "Why do I give you a sociology lecture? You've seen the same everywhere on Haven. You've heard it from everywhere in the Empire. Come, let us look at something more attractive."

That had been the reception chamber into which I was now ushered. My group and the two men who waited for us were lost in its wainscotted stateliness. I glanced up at the ceiling, where crossbars made a set of niches for holding coats of arms, those of the aristocratic families surrounding those of the Imperium. No, they had not replaced the latter with the White Eagle . . . yet. And, yes, in the courtesy space left vacant for distinguished visitors, there were the twin lightning-bolt sevens.

It similarly boded well, or less than ill, that two important individuals greeted me in the flesh—unlesss they wanted to gauge me better than you can in a com screen. True, neither of them was the Wojewóde; but I got a polite if unapologetic explanation that he was chronically overbusied and that Lis' call from the car had given very short notice.

Brigadier Jacek Skarga was stocky, bald, iron-faced, a Marine called out of retirement to lead the lately formed Home Guard. His years had only toughened the leather of him. He showed tact, saluting simultaneously with me before shaking hands in spite of the gap between our ranks. (Abruptly, I wondered whether he was telling me I represented a foreign power.) "Since you are largely concerned with Major Soltyk, I hear, it seemed best I discuss this with you myself," he rumbled. "First things first, however. The Plague." He nodded at his companion.

Professor Zygmunt Geremek was dean of the school of medicine at Copernican University: a lean man with a gray beard and relaxed manner, except for his eyes. "Welcome, Colonel Raveloe," he drawled. "Shall we sit down?"

Before the great fireplace and its flanking statues of the Angels of Victory and Mercy stood a table of heartfruit wood, flame-grained, gloriously carved, inset with tamerlane bone. We took seats; after I gave him a sign, Jezierski settled at my far side. A couple of servants padded in with cakes and authentic coffee.

Professor Geremek smiled, while never letting his blue gaze waver off me. "The delay in conveying the antiviral to your division has been unfortunate," he said. "But we have at least put the time to good use. Such chemosynthesizing units as we possess and can spare have been producing Agent Beta at full capacity. That is the cure, you understand." He smiled again, still more carefully. "We had to give it some name, no? A substantial quantity is ready for Fort Kursk— more than enough, I am sure, to deal with all cases there and in the environs. Needless to say, we will transmit the production program and other relevant information. In fact, we plan to distribute printed copies to regions which do not possess reliable electronic communications but may still have synthesizers in working order."

Recalling Slaunch, I could not but ask, "What does this stuff do?"

Geremek raised his brows. "You do not know?"

"I was brought in on the business just hours ago, sir. It's been under wraps."

"Ah, yes. The Imperial mind. . . . Well, then, as for application, the agent is a liquid to be injected intravenously. Depending on how advanced the case is, from one to six shots are required. The kit includes a blood test to make certain the virus has been wholly destroyed. Thereafter the patient gets nursing care while he recovers from the damage done his system. Of course, he must be protected against reinfection."

The implications of that slipped past me at the moment, like a night wind I barely felt. My interest was too aroused. "You realize this is a remarkable phenomenon," Geremek was continuing. "I believe something analogous occurred long ago on St. Ekaterina, but I have found no technical account here on Haven, and in any event that was merely a plant disease."

"What do you mean?" I asked.

"You were not informed?" His tone expressed mild surprise, which was a way of putting me in my place. I wasn't dealing with an unworldly academician. "The Red Plague is an attack by native life."

"What?" Briefly, ridiculously, I had before me images of a cliff lion, a land gator, a swordfin—sure, the big carnivores of Haven sometimes killed and ate people, while people ate muskylope, humphrodite, clown-fruit, the sweet gel we misnamed "honey"—"But that's impossible."

"Why?"

I must needs rise to his challenge, prove that I did know elementary biology. "Incompatible chemistries. Haven proteins have some of the same amino acids as ours, but not all; similarly for lipids, sugars, the whole range of nutrients, vitamins, trace elements in compounds our bodies can break down. If we tried to live off native plants and animals exclusively, we'd soon be dead of a score of deficiency diseases. Neither can Haven microbes live any length of time off us."

"What of viruses?"

"Still more impossible. The genetic material here resembles DNA and operates like it, but is not identical. The nucleotides—" I broke off. "Evidently something weird has happened."

"Good, Colonel," Geremek murmured. "Excellent." Did I see wariness strengthen in Lis and Skarga? "Yes, it was doubtless inevitable sooner or later, as nature played her eternal game of changes and permutations. A Haven virus has linked with one of Earth origin—an ordinary influenza virus, which has the means of invading human cells. The Haven component is a simple thing which requires only those amino acids common to both ecologies. It coils around its carrier so as to block the action of our immune system and of every antiviral we have hitherto known, since none of those 'recognize' molecules so alien. The result bears superficial resemblances to porphyria. However, it progresses too fast for conventional treatment to be of significant help.

Without Agent Beta, it must be one hundred percent fatal."

Sweat prickled under my arms and down my backbone. "But this drug will cure it?"

Geremek nodded. "Oh, yes. Once we had the idea of what was happening, we knew what to look for and how. The molecular structure was soon analyzed. Thereafter we could design a suitable reactant." He repeated his sharp smile. "If you are interested, it is a perfusive enzyme. It breaks the chemical bonds between the two viruses. Both become impotent and quickly perish. Then the body is free to flush out the toxins and set about repairing itself."

Jezierski stirred in his chair. He uttered a few words. The others stared at him. Recognizing his faux pas, he looked down at the table, where his fists lay knotted. His cheeks blazed. "I'm sorry, sir," he mumbled. "Got too excited."

"What did you say?" I inquired.

"Why, uh, well, I asked . . . whether a man, a recovered person . . . can catch the sickness all over again."

The tension which had been gathering in me uncoiled itself in action. "You're quick, son," I said, and flung at Geremek: "That's true, isn't it? You don't have a vaccine."

"Not yet," the scientist answered blandly. "A more difficult problem. We are working on it."

"When do you expect to have an answer?"

"If we knew that much, there would scarcely be a problem, would there?"

"In frankness," Lis added, "work will go faster if outsiders leave us alone. Take the cure and go."

I shook my head. "No." Caution intervened. "I'm grateful for what you've done. The whole planet soon will be. But you realize it isn't enough. The disease is highly contagious—also during an incubation period which may be several hundred hours—right?"

Geremek nodded as before. "Then without a vaccine, we can't conquer it, we can just contain it," I went on, my voice harsh in my ears. "We dare not risk letting it into space. It could outrun any health care, overrun the Empire."

"We intend to point this out to the Governor," Lis said.

"But they need us—the Marines—" I collected words. "Restoring the Imperial peace may well require every military resource we have."

Skarga stopped bothering to veil his scorn. "Fighting the civil war will require it," he rasped. "That is what you mean. You withdraw and leave worlds like this defenseless. The Imperial peace!"

"We follow our orders," I cast back. "I thought a *former* officer would understand that."

"Gentlemen, please," Geremek broke in, soft-toned. "Let us avoid pointless quarrels. We have a cure for the Plague. Any recurrences can be quickly, almost routinely treated. The Marines alone have the organization and resources to get established a global system of production, delivery, and application. I would guess this as requiring two thousand hours of intensive effort. That is your first duty, Colonel."

My mind automatically translated his precision into round figures. Twenty-five or thirty days— The division wouldn't likely be called that soon, and meanwhile doing something real would boost morale no end. "Very good," I replied, and refrained from adding, "As far as it goes." Instead: "Let's get cracking. You don't have a suborbital vehicle of your own, do you? No? Well, please bring everything necessary to the one I came in, at once, including experienced personnel to demonstrate for our medics. My pilot will take off for Fort Kursk the minute it's aboard."

"What of yourself?" Lis demanded.

"And the enlisted men with you," Skarga said.

"We stay a while," I told them. "The reason you weren't simply requested to send the shipment by your fastest conveyance is that our man who came to take possession of those first few grams you informed us you'd have ready, he's gone."

Skarga drew his brows together. "So I have gathered,

from *Pani* Lis' call. Why do you make so important a business of it?"

"My commandant does. Your good faith is not necessarily denied, but you can see why we had to make as sure as we reasonably could that nobody was planning some lethal trick. Besides, Major Soltyk is our service brother. We are not about to write him off. Sir, in the name of the Emperor, I require the facts of the case."

Skarga sighed. "They are few. The advance information was that he would land at the municipal airport but did not know the precise time. He did not explain why, but said he would call the Palace when he arrived. A four-seater stratojet with Marine insignia did put down. It is in charge of the Guard and you are welcome to inspect it and take it back. Airport personnel paid little attention. From casual witnesses we have learned that a single man was inside. He wore civilian clothes. After the vehicle was in garage, he took the slideway up to the terminal. That is the last anybody knows." His grin was cold. "The city police are not accustomed to tracing missing persons. Nor is the Guard, which has much else to keep it busy. Besides, by the time Fort Kursk inquired of us, hours had passed."

"What do you think, sir?"

"I have not had an opportunity to think about it until now. Do you realize that airborne pirates have been raiding northern Cracovia? Hit-and-run attacks from Gletscherheim. The king claims he is powerless to stop them. We do not believe him, but it does not matter. We are preparing for hot pursuit of the next squadron, and will clean its home base out. Further incidents will bring punitive action more widespread." His eyes reminded me that this was the proper work of the Marines. Mine replied that we were spread too thin.

"Soltyk could have met with foul play," I insinuated. "For instance, your pirates may be shrewd and well-informed. Delaying a campaign against the Plague would mean more chaos for them to operate in."

"Far-fetched," Lis scoffed; but I knew how the specter of terrorist tactics must stand before her.

"Or it's possible Soltyk made . . . a mistake," I said. "If so, I must speak with him. He's too valuable an officer to let go. My lady and gentlemen, I have a printout from the Governor directing your cooperation."

"Its legal force is questionable," Lis answered stonily. After a silence which brimmed in that cavern of a chamber: "Be that as it may, we have nothing to spare for you. You must work by yourself."

"I shall so report," I said. "You will not obstruct an agent of the Imperium."

"No, no," she promised. I thought how empty that was.


We were quartered at the Hotel Wasa. It was a dignified old place, four stories of mullioned windows and pastel wall overlooking the shops along its street. Their wares were as sparse as its guests. We four were alone in the dining room, except for a waiter who probably had his job in lieu of a pension. Most items on the menu were unavailable. We ate adequately, though, with scarcely a word between us. Afterward I told Jezierski to accompany me back to my room. The corridors were empty and still. Portraits of forgotten magnates stared at us.

When my door had closed, I said. "At ease. Sit down. Would you like a drink or something?"

"The colonel is too kind," he almost whispered. "No, thank you, please." He settled on the edge of a chair.

I took my seat opposite him, leaned back, crossed shank over knee, bridged my fingers, and peered across them in the most fatherly way I knew. "You're my consultant, remember," I said. "My guide, assistant, and bodyguard if needful—comrade in arms." Despite the trouble in him, he dropped his glance and blushed like a girl. "I want you to speak frankly. You can't offend me with the truth."

"I will . . . do my best, sir."

"I'm sure you'll continue to be a credit to the service. Now, what do you make of that scene at the Palace? Of this whole situation?"

"I don't know, sir. What can I?"

"You mean you're just a country boy? Come, come, Private. For openers, all your life you've known your uncle, his family, the entire society that made him what he is. He had clear orders. Does it ring true he'd be vague about his time of arrival? That he wouldn't promptly report in, but disappear?"

Jezierski ran tongue over lips. His eyes lifted, and I saw abrupt desperation. "Sir, he cannot be a traitor. He cannot. It's impossible."

"That's my impression too," I reassured him. "Naturally, Intelligence has questioned his wife and children. They seem as honestly bewildered as you. Jadwiga— *Pani* Soltyk wants to come here with the youngsters and, mmm, wait things out in familiar surroundings. Would it be wise to allow that?"

"Oh, please, sir—"

"It's up to the commandant, of course. I daresay he'll let them. For instance, they could ride with the returning Cracovian doctors. After all, when the division leaves there'll be nothing to prevent them going wherever they like, if they can get passage and if the crossing can be made safely. But first we need to know what's afoot. Suppose Major Soltyk has been—lured astray and kidnapped. Better not expose innocents to the same danger."

"How could he have been, sir?"

"Well, someone may have contacted him clandestinely. That would be easy. But who? And what's he—they—up to?"

The pain sharpened in Jezierski. His face had gone chalky. I could practically see the turmoil behind it. If Uncle Adam was loyal, a faction among his people must be enemy.

I doubted matters were that straightforward. If Jezierski reflected on the nuances of the conversations I'd been in, he'd likely feel the same doubt. For the present, it seemed desirable to steer him off with hints of melodrama.

"Another strange thing," I said. "We had the distinct

idea originally, back at base, that not just a medicine but a vaccine was ready."

"Surely a m-m-misunderstanding, sir. Technicalities—and Anglic is not our, not the Cracovian language."

"Well, it still looks odd to me. I'm a layman, but I do know some molecular biology. Cadet officers in my day got the kind of education they don't any longer. Assuming development of the vaccine has lagged, what's the reason? Or has it?"

"The professor told us, sir. A harder problem."

"Really? Once the chemistry of the Plague was understood well enough to tailor an enzyme that stops it, I should think it would be a fairly standard matter of genetic engineering to make an immunizing agent. How about a modified strain of human intestinal flora to manufacture the enzyme and release it into the bloodstream? That sort of thing's been done for centuries, against everything from diabetes to Greenstein's Syndrome. Inject everybody on Haven—or, I suppose, just everybody who may have been exposed—and you eradicate the Plague entirely. Agent Beta is a mere stopgap." I paused. "Or else it's an unnecessary detour."

"But, but why would—anyone—falsify the work?"

"To keep the Seventy-Seventh on this planet?"

"Cracovia doesn't have the only experts." A touch of pride: "The best, but not the only ones."

I nodded. "Given the information that Geremek's team is providing, we can find people to go on from there. They'd be slower, but in due course—an Earthyear or two?—they'd have the vaccine. Then the division can ship out." Again I gave him a moment to think. "That may be too late for a certain party in the war."

Jezierski gaped.

"Do you begin to see why this is a mystery we *must* crack?" I pursued. "Geremek and company may have been truthful. Or they may not have been. Our mission begins with finding out which."

After a long career, I could put on an excellent show of decisiveness. The fact was that I had only the vaguest notion of what to do. A few fragmentary ideas had come to me in the past couple of hours, but I depended on Jezierski's leadership, and on making him believe it was mine. "Before enlisting, you studied at the university, didn't you?" I asked rhetorically.

"Yes, sir. Physics. I didn't finish."

"Why not?"

"Oh, it got to feel so . . . futile. Nothing but memorizing texts and repeating experiments. Who's made any real discoveries these past two or three hundred years? Better to enter the priesthood. That would mean something."

"But you chose the Marines. With us, you could hope to get into the Deep."

He swallowed hard.

"Well," I said, "you did acquire learning we need. You know your way around that place."

Cracovia used the regular Haven calendar; but unlike people in Castell, here they didn't ordinarily stagger their schedules. They preferred working and playing together as much as possible. I suppose somehow this arose from a unity that most civilizations within the Empire have lost. The sun was approaching noon when Jezierski and I went forth into an empty and utterly quiet street. We'd planned for that.

I'm not in Intelligence, but in the course of pacifications I've necessarily picked up techniques. A detector from my baggage indicated we were free of electronic surveillance. Once outdoors, my eyes soon verified we weren't being followed. I had decided we should keep our uniforms, because they lent some show of authority and a change to civilian garb might excite suspicion if reported. Let any stakeout assume we were just taking a stroll, working off restlessness brought on by the day zone shift.

Though we walked along in the most ordinary fashion we could manage, our boots racketed loud in our ears. I caught echoes off high walls and out of twisting alleys. Among the parked vehicles I saw as many unpowered as not. With scarcity upon them and worse to come, folk were breeding horses. Nevertheless the city remained clean. So did fronts and windows.

Catscye had risen, close to half phase, dayside luminous with stormswirls, darkside showing ember glows even through a sunlit sky. The spire of St. Jan Pawel's pierced it like a spear. Three companion moons were wanly visible. A few clouds drifted on a cold breeze, tinged coppery toward the planet, silvery toward the star. Beneath them on the ground, the mingled lesser shadows came and went.

Copernican University was in the middle of town. It didn't have a campus like American (where native weeds were crowding in around mostly abandoned halls). A number of buildings stood near each other. The four oldest defined a paved quad. A guard—Home Guardsman, uniformed and armed—stood at its gateway. Jezierski and I halted. We exchanged looks. His said he hadn't expected this either.

After a second he trod close and spoke in Polski. The sentry, a young fellow like him, answered with a smile. Jezierski turned to me. "This is a friend of mine from student days," he said. "They have begun keeping watch during sleeptime because there has been crime, theft, wanton destruction." His mouth writhed. "In Nowy Kraków, sir! . . . What shall I tell Sergeant Michnik?"

If yonder boy had already made sergeant, and nevertheless drew sentry-go, it said much about Skarga's command, and little of that was favorable. Not that I blamed the brigadier. He was able and conscientious—no genius, but Alexander or Napoleon couldn't have created an army all by himself. How many good officers did Skarga have? They were few enough in the Seventy-Seventh.

I thought fast. "Explain I have a mission, which you needn't describe," I directed. "Say this is a free spell, and I'd like to see your famous institution."

Jezierski winced. He must hate lying to his compatriot. He did, though, and Michnik gestured us through, without a salute for me. He seemed amiable, so perhaps it hadn't occurred to him—nobody had ever told him—I was his superior in the Imperial service.

Cloisters surrounded the quad. I imagined students colorful and cheerful, professors serene and honored, in waketime; and I wondered how much longer they would be. "Hurry up before somebody else notices us," I muttered.

We passed by the stargazing statue, through a bronze door where the Great Equations stood in relief, down a row of time-dimmed murals to another door, and on through. Jezierski had told me it was traditional to leave this holy place unlocked. Evidently a youngster with a rifle was still believed to suffice. Beyond lay a dim chamber lined with books, codices as well as micro. Atop one shelf, I recognized a bust of Alderson. My attention flew to the desks and office equipment, yes, *that* computer terminal.

I sat down before it. Jezierski and I had already discussed procedure. The board was standard, but he didn't know every trick you could play with it, whereas I didn't know the language in which Geremek doubtless kept his records.

Jezierski leaned over my shoulder. "First we must obtain the file code, sir," he said needlessly. "Touch KOD—*kodeks*. Now spell out G, E, N, E, T, Y, K, A." In a couple of minutes the display was giving us the data on Red Plague research.

Time dragged then, scraping my nerves, for he must pick his way through unfamiliar technicalities. I could only help by telling him when a report was obviously irrelevant and by gradually deducing the form of logic tree used.

In the end we had a name. Agent Alpha. The immunizer.

That was what we had. Nothing else. We went back over the ground twice to make sure.

I swiveled my chair around and looked up into Jezierski's eyes. Light from the screen and a narrow window picked them wide out of dusk. "We-ell," I breathed through the silence. "Most interesting. Not a word about it in the whole damned database."

"Sir, there is—I saw implications mentioned—"

"Sure, that was inevitable. The professor hasn't had time to censor everything out."

"Maybe they have n-n-n-not begun this next stage of the work."

"Impossible. I told you, the cure and the preventive have got to be two parts of the same thing. You can no more learn about one without making progress on the other than you can design a new missile without regard to the propellant. No, somebody's wiped the file on Agent Alpha."

He lifted his hands like a man fending off a blow. "Destroyed, it, sir? *Nie! Nigdy!* I will not believe!"

I rose and laid a hand of my own on his shoulder. "Easy, son," I said in my gentlest tone. "The information would've been copied off first. The disc is hidden somewhere, likeliest in somebody's possession."

"In God's name, why?"

"I'd guess because the research is in fact complete. A program for making Agent Alpha exists. Come on, let's get the hell out of here. We've been lucky so far, sort of, but it can't last."

Jezierski was stunned. After I'd removed the traces of our visit as best I could, he shambled along beside me, staring ahead. I tried to cover by staying between him and Sergeant Michnik as we went out. But the gaze followed us. Soon after the guard went off duty, word would be going around about this curious visit.

I wasn't sure how long it would be before Skarga heard—Lis, Geremek, the whole gang. The chances were we were dealing with a handful of amateurs. Still, they were tough, smart, determined. If I didn't act fast, I might well find myself blocked off from acting at all.

What were they after?

My thoughts rattled in the hollow streets, between the blank walls. To Jezierski I'd suggested that a faction in Cracovia favored a faction in the war for the Empire. Maybe one contestant had promised special treatment if Double Seven was kept off his neck. Then doubtless the promise was to the nation, not to individuals, considering what a fierce sense of community most Cracovians had. Lis and her associates weren't monsters. They were releasing Agent Beta, lest millions die. But they were withholding Alpha until the military situation had changed beyond retrieval.

None of that conjecture felt right. Space traffic was thin these days; the Marines monitored it without difficulty. You'd need a considerable volume of clandestine messages to and fro to work up a plot like this. Moreover, it would have had to have reached its decision point very recently. Though Geremek denied it now, the original word to Fort Kursk, that brought Adam Soltyk here, indicated that both Alpha and Beta were on hand. The leaders in Nowy Kraków had changed their minds almighty quickly, and tried to cover their tracks.

They'd tried too thoroughly. That blank file gave them away. If Geremek planned to insert a convincing fake, I'd anticipated him.

His group was bound to find out soon. I had to keep ahead of them.

But how? Going where?

I looked around. Nobody was in sight. Just the same, I drew Jezierski into a lane. A cat lying on a window ledge watched us, idly curious. The breeze had sharpened to a wind. It whined and bit.

I shook Jezierski out of his daze. He looked at me the way a trapped animal might. "Listen," I said. "We've come upon treason. Without that vaccine, our division is stranded on Haven, effectively crippled. We can't serve." I didn't add that we were unsure of whom we would be serving. "We can't get into the Deep.

"Now I don't for a minute imagine that more than a few individuals are involved. We've got to let the high command know what we've discovered. However, I think we—you and I, Lech—are in a position to discover more. A unique position. Let's take advantage of it.

"Think what'll happen if the Marines come to search for the traitors and Agent Alpha. They'll ransack the island. The innocent will suffer along with the guilty—or much more, because the guilty won't wait to be arrested, they'll disappear. Cracovia considers itself a nation. People will furiously resent troops coming in to occupy it. Incidents will lead to bloodshed, maybe to a little war, the kind this world has already seen too many of. Do you agree?"

He nodded mutely.

"Adam Soltyk's vanishment can't be a coincidence," I went on. "I am not, repeat not, accusing my friend of anything. I'm certain he's incapable of treachery." That was an altogether honest statement. "He may have been fooled, himself betrayed. In that case, I'll do what I can to smooth things over." I hoped Jezierski didn't notice my voice stumble there. "Or he could be a prisoner, or—Well, we need to find out, don't we?

"Have you any idea where he might be?"

Jezierski must try three times before he croaked, "Sir, this is a big island. Farmhouses, villages, wilderness—"

"I know. Or he could be dead." That battered at the boy's resistance. "However, the indications are he moved about on his own. Suppose he felt, for whatever reason, wise or unwise—suppose he felt he'd better lie low a while. Can you guess where that might be? Someplace out of the way but familiar to him, with emergency exits or hidey-holes. Sure, it's a long shot, but give me your best guess."

I waited a moment before finishing, "On your honor, Private Jezierski."

Reinhardt, Rostov, and Li were playing cards in the sergeant's room. The air was blue and bitter with smoke. They sprang to their feet when I entered. "At ease," I told them. "You'll have a spell more to cool your heels."

"No action, sir?" Li was obviously disappointed.

"Not expected," I answered. "Stand by." I handed Reinhardt a sealed envelope. "If it happens you return to base without me, this must go to the high command. Under all circumstances. Understood?"

They stared. "Sir," ventured Reinhardt, "you aren't headed into danger alone, are you?"

I suspected he was as much shocked by the irregularity as by anything else. A commissioned officer puts his life on the line where necessary, yes, but otherwise he issues orders to his juniors. I forced a grin. "No reflection on you three. This is a delicate matter. Private Jezierski will be my interpreter and backup. I rely on my experienced men to convey my message in the unlikely event of trouble. There's a Marine flyer available for our use." I briefed them, having earlier obtained the information at the Palace. "Or if you must, commandeer whatever else you see fit. But that's strictly contingency. Give me thirty hours to contact you before you start worrying."

They had already begun. I felt it as I left.

Jezierski was in my room, crouched before the com. Forgetting to rise, he turned a stiffened face toward me. "They w-w-will not release a military vehicle, sir," he reported. "You must call yourself." He pointed to a display cell. His finger shook.

"Oh, I expected that," I said. "I had you try making the requisition for me just to expedite matters." He left the chair and lurched aside. I sat down and punched. It was scant surprise when Lis' countenance appeared. Her or Skarga, I'd thought; the circle of conspirators must be small.

I went straightway on the offensive. "Greeting, *Pani*. You pledged full cooperation with his Majesty's investigators. But your depot refuses us transportation, apart from the inadequate vessel Major Soltyk arrived in. Why?"

"It is . . . most unusual, Colonel Raveloe," she replied. "In the middle of sleeptime—"

"Not unexpected, though, since you left standing orders you be called. What other possibilities have you covered?"

"Furthermore," she continued as if she hadn't heard,

"you demand a fighter craft. What do you intend, that an ordinary transport will not serve?" With a slight sneer: "You could send for a taxi. I am sure you have a generous expense account."

"Converting Imperial credits to gold isn't simple, Pani, especially at this hour. As for thc haste and the type of flyer, let me remind you that my duty is to learn what's become of one of our most valuable officers. Suppose he's been captured by those pirates I heard mentioned. Far-fetched, maybe, but— My duty is also to return alive, in order that I may serve the Empire further. It's basic to provide myself with means of protection." I put a knife edge on my tone. "Do you deny me this? Please think. His Majesty's Governor has been patient with Cracovia, but he cannot overlook outright rebellion."

"You exaggerate, Colonel. This is a difference of judgments." She bit her lip. "May I ask what you plan to do?"

I was prepared. "A reasonable question. Look, I don't know why you're so antagonistic, but I'm willing to be frank. The odds are all against my success in this assignment, and the time I can devote to it is limited. But I must make my best effort. It seems to me that that should start with an aerial survey. Maybe I can turn up a clue. For instance, in spite of having bandits to combat, your people might not recognize a guerrilla encampment for what it is, whereas I might well. Then I'll make inquiries in Major Soltyk's home area, around Wielki Lato. You remember I have a kinsman of his with me. If we get a lead, we'll try to follow it. If not, which I admit is much more likely, we'll return here, consult with you and headquarters both, and probably go home."

Relief struggled with vigilance. "I see. Thank you. How long do you propose to search, and in what pattern?"

"Unless I do discover something, I have about two hundred hours. Private Jezierski suggests a preliminary zigzag flight path, southeast to, uh, Cape Wrak, then to-and-fro northward."

"Yes, that will be best," Lis said hastily. "Very well, I will give an authorization. It will take perhaps an hour to clear channels. Do you wish to be at Gwiazda Field at that time?"

We went through brief courtesies. I switched off and turned to my companion. "All right," I said. "Go rouse 'em in the kitchen and get us a well-loaded food basket." Squinting: "What's wrong?"

He shivered where he stood. "Sir, you—you lied to *Pani* Lis."

"Well, I was diplomatic." Sharply: "No more haggling, you hear?"

"Yes, sir. I, I did not mean to be—insubordinate—"

No, I reflected, not exactly. He had only, wildly, insisted, there in the alley, that action was futile if I didn't follow his advice. *"Sir, I do know where he may have gone. But we must not take the others. The colonel understands? Private talk."* Tears came forth. He wiped them with his wrist. *"Y-you wanted me along because I know the country and my people."*

I had refrained from requiring him to tell me what he meant, regardless. He might have refused, and tried in some incoherent fashion to justify himself at the court-martial.

"Go fetch that chow," I said. "Include plenty of coffee."

Alone, I got out my sidearm and secured it to my belt. That would be our single weapon. Guns and missiles were not what I wanted a pursuit craft for.

I went to the window and stood, not really seeing the gracious roofs and the spires above them. My thoughts were colder than the wind that whistled down the street.

The flyer was a Lance-15 two-seater, part of the equipment the Cracovians had "inherited" when the Forty-Fifth left Haven. It wasn't the best they had, I knew, but it was well maintained and the gauge showed fusion potential sufficient to circle the globe three times. I took it straight up and lined out southeast at its top stratospheric cruising speed.

From the fire control seat at my back, Jezierski's awed whisper cut through the murmur within the cabin. "How beautiful our world is, sir. We must keep it."

The sky engulfed us in purple. Away from the mighty shield of Catseye and the diamond glare of the sun, stars glittered. Haven curved underneath, silver-swirled with clouds above wrinkled land and gleaming sea. "But it is not like the Deep," he added.

That gave me hope he was strengthened for what lay ahead.

Which might be nothing, of course. He hadn't claimed certainty.

From afar I spied a squall. They're common west of the Catseye dawn line in the lower latitudes, where air masses of different temperatures collide. My instruments declared this was a big one. Good. "Hang on," I warned, and dived for its darkness.

We pierced chaos. Wind roared, yelled, dashed rain over the canopy till all I could see was lightning. The craft bucked, dropped, yawed. Twice we nearly went into the drink. But I had full control throughout. After ramping about in the storm for minutes, I broke free and streaked low above the water. Grayback waves snatched hungrily after us, then damped out until we jetted over blue-green brilliance adance with whitecaps.

"That was, uh, uh, that was amazing, sir," Jezierski stammered. "I expected m-my jaw would pop out the top of my head."

I laughed, mainly to encourage his show of spirit. "Well, maybe it was a bit much, but it seems to've worked." I'd taken for granted that the Cracovian air corps had us under surveillance both by ground-based radars and by at least one craft with more legs than this. Why else had Lis kept us waiting before we could board? Now, according to my instruments and intuition, we'd shaken any watchers. Given their limited capabilities, they might take several hours to reacquire us.

I didn't think Lis or Skarga would question me very closely about my maneuver if I returned to Nowy

Kraków. They didn't want an open break with the Imperium.

"No time to waste," I said, skimming along, and displayed a map of the west coast. "Here, lean over and point. I'll switch to progressively larger scales till you've zeroed the destination."

"Reda Bay, I told you, sir. South shore, about seventy-five klicks from Port Morski, which is the nearest town."

The ultimate detail was a satellite picture of a small house on the edge of a cliff. Behind it and on either side was wilderness, native forest. "A *domek*, sir, a holiday home that belonged to my parents. Uncle Adam—Major Soltyk often joined us there. It's my other uncle's now, but he and his wife don't like the location. The last I heard, they had not sold it. Who has money any more?"

"Vacant and isolated. Uh-huh."

The voice at my back, which had been intent, cracked across. "But why would he hide, sir? He can't be—a deserter—before God, he can't be!"

I thought that the prospect of leaving Jadwiga and the kids for years, possibly forever, could give motive. Not enough, though. They had faced the possibility when they married, and he had not resigned, because he believed that guarding civilization mattered too much. Today no resignation would be accepted—not till after the war—but eventually he might hope for discharge and some way of getting home, if any Imperial ship dared by then to cross this part of space. And if he remained alive. Would any? Civilians went in terror of being left to defend themselves. That was why we downplayed the likelihood.

"No, he's not a quitter, absolutely not a coward," I agreed. "But something strange is afoot. Shut up and let me pilot." Let me think. Let me grope in winter blindness.

At our speed, we approached the goal within half an hour, rounding the southern end of the island, swinging north, veering east. Land fairly leaped over the horizon. Here it was rugged, standing a hundred meters above a white fury of breakers. Reefs and shoals must make the tides higher and rougher than elsewhere, and they are more so on Haven than on most habitable planets. Above the tawny limestone, russet treetops billowed before the wind. The far shore of the bay was invisible from this height; the one sign of man was the cottage. Low and sturdy, with vines blossoming scarlet over whitewashed walls, it belonged to this landscape in which it had stood for centuries.

A landing strip lay vacant at the rear. I set down vertically, threw off my harness, flung the door open and sprang forth. My hand was on my sidearm. Wind soughed, full of salt and chill; the sea-thunder came over the cliff edge like an endless drumbeat; wings soared lonely overhead. Already wireweed and prickle bush were reclaiming what had been a garden. They surrounded the strip. Our jets had scorched them a trifle. Nothing stirred within the house, nobody stepped out.

I beckoned Jezierski to follow me and walked to it. The door was unlocked, as was customary almost everywhere in Cracovia. (How much longer would it be?) We entered. Light slanted through windows, over a snugness of generations-old furniture, books, discs, heirlooms, antiquated but serviceable electronics. When Jezierski shut the door, thick walls enclosed us in silence.

We looked through the four rooms and came back to the first. "It seems I was wrong." Jezierski sounded glad. "Nobody here. I'm sorry, sir. But it was only a guess."

I shook my head. "Somebody's been around till, I'd say, an hour ago or less. Food in the pantry, well, that's stuff that would keep. The beds are stripped, but used linen could easily be squirreled away in the woods. What I notice is that there's no dust, and that the heat's turned off but the interior's warm."

"Somebody else—maybe gone for a walk—"

"Without a made-up bed to welcome him home? No, Adam Soltyk got out. He hoped we wouldn't show, at least not immediately."

A noise like a sob, then: "Do you mean . . . somebody called and warned him? How could they know?"

"They didn't, for sure. They must have contacted him on general principles, told him he'd better hide himself more thoroughly till they gave him the all-clear. It could have worked, if we'd arrived much later."

"They took him away?" Jezierski asked eagerly.

"I think not. No char marks on the brush, except ours and some so faint they're many hours older. Fetching him would be kind of chancy. An aircraft descending to this empty spot could well be noticed in Port Morski or aboard a ship at sea. Investigators could pick up the gossip. That would be a clear sign he had help, which could bring on disastrous consequences. No, I think a strong reason he went to earth here is that the location has more than one covert." I turned to confront him. "You'll know where."

He backed away a step before he caught himself. "No, sir. We have a whole forest around us."

I caught his gaze and hung on. "You've got a better idea than that, son. You're not a skilled liar."

He broke. Again I saw tears. "Please, sir!"

"Has the situation changed? Has our duty? Doesn't the fact that Soltyk scuttled from us make it the more urgent to track him down?"

Anger brought blood to cheeks. "He didn't scuttle!"

A gulp, a shudder. Flatly: "Very well, sir. For the honor of my kindred." The phrase did not sound pretentious. Jezierski looked beyond me. His fists clenched, unclenched, clenched. "There is a cave at the foot of the cliff. Pieczara Syreny, we children always called it. Uh, M-mermaid Grotto. One must be careful, because the water is crazy. But places inside are above high tide. Sometimes for an adventure a grown-up took us down. We played pirates or—"

"Well, let us go!" he screamed.

"Good for you, Marine," I said softly.

Flashlights were in a cabinet from which other items of camping gear seemed to have been removed. We helped ourselves and departed.

Brush screened the head of a trail down the heights. Without my guide I'd never have found it, for it was little better than a set of precarious footholds, snaking along natural projections and cracks. My muscles strained to hold me. I kept having to clutch rock or gaunt bushes lest I go over. Wind hooted and slashed. As we neared the sea, spindrift blew blinding in our eyes, bitter onto our lips. Surf crashed and spouted. I felt its impact tremble through the stone. Jezierski led the way, agile, joyless.

The tide was flowing, but had not yet covered a strip of beach at the bottom. I slipped on wet cobbles, skinned a knee, regained my feet and slogged on. Chill smote me. My clothes were drenched. But my sidearm didn't suffer from it.

I'd never have seen the grotto from the bay, either. A holm, on which the waves burst in white curtains, blocked that view. Through the scud I descried a blackness which was the mouth. Military reflex made me scan the terrain past it. There also, the cliff didn't rise quite sheer. Crags, ledges, erosion holes would enable an active man to climb. If he went up, he'd emerge, breathless, in the woods. Desolation like this was right for what we had to do. A sunlit meadow or a Catseye-lit lakeshore would have been mockery.

We halted before the entrance. "What now, sir?" I could just hear Jezierski's hoarseness through the racket. He'd lost his cap; the blond hair clung to his skull.

"Does the cave have any traps for the unwary?" I asked.

"No, sir, if you are careful."

"Then I'd better lead." Else he would be my shield; and I was his commanding officer.

At first light from outside touched the vaulting of the roof, the water that churned and snarled over the floor. A ledge on the right led into flickery shadows. They deepened as we went inward, until I thumbed my flash against them. That left me alone in a shifting puddle of paleness. The currents and rips filled it with their echoes. Ahead of me, the passage bent around a corner.

"Douse your glim," I ordered Jezierski, softly under the noise, and did likewise. We stood for what felt like a long time. My eyes adapted. I picked out a dim glow seeping around the edge. Crouched, I slipped forward for a peek.

The cave ended several meters beyond. Most of the space was occupied by a shelf whose roughness loomed above high-water mark. The glow was from a portable heater-cookstove on top. Adam's sleeping bag and food supplies must be there too. Himself? I moved ahead, onto a wide space below the shelf, keeping rock always next to me.

Brilliance struck. I stood dazzled. "Hold!" rang a remembered voice. "Not a move. Either of you." A shot cracked. I heard the bullet whang off the wall behind us. "You are covered."

He'd outwitted me, I realized with my guts. Probably he'd kept watch near the cave mouth, seen us approach, retreated to ready his ambush. He had the drop on us. I couldn't even have seen where to aim.

"Hands on heads," he commanded. I let my flashlight fall and set the example for Jezierski. Should I force my friend to kill us?

Through the wet surge at my heels, I heard his footfalls approach. They stopped. The beam wavered. "Colin," he choked. "Lech. Not you."

"Nobody else," I retorted. "Can you fire on men of Double Seven?"

"I will . . . do what I must," Soltyk answered. "Have care. Why did you betray me, Lech?"

His nephew cried aloud.

"Don't blame him," I said, for that pain was hurtful to hear. "The top brass sent me after you. I co-opted Jezierski; he had small choice about that. True, he could have played dumb and left me without any realistic hope of finding you. I'm not saying he would have, but he could have. What made him help, made him suggest we look here, was the absence of any data on Agent Alpha, the Plague vaccine. It had to have been concealed. That was too much. Who is the betrayer, Adam?"

"Sir," Jezierski pleaded, "Major Soltyk can explain. He is honest, he has good reasons for everything, I know he does."

"You have the program with you, don't you?" I hammered.

"What makes you imagine that?" Soltyk growled.

I sighed. "Adam, after these many years I can tell when you're bluffing. But in this case, it's only logical. The higher-ups in Nowy Kraków had pretty clearly connived with you. They had also, pretty clearly, abstracted the Alpha file. That was scarcely a coincidence. If they were helping you hide, the chances were they'd leave the disc in your care."

"You're a quick one, Colin. Nobody expected you'd search the medical database right away, as it appears you have. I won't waste time denying the program exists. It's lying up there with my duffel. Can you guess why?"

"Kuron's people—I suppose the Wojewóde is party to this— they made it plain in retrospect. Their intent is that we shall think Alpha is still under development. That'll give them leverage against us. We could complete the project ourselves, but much slower and at high cost to our limited technical resources. For a start, they can insist we drop our hunt for you, because on the scale necessary, it would be too bothersome; their scientists would go on strike. You're a mighty important man in Cracovia, aren't you, Adam?"

"Yes," said the voice from behind the mask of light. Slowly: "The question is what to do about you two. You must have left a record of what you know and what you were about to try. This won't be a safe place for me any more. But I have an entire island full of refuges, and Alpha for my hostage."

"Nie," said Jezierski. Sweat sheened on the highlights of his face. He breathed like a runner at the end of a marathon.

"Be reasonable," Soltyk urged. "Let me see . . . Yes,

I'll go up the trail first. Don't follow in my sight. You'll have ample time to get on top before the tide. I'll have taken your flyer, but somebody will be along in due course, or it's not too long a hike to Port Morski. Then for God's sake—for everybody's sake, Colin—see if you can't keep matters from reaching a crisis."

"*Nie*," Jezierski said again. "You must not. For our honor."

He sprang. Soltyk shouted. Jezierski paid no heed. He landed between me and yonder firearm.

"Sir," he called, "please do not kill him if you can avoid it. Let him explain."

He held his right hand out. Though he spoke in Polski, I knew what it meant. "Give me your weapon, Uncle." Behind him, I drew my own. He would not die unavenged.

Soltyk cursed, once. His pistol clattered across the rock. I retrieved my flashlight and pinned him in its beam. The old half-grin of battle lifted his mustache. "You called my bluff," he said almost merrily.

"Well done, Private Jezierski!" I exclaimed in my poverty of words.

"Tell the colonel why," the boy coughed forth. "Tell us, tell us."

Soltyk shrugged. "Shall we make ourselves more comfortable?" he asked.

"Sure." We took our various flashlights and aimed them aside. Diffused, the beams brought us halfway out of darkness.

"You are not a traitor, not a deserter," Jezierski said, barely hearable in the hollow noise around us.

"Not the usual sort, anyhow," I declared. "Those top-flight people wouldn't have taken the risks they did if you were simply quitting, Adam. There must have been some contact before you flew to Cracovia; I imagine you pulled a few wires to get the assignment. How long did you intend to withhold Agent Alpha?"

"Only till the division is sent for." Soltyk's tone stayed level. "We could have delayed that embarkation, but not by much, and it might have caused the worst of the war lords to win, when we hope that the least bad will. No, the Wojewóde means—meant to announce at the proper time that the research was completed. In fact, a supply of the immunizer would have been secretly produced, sufficient for the Marines. In exchange, in the hurry of departure, we'd try for certain concessions, certain amnesties, a transfer of weapons and other equipment to us."

"Try," I said. "You couldn't be sure. But if everything had gone fairly well, the scheme would have protected Adam Soltyk. That's what it was mainly about."

He nodded. "Correct. Not because I'm so great, but— The last Marines are leaving. The wars, the reavers, the barbarians are coming. We must prepare ourselves, and our defense force is desperately short of everything."

"Especially good officers," I said. "And you were always among the best. Yes. As soon as you could appear in the open, I suppose, you'd become Skarga's second in command. Shortly you'd succeed him; he's elderly, and the time ahead is terrible."

He reached out as if to take both my hands. "Right, Colin, right. I came to understand— What's one man more or less, in that dance of death among the stars? This is my country, these are my people, I could not forsake them."

Never had I seen such joy as burst from Jezierski. "You hear, sir! No traitor! Patriot! I knew it!" He cast himself into his uncle's arms.

Above his shoulder, Adam Soltyk sought my gaze. "What will you do about this?" he murmured.

"Stand aside, Private Jezierski," I directed. Shakily, he obeyed. I gestured at the floor. "Take the prisoner's weapon." He hesitated. "Take it, God damn you!" I yelled.

When he had, I stood before them and said: "Private Jezierski wanted us two to come by ourselves. That was rotten military practice, but I agreed, because otherwise— Well, he realized that in the presence of witnesses, plain talk and quiet compromise would be impossible.

You're a bright lad, Private. May you go as far as your talents deserve."

"You don't intend to bargain, then?" Adam asked, as calmly as before.

"How could I? I have my orders, and . . . the Imperium has my oath. I must bring you to Fort Kursk, Major Soltyk."

He nodded.

The pistol shuddered in Jezierski's hand. "What will they do with him, sir?"

"He'll be court-martialed," I answered. "Probably he'll be shot."

Jezierski moaned.

"We're having too many desertions," I said. "We need to make a conspicuous example." The waves clashed and hissed. "But I wouldn't expect any attempt to prosecute the rest of the conspirators. That part is best hushed up."

"I hope so," Soltyk put in. "We shouldn't undermine what's left of civilization on Haven."

"We're supposed to defend it."

"I know."

"Sir, please, please," Jezierski begged.

"Shape up, Private!" I rapped. "Stand clear. Don't give the prisoner a chance to jump you. If he tries anything funny, shoot. That's an order.

"Major Soltyk, you told me the Alpha disc is on the shelf. Very well, I'll fetch it."

When I climbed back down, neither man had moved. The murky light showed both their faces congealed, like metal that has set.

"Now," I told them, "the craft we came in won't hold three. I'll go topside and call our men in Nowy Kraków. They'll claim the vehicle you brought, Major Soltyk, and we'll fly home in tandem. For the time being, though, you two stay in this cave. Then if a Cracovian party lands, I can try to explain things away, stall them till Reinhardt's squad arrives. How long before high tide closes off the mouth?"

"Perhaps two hours," Soltyk replied.

"Time enough. Private Jezierski, I leave you with your responsibility. Carry it out as honor requires. Major Soltyk, whatever happens, I will convince my superiors your wife is blameless."

"Thank you, my friend," I heard him say. He saluted.

I returned the gesture and left them.

The sea licked at me as I made my way out. On the beach and the lower trail, it whipped me with a salt storm. The rising violence of it rang in my head. The climb was stiff.

When finally I reached the jet and got in, I was so cold, wet, and tired that I must sit with my hands to the heater duct till the numbness left them and I could code transmission for Reinhardt. "All right," I instructed, "get that vehicle and come join me." I gave him the coordinates.

"Is there a big rush, sir?" he asked. "Unless we bull through, it may take an hour or two, the way people seem to drag their feet around here."

"No, take it easy, don't give offense, things are under control. But destroy those sealed orders I gave you. They're obsolete."

I stayed put as long as seemed wise, against that possibility of Skarga's men appearing, At last the waters had risen so far that I'd better go lead the others up.

Hip-deep, I fumbled and stumbled into the Mermaid Grotto. The currents hauled at me. Their chill bit my bones. I waved my flashbeam about and shouted. Surf and echoes gave answer. Darkness thickened.

If I didn't leave at once, the sea would eat me.

Back in the jet, I raised Reinhardt. He, Li, and Rostov were on their way. "Change of plan," I said. "Proceed straight to Fort Kursk."

"Yes, sir," he acknowledged. "Who shall we report to?"

"Me. I should reach it first."

His silence pressed inward. I drew breath. "You may as well hear the news at once," I proceeded. "I have what we came for, not just a cure for the Plague but an immunizer against it. A deserter—his name will be spat on—he'd stolen the program, meaning to use it for a bargaining chip. The Cracovian authorities were dismayed but incompetent. With Private Jezierski's help, I tracked him down and retrieved the disc. Unfortunately, it now appears he made a break for it while I was calling you earlier. Private Jezierski seems to have died gallantly in an effort to prevent that. At least the deserter died also. Keep this confidential for the present, Sergeant. I must inform the high command in more detail."

"Oh, sir! That poor kid."

"A pity, yes. He really longed to go with us. Well, we can't make a big thing of an incident. Carry on."

I secured my harness and took off.

The sun ahead is only the brightest among a thousand thousand stars. It waxes ever faster, though, as our troopship accelerates inward from the last Alderson point to the next battle.

We can still take some ease. Yesterday evenwatch, Ashcroft and I got a little drunk together in his cabin, after we'd finished discussing problems of morale and discipline. My promotion has been quick, same as in the lower ranks, given the casualties we've taken. "I do sympathize with the men," he said, somewhat blurrily. "The girls we left behind us— We won't see them again. That's become unmistakable. Forget them. Except we can't, can we?"

"Not easy," I admitted. "But you're coping."

"And you're lucky, you're free of ghosts." He ran fingers through his gray hair. "Or are you, Raveloe? I don't want to pry, but—Soltyk's widow— She is a remarkable woman, and you did help her a lot. I thought for a while— But, sorry, I don't want to pry."

I shrugged. "Nothing to pry into. She accepted my protection and my making arrangements, for the sake of her children. She never pretended any different. When I saw them off on the flight to Cracovia, all she said was, 'Perhaps when we meet on the Judgment Day, perhaps then I can forgive you.'"

It wouldn't take that long, of course—only till she had been brought to where her husband and young kinsman were lying low. By now they must long since be back in the open, he taking a lead in arming his country against its future. Maybe he will at least give it some years or decades that can be lived in, with afterward a legend to live by. Surely he's grateful to me. But what does he think of my honor? What does she?

Catseye had been alone in heaven. Its light made coral of those high cheekbones and big eyes. There was frost in her breath and her hair.

"I wonder how they're doing," Ashcroft mused.

"We'll never know," I said, and drank.

Our ship drives on through the Deep.

## Introduction

First, an elementary example of false inference: because an idea is at the heart of liberal-chic dogma it is necessarily *untrue*. Second, a confession: I have been guilty of that very example of flawed reasoning. I am not certain that Mr. Stirling has proved his case beyond cavil, but most assuredly he is not, prima facie, *wrong*.

Now for a funny story. Both I and an editor/publisher from another house had summarily rejected the same medieval-milieu fantasy novel featuring a co-ed mercenary cadre on the grounds that ladies just can't hack it with broadswords, or any pig-sticker less dainty than, say, an epee. Boy, was that author mad. Seems us two New York desk jockies with our ineffable male wisdom were patronizing an officer of the United States Marine Corps.

*Marching Through Georgia*, S.M. Stirling, May 1988.
*Sheepfarmer's Daughter* by Elizabeth Moon is scheduled for publication in June 1988.

# THE WOMAN WARRIOR

## Or, Rebutting the Editor

### S. M. Stirling

Thomas Jefferson once remarked that it is almost impossible to avoid despising those with whom we profoundly disagree; but that to accomplish it was the mark of a civilized man. Jim Baen passes the test.

Recently, I had the good fortune to sell a novel, *Marching Through Georgia*, to Baen Books. The book is alternate-history, and set in the Caucasus Mountains during that timeline's version of World War II; they call it the Eurasian War. One of the nations involved does not exist in our history; their culture is a rather extreme variant of Western civilization, and among other peculiarities their military uses female personnel in combat roles. Jim Baen thought this (besides being almost a cliche of modern science fiction and fantasy) was not realistic. I managed to convince him that I had done my homework on this issue, and he invited me to cover the question—and to entitle the article "Rebutting the Editor."

Arguments against the use of women in combat can be broken down (with some overlap) into two categories: that they *should not* be used in combat, or that they *cannot* perform effectively under combat conditions. The first is largely an emotional attitude, while the latter at least pretends to be a matter of provable fact. Accordingly, I will deal with emotional repugnance first.

Social reality is a matter of perception; the limits of the possible are set by what is thinkable. This is observable in athletics; for generations, the four-minute mile was thought to be an impossible feat. Then one man did it, and pretty soon it became routine. In the same manner, the men's Olympic records of the 1930s in many sports are now routinely broken by women athletes, and while men's performance has also increased, the gap is much narrower. The genetic differences between men and women have grown no less in the intervening decades; what has changed is the *perception* of what it is possible for women to accomplish.

Thus, much opposition to women in combat is based on a sense of cultural discontinuity—a queasy, visceral feeling that some basic law of nature is being violated. In Western civilization, this is often verbalized as a desire to "protect" women from the horrors of combat; the argument usually starts with a listing of the meat-grinder brutalities of war, and is followed by a rhetorical question as to whether we should "expose women to that." The obvious answer is that nobody should be subjected to such misery, but that if somebody must be, why should women be exempt?

At this point the allegedly "natural" desire of men to protect women is introduced. Unfortunately, no such desire is evident in most societies, or through most of human history. In most of the world, women are considered beasts of burden and treated as such; in Kenya, where I was raised, the predominant waKikuyu ethnic group accepts it as a fact of nature that women are stronger than men and should do the physical labor. The sight of 130-pound women trotting for miles across the hills with 200 pounds of firewood on their backs, while their menfolk stroll behind with a walking stick,

is enough to dispel any myth of feminine frailty![1] The enormous scale of domestic violence against women in our own culture also gives the lie to this allegedly natural desire to protect.

There may be some genuinely and unselfishly chivalrous souls out there; let them be put aside with the gentle consideration due to the hopelessly old-fashioned and amiably insane. Far more commonly, "protectiveness" turns out to be ideology in the sense that Marx used the term—mystification, false consciousness, and a cover for exploitation. A good example occurred here in Canada recently; women were being excluded from one of the better blue-collar jobs in the Canadian National rail yards because they could not pass the "knuckle test"—could not carry a sixty-pound lump of steel used for coupling boxcars single-handed. Several women were injured trying, and the cry went up that women must be protected from this dangerous, demanding toil.

The Human Rights Commission then sent in an undercover observer. And in the next several months he observed that never, not *once*, did any of the male railwaymen lift a steel knuckle by himself. Instead, two men ran a shovel handle through the hole in the center and carried it that way! Lo and behold, when the women applicants were allowed to do likewise, every single one of them passed.[2]

When the first women were assigned to Table of Organization support-units in the U.S. army, many men tried to protect them by doing their work—protecting them, that is, from acquiring the knowledge and skills necessary to do their jobs. They were being protective, all right; protective of their turf, pay and perks. The so-called protective legislation that unions fought for, excluding women from shift work, steel mills and coal mines, fulfilled much the same purpose, protecting women right into the pink-collar ghetto and domestic drudgery. This form of protectiveness is functionally identical to the sabotage and sexual harassment that usually greets the first women into an all-male work environment. Strange, that no men chivalrously stepped forward to take over the badly-paid migrant stoop-labor so many women have always done. . . .[3]

However, more than simple selfishness is at work here. A related issue is brought to the fore when the question of capture in the field is raised; combat for women is unthinkable because it would involve the prospect of being raped by the enemy. Yes; and Lawrence of Arabia was, too. (The moral being that one should not be taken prisoner by Turks.) Note that the ultimate horror here is not seeing female comrades killed, not seeing them horribly burned or mutilated, but seeing them sexually violated. Granted that this is traumatic for the victim, but why the particular shrinking? Note also that most women stand a very good chance of being sexually assaulted at some point in their lives (most often by a relative or acquaintance) and that the "protectors" of women seem to accept this without the cries of horror the thought of wartime rape arouses.

The answer, again, is not a genuine protectiveness, but a defense of psychic "turf"; a masculine identity bound up with maintaining exclusive sexual access to *our* women. A man who cannot protect *his* women is castrated, impotent, reduced to the status of . . . well, of a woman. Likewise, to be a warrior is to be a "real man," protecting dependent women; if women can take up guns and defend themselves . . . at this point a look of terror and metaphorical clutch at the genitals follows. To put it gently, such individuals need to be resocialized; the means I would select would be a vigorous whack up alongside the head with a tire iron. War, as our ultimate means of political communication, is far too important to be left to this sort of caveman nonsense.

To those who have followed the "great rifle controversy" of the past two decades, there is an amusing parallel in the dispute over the move to smaller, lighter rifle bullets. This was advocated as far back as the 1930's by that bastion of coldly analytical rationalism, the German General Staff, but still one finds laments for the declining manliness of the modern soldier, unable to handle the "big" bullet of his father's time. How big, how long, how hard, how far . . . There may, perhaps, be non-rational elements involved here?[4]

Another argument of this type is the complaint that the enforced lack of privacy in the front lines will lead to sexual immorality and loss of feminine "delicacy." As for delicacy, an article in *Armed Forces & Society* comes to mind: At the beginning of a three-week field problem in a desert winter, everyone in a mixed signals unit took great trouble to keep blanket barriers up and guard the latrines. By the end, everyone was exhausted and filthy and the general attitude was "if they want to look, let 'em look." We are talking about *war*: life and death, the fate of nations. And someone is getting upset at the thought of seeing a member of the opposite gender pee? Really, now.[5]

As to sex, another anecdote suggests itself. In the brief honeymoon after World War II, an American general inspected a mixed Russian tank unit. Unknown to the Russians, he had his own interpreter, who translated a sign on the barracks wall which his hosts had told him meant "Long live Soviet-American friendship." It actually read: "Due to the visit of the *Ami* general all fornication in this barracks is forbidden for the next 48 hours."[6] Sexual fraternization that threatened discipline, and sexual harassment, could be dealt with by normal administrative means. Under fire, everyone would be too busy; out of the line, the troops would undoubtedly "make like bunnies." What of it? From a strictly military point of view, it would probably help reduce the prostitute-spread VD which has often disabled more soldiers than has combat. And otherwise, if the soldiers are old enough to fight, they are old enough to pick their own partners and it is nobody's business but their own. The issue of sex is therefore a red herring, again for questions of territory and power; and the same accusations have been used to oppose the entry of women into every previously male stronghold since Victorian times.

In fact, if properly handled, the "bonding" process so central to military cohesion and morale could be strengthened. In ancient Greece lovers (admittedly, same-sex ones) were considered the best soldiers, because their devotion to each other made them fight the harder and risk death for each other's sake and to avoid dishonor before the beloved's eyes. The Sacred Band of Thebes, 300 strong, was composed exclusively of lovers who took a lifelong oath before the shrine of Ialos, the beloved of Hercules. Their oath was never to retreat without orders; at the battle of Chaeronea, they met the charge of Alexander the Great and his household cavalry and died in their tracks to the last man although offered good terms of surrender.[7]

A good army *must* have strong small-group bonds, and strong bonds between "buddies" in the ranks. However, this by itself is no guarantee of good military performance; that depends on the sub-culture of the army in question. If the consensus is that shirking is "letting your friends down," and the soldiers are ashamed to show fear before their comrades, you get aggressive competence. If the consensus is that glory-hounds expose everybody to useless death, the same strong feeling of group solidarity produces disaffection, mutiny and "fragging."

Gender mixing would produce new problems, but no more so than racial integration did in the U.S. army of the early 1950's. This went surprisingly smoothly, considering the depth of ethnic tensions and the largely Southern cast of the American army. A recent (and extremely realistic) fictional portrayal has a drill instructor at Parris Island telling a group of Marine recruits: "I am hard, but I am fair. There is no racial bigotry here. I do not hate niggers, wops, kikes or greasers. Here, you maggots are all *equally* worthless!" Intelligent modifications of classic training methods would no doubt produce similar results.

There is a final and less irrational argument that women should not be exposed to combat based on the greater biological dispensibility of young males. And there is a certain sense to it: one male can father thousands of children (if he could get the chance) while a woman cannot generally have many more than ten offspring—and usually far fewer, even in cultures with high birth rates. Thus, in terms of a society's reproductive potential, wombs are less expendable than testicles.

In my opinion, this argument has the sort of specious pseudo-plausibility that sociobiological logic often does. And if humans had the same sort of reproductive pattern that, say, horses or antelopes do, it *would* make sense. Herd animals of this sort have an exaggerated harem pattern; males fight among themselves to collect large groups of females during a brief mating season, and most of the infants are sired by a small minority of bucks. However, even in the most *outré* of human cultures, even in the classic Middle-Eastern societies where the harem was the ideal, monogamy was the commonest family pattern.

And whatever the structure of clans, extended families, etc., the *reproductive* unit is almost invariably one man and one woman, or at least a balanced number. Humans have year-round sexuality, and a long period of dependent infancy; successful reproduction requires some sort of fairly stable partnership to rear children. In Western society, where monogamy is customary, this is even more evident. In statistical terms, *women* do not reproduce, *couples* reproduce. If you kill off a large number of men, especially young men who have not yet formed families, then there will be a corresponding dip in the marriage and birth rates. This is precisely what happened to Britain and France after the slaughters of World War I: a generation of spinsters and a sharp dip in the birth rate. The same phenomenon hit the Soviet Union after World War II, particularly the Slavic groups that bore the bulk of the military casualties.[8] In other words, the effect of killing off large numbers of young men is, in reproductive terms, *exactly equivalent to killing off a sexually balanced group of twice the size*.

From the realm of mythology, we move to that of physical possibility. Can women stand up to the physical and mental strains of modern combat?

No. Neither can men. Nobody can; modern infantry combat is a uniquely horrible experience, if only because the ordeal is so much longer than that of pre-industrial warfare, where battles generally were over by sunset and you were safe once farther away from the enemy than human muscle could throw. If one thing is clear from the research done on combat soldiers in the World Wars and since, it is that in the end being up at the "sharp end" destroys *everybody*. Either the enemy kills you, or you break. The only reason that psychiatric casualties do not reach 100% is that most soldiers are not exposed to enough continuous combat; the amount needed varies with personal toughness, unit morale and other factors, but after the equivalent of a year or less of heavy fighting, a soldier becomes essentially useless. Endurance and courage are non-renewable resources, like oil; once used, they are simply *gone*.[9]

To digress briefly, the same research shows that an understanding attitude and elaborate psychiatric care is, from a military point of view, useless. The best way to keep down combat fatigue is to let nobody out of the front zone without crippling wounds, and shoot out of hand anybody who disobeys orders or becomes non-functional. This is what most World War I armies did, and they had a shell-shock rate of about nine per thousand per year. The Russians and Germans did the same in World War II, and had about the same combat fatigue rate; the U.S. and Britain were much more humane, and quadrupled the rate of loss to their fighting strength. Not that men were faking, but the human subconscious is no fool; if going mad gets you out, substantial numbers will go genuinely "bugfuck." If it only gets you a pistol bullet in the back of the head, most hold out longer before breaking. Fear alone will not keep soldiers in the line and fighting, but it can certainly help.[10]

The question therefore becomes, more realistically: can a substantial portion of women show enough physical and mental stamina to make useful combat troops?

We shall leave the "women are inherently cowardly

hysterics" argument where it deserves: on the manure-heap of history, along with "burn the heretics" and "death to the Jews." It is true that human beings tend to act more or less as their society expects them to; hence (even without corsets) the Victorian middle-class women's sport of swooning. To introduce a personal element: While helping to teach a women's self-defense course, I found that a substantial number of the students had a fixed inhibition against hitting anybody; however, with careful drill this could be overcome easily enough. Basic military training has to overcome a substantial degree of inhibition against hurting and killing people anyway, if the recruits are 20th-century Westerners; it does so, and instills self-confidence and aggressiveness, very effectively.

In fact, again from personal observations, once the initial inhibitions are overcome, women may have some substantial advantages, mostly in terms of having less to unlearn. Actual hand-to-hand fighting is nothing at all like the bull-baboon posturing you see in the average bar brawl, which is mostly display and noise. In a real fight you strike without warning, without subliminal clues of aggressive intent, and to kill. Without the macho conditioning most males in our culture suffer, women are readier to treat combat as a difficult skill to be mastered. In military terms, other things being equal, I think their socialization would make women less prone to berserk displays of heroism and more likely to do what they were trained to; the range of individual behavior would undoubtedly overlap broadly, however.

Accepting that trained women would show roughly the same range of mental responses, what of the undoubted *physical* differences between the sexes? Here we must examine the actual extent of differences between the sexes, define the requirements of the various forms of combat, and ask what the requirements for an effective soldier are in each category.

Certain facts are indisputable. Women are smaller and lighter than men. They can take more acceleration before blacking out, due to small differences in the distribution of the blood. Given equal training, they are somewhat weaker in upper-body strength (although our culture exaggerates this); they have slightly less sprint and slightly more long-distance endurance than men; on average they have rather better balance and reflexes, and a higher *biological* resistance to pain and fatigue—although this is less important than willpower and training. Women have a higher proportion of fat to muscle, although training reduces this sharply; they are more resistant to disease, on average, less likely to have heart attacks or strokes, but slightly more prone to bone injuries. There are areas of uncertainty; the alleged male superiority in spatial/mathematical perception, or the female advantage in verbal skills, which may be either genetic or the result of differential socialization.[11] Personally, when dealing with humans I follow a version of Occam's Razor: Never assume a biological explanation when a cultural one will do.

An important point to keep in mind is that the above differences are *statistical averages*, not absolutes. They express the *ranges*, which have a substantial overlap in the middle. Thus, even in a totally egalitarian culture the best weightlifters and shotputters would almost certainly be men, and the best long-distance swimmers and runners women. Many women will be larger and more muscular than many men; many men will have higher pain tolerances and greater manual dexterity than many women. And differences between ethnic groups may be as great as that between the sexes in one group; for example, the difference in size and weight between men in North America and men in Southeast Asia is almost exactly the same, on average, as that between men and women in North America. Not to raise painful matters, but in a certain Southeast Asian country . . .

There is no question that women can roughly equal men in terms of endurance and tolerance of hardship. Women peasants and laborers have always done their share of the fieldwork and much else besides; women have fired steam locomotives, hewed coal by hand, dragged carts through mines on their hands and knees. While they may not, on average, have as *much* raw muscle power as men, this is not to say that they cannot be very strong indeed, given the proper training and incentives. Those African women I mentioned earlier were carrying their own body-weight of firewood on their backs, at 6,000-feet altitude, up and down 40-degree slopes on a diet of cornmeal porridge. And they often traveled twenty miles a day to the forest, then put in hours of fieldwork, then cooked for large families. As often as not they had a child at the breast; sometimes they were pregnant.

There is therefore, I think, no serious dispute that there are *some* combat tasks which women can and have fulfilled. Women have been flying aircraft almost as long as men have, and just as capably. Even before the sophisticated power-controls of the jet age, women ferry pilots in World War II flew every type of aircraft, from four-engine B-17's and B-29's through the "hottest" fighters—Spitfires, Mustangs, and massive P-47 Thunderbolts. The Western countries did not allow them to pilot in combat, but there were no serious complaints about their abilities—though many instances of bitter hostility and ingratitude, not to mention fear of postwar job competition. [12]

However, in 1941 the Soviets were desperate. They had lost much of their cadre of trained pilots to the initial German attack; and being a tyranny of the most ironfisted sort, their leadership did not have to consider public opinion as to the "proper" role of women. Accordingly, a call went out for volunteers and a number of all-female units were formed (including mechanics and ground crew). These units performed everything from reconnaissance and ground-attack to fighter cover, and performed it on the average neither better nor worse than their male counterparts—in spite of the fact that some of the pilots had to have wooden blocks fitted to the rudder pedals to reach them from the seat! (After all, Douglas Bader of Britain became an ace after losing both legs above the knee.)

So several Russian women became aces—against the Luftwaffe, which was no mean opponent. This was in relatively primitive aircraft, even by 1940-45 standards; Russian fighters were soundly designed, but not state-of-the-art by any means. German, British, Japanese and American women could undoubtedly have done the same, given the opportunity. Flying those aircraft took considerable physical strength; you had to *wrestle* with the stick, and the pedals on a multiengined ship of the period were often very heavy indeed.[13]

The aircraft of our own day are rather easier to fly; on strictly physical terms, the smaller size, greater g-resistance and faster reflexes of women should make them *superior* pilots, particularly for fighters. It seems logically inescapable that the only reason women are kept out of combat aircrew is sheer, loutish bigotry. Happily, Canada has just announced that women will henceforth be accepted for air-combat positions; the Netherlands already has such a policy, and the rest of the Western world at least must inevitably follow.

There are a number of other "combat" positions in the same category. Operating a nuclear reactor or missile computer aboard a Polaris or Poseidon boat, for example. The U.S. air force very sensibly allows women to be posted to the missile-silo crews of land-based ICBMs; the main difference between these and those on a submarine is that the submarine, being a concealed and moving target, is much safer. The same applies to virtually all sea duty; much of it is fairly strenuous, but no more so than the same tasks on merchant vessels with mixed crews, or on the logistics ships of the U.S. navy that have female sailors aboard. And these would be targets in time of war; it seems the objection of conservatives in these cases is not to women being shot at, but to their having an opportunity to shoot back! Perhaps another case of "manhood" being threatened by accepting the protection of armed women?

Moving on to the land, a whole range of *near-combat* tasks are now or have been routinely assigned to female personnel in many armies. During World War II many of the anti-aircraft, radar and searchlight positions which defended Britain were "manned" by young women of the WAAF; in all cases, they won high marks from their often surprised male commanders for efficiency, discipline and coolness under fire—in one instance, staying at their posts while the male aircrew of the base took to the shelters and refused to emerge. Many were killed in the line of duty, as the command centers were prime targets for air attack.[14]

In more recent times, the American army now assigns women to units which would be routinely under fire in action: anti-aircraft missile units, Military Police and forward combat-support outfits, and headquarters down to battalion level. Of necessity, these soldiers are armed and trained in infantry combat, as their units would be expected to do their own perimeter defense and provide reaction-forces against infiltrators and paratroops.[15] And in the event of an emergency, support troops of all types can and would be shoved into the line as emergency infantry replacements.

Incidentally, this makes utter and hypocritical nonsense of the claim that women are not assigned to "combat" units; they are not usually assigned to rifle companies, armored fighting vehicle crews or tube artillery, which is *not* the same thing. Taking a more realistic definition of "combat unit" as one likely to shoot and be shot at, the U.S. armed forces depend on female combat troops to such an extent that any attempt to pull them out of harm's way would result in immediate and total military collapse. If, God forbid, a major conflict were to break out, women would be in combat from the beginning and would, as a female captain of M.P.'s once said (*Time* magazine): "All go, all fight, and all get an equal crack at the Order of the Green Body Bag."

In the Soviet Union, the disasters of 1941 produced a crisis in other fields than aviation. The Russians had the world's largest tank park: the panzers hammered it into scrap, and most of the trained crews who survived went behind the wire of German prisoner cages, never to return. In a society where the internal combustion engine was still a rarity, this was a catastrophe; peasants can be taught how to handle a rifle fairly quickly, but a tank is a highly-stressed and delicate piece of precision machinery. Another call for volunteers went out; this time for female tractor and truck drivers to ferry tanks from the plants, and then to crew them in combat. Again, the experiment was an unqualified success, and the practice was continued until peace, victory, and a smaller army enabled the Russians to relapse into comfortable sexist ruts.

Crewing a tank is not an easy task. The T-34's and KV-1's those Russian women drove into battle with Guderian's and Manstein's tankers were superb designs for their day, well protected, fast and hard-hitting. But they were primitive steel coffins in other respects: no power turret-traverse, manual gun-training, manual loading, transmissions whose constant problems were often solved with a hefty whack from a sledgehammer. And they were, contrary to myth, unreliable; Russian tanks often went into combat with spare transmissions strapped to the rear deck. The constant grind of maintenance involved the heaviest sort of labor—ask somebody who has tried to change a broken track in the inevitable mud.[16]

Again, compared to these, contemporary tanks are creampuffs, far easier to operate and maintain. Russian tanks, with their customary over-functionalism and contempt for ergonomics, are so cramped inside that their crews cannot be over 5′4″! Western vehicles are more spacious but still cramped, and the reason their crews are all men has very little to do with the inherent capacities of women.

The final and most problematic category of combat soldiering is undoubtedly the infantry. The infantryman must be able to "yomp" heavy loads of gear and supplies, march, dig, even *run* under all this impedimenta; manhandle heavy, cumbersome weapons about, endure endless fatigue and stress, constant danger for weeks on end, bad food, wet bedding . . . and the endless knowledge that beyond each day of fatigue or terror lies another, and another, until death or rotation ends it. Can an appreciable number of women sustain this burden?

Well, appreciable numbers *have*. In preindustrial times, when war was a matter of muscle-powered impact weapons, women warriors were rare but by no means unknown. The Sarmatians were an Iranian people living in what is now the eastern Ukraine and western Central Asia; classical historians claimed that their women were not allowed to marry until they had taken the head of an enemy warrior. Archaeology supports this; about one-third of all Sarmatian-period burials are of women interred with weapons—the rare, costly, and treasured weapons of a nomadic knight of the steppe. For the Sarmatians, these included a 13-foot lance, full suits of scale armor, long double-edged slashing swords, and horn-backed composite bows with a draw of over 75 pounds. None of them weapons to be used by weaklings!

Individual female warriors crop up elsewhere: in Japan, where several martial-arts schools evolved around "women's weapons" such as the *naginata* (a three-foot curved blade on the end of a seven-foot shaft), and among the Plains Indians of North America. On a large scale, the most impressive recent example would be the West African kingdom of Dahomey, where the famous corps of Amazons made up half the standing army. These women (technically "wives" of the king) were raised by conscription, armed partially with flintlock muskets but mainly relying on bows, spears, small axes and long knives. For most of the 18th and 19th centuries they were the terror of west Africa, constantly employed in the slave-raids and expeditions of conquest that were Dahomey's national industry.

When the French overran Dahomey in the 1890's, the Foreign Legion met the Amazons and soon developed an ungrudging respect for their disciplined valor and ferocious will to combat. Unable to meet the long-range fire of the Europeans' magazine rifles, they laid ambushes in bush country and made repeated rushes, always trying to close with cold steel. Often they did, and the Legionnaires soon lost any inhibitions they may have possessed against using bayonet and rifle-butt on women; watching the woman gutting your comrade with a machete proved to be a powerful solvent of prejudices.[17]

Turning to Western history (and leaving aside the female head-hunters of legendary Celtic days), there are repeated instances of women disguising themselves and serving in the ranks. This was perfectly possible in an age with no medical inspections or birth records or dress-stereotypes so strong that the eye could not "see" beneath the visual clues of breeches versus skirts. Instances occurred in the American Revolution and Civil War; in those cases some women were discovered when brought wounded to aid stations, and presumably many more survived undetected—or were tumbled into anonymous mass graves along with the other casualties. One officer in the British army served for thirty years, saw active service, fought several duels, and was only discovered to be female on her death bed—despite being less than five feet tall![18]

In more recent times peoples whose backs were to the wall have drawn women into the ranks of their infantry forces: Tito's partisans did so in World War II, the Jewish rebels in the Warsaw Ghetto, the Viet Minh and Viet Cong (occasionally) and the Palmach in Israel's War of Independence. And of course there have been female terrorists and so forth without number; anyone who still believes that women are somehow less bloodthirsty than men need look no further than the Baader-Meinhoff gang for cold-blooded atrocity and fanatical contempt for death.[19]

The examples above have been largely swept under the rug, or treated as curiosities of no account; in my opinion, largely because of the unconscious cultural "filters" which censor information to reduce cognitive dissonance. There may be more mental stress in modern combat than there was in the last century, due to the greater length of battles and the larger size of the combat zone, but I'll be damned if carrying an M-16A2 and pack in 1987 is any more physically demanding than humping a Springfield rifle-musket and kit through the dust of Virginia in 1862, or rushing a line of Legionnaires with spear and knife in the African savannah in 1896, or trudging through the mountains of Serbia under a Kar-98 and everything you owned in 1943.

On a more personal note, there is no more demanding form of combat than hand to hand. I have had fifteen years of training in mixed martial-arts dojos (most lately in Tao Zen Chuan, a power-style if there ever was one), and have seen the knowledge applied outside in real-life situations. The men involved are usually strong, fit, very fast for their size—and I have repeatedly seen them outfought by women as little as half their weight. If size, arm-and-shoulder strength and heavy bone structures were all that mattered, they should have been able to roll over the women like tanks. Those that tried didn't do so well.

I emphasize, this is not a sport; it is as close to fighting as you can get without killing people. I have suffered three broken toes; a broken thumb; three broken ribs; chipped teeth; concussions . . . If the fighters were to stand toe to toe and noogie on each other's heads with cinderblocks, the women would be at a considerable disadvantage. This is not the way things are done, and the higher the level of skill the less raw strength matters. It is necessary to have a certain *minimum* strength, but beyond that extra muscle is largely overkill.

One instructor I remember was about 5' tall and weighed in at a little over 90 lbs. When we got macho street stud types who objected to learning about fighting from a woman, we would tell them that unlike everybody else they would not have to train for a year before being allowed to free-spar; this instructor would then proceed to systematically beat them to a pulp. This was a wonderful educator, for those who stayed. And once when she was groped in the casbah of Marrakesh, she reached down, dislocated the man's thumb, locked and smashed his elbow-joint and broke his nose with a backfist in less time than it takes to read these words; she skipped the follow-up killstrike with the heel of the palm, but she held his life in her hand.

Granted that unarmed combat is only a small part of the modern soldier's repertoire, I think the above examples show that small size and slight build do not prevent an individual from becoming a formidable fighter in this most personal type of conflict. There is no question that some women, at least, can endure the hardships of an infantry soldier's life; nor that they can develop enough muscular strength to handle the tools of the trade. In our culture, which has discouraged physical development in women, this might require a good deal of remedial training. To give a fictional example most readers of this magazine are probably familiar with, consider the "Vasquez" character in *Aliens*; she had enough muscle to throw a 30-lb. machine-gun around with considerable authority. The actress in question went on a crash course for two months and gained twenty-odd pounds; all of it muscle, most of it on arms, shoulders and neck. Chipped beef on toast and a daily course of weights and assault courses could probably do it for most. Also I think it looks wonderful, but that may be personal prejudice.

If personnel assignments were made on the basis of ability alone, women would probably be rather less than half of the infantry; and rather more than half of the fighter pilots and tank crewpeople. The barriers are ones of culture, perception and will rather than differences in the capacities of the sexes. These barriers are crumbling; my own nation, Canada, has opened the air-combat specialities to women, is planning to have a destroyer with a 25% female crew by 1988 and is already forming the first experimental mixed infantry and armor battalions. Demography (the baby bust), military necessity and sheer logic will almost certainly force the rest of the Western world to eventually follow suit. Our perceptions of what is possible, natural and thinkable will have to change too, whether we like it or not. —Which brings us full-circle to *Marching Through Georgia*. In that alternate history, southern Africa becomes a British colony during the American Revolution, and is afterwards heavily settled by Loyalists and Hessians, among others. To cut a long novel short, a new society (the Draka) develops; militantly expansionist, with a fear-driven cycle of conquest, repression, war, conquest and repression. The dominant caste produces a brilliant, efficient but brutal and depraved culture; one that is overwhelmingly martial in orientation but rightly afraid to trust many of its lower classes with arms or any position of responsibility.

In other words, an emergency personnel shortage that gets steadily worse generation after generation. Not liberalism but sheer necessity forces the rulers to use the women of their own class in wider and wider roles, and since there is never any period of peace or relaxation this gradually becomes ingrained into the culture and fairly complete by the 1930's. Of course, the savagely hierarchical structure of the "Domination of the Draka" allows me to cheat on some of the stickier points: traditional female functions like child rearing are not shared, they are dumped on the subject classes, while the ruling Citizen caste becomes as specialized as warrior ants . . . Well, I'll save all that for the book!

## REFERENCES

1. Personal experience. I was unable to even lift several of these bundles.

2. *Dominion Law Reports* (1980). I studied this case in law school.

3. "Gender Integration: A Study of G.I. Joe," *Armed Forces and Society* Vol. 11, Number 4.

4. *Soldier of Fortune*, interminably.

5. "Gender Integration: A Study of G.I. Joe."

6. Testimony from someone who claimed to have been there. Well, he was certainly in Germany in 1945 . . .

7. Pierre Ducrey, *Warfare in Ancient Greece* (Fribourg: Office du Livre S.A.).

8. Colin Dyer, *Population and Society in Twentieth Century France* (London: Hodder and Stoughton, 1978), pp. 33-46., and R.M. Williams, *British Population* (London: Heinemann, Ltd., 1972), p. 38.

9. Paul Keegan, *The Sharp End* (MacMillan and Co., Ltd.: London, 1983).

10. Keegan, *The Sharp End*.

11. G. Mitchell, *Human Sex Differences: A Primatologist's Perspective* (Van Nostrand Reinhold Co.: New York, 1981), p. 10. and K.B. Hoyenga and Kermit Hoyenga, *Sex Differences: Psychological, Cultural and Biological Issues* (Little, Brown and Co.: Boston, 1979), p. 320.

12. Oliver La Farge, *The Eagle in the Egg* (Arno Press: New York, 1949), pp. 129-143.

13. R. Holmes, *Acts of War: The Behavior of Men in Battle* (The Free Press: New York, 1985), p. 102. and S. Saywell, *Women in War* (Penguin Books: London, 1985), p. 139.

14. Saywell, *Women in War*.

15. A.T.R. Hadley, *The Straw Giant: A Report From The Field* (Random House: New York, 1986), p. 259.

16. Saywell, *Women in War*, pp. 131-158.

17. E. Isichei, *History of West Africa Since 1800* (Holmes and Meier, Publishers: New York, 1977), pp. 80-87.

18. "Women in Combat", *Armed Forces and Society*, vol. 7, Number 2 pp. 217-218 and H.V. Morton, *In Search of South Africa*, (Metheun and Co. Ltd.: London, 1948).

19. Saywell, *Women in War*.

## Introduction

In the face of radical new technology some people lose their heads. Others lose their hearts. A few just completely fall apart. All of which goes to show that when embracing scientific miracles one should move slowly and with great care.

# WIRES

## F. Paul Wilson

### 1

Being decapitated will always rank as my most memorable experience. Not my favorite, but very memorable. Happened right in my own home, too.

Someone had strung a strand of molly wire across my compartment doorway. Neck high. Couldn't see it, of course, so I stepped right through it. Correction: It stepped through me. A submicroscopic strand of single molecules strung end to end. If it hadn't made that faint little *skitch* as it cut through one of my neck bones, I don't know what would have happened.

Yes, I do. I would have died right inside my doorway.

Wouldn't have been pretty, either. A turn to the left or right, or a slight lean forward, and my head would have fallen off and bounced along the floor with a gaudy spray of red.

Didn't feel a thing. But that's supposed to be typical of molecular wire. Could guess what brand it was, too: Gussman Alloy. Hundred-kilo test. Cuts through a human body like a steel razor through cheesoid.

As the door slid shut behind me, I felt my skin begin

to burn from a line just below my Adam's apple all the way down to my toes—a million white hot needle pricks. My knees were getting soft. That was on the outside. Panic was roaring to life on the inside. Had to do something—but what?

Gently clamped my weakening fingers around my neck and shuffled across the single room in the direction of the only chair like someone balancing live dissociator grenades atop his head. My legs were starting to give way as I neared it. If I fell or even stumbled, my head would slip and loosen all the connections with the rest of my body and it would all be over. Forced myself to turn slowly, got the backs of my knees against the seat, and lowered myself down as gently as I could. My arms were getting tired from holding my head on, but at least I was seated.

Relief, but not much. Had to stay stiffly erect. Couldn't last like this very long, though. Risked taking a hand away from my neck to press the REFORM button. Felt the chair move up against my spine and the back of my neck and head, fitting itself to me. Kept the button pressed for maximum fit until the padding had formed forward to my ears and had wormed its way between my arms and body. Thanked myself sincerely for investing in a top-of-the-line chair like this.

Safe for the moment. I swallowed and felt something tear free in my throat. Got my hand back up there real fast. But how long could I hold it there? Everything was going numb.

At least now I could think. Still alive—but how? Even more pressing— Why and who? Who would want to behead me? Could only be one—

Saw movement outside my door and had the answer to my question. But not quite the answer I had expected. The custom chair and the one-way transparent door were a couple of instances of inconspicuous consumption I'd splurged on since the windfall of the Yokomoto affair two years ago. The door appealed to the voyeur in me, I guess. Mine is an end-corridor compartment and my door faces down the hall. The door lets me get to know all my neighbors without them knowing me. Nice that way.

But the guy coming down the hall now was no neighbor. He was pale and pudgy, had a high forehead, with beady little eyes and a small mouth crowded around a fat nose. Never saw him before. He came up to the door, glanced around, then pulled a tiny aerosol cannister from his pocket. Thought I saw a brief blur of motion back in the hall but my attention was centered on him as he sprayed the air in front of the door at the neck-high level. He waited a couple of seconds, then waved the cannister through the fading spray. The molly wire was gone, its molecular bonds dissolved. The murder weapon was now just a bunch of Gussman Alloy molecules floating randomly through the air of the hallway.

The guy didn't leave right away. He stood and stared longingly at the door. Could tell from his expression he wished he could see through it so he could dwell on the end result of his handiwork. Almost wished the door could go transparent both ways so he could see me sitting here looking back at him, giving him the finger. With a sigh and a wistful little smile he turned and walked away.

Who the hell *was* he? And why had he tried to kill me?

*Tried?* He hadn't failed yet. Didn't know how I had hung on this long and didn't know how much longer everything in my head would stay lined up with my neck. Needed help, and fast! Wheeled the chair over to the comm unit and told it to call Elmero's private number. Knew he was there. Just left him.

"El!" I said when his sallow, skeletal face appeared on the screen. My voice was soft and hoarse.

"Sig! Why're you whispering? And why're you holding your throat? Sore?"

"Need help, El. Real bad."

He smiled that awful smile. "What you into now?"

"Trouble. Doc still there?"

"Out in the barroom."

"Send him over. Gonna die if you don't get him here real quick. Molly wire."

The smile disappeared. He could tell I wasn't joking. "Where are you?"

"Home."

"He's on his way."

The screen blanked. Swiveled the chair around and stared down the empty hall, trying to figure out why that guy wanted me dead. Had only been back in business for two weeks . . .

## 2

The life of the idle rich had become a real bore, mainly because I couldn't act rich. All I could do was be idle. That was the problem with getting a windfall in something illegal like gold. Had to fence it through Elmero and keep my spending at a level that would not attract attention in Central Data.

But even if it had all been legal, it was hard for me to spend anything near what I had. Didn't like to travel, didn't drink or sniff much, didn't do luce or stim, didn't have friends to squander it on. Did buy some top-quality buttons as a treat. Spent a lot of time in pleasureland with a succession of them snapped onto my scalp, trying to saturate my limbic system before I began the slow, painful process of weaning myself off. Determined to stretch myself out to the point where I'd feel safe getting dewired. Been weaning off for almost a year now. It was hard, and idleness only made the weaning harder.

So I opened my office again. Thought that would be pretty idle for a while, too, but who shows up the first day? Ned Spinner. Didn't call, didn't knock, just strutted into my office and started yelling at me.

"Dreyer, you lousy rotten dregger! I knew you'd be back sooner or later! Where is she?"

"Where is who?"

Knew he meant Jean. Spinner had hounded me for months after her "disappearance." Finally I'd moved to an outer wall compartment and lost him for a while. Now he was back. Must have had my office watched all this time.

Hated the guy. A short strutting roosterish creature, slightly older than me, with curly blond hair banged in front. Always wore the same dark green pseudovelvet jumpsuit. He thought he had friends, thought he had influence, thought he was a talented entrepreneur. And he was . . . but only in his own mind. In real life he was a lousy pimp. Easy to see why he wanted Jean back. He'd given up his right to have a child and had invested a load of credit to buy a clone gestated from Jean Harlow's DNA. Then he'd set her up in a Dydeetown cubicle and lived off her.

And he called *me* a dregger.

"Don't know any more than Central Data tells you, Spinner: she took a shuttle off-planet and from there emigrated to the Outworlds."

"Dreck! She's still on-planet and you know where!"

"In all honesty, I don't know where she is. But if I did know, I wouldn't tell you."

His face reddened. "If that's your game, fine. But sooner or later you're gonna slip up. And when I catch you with her, it'll be all over for you, Dreyer. I won't bother with grand theft charges. I'll take care of you myself. And when I'm through with you, even the garbage chute in this roach-hole building won't accept you."

The man had a way with words.

Shortly after he left, a real customer showed up. He was slim, smooth, maybe thirty, his shiny hair leaf-sculpted in the latest, tinted perfectly to match the lemon yellow of his feather-trimmed clingsuit. The height of fashion. Up on the latest. Hated guys like this. Maybe because his clothes would look ridiculous on my cuboid frame, but mostly because he dressed to proclaim that he was up to the minute on style and all he really advertised to me was that he didn't have a mind of his own.

His name was Earl Khambot and he said he needed help finding someone.

"My specialty," I said. "Who're we looking for?"

He hesitated, uncertainty breaking through the high-fashion façade for the first time since he'd stepped in. For an awful minute I thought he was going to name some clone that had wandered off. I didn't want any more clone work. But he surprised me.

"My daughter," he said.

"That's a job for the CA, Mr. Khambot, and they don't like independent operators making waves in their pond."

"I . . . I haven't told the Central Authority."

A definite glitch here. A missing kid was cause for hysteria. After all, you were only allowed one. That was the law. You had one chance to duplicate yourself and after that the population problem was left to natural attrition. That one chance was damn valuable to you. You couldn't buy a second for anything. *Anything*. If that one precious child disappeared, you went screaming to Central Authority. You sure as hell didn't come to some hole-in-the-wall independent operator. Unless. . .

"What's the glitch, Mr. Khambot?"

He sighed resignedly. "She's an illegal."

*Ah!* That explained it. An extra. An above-and-beyonder. A one-more-than-replacement kid.

"I take it she's an urch now? You want to hire me to find an urch? How long since you placed her with a gang?"

He shrugged sullenly. "Three years ago. We couldn't let them terminate her. She was—"

"Sure," I said. "Save it." Hated irresponsible people. No excuse for having an illegal. A no-win situation. The only alternative to risking the kid being yanked and terminated by the C.A.—a retroactive abortion, as some called it—was to give it over to the urchingangs. And that was no picnic.

I thought: *You idiot*.

My thoughts must have shown. He said: "I'm not stupid. I got sterilized. Guess it didn't take." He read my mind again. "And yes, the baby was mine. Chromosomes proved it."

"And you wanted your wife to carry it?"

"*She* wanted to. And if she wanted it, so did I."

Earl Khambot went up a notch or two in my estimation. He could have sued for a bundle of credit—malpractice and wrongful conception and all that—and got a nice settlement. But he passed it up. Odd to find someone who's not for sale. Can't figure some people.

"Let's get clean," I told him. "What's your angle?"

His expression was all innocent bewilderment. "I don't understand."

"Come *on!*" Patience was slipping away real fast. "Even if I find her for you, you can't take her back! So what's the angle?"

"I just want to make sure she's all right."

That got me.

" 'All right'? What's that supposed to mean?" The guy had given up his kid. She wasn't his anymore. She belonged to the urchingangs now.

"Don't you tap into the grafitti?"

"Only sometimes." Didn't want to tell him I'd spent so much time buttoned up over the last half-dozen or so years that I'd got out of the habit of checking the grafitti. "Never been too sure how accurate that stuff is, anyway. Those grafitti journalists always seem to have an ax to grind."

"They're more reliable than the Central Authority datastream, I assure you."

"If you say so." Wasn't going to argue with him. Some people swore by the underground journalists who spend their days slipping uncensored capsules into the datastream, supposedly reporting "news that won't stand the light of day."

"Then I guess you haven't heard about the two urchins they found splattered at the base of the Boedekker North building two days ago."

I shook my head. No, I hadn't. It wasn't something you'd find on the standard newsnet. Two dead kids with no registered genotype were undoubtedly urchins. Officially, urchins didn't exist, therefore news of their deaths wouldn't appear in the datastream. Everyone knew the Megalops had its share of urchins, but their existence was never mentioned by anyone connected with the CA or the official media. To admit the existence of urchingangs was to admit there was a problem, and that would lead to someone having to find a solution to that problem. Nobody wanted to tackle that.

So the urchingangs lived on in legal limbo: illegal children of Realpeople, as real as Mr. Khambot or myself, but non-existent as far as Central Authority was concerned. Even clones had higher status.

"You mean you want me to check and see if your kid is one of the dead ones?" That would be easy. I'd just have to—

"I've already done that myself. She's not. I want you to find her and bring her to me."

"What 'round Sol for?"

"I just want to know she's alive and well."

Mr. Khambot went up another notch. Beneath the window dressing lurked a guy who still had a lot of feeling for the kid he had been forced to dump on the street. There was a real human being under all that make-up.

Didn't like the odds of locating a particular kid among the urchingangs, though. Kids were picked up as infants and had no identity outside their particular group. The one I was looking for would have no idea that she was Little Khambot, and neither would anybody else.

"I don't know . . ." I said slowly.

He leaned forward, hovering over the desk. "I've got prints—finger, foot, and retinal. Even have her genotype. You've got to find her for me, Mr. Dreyer. You've *got* to!"

"Yeah, but—"

"I'll pay you in gold—in advance!"

"Guess I could give it a try."

## 3

That afternoon I went down to the Battery Complex. Three years ago, according to Khambot, he had left the kid near the base of the Okumo-Slater Building where it arched over to Governor's Island. Before heading down there, I'd stocked a big bag with bread, milk, cheesoids, and soy staples. Now I stood and waited.

Gloomy down here at sea level. The calendar said summer but it could have been any season for all the sky you could see. The tight-packed skyscrapers with all their show-off overhangs did a great job of keeping the seasons out. Their shadows blocked the sun in the summer, and the heat leaking from their innards nullified the cold of winter. No day or night, just a dank, perennial twilight.

Far above I could see the gleaming southern face of the Leason Building looking like something from the Hanging Gardens of Babylon. Outside every window that opened—and some that didn't, probably—hung an overloaded window box festooned with green. Window gardening was the latest rage in the Megalops. Had a little plot right outside my own compartment window. And why not? With the price of fresh vegetables, it made excellent sense to grow your own wherever you could. And if you were on the north side or on the lower levels in perpetual shade, you grew mushrooms.

And further down, way down here in the shadows, the urchins grew.

Thought about what it must be like to have to give up your kid. Didn't think I could ever do that. I'd lost Lynnie, but that was different. She was taken from me by her mother—one day I looked around and she was gone. But at least I knew she was alive and well. Better than having her in an urchingang. And a hell of a lot better than having the CA terminate her for being excess.

No reprieve for a kid who went beyond replacement value. The state extended the old Abortion Rights laws to itself and dictated mandatory termination in utero. If the kid was somehow carried all the way to term, the child was terminated post-term. You couldn't even trade your own life for the kid's. No exceptions. The CA was ultrastrict on that. Only way they could make the Replacement Quota stick was to enforce it across the board. If news of one exception—just one—got out, there'd be chaos. The population would be up in arms and the whole Alliance would come crashing down.

Maybe it had been necessary a couple of generations ago, what with the planet on the brink of starvation and all. But times were better now. Population had dropped to a more manageable level, and with photosynthetic cattle in Antarctica and the deserts, and grain shipments coming in from the outworlds, food was getting steadily more plentiful. Wondered if we had to keep up the quota system. Maybe the CA was afraid that loosening up even a little bit would lead to a people explosion, the biggest baby boom in human history.

Even though it had started long before I was born, the whole thing had always seemed pretty drastic to me. Most people figured the end justified the means —if the CA hadn't taken Draconian measures, we *all* would have starved. Mandatory sterilization after you'd replaced yourself wasn't so bad, but termination of babes born in excess of replacement never sat well. One good thing seemed to come out of the Replacement Act: at least parents really appreciated their kids.

I had appreciated mine like crazy while she was here. And it had hurt like hell when her mother took her away.

"Can you give me somethin', Mister?"

Looked down and around and there was this three-year-old beaming up at me and holding out her hand. She was dressed in a little pink jumper, face scrubbed, cheeks glowing, smile beatific, her hair a blonde cloud around her head. That little face made you want to empty your pockets and take off your rings and shoes and give it all to her.

I looked around for her guardians and found two groups of them—a couple of twelve-year-olds at the

corner, and a slightly younger pair fifty meters away
in a doorway. If I tried anything cute with her, they'd
be on me like a pack of wild dogs. I pulled off a cheap
ring I'd bought just for the occasion.

"Take this," I said, handing it to her. "And tell your
friends they can have all the food in this bag if I can
have a talk with them."

Her smile widened as she grabbed the ring and ran
down the block. Watched her talk to the two on the
corner, saw them signal to the two in the doorway.
Suddenly another pair appeared from the other direction. Six guards for one little beggar—either she was as
valuable as all hell or they were *very* nervous about
losing her. In no time I was surrounded by the whole
crew. Something was up.

"Wan jaw, san?" the leader said in urchin pidgin.
Looked barely thirteen, but he and his friends were all
lean and angular, armed and wary, ready to fight.

"Want to ask you some questions."

"Bow wha?"

"About a babe someone left right here three years
ago."

"Lookee bag firs, san. Den jaw."

"Sure." I opened the bag and let them all take a long
look at the goodies. A couple of them licked their lips.
Hungry kids. Gave me a pang in my gut. I pulled out a
bag of cheesoids and unsealed it. "Here. Pass this
around."

Their dirty hands dug in, then stuffed the soft creamy
balls into their mouths. Noticed that the bigger ones
made sure the little blonde got her turn. I liked that.

The leader swallowed his mouthful and said, "Who
dis babe? Lookee how? Got pickee-pickee?"

"No. No picture. I guess she'd be her size" —I pointed
to the little beggar blonde— "but with black hair."

He shook his head. "No Lost Boy dat."

" 'Lost Boys,' eh? Well, do you remember any babe
like that three years ago?"

"Nine den. D'know. Probee trade, stan, san?"

I nodded. *Traded.* Damn! Hadn't thought of that.

Obvious though. The older kids took care of the babes until they were old enough to beg. If one urchingang was low on babes or beggars, it would trade for them with another. As the beggars grew older, they became nurturers, then graduated to guards, then to gang-leaders, then out into the underworld. An endless cycle.

"Take me to your leader," I said. It was lost on him.

"Takee halfway. Wendy meetee."

*Wendy?* Had someone been reading stories to the Lost Boys?

"Fair enough, I guess."

They led me north for a bunch of blocks, then down a stairway into the ancient subway system. Unimaginable that people used to prefer traveling underground to traveling in the air, but these tunnels were real, so I guessed those old stories were, too. The kids all pulled out pocket lights as we made our way along a white-tiled corridor. The leader stopped and faced me after we had descended a second stairway.

"Waitee here, san. Wendy be back. Waitee here."

"Okay. How long?"

"N'long, san. Waitee. We takee bag. Giftee. Kay, san?"

I handed over the bag of food. "Okay. But don't make me wait too long."

"N'long, san. N'long."

They left me one of their lights. As they hurried off into the darkness with my bag of goodies cradled in their midst like the Ark of the Covenant, I listened to the sound of their giggling and it occurred to me that maybe I was being played for a Class A jog.

After an hour of sitting alone in that damp, tiled hole with no sign of Wendy, I was sure.

*Well,* I thought, *not the first time.* Surely not the last. In truth, I'd half expected to be ripped but figured it was worth the risk. After all, the food hadn't cost me much. Felt bad, though. Sort of hoped for better from them.

Headed upstairs and back to my compartment, realizing for the first time what an impossible job this was:

trying to find a kid with no identity, a kid who didn't know who she was, with no picture, not even an identifying characteristic to go by, along a trail that was three years cold.

And to think I'd left being idly rich for this. Sometimes I think I'm crazy.

4

As I turned on the compartment lights, Iggy scrabbled across the floor and chomped on a fleeing cockroach, then retreated to a corner to chew. He wasn't much company. Iguanas are not known for their warmth.

One minute home and I knew I had made a mistake. I was feeling down and that was when my resistance was at its lowest. No sooner had I loosened my jump than the buttons began calling me from the back of the drawer where I kept them.

Twenty days now. Twenty full days since I'd snapped on a button. A record. Proud of myself. But felt myself weakening steadily. Hard to resist after that length of deprivation, no matter how much you wanted off. Began thinking of that group button I had bought during my first flush with the gold—all those bodies going strong, all funneled into that one little button. Threatened me with overload every time. Very hard to resist. Nothing I would have liked better right now than to snap it on and just lose myself in all that sensation. But I was never going to kick this if I didn't show a little more spine.

Maybe I should have gone the cold turkey route and just had the wire yanked and let it go at that. But I'd heard horror stories about guys who'd got themselves dewired that way and went black hole shortly after. Not for me, thanks. This wasn't the greatest life, but it was the only one I had. So I chose the wean. And by the Core, it was killing me.

Tried to keep busy tilling the window garden but it wasn't working. Finally I closed up and ran out into the night, vowing to find some real flesh, even though I knew it wouldn't help much, even if I had to go to Dydeetown and pay for it.

## 5

In the morning I was about to put a call in to Khambot to tell him what a lost cause this case was when a kid came through my office door. A skinny little twelve-year-old. He had thin lips, dark hair, and dark eyes that darted all over the place. He was wearing the upper half of a blue jumpsuit and the lower end of a brown, and they weren't joined in the middle. He looked dirty and scared.

An urch. No doubt about it. Certainly not the Wendy they'd told me about. Maybe a young lieutenant.

"You Dreyer-san?" he said in a voice that had a good ways to go before it would even consider changing.

"That's me. What can I do for you?"

He took a seat. "Still lookee three-year babe?"

"Maybe. Why didn't Wendy show up yesterday?" I said, leaning back in my chair.

"Din know you, san. So we wait, watch, follow home, then out, then home, then here." He was speaking very carefully. Probably thought he was putting on a good show of Realpeople talk. That was a laugh.

"She satisfied?"

He shrugged. "M'be."

"She send you?"

A nod.

"And you think you can help find this kid?"

Another shrug, another, "M'be. But cost."

"Never any doubt in my mind about that."

"N'hard barter—soft f'soft."

*Soft barter?* "Like what?"

"Info for us."

"Who's 'us'?"

"Urchingangs."

"You're an 'us' now? Thought you were always scrapping with each other over begging turf and spheres of influence. Thought you got together for babe trades and that was about it."

"Used t'be. Be again, san. B'now lookee—look for—answer to same question."

"Which is?"

"Dead urches."

"Ah! That means, I take it, that the gangs don't know what happened to them either."

"B'blieve no, san—" He coughed and raised the level of his dialog. "No, but we find out sooner-late."

"If you're so sure of that, why do you need my help?"

"Need Realworld connect."

"You mean to tell me that with all the graduates from the urchingangs floating through the Megalops, not one of them will help out?"

He lowered his eyes and shook his head. "No lookee backee."

"Oh. Right."

Remembered: Once you're out of the gang and topside in the shadow economy where everything's barter and nothing's connected to Central Data, you're who you are—no past. No one admits they're from urchinland—*ever*. Urchins don't exist.

The more I thought about it, the better this looked to me. The urchins would search out little Khambot among the gangs for me while I worked in the Realworld for them. Didn't see why they were so determined to find out what happened to the two little kids. No one had mentioned foul play. But why argue? The way I saw it, we'd both come out ahead.

"Okay. I've got a good contact who can help us out."

"Come?"

Shook my head. "No place for a kid. Especially an urch."

True. Elmero's was not for kids, but even truer was that I didn't want to go sliding into Elmero's with an urch in tow.

"Nev know," he said.

"They'll know as soon as you open your mouth. The only kids who talk pidge are urchins."

"Helpee Realfolk?"

Shook my head again. "No time."

He lowered his voice and spoke haltingly. "I . . . know . . . some. I . . . can . . . do."

Had to laugh. "You've been practicing that? Getting ready for the Realworld?"

He looked at me with his big brown eyes. "Please, san?"

Something in a dusty, almost forgotten corner inside went soft and mushy.

"Okay," I said, wondering why even as the words came out. "Just keep your mouth shut. And if you have to say something, don't use 'san.' That's a dead giveaway. It's 'Mr. Dreyer.' Got it?"

Now he smiled. "Kay."

"*Okay.*"

Called Elmero's. The man got on the screen. After exchanging pleasantries, I asked him if he could do a jack for me later today.

"How deep?"

"Top sector."

"That will cost."

"Don't I know. I can pay the freight if you can do the jack."

"Do I ever let you down?" Elmero said with his awful smile.

"Not never," I said, "but hardly ever. Doc around?"

"Should be soon. Bout time for his midday wiff."

"If you see him, ask him to wait around for me. Be by in a tenth or so."

"Sure." The screen blanked.

"Fees fren, come he—?"

"Say it in Realtalk," I told him.

"If . . . he's . . . you . . . friend, how . . . come . . . he . . . charge?"

" 'How come he char*ges.*' " Felt like a tutor machine. "He charges because that's his business—*one* of his businesses. We're friends, but that doesn't mean I dip into his trade whenever I want. Business is business."

Could tell he wasn't following me too well so I shifted

to a topic I was sure he could track. "Interested in lunch?"

"Course. Y'got?"

"Not here. A restaurant."

His eyes saucered. "Mean sitdown?"

You'd think I'd just offered him a trip to Skyland Park.

"Yeah. There's a nice place on level 12 that has—"

He was out of his chair and heading for the door. "S'go!"

## 6

"Don't make yourself sick, now," I told him. The urch was ready to order two of everything on the menu.

"Never had steak." He was talking more carefully now. I guess sitting in a roomful of Realpeople was influencing him.

"Won't get one here, either."

"Said 'steak'?" he said, pointed to the glowing table-top menu in front of him. The table had read off the menu selections in its feminine monotone, brightening each line as it went. I searched through the printed list. My reading skills left much to be desired, though I'd improved them a lot in the past year.

"Yeah. Here it is: steak with mushroom gravy. But it isn't real grass-fed steer steak." Not with the economic stratum this place serviced—no one could afford it. "You can either get chlor-cow or soysteak."

" 'Chlor-cow'?"

Didn't want to go into an explanation of photosynthetic cattle so I told him, "The soysteak tastes pretty much like the real thing. And it's bigger."

"Soysteak me. Two."

" 'I'll have two soysteaks, please,' and no, you won't. You'll have one. It's a big one—half a kilo." He made a face so I said, "If you finish it and you're still hungry, I'll get you another."

He smiled and for a fleeting moment he was a real little boy.

Ordered a shrimp culture sandwich and a beer for myself. Felt like his father or something as I helped him punch his order into the console, letting him add sides of chocolate soymilk and double speedspuds. Hadn't been called on to act like a father in an awful lot of years. Gave me an odd little warm feeling, one I might get used to if I wasn't careful.

"What's your name, kid?"

"B.B."

That was easy enough. "Okay, B.B. Your meal will be here soon. Just sit back and relax."

Watched him as we waited. He couldn't take his eyes off the servers wheeling by. On two occasions I thought he was going to lunge at the dessert cart. Finally a server wheeled up and slid our meals onto the table. When it asked if we wanted to modify our order, I told it no and stuck my thumb in its pay slot. As it trundled away, I turned back to the urch. He had the steak in both hands and was gnawing at it.

"*Put that down!*" I said in as forceful a whisper as I dared. To his credit, he didn't drop it, and he didn't buck me on it. He eased it back onto his plate.

"S'matter?" he said with a wounded expression as he licked the gravy off his lips.

"You trying to embarrass me? Ever hear of a knife?"

"Course."

"Well, unless you want everybody in this place to know you're an urch, use it!"

He proceeded to hold the steak down with his left hand while he cut with the knife in his right. I was ready to get real angry when I realized he wasn't trying to turn my screws.

"Okay, drop everything," I said softly. He did, reluctantly, and sat there sucking his fingers.

If I was going to have to sit here with him, I didn't want him making a spectacle of himself. I held up my fork and said, "This takes the place of your fingers when you're eating with Realpeople. It's called a fork. Here's how you use it."

As I picked up my knife and reached across to demonstrate, he lunged forward and covered his plate with his hands. Just as quickly, he pulled them away and leaned back. Instinct, I guessed. I speared the gnawed corner of the soysteak, sawed through his teeth marks, and handed him the loaded fork. Watched him grab it and shove it into his mouth, watched him close his eyes as he chewed.

"S'steak?" he said in a hushed voice after he had swallowed.

"Well, something that tastes a lot *like* steak. Only the mushrooms are real."

He attacked the meal. My shrimp culture sandwich was only half gone when he looked up at me from his empty plate. Nice thing about soysteak—no fat, no bone, no gristle.

"Said nother."

"Look, if you're not used to gravy and that sort of—"

"*Said!*"

"All right, all right!"

Punched in a reorder of the soysteak but skipped the speedspuds. Finished my sandwich and watched him work his way through the second steak. Knew he was going to have a bellyache by the way he was wolfing it down. Surprised me, though. Asked for dessert. Treated him to a chocolate gelato-to-go as we left. He had it finished by the time we got up to midlevel. As we waited on the platform for a slot in the crosstown tube, he turned green.

"You feeling all right?" I asked.

"Na s'good, san."

"Not surprised after the way you—"

And then he was running for the pissoir. Never made it. Chocolate-colored soysteak-speedspud stew splattered the platform. When he was empty, he returned to the boarding area, wiping his mouth on his sleeve.

"Told you not to have that second soysteak."

He smiled up at me and jerked his thumb at the gravity chute that led back to the restaurant. "Third now?"

Took a half-hearted swing at his head. He ducked easily, laughing.

## 7

"An urch search, ay?" Elmero said, smiling horribly after I'd explained the Khambot case. He repeated the phrase. Seemed to like the sound of it.

Doc was there, wiffing a pale yellow gimlet. He had a round black face, a portly body, and owlish eyes. He still had a year to go before his license suspension ran out and tended to spend a lot of time here.

"Where do I come in?" he said.

"Need an opinion on the autopsies of those dead kids. What's your consultation fee?"

Doc snorted a laugh. "I believe it would approximate my tab at this establishment."

I glanced at Elmero who shrugged his narrow shoulders. "Not unreasonable," he said.

"But I don't have access to those data," Doc said. "Can't tell you anything without data."

"That's okay. Elmero can jack into—"

"Elmero can't jack *anywhere*!" Elmero said, his face a stony mask. He was looking past me at the urch.

"He's secure," I said quickly, placing a hand on the kid's shoulder. He'd been good. Hadn't said more than one hello since he came in. "B.B. is tight. Tight as can be."

Elmero arched his eyebrows and cocked his head. "You guarantee that?"

"To the Core." Knew I was safe saying that. Not being Realpeople, urches couldn't testify in court.

"Good enough."

Elmero rode his chair over to his comm chassis and began his jacking procedure. He broke into the coroner's datafile and then we began to search. In the Under Age Five category, we found one John Doe and one Jane Doe, each with an unregistered genotype, deceased on the date in question. Doc took over then and scanned the data. Twice.

"Nothing here but trauma, all simultaneous, consistent with a fall. No biological or chemical toxins or contaminants, no molestations. Generic foodstuff in the intestines. What we have here are two otherwise healthy kids dead as a result of a fall from a height consistent with the middle sixty floors of the tower complex they were found next to."

B.B. piped in. "No drug? No sex?" It was the most he had said since we'd entered Elmero's.

"I believe I covered those fields," Doc said.

"*Has* to be drug!"

I looked at him. "Why does there 'has' to?"

He glared at me, then turned and stalked out.

" 'B.B.' is an urchin name," Elmero said.

"Really?" Hadn't known that.

"Common one. The other most common is 'B.G.' "

"That's all very interesting," Doc said, "but what I'd like to know is what a couple of toddler urchins were doing up on the middle level of the Boedekker North building in the first place."

"Something nasty, I'll bet," Elmero said with a sour grin. "Something *very* nasty."

This was getting interesting. Intriguing, even. But it was time to settle up accounts: Elmero canceled Doc's balance, then deducted that amount plus his jacking fee from the big store of credit I had with him from the gold he'd fenced for me after the Dydeetown girl job. Then I hurried out, looking for B.B. Found him watching somebody playing the new zap game. Procyon Patrol was passe now. Bug Wars was the current rage. Grabbed his arm and pulled him to an empty corner.

"We've got to talk, urch. You're not telling me everything you should be telling me."

"S'n'true, san—" he began, then stopped himself. "That not true."

Caught and held his eyes with my own. "Why were you so sure of drugs? Truth now, or I walk."

He looked away and took a deep breath. He spoke carefully.

"Beggee kids be snatched."

"Snatched?" It was the first I'd heard of it. "By who?"

"D'know."

"How many?"

"Lots."

"Why?"

"D'know."

Was almost glad he didn't know. Wasn't sure I wanted the details on why someone was kidnapping little urchin beggars. Was sure it wasn't for ransom. But now I knew why there had been six urchin guards for that little blonde beggargirl down by the Battery yesterday.

"Were the two dead ones snatched?"

He nodded.

"Have any others been found dead besides the ones at Boedekker North?"

He shook his head. "Jus' th'two. Get others back."

"You mean they're snatched and then returned to you?"

"Drop off where they snatchee."

This was making less and less sense.

"Unhurt?"

B.B. shook his head vehemently. "No! N'same. Even after back, still gone. Dull, dumb, stupee, bent."

Now I understood. Whoever was snatching the little urches was returning damaged goods. That was why B.B had been so sure we'd find drugs in the post-mortem report.

"So you think they're being dosed up and—what?"

He shrugged. "D'know. Can't tell. N'good sure."

"No signs of . . . abuse?" I thought of my own daughter. For perhaps the first time since Maggs had spirited her away, I was glad Lynnie was out among the Outworlds.

"Nup," he said, shaking his head. "Checked by Wendy. Sh'say bods okay, b'heads f'blungit."

"Who 'round Sol is this Wendy? She a doctor or something?"

B.B. was suddenly flustered. "Sh'Mom. D'worry. Sh'know. An'way, kids get better, b'ver' slow. Weeks."

They're returned slow and stupid but get better with time. Sure sounded like a drug to me. This was getting stranger and stranger. Little urches snatched and re-turned, physically okay, but dosed up on something. To what end? Maybe just dosed up and posed? Or maybe overdosed on purpose so they couldn't talk afterwards? But why bother with such elaborate precautions? Urchins had no legal existence. They couldn't bring charges or testify against anyone. So why coagulate their minds before returning them?

Why return them at all?

"How many days were the two dead kids missing?"

He thought a moment, then said, "Old one three, young one four."

Missing three to four days—were they so gelled on something that they walked right off the outer walkway? No, wait: no trace of foreign chemicals or toxins in their systems.

My own mind was beginning to feel a bit gelled.

"Post-mort said they were clean."

He looked at me as if I were stupid. "Druggee-druggee!"

Maybe he was right. Suddenly I had an idea.

"Come on," I said, pulling him toward the chute up to the tube level. "We're heading uptown."

### 8

Boedekker North was the biggest thing in the Danbury borough. It towered above everything around it like a giant stack of rice cakes on an empty table. We tubed into the midsection and hunted up a directory.

"Lookee, san?" When I glared at him, he sighed and said, "What we looking for?"

"A pharmaceutical company."

"Farmers—?"

"No. Pharmaceutical. As in 'pharmacy.' They make drugs. You know—medicines?" He gave me a puzzled look. "Wait," I told him. "You'll see."

I'd had a brainstorm. Suppose somebody was using the kids as lab specimens to give some new drug a clinical trial? Something so new and unique that the coroner's analyzers wouldn't spot it? Suppose this new drug backfired? And suppose the testers weren't pre-

pared to house the damaged kids? What would they do
with them?

Send them back where they came from, of course.
That would take the kids off their hands and allow the
researcher to observe the longterm effects of their
botched trial.

Urchins as human lab rats. What a wonderful world.

There were a few bugs in my scenario but it fit most
of the facts. A little more information and I was sure I
could fill in the empty spaces.

"Sh'tell more," B.B. said as we sorted through the
midlevel directory's stores and services.

I gave him a sidelong look. "What else you been
holding out on me?"

"N'hold, san—" He stopped and cleared his throat.
"Not hold out. Jus' membered. Saw comet on side of
flitter snatched little Jo."

"Why didn't you tell me this before!" It would have
made things *so* much easier!

He shrugged. "Din think—"

"Never mind. What color was it? Red, yellow?"

"Pointy silver star with long silver tail."

"Any words?"

He shrugged again. Right. Remembered he couldn't
read. No matter. Starting to get real excited about this
case. A stylized comet in silver. Obviously a company
logo. Now we were getting somewhere.

Or so I thought.

Boedekker North housed thousands of lessees. We
sorted through the entire mid-section directory and
looked up every single firm or store that might conceivably have anything at all to do with drugs, medicine,
research, doctors, even kids. Then we ran a match
search to see if any of these had a silver comet in their
logo. No match. Another run looking for the word
"star" or "comet" or "meteor" or any celestial body
associated with their company name. No match. So we
searched for *any* company name that contained any
reference to outer space. Even checked out names re-

lated to speed. We found quite a few, but none of them had a silver comet for a logo.

We came up equally empty on the top-section and under-section directories.

The hours had slipped by. It was dark out. We found a roving soyvlaki cart and I treated B.B. to a couple. He wolfed them down as we sat and watched a lot of the workers head home for the night.

"Howc y'don work l'them?"

"You mean a steady day job?"

He nodded.

Thought about that. Maggs had asked me that same question maybe a million times during our marriage. Couldn't come up with a new answer on the spot so I gave him the stock reply:

"Too much like being a robot."

He gave me a strange look so I explained.

"You know—everything on a schedule. Be here now, get there then, do this before lunch, do that before you go home. A regimented existence. Not for me. Like to make my own hours, be my own boss, go where I want, when I want. Work for myself, not some big corporation. Be a corporation of one."

He gave me a half-hearted nod, like he wasn't really convinced. I couldn't believe it. An urch who'd lived by his wits as long as he had—how could he have the slightest doubt?

"Don't tell me you'd want to be like *them!*"

He watched the scurrying workers with big round wistful eyes. His mouth was pulled down at the corners and I could barely hear his voice as he said, "Love it."

Couldn't fathom that at all. Struck me speechless a moment, then I understood. Here I was talking about bucking the system to a kid who'd have to spend his entire life scratching out an existence in the underworld, who would never get a hand on the bottom rung of the system's ladder no matter how hard he wished, hoped, or tried. From where he was, that bottom rung looked like heaven.

Somebody should have come by then and daubed my

face white, painted my nose red, and turned on a calliope. What a clown I was. An idiot clown.

Suddenly my appetite was gone. Offered the kid my second soyvlaki. He took it but ate it slowly.

When he was finished he said, "Where fr'mere?"

Wasn't sure. Tired. Knew we weren't finished here at Boedekker North, but I didn't want to go back to Manhattan tonight and have to tube up here again in the morning. Wanted to milk this trip.

"Back to the directories," I told him. "We're going to go through the mid-section firm by firm and look at every logo of every lessee in Boedekker North until we find something that looks like a comet."

"Cou b'wrong," he said.

"About the comet? Don't think that hasn't occurred to me. That's why you aren't going home till I do."

We seated ourselves at the directory console, queued up the ads of each lessee in alphabetical order, and let them run in the holochamber. Started getting bleary along about "J" and was nodding around "M." Suddenly B.B. was yanking on my sleeve.

"It, san!" He was bouncing in his seat and pointing at the chamber. "It! *It!*"

Opened my eyes and stared at the holo. Felt my blood run cold at sight of the name: *NeuroNex*. But the logo was all wrong.

"That's no comet!"

The kid's finger was wiggling in the chamber, intersecting with the NeuroNex logo. His voice had risen to just shy of a screech. "It, san! *It!*"

And then I saw what he meant. Underlining the NeuroNex name was a stylized neuron trailing a long axon—all silvery gray in color. It did look like a comet.

*Found it!*

I noticed the kid looking at me with something like adoration in his eyes. "You plenty smartee, Dreyer-san."

"If I were really smart," I said, trying to hide my dismay as I stared at the NeuroNex logo, "I wouldn't be involved in this at all."

"Where place?"

"Doesn't matter," I told him. "Place is closed now anyway. Be open tomorrow. I'll come back then."

"We—"

"No! *I. Me*. Alone. You can't get into a NeuroNex shop—no minors allowed—and you might give it away if you did." Stood up. "Come on. Time to get back to the island."

He was pouting as I guided him to the tube platform. The pod came and I spent most of the trip home staring through the wall at the progression of lighted stops and semidark in-betweens, thinking of NeuroNex.

NeuroNex. I hadn't included it in the sort, probably because I hadn't wanted to see that name.

Of all the places that could have been involved, why did it have to be NeuroNex?

Something bumped my arm. I looked around and saw that the urch had fallen asleep and was leaning against me. The other people on the tube probably thought he was my kid. He shivered in his sleep. I put my arm over his shoulder. Just to keep up appearances.

## 9

"My stop's next," I said, jostling him awake. Got to my feet as he yawned and stretched.

"Tired," he said. "Sleep y'place, san?"

Shook my head. "No chance."

He looked surprised. "Please? Tired. Nev spen night in real compartment."

"Haven't missed much. Once you're asleep it's all the same. Besides, I've got work to do. Can't have an urch hanging around."

"I can help," he said in his best Realpeople talk.

Could see he was getting too attached, imprinted on me like some baby duck. Had it introduce a little distance here.

"No, you can't. Check with my office in a couple of days. May have something for you then."

The tube stopped and I got out. Walking away, I felt

his hurt gaze on my back like a weight until the tube shot him further downtown. Could have used some company but I had to be alone tonight. No witnesses.

Learning that the "comet" we had been seeking was part of the NeuroNex logo was pushing me toward a decision. A big one. One I wasn't sure I was ready for yet.

Years ago, NeuroNex had wired me for my button. Now NeuroNex—or at least this particular branch office—was linked to the snatches and deaths of a couple of urchins. And I'd managed to get myself tractored into finding out the who, the why, and the wherefore.

Which meant I had to find a way of presenting myself to NeuroNex and asking lots of questions without raising too much suspicion. There was a foolproof way for me to do that:

Get myself unbuttoned.

Not a pretty prospect. Been preparing myself to have it done, been planning to have it done . . . *someday*. But not so soon. Next year maybe. Next quarter maybe. Sure as hell not tomorrow.

*Not* tomorrow!

But what better way to get next to NeuroNex? Tried desperately to think of one and came up blank.

Dropped into my new formchair—just like Elmero's —and buttoned it to adjust to my posture. Sat there looking down the hall through my door. Watched for a while but nothing was moving out there so I rode the chair over to the button drawer and opened it. Sat staring at those little gold disks. A lot of money invested in those things over the years. Some were played out but I kept them anyway. Nostalgia, maybe. The Good Old Days—when a good simple single-input orgasm was quite enough for a long while. But then I graduated to doubles, then triples. My latest was a five-couple orgy multi-channeled into a slow build that crescendoed through a series of minor eruptions into a major simultaneous explosion.

Picked it out of the pile and backed the chair into the

middle of the compartment, turning so my back was to Lynnie's holo. As the chair reclined supineward, I hesitated. Shouldn't do this, I told myself. You've been weaning yourself down all year. Three weeks now without buttoning up once. A record. As good as clean. Why set yourself back now? The day after tomorrow will be a lot easier if you put that damn thing back in the drawer right now and go to sleep.

Good arguments. Made a lot of sense. But they couldn't overcome one little slice of reality: After I was unbuttoned tomorrow, there'd be no choice for me unless I decided to get rewired, and that wouldn't be possible for at least half a year. Tonight was it. After this, I'd be like the rest of the walkarounds except there'd be a part of me so callused by years of buttoning that no one in the real world could get through to it. An important part of me would be permanently—or *almost* permanently—numb. I needed one last jolt, one last hit, for old times' sake. Auld Lang Syne. No rational arguments were going to keep me from buttoning up one last time.

Was just fitting the button into the dimple in my scalp when I noticed movement through the door. Held off and watched the urchin steal down the hall toward my door. Felt my jaw muscles tighten. If that little bastard thought he was going to barge in here and whimper and whine his way into spending the night, he had another think coming. I needed my privacy, needed to be by myself for a—

He didn't knock or push the buzzer. Just stood there looking at the door for a moment, then slipped to the floor and curled up with his back to me.

The little jog was going to spend the night camped outside my door and he wasn't even going to tell me!

Watched the slow rise and fall of his skinny little back as he dropped off to sleep. Fingered the button in my hand. Could still button up just like I'd planned. The door was soundproof and he'd never know what I was doing.

But *I'd* know he was there.

Stared at him. He looked so frail lying there, scootching around to get comfortable. Thought of him staying there on the hard floor all night in the cold white light while I slept calm and soft in my dark compartment. So what? It was his choice, wasn't it? He could have been back with his gang now, sleeping with them. Safe. Secure. Underground. In the old subway tunnels.

Sighed and floated the chair over to the drawer, dropped the button back in, then returned to the door. Maybe it was for the best, I told myself. Make it easier in the morning . . . and all the empty nights thereafter.

Opaqued the door—saw no use in letting him in on that little secret—and slid it open. Nudged him with my foot.

"Get in here!" I said in an angry hiss. "What'll the neighbors say if they see you out here?"

He gave me a shy smile as he stumbled to his feet. Growling, I pointed him toward the couch and turned out the lights.

## 10

B.B. had the big thrill of waking up in a real compartment and eating a compartment breakfast. After he was finished, I sent him on his way happy and smiling, telling him I'd meet him at the office later. When I was sure he was gone, I emptied my button drawer into the pocked of my jumper and headed for the tubes. Tried to keep my mind blank as I headed for Boedekker North. Didn't want to think about what I was going to have done to myself this morning.

The word *castration* drifted through my mind.

Not that I was much use to the female of the species now, but without the wire I wouldn't even be useful to myself. They say that after you get unbuttoned, you can relearn to be with a woman again. It was never as good, but you *could* relearn.

Wasn't sure I'd even want to try.

Wandered around Boedekker North for a while, killing time. Finally I decided that I'd put it off long enough. Wasn't going to accomplish anything by delaying any longer. Strolled onto the premises of the NeuroNex franchise and . . .

. . . got in line.

Hadn't expected this. A bunch of official-looking types in executive jumps were waiting for the human tech. She took each into the back office; a few minutes later they were out again and on their way. It looked like they were making purchases, but that didn't make sense. Simple purchases of 'mones or buttons could be made more quickly—and with greater confidentiality—via the slot consoles along the wall. Needed a human myself. After all, I was here for a procedure.

"You alone here?" I called over the heads of the others.

"Until the sales girl comes in, I am." She smiled. "We let her sleep late one morning a week."

"I was here before you," said a thin, worn out looking guy two seats away.

"Nobody said you weren't."

"Just remember that," he said sullenly.

Finally they were gone. Only me and my polite fellow dallier—the one ahead of me—remained. He shuffled up to the counter. "Wanna donate a few nanos."

The tech gave him the up-and-down. She was red-haired, round-bodied and round-faced, with ruddy cheeks. A plump little angel, except that she was scowling.

"Weren't you here last week, Stosh?"

"Yeah, but—"

"No 'buts.' Two weeks between donations, not a tenth less. You know that. See you in a week."

He stalked out, averting his eyes as he passed me.

"What can NeuroNex do for you?" she said to me.

"A procedure."

Her interest level rose visibly. "Oh? Which one?"

Looked around to make sure the office area was empty. This wasn't something I wanted to advertise. "Want to get dewired."

Her eyes widened, revealing more blue. "Really?"

"Something wrong?"

"No. Of course not. It's just that you don't look like our typical . . ." Her voice trailed off.

"Buttonhead?"

"Not a nice term. We prefer 'direct limbic neuro-stimulation.' "

"And you think I should probably look like the guy you just chased off, right?"

"We try to discourage that stereotype. By the way, you'll have to sign a release."

"I know."

Expected that. The NeuroNex people had installed the wire a year or so after Maggs had run off. Had to sign a release then saying that I'd heard and understood all the listed potential physical and psychosocial side effects of becoming a buttonhead and absolved NeuroNex of any liability connected with same. Now they'd want me to absolve them of any and all liability associated with *not* being a buttonhead.

Sure. Why not?

We got down to business. The releases were signed, then we discussed price. That was not negotiable, I knew—the fee was set at NeuroNex's central office— but I haggled anyway. Got nowhere, as expected, but did manage to get a trade-in allowance on the unused plays left in my buttons.

After the sales girl arrived, the tech led me back to the sterile room and laid me down. I watched the monitor as she prepped the top of my scalp. Had an odd, disembodied sensation as I looked down at the back of my own head in the holo chamber. She depilated the area around the dimple, disinfected it, then readied her scalpel.

"No blade?" I said.

She was seated at the top of my head as I reclined on the table. Couldn't see her face, only her hands in the monitor, but her voice was calm, matter-of-fact.

"It's there. You just can't see it. It's a loop of Gussman molly wire. See?" She passed the visible part of the instrument within a couple of centimeters of my scalp and the flesh parted magically. "Beautiful stuff—a single strand of Gussman Alloy molecules strung end to end, submicroscopic but still 100-kilo test. Wonderful to work with."

Her unbridled enthusiasm did not keep my stomach from lurching as I saw my own blood start to well in the lengthening incision.

"Could you turn off the monitor, please?"

"Sure."

A hand disappeared from the field and then the holochamber went blank. Couldn't understand why some people like to watch. Looking at the blank ceiling now, I heard my voice yammering on. Usually I let other people talk, but I was nervous, shaking inside, feeling cold and sick, and it seemed to help to talk.

"You do this often?"

"No. Hardly at all. I used to put in a lot of wires when I was back on the island. We refer all our button jobs there. You really need a team of two to do an implant right. These little branch offices don't have the volume to warrant two techs."

"Didn't look that way this morning."

"Those were special orders." I heard her shift position. "Okay. We're ready to dewire. Last chance: You sure you want to go through with this?"

"Absolutely . . . I think. But what if I feel I'm starting to go crazy after the wire is gone?"

There was a pause. "I think we can help you."

"Yeah? How?"

"You've heard of NDT, right?"

"Of course." Had forgotten what the letters stood for but knew it was a neurohormone—NeuroNex marketed their own brand under the name that had become generic for the stuff: BrainBoost.

"Right. Well, new research indicates that NDT might prove to be of some benefit in the button withdrawal stage."

That was good news. Anything to ease the withdrawal would be a blessing. I'd tried some NDT in my younger days to help me pass the investigator's exam and hadn't been too impressed. NDT was the last thing I would have expected to help.

"Isn't that for memory and the like?"

"Right," she said. "There's some perceptual enhancement, but basically it's a cognitive booster. Better recall, heightened deductive and analytical capabilities."

"That's what I thought." Students used a lot of it, so did business people for meetings and negotiations, and so on. "So how's it going to help me?"

"It appears to concentrate attention on the cognitive functions and distract it from the vegetative-reproductive areas. In other words, you're still withdrawing but you don't notice it as much."

Just then a disturbing thought struck me. "By the way, what did that guy just ahead of me want to 'donate'?"

"NDT."

"Afraid you'd say that. Not exactly anxious to have any of him floating around in my brain."

She laughed, a deep chuckle. "Don't worry! By the time we finish concentrating and distilling our NDT, it is *pure*. Not a trace of contaminant."

"Sounds like it's worth a try."

"Oh, it's definitely worth a try. In fact . . ." She hesitated here and I wished I could have seen her face. "There's a special high-potency NDT that would be perfect for you. It's a new synthetic."

"Thought the synthetics weren't worth the trouble."

"They weren't. But this is something completely new. Unfortunately, it's not officially on the market yet."

"Too bad."

"I could get you some, but I can't sell it to you through the usual channels, if you get my meaning."

Got her meaning, all right: a barter deal. Very interesting. NDT was growing in my mind as a two-edged sword: it could get me over the hump of withdrawing from the buttons, and it would give me an excuse to keep coming back here until I found a connection between NeuroNex and the snatched urchins. If indeed there was a connection.

"What's so special about this synthetic?"

"Super high potency."

"Why not just take more of the regular NDT?"

"Because there are only so many receptor sites in the brain available to regular NDT. Once they're all engaged, that's it—you've got your maximum effect no matter how much you pour in. The super NDT has quadruple the bio-activity of regular."

She did a little more fiddling around on my head, then said, "That does it. The wire's out. Now . . . I can either close you up tight or implant a membrane patch so you can put NDT to use on a regular basis."

"How about a free sample of the super stuff? If it helps, I'll come back for the membrane and you'll have yourself a regular customer." Didn't want to trade one dependency for another, but if NDT would help me over the rough spots, I couldn't pass it up.

There was a pause, then, "Sounds fair. I'll get some."

She left me alone. If not for my open scalp, it would have been a perfect opportunity for some quick snooping. I stayed on the table and waited.

"I'm going to add a drop of NDT suspension directly into your CSF and then—"

"CSF?"

"Cerebrospinal fluid. The juice your brain floats in, so to speak. Then I'm going to close you up. You'll get a short, quick, intense reaction to the NDT. It lasts much longer through a membrance patch."

"This is the super stuff you're giving me? On the house, right?"

"On the house."

It didn't hit me until I was off the table and thumbing my bill in the outer office. Suddenly noticed that colors seemed brighter, clearer, objects more sharp-edged. Was aware of all my nerve-endings, could feel the scanner read the processor in my thumb and deduct the unbuttoning fee. Felt the blood racing through my capillaries, felt the slow coiling peristalsis of my intestines, the microturbulence of the air currents in my lungs, the electric currents arcing through the walls of my heart. If this was the effect of super NDT, I could see how it would make it easier to forget how lost and alone you felt without your button collection.

The NDT I'd had in the past had never been like this. Super NDT . . . nordopatriptyline . . . everything I'd ever learned, ever read, ever heard about it came back to me and swirled with my latent thoughts and questions about the snatched urchins, living and otherwise. And suddenly it was all clear. All the pieces fell together into a seamless could-be that needed only a few more facts to make it a must-be.

"Of course!" I heard my own voice mutter as I withdrew my thumb from the payment slot. "That's why you snatch the urchins!"

"What did you say?" the tech asked with suddenly narrowed eyes.

"Nothing." *Loose-lipped idiot!*

"No, you said something about urchins." Her smile had shrunken to a tight thin line, her cherubic face had settled into a petrous mask.

I didn't hesitate a microsecond. " 'Luncheon.' I said, 'I still have time to make a luncheon.' "

"Oh," she said and nodded, but I knew she didn't believe me. Got out as fast as I could and headed for Elmero's, hoping Doc was there.

## 11

"Seems kind of a waste to me," Doc said, his black face gleaming in the bright lights of Elmero's office. "I mean, we've already been into Central Data once and found nothing useful in the p-m report. Why go back?"

"Because I don't think we asked the right questions."

While I argued with Doc, Elmero was already at his console, working his jacking procedure. The super NDT was still buzzing through me. My thoughts were flying.

Doc shrugged. "Well, it's your money."

"Right. So tell me: Is a cerebrospinal fluid analysis done on a routine post-mortem?"

"Of course. Protein, glucose, chlorides, bacteria, viruses, toxins, and other sundry things."

"Neurohormones?"

"Hell, no!"

"Why not?"

"Be like checking for subcutaneous fat on your ass: everybody's got it to varying degrees. Why should they check for neurohormones? Everybody's got those. Besides, those assays are expensive. You'd have to expect a problem along those lines before trying to justify that kind of expenditure. Certainly wouldn't do it on a John or a Jane Doe that's undoubtedly an urchin."

That was what I had figured. "How long do they keep tissue samples in the coroner's dept?"

"Depends. On a Doe case, probably a month, tops."

"We're in," Elmero announced from the console.

"Can you requisition a test on one of the dead kids' CSF?"

Elmero gave a me a look that eloquently mixed disgust with annoyance.

"Sorry," I said. "Don't know what came over me. Get a nordopatriptyline level."

He told the coroner's computer to run the test, then leaned back in his chair and glided it back to the desk. Doc went out to the barroom for a fresh whiff, saying this would take awhile. His timing was perfect: the result of the NDT assay popped into view just as he returned. He stepped over and looked at it.

"Damn me!" he said.

I joined him and scanned the result: "*NDT level in subject CSF = 2.7 ng./dl. Normal level in age group = 12.5–28 ng./dl.*"

"Figured that," I said.

Doc gave me a sour look. "And just *how* did you 'figure' that someone had sucked off this kid's NDT?"

Told them how B.B.'s "comet" had led us to NeuroNex, what the tech had said about the super synthetic NDT, about my earlier guess that NeuroNex might be testing a new substance on the urchins.

"But if that's the case, the kid's brain should have been *loaded* with NDT!" Doc said.

"Not if the assay doesn't pick up the synthetic," Elmero said.

Doc scowled. "Then why the depressed levels?"

Waited a few beats, then said, "Because everything the tech told me about the new synthetic super NDT was true, except the part about it being synthetic."

They stared at me uncomprehendingly. Nice to be the smart guy, the guy with all the answers for once. Allowed them to stew for awhile. Finally:

"Think about it. NDT is a normal component of the CSF. It's necessary for normal cognitive functions, and in increased concentrations it can enhance those functions. Now . . . at what time in your development is the brain most actively sorting, analyzing, filing, matching, compounding, linking, correlating, and so on?"

"Childhood," Doc said.

"Right! The whole world is new. The mind is relentlessly bombarded with a seemingly endless flow of new data."

Doc bit his lower lip. "I don't like where this is heading."

Elmero said nothing. He just sat there and absorbed it all.

"Bet there's an obscure piece of research somewhere that recounts the remarkable enhancing power of toddler NDT on adult cognition. Quadruple bioactivity.'"

Doc whiffed and exhaled slowly. "NeuroNex is a reputable company. I can't believe it would get involved—"

"It's not," Elmero said. "If this was being done on a corporate level, I'd have heard about it."

I nodded in agreement. A big operation would cause supply problems, creating a black market in toddler NDT, and there wasn't a black market in Sol System that Elmero didn't know about.

"Right. This is strictly small time. The tech and the local franchise owner are probably working it on their own, snatching the kids, siphoning off their NDT, and bartering it away as an 'unapproved synthetic' at a very stiff price per nanogram."

"There's people who want it that bad?" Doc said.

"Definitely." The effect of my test dose was fading a little now and I could see why you'd want some more. Especially if you were a businessman or analyst. Never thought so clearly, never saw so many relationships and correlations between seemingly unrelated facts in all my life. Like being terribly nearsighted since birth and then having your focal length corrected—a whole new world is suddenly available to you. Probably never feel this way again. Would miss it.

"And then they kill the kids?" Doc said. His face was drawn and tight. Real anger there.

"No. Those two were accidents. My theory is that adults can donate a unit of NDT without much after-effect, but kids really notice the difference. They're dull, dim-witted, sluggish after their NDT's been siphoned off. At least that's the way B.B. described the kids that were snatched, then returned to the gang. I think the two dead kids were going to be returned like the others but got loose. They were dopey and disoriented and I think they just fell by accident."

"Sounds to me," Elmero said, "that killing them would be safest. No trace."

"There's no trace anyway," I told him. "An urch has no legal status, and besides, these kids don't remember anything about the weeks preceding and following the time they're robbed of their NDT."

Elmero was insistent. "Still safer dead."

"But don't you see, Elm? They're the Golden Geese. Put them back with their urchingang and they'll gradually replenish their super toddler NDT over a period of months, and then they'll be ripe for milking again, like a herd of cows."

This, unfortunately, elicited a smile from Elmero, "Good plan!"

"It's a monstrous plan!" Doc said, the dark skin of his face getting darker. "It's got to be exposed! They're doing untold damage to those kids! NDT deprivation at their age, even for limited spans, has to curtail their intellectual development, may even retard it permanently. And an urch needs every bit of brain he can muster to make it in this world. No, this can't go on. I've got to bring it to the attention of the medical authorities." His head snapped up, as if startled by a thought. "Why, they may even reinstate my license for this!"

"Got to invoke privilege on this, Doc," I said.

He looked crestfallen. "Really? Why?"

"Client's wishes."

In a way, that was a lie. Mr. Khambot didn't know a thing about this super NDT angle, but I was sure he wouldn't want it spread around. Publicity would only encourage open season on little urchins by NDT vultures. I had to figure out a way to settle this quietly, on my own.

Settled up with Elmero and Doc, then headed home.

That was when the molly wire beheaded me.

## 12

Had to hand it to Doc—he didn't waste any time getting to my place. My head was still on my shoulders and my fingers were still clasped around my lower neck, although I'd lost all feeling in my hands when he arrived, black bag in hand. My chin and the front of my jump were soaked with saliva. Wanted so bad to swallow something.

"Siggy, Siggy," he said in an awed whisper as he inspected me. "Who'd do this to you?"

Resisted the temptation to shake my head as I whispered, "Not sure. NeuroNex a good bet."

He nodded. "Maybe."

"Why'm I still alive?"

"I don't know," he said. His hands were trembling as he dipped into his black bag. "I've heard about cases like this, read about them, but never believed I'd ever see one. I think you're alive due to a mixture of fantastic luck and good balance, combined with more fantastic luck and surface tension."

"Surface—?"

"Makes wet things tend to stick together. There's a natural cohesiveness between cells. I'll venture to say that your would-be assassin used pristine new molly wire. That was luck on your part. The older stuff picks up garbage on its surface that makes it relatively dull. Still sharper than anything else in Occupied Space, but nothing like the fresh stuff. Your cut is so fine and clean that all your blood vessels and neurons and other tissues have stayed in physiological alignment. The chair, the gentle pressure from your hands, the fact that you haven't turned your head or done much swallowing and, of course, surface tension, have kept things lined up where they belong."

"Can talk."

"The wire passed below your vocal cords."

"Still don't see how—"

"Look: molly wire's only one molecule thick. Mammalian cells can pass particles much much larger right through their cell walls. It's called pinocytosis. A lot of your cell walls are probably healed up already. Why— why, I'll bet most of those cells don't even know their membranes have been ruptured!"

He was babbling. "Doc—"

"Do you realize that your neurons are still sending impulses from the brain to your arms. Oh, this is amazing, simply amazing! There's a little hematoma by the right jugular, but in general this is—"

Wanted to kick him but didn't have the strength. "Doc. Help. Please."

"I *am* helping."

He pulled out some gauzy stuff and started wrapping it around my throat, working it under my fingers and finally pushing them out of the way. Reluctant as hell to take my hands away, but it was an immense relief to finally let them drop to my sides.

Doc continued to babble as he worked.

"Amazing! Just amazing. I've got to hand it to you,

Siggy. You showed real presence of mind. I mean, to know what had happened to you and assess the situation and do just what you had to do to keep your head on straight. Took real guts. Never knew you had it in you. I'm proud of you."

Thought about that and realized it must have been the residual effects of the super NDT that helped me zero in on what had happened and what to do about it so quickly. Doubt very much I could have done it purely on my own. Kind of liked the irony in that.

Doc looped the gauze over the top of my head, then sprayed the whole mess with a pungent liquid. It hardened.

"What—?"

"It's a cast of sorts for your neck. It'll hold everything in place until I can get you to a hospital."

"No hospital."

"No choice, my friend."

"They think I'm dead." Wanted to keep it that way until I was fully recovered.

"They'll think right if I don't get you to a facility where somebody can staple that split vertebra together, reanastomose your major blood vessels and nerve trunks, and repair the damaged musculature. Even if you live, your spinal cord could start demyelinating and leave you a paraplegic, or a best a paraparetic."

"They'll come to finish me."

"I know a small private hospital where they can hide you away indefinitely. They'll—"

There was a thump on the door. I glanced over—with eyes only—and saw B.B. the urch slumped against my door, half-heartedly pounding on it. He was sobbing.

"Open it," I told Doc.

The door slid open and dropped one surprised urchin into my compartment. He looked at me and his reddened eyes fairly bulged out of his tear-streaked face.

"Dreyer-san! You . . . you're . . ."

"Alive?" I said.

"But I see'm spray, see'm smile—"

"You were out there?" And then I remembered the

blur I had seen behind the guy who mollied me. Must have been B.B.

"Follow you from Elmero's, see'm spray, then follow him all way back."

Wanted to cheer. "Back where?"

"Boed North. NeuroNex."

All right. That clinched it. My slip about urchins in front of the tech had put me on a hit list. I'd have to risk Doc's private hospital. And when I was well enough —*if* I ever got well enough—I'd have a score to settle.

B.B. came over and grabbed my hand. Could barely feel it. There were fresh tears in his eyes.

"S'glad y'live, Dreyer-san."

"*Mr.* Dreyer, urch."

## 13

A week later I was home. They hadn't wanted to let me go but I didn't care. Enough was enough. Would've had me living there for months if I'd allowed it but I was more than ready after a week. After all, they'd put everything back together the first day, then started electrostim treatments to make the bones and nerves heal faster. Felt like a lab rat after a while. They all wanted to talk to me, examine me. Sickening.

Made them send me home, but they insisted on rigging this steel frame around my neck. It was screwed into my collar bones, the back of my neck, and my skull. Couldn't rotate my neck at all—had to turn my whole upper body to look left or right. Felt like a cyborg.

All the medics wanted to write about me, but Doc had first call on that. Said it would help him get his license back. How could I refuse after the way he'd shown up when I needed him? Put two restrictions on him, though: he couldn't use my name, and he had to wait till I'd settled the score with the NeuroNex people.

Doc brought me home. The urch opened my compartment door before we reached it. Iggy was sitting on his shoulder.

"Mr. Dreyer, Mr. Dreyer! You're back home!" He was fairly trembling with excitement. "So glad, so glad!"

"What're you doing here?"

"Living. Keeping clean. Feeding doggie." He stroked Iggy's flank.

"That's not a dog, that's a lizard."

Doc said, "B.B.'s going to help take care of you, Sig."

The urch tried to take my hand and lead me over to my chair. Shook him off.

"Don't need help." Eased myself into the chair and let it form around my back. It accommodated the brace easily.

"You most certainly do," Doc said. "I'm going to teach B.B. here how to apply the neurostimulators to your neck to keep the healing process going at its accelerated rate."

Glanced around my compartment. It was clean— much cleaner than the autoservice ever left it.

"How'd you get in here?" I said. The door was keyed to my palm. There was a key I could give to someone else if I chose, but I hadn't given it to anyone.

"Never left."

"You mean to tell me you've spent a whole week here without leaving even once?"

He smiled at me. "Sure. Got food, got bed, got shower, got vid. Lots of vid. Watch all day and night." He spread his arms and turned in a slow circle. "Heaven."

Looking at his scrubbed, happy face I could see that he really believed he had found heaven. Maybe he had. He must have been living around the vid set, and must have been practicing his Realpeople talk because he was much better, much smoother. And his body looked a little plumper. He was still a stick drawing but with heavier lines.

"Leave me any food?"

"Oh, yes!"

"Think you can fix us some lunch?"

"Lunch? Oh, yes! Most certainly yes!" he said as he scurried over to the kitchen console. He had definitely been watching a lot of vid.

Doc winked at me. "He's going to work out just fine!"

Said nothing as I watched that skinny little monkey dart around my compartment like it was his own. Didn't like the idea of living with someone but could see I was going to have to get used to it, at least for the time being.

## 14

Had to admit it: the urch came in handy. He learned to handle the bone and neurostimulators in nothing flat and was religious about the treatment schedule. He massaged my slowly strengthening limbs, maintained the compartment, and ran errands. He also kept up a constant flow of chatter. Mostly questions. The kid was an information sponge, a black hole for knowledge. He knew next to nothing about the world and anything I could tell him was a major new discovery. B.B. looked on me as a font of learning. Thought I was the greatest guy walking this earth. Didn't know anyone else who saw me that way. Kind of nice. Made me want to live up to his expectations.

He also kept me distracted enough with the treatments and his incessant talk that I didn't miss the buttons too much. Not yet, at least. Wasn't sure how I'd have made it through those first few days without him.

"Never did tell me how you knew somebody'd used molly wire on me," I said on my third day home as he ran the bone stimulator against my neck. The hum traveled up the back of my head and buzzed in my ears.

"We use alla time un'ground."

"So you told me, but you didn't tell me what for."

"Rats."

"Explain."

"We tie across runs and over hidey-holes, sort like . . ." His voice trailed off.

*Sort of like what happened to me.* Could tell he was embarrassed, so I let him off the hook: "I guess that keeps them away from your food stores."

"Uh. Rats *are* food un'ground."

My stomach did a little flipflop. "I see." Decided this was a good time to change the subject. "By the way, what does 'B.B.' stand for, anyway?"

"Baby Boy."

"Oh." My throat was suddenly tight and achy.

Just then we had a visit from officialdom: Complex Security came calling. Recognized the uniform and the droopy-lidded face that went with it. Had seen him around the complex over the years.

"You Sigmundo Dreyer?" he asked from the threshhold after the door had been cued open. He was staring at my neck brace.

"Who wants to know?"

"We had a complaint about a foul odor coming from this end of the corridor."

"Really? What kind of odor?"

"Said it smelled like something dead."

A chill raced through my bloodstream. "Well, sniff for yourself. You smell anything?"

He shook his head. "Not a thing."

"Who made the complaint?" Already knew the answer, but wanted to hear it confirmed.

"Anonymous."

Thought so. "Consider the source," I said.

He smiled, gave me a little salute, and left.

"We got trouble."

"S'wrong?" B.B. said. I'd been talking to myself—sometimes I think better out loud. Decided to bounce my thoughts off the urch.

"That wasn't a crank complaint, or a mistake. That was somebody checking up to see why I haven't been reported dead."

"How they know you not?" His face screwed up in

concentration. "And how they find out where you live so they can wire door?"

Held up my right thumb. "The cashless society. Every time I use my credit I leave all sorts of vital statistics behind—name, address, credit record. They've doubtlessly been checking with Central Data to see official confirmation of my death. Naturally, it hasn't appeared. They figure my body's rotting in here so they try to get the complex's security force to do their checking for them. When my name fails to be listed as deceased tomorrow, they'll come by to finish the job."

Didn't know what to do. Still too weak to take the battle to them, but didn't want to go back to the hospital.

B.B. was suddenly very agitated. "You think they c'mere? Really try again?"

"That's what I'd do. But don't worry," I said with a confidence I didn't feel. "We'll just keep the door sealed tight and wait till I'm fully healed up."

"W'if they blow door?"

Hadn't thought of that.

"That would make a little too much noise, I'd think."

Tried to sound confident, but if they wanted me bad enough, it *was* an option: blow the door, strafe the room with blaster fire, and take off.

"N'good, san," B.B. said, up and pacing about. His speech was deteriorating by the minute. "N'good, n'good." He turned and darted for the door.

"Hey! Where're you going?"

"Y'stay, san. I go. Gots go now."

And he was gone.

Thought he'd be back soon but dark came and still no sign of him. Missed two treatments for the first time since coming home from the hospital. Finally it got late and I got sleepy and so I turned in.

Had trouble sleeping. Not much. Just a little. Kept thinking how I'd been smart all along to be alone. Have somebody around all the time and before you know it, you're depending on them. And then what? The first sign of trouble, they run out on you. Should have known better. The whole thing made me mad. Wasn't hurt. Just damn mad.

Thought I heard someone at my door during the night. Worked my way to the transparency control, hoping to see B.B. there but found the corridor empty. Probably my imagination. Besides, B.B. had the key I'd given him. He didn't need to fiddle with the door.

This whole situation was getting me spooked. Decided to sleep in the chair for the rest of the night. Left the door transparent. Usually the light from the corridor bothered me when I was trying to sleep, but tonight it was comforting.

Awoke later to the sound of the door sliding open. The pale-faced, fat-nosed fellow who had mollied my neck was standing in the hall behind the redheaded tech. His eyes were wide as he looked me up and down.

"You're really alive! It's not possible!"

Felt like a half-crushed roach pinned in a flashlight beam. But all I could see was the little stub of plastic in the redhead's hand. My mouth was dry as I spoke.

"My key . . .?"

He smiled. "Your little friend sold it to us for a meal credit."

My fear was suddenly washed away in a gush of abysmal sadness. B.B. had sold me out for another soysteak dinner. As the pale-faced guy nudged the redhead into the room, I found I didn't really care all that much about dying. Too tired, too weak, too many troubles, too much disappointment. Sick of everything. Almost welcomed her.

As she moved toward me, her eyes suddenly bulged in alarm. She started to turn around, and as she did I saw fine crimson lines appear across her throat, across the white of the uniform overlying her breasts, abdomen, and legs. She began to fall, and as she went down she came apart like an overbalanced stack of boxes. The crimson lines quickly spread to blotches which became geysers and torrents of red as her head toppled to the left, her lower arms dropped straight down, and the other pieces tumbled to the right. In a matter of seconds the ceiling, the walls, the pale-faced guy, and I were all dripping warm red sticky fluid. But most of the red was pooled around the still twitching horror just inside the doorway.

Wiped my eyes and looked up. Saw the guy staring dully at his former associate. Swallowed back my stomach contents and tried to think of a way out of this. An idea of what had happened here was forming in my brain and suddenly I was very anxious to stay alive. Figuring it was now or never, I started my chair toward the drawer where I kept a small popper. The movement must have shaken Paleface out of his shocked stupor. Suddenly he was reaching into his jump and pulling out a mean-looking blaster. As he raised it, I heard a shrill cry from down the hall. He turned, I looked.

B.B. was in full charge toward Paleface. The kid caught him off balance halfway through his turn. He fell backward, his arms whirling like flywheels. Did him no good. He stumbled through the wired doorway and went to pieces. More pumping, twitching sections of body bounced and rolled along my compartment floor.

Looked away in time to see B.B. skid to a halt at the threshold, then to my horror, saw him slip on a splatter of blood and lose his balance. One hand grabbed onto the jamb while the other flailed—

—and crossed the plane of the door.

Saw his hand fly off, saw him drop to his knees and stare stupidly at the geysering stump of his wrist.

Without even thinking I had the chair in motion toward the door but it caught up on the bloody meat all over my floor.

"Grab it!" I shouted. "Squeeze it off!" But he didn't seem to hear.

Stumbled out of the chair and up onto my feet. My legs gave out after two steps so I crawled on hands and knees through the gore, praying that my brace would hold my head on and that I'd healed up enough inside so that nothing would slip around. Shouted encouragement all the while, but he just sat there and stared at the stump.

Reached the threshhold and stretched my arm through,

holding my breath and hoping I was between the wires. When none of my fingers fell off, I grabbed his forearm just above the amputation site and squeezed, working my fingers and thumb into the scant flesh, trying different spots until the blood stopped pumping out, then held onto that spot with every ounce of strength.

He looked at me and blinked. His face was death white and his eyes seemed to have retreated into his skull. "Got'm, yeh. Won't hurt y'no mo, san."

Then he collapsed onto the floor in a heap.

Held onto his wrist and started shouting at the top of my lungs. When doors started opening down the hall, I turned back to the kid and said,

"You die on me you little bastard and so help me I'll wring your skinny little neck!"

Thought he was dead or in a terminal coma at best but swore his lips curled into a tiny smile.

## 15

Two neatly sliced up bodies on the floor of one's compartment tends to raise questions among officialdom. Had a lot of explaining to do. Leaving out all mention of the super NDT, I told them that I'd learned about the pair's urchin-snatching activities—said I had no idea why they did it—and that they'd tried to kill me with molly wire. Because I had an investigator's license and had the wound to prove prior assault, and because Redhead and Paleface still had blasters clutched in the hands at the ends of their severed arms, I managed to stay out of confinement. But the incident was still under investigation while the bodies were being pieced together and posted, and I was not to leave the Megalops until all questions were answered.

Didn't matter to me. Wasn't going anywhere for some time anyway.

My arms and legs were stronger now and I could walk around and take care of myself. Even worked the window garden a little. Doc was allowing me out of the brace for short periods during the day. B.B. had come through fine—I'd guaranteed his medical expenses to make sure of that. His right hand was grafting on nicely but it was still in an immobilizing brace. He had full use of his left hand, though. Together we made one marginally competent person.

"Fine pair we are," I said as we watched the vid.

B.B. popped a cheesoid into his mouth and tossed another to Iggy. "Lazy."

"Yeah. Lazy. Got to get back to work someday."

*Work.* Reminded me of my only client—Mr. Khambot. A number of local urchingangs had checked all of their females in the age range of the Khambot girl and had found no one with footprints that even came close to the infant prints the father had given me. Didn't know if I could trust their comparison skills, but had no alternative. A retinal check would have been better but that was impossible.

Time to call my client and tell him I was still looking but had come up with zero. Strange . . . it had been weeks and he hadn't called once to check up on my progress. Doubly strange after his generous downpayment in gold.

Called his number but the man who answered was not my client and he'd never heard of Earl Khambot. Spent the rest of the day calling every Earl Khambot in the Megalops. There weren't too many, and none of them was my client.

"What's going on?" I said as the holochamber faded after the last call.

"S'wrong?" B.B. said.

"Hired by a paying customer who doesn't exist to find a child who can't be found. That make sense to you?"

"Maybe no child."

"Maybe right."

"S'mystery, san."

" 'Mr. Dreyer.' And yeah, it's that all right."

"S'okay. Got friend for life, right?" he said, pointing to himself and tossing me a cheesoid.

Laughed and winged it back to him. Maybe that was enough. For now.

## Introduction

Sometimes, as at Nagasaki, the future arrives in a blinding flash. Sometimes it is heralded with a seemingly anticlimactic thud, as with desktop computers. And occasionally it steals up on cats' feet, with the gentle whir of a floppy disk.

According to David's Sling author, Mark Stiegler, that's what's happening with hypertext: though it's arrival has caused the barest ripple of excitement, the world will never be the same; you will barely be able to imagine the interior lives of those who "fly through information space," unless you are one of them.

David's Sling, $3.50, Baen Books, January 1988.

# How David's Sling Met Hypercard

## Marc Stiegler

The media doesn't fully realize this yet, but Bellevue, Washington of the late '80s may be to computer software what Silicon Valley is to computer hardware. For a software engineer it's an exciting place to live because there's something new every day; it's also scary because you can get so obsolete so fast. At times it feels like a white-water rafting expedition—one of the recent series of rapids swirls around the evolution of the concept of *hypertext* into *hypermedia*.

Hypermedia is to the information age what the Gutenberg press was to the industrial age.

I can already hear a lot of people muttering: "Oh yeah? Probably just another load of plain old computer hype. What is hypermedia, anyway, and why should I care?" Well, I sympathize with your skepticism, but there *is* more than hype to hypermedia. Trust me.

Ted Nelson coined the term "hypertext" in the '60s to cover any form of text presentation that allows the reader to jump effortlessly from place to place—text

presented in such fashion that it is neither necessary
nor desirable to follow a set sequence from page one to
two to three *ad nauseum*. Anyone who has ever read
the ending of a story to decide whether he should read
the words in the middle has performed nonlinear reading, though hardly in a format designed to encourage
that approach. Nonlinear *writing*, on the other hand,
aids and abets the nonlinear reader.

Hyper*media* is the obvious extension of the term
"hypertext" to include sound, pictures, and animation:
a collage of sensory inputs cut and spliced in nonlinear
order and intended for nonlinear access. (We will come
back to the merits of this seemingly chaotic stew in a bit.)

Though the general concept is now decades old,
hypertext/hypermedia has only recently become a hot
topic—at least *I* hadn't heard of it as late as 1984, and I
had a master's degree in computer science. What I did
have in 1984 was the idea for a novel.

*David's Sling* was to be a complex book with many
characters and numerous subplots. It was to be about
the dawning of a true Information-Age society and the
inevitable combat with the old Industrial-Age power
structures that will be destroyed by it. In order to
guarantee the internal consistency of such a complex
book while writing quickly and yet holding down a real
job, I knew I needed a more powerful tool than just a
word processor. I defined the concept of a "multidimensional book," a book that you could read in several
different ways—you could follow a character through
time; read just those scenes where that character was
involved; or read just the subplot that interested you,
much as an excerpt from the book might appear.

I found a tool, Dayflo, that allowed me to write in
this fashion. Dayflo is a database management system
that is well optimized for handling text, designed for
handling the random pattern of tasks encountered by a
manager in an average workday. The creators of Dayflo
didn't know it, but they had created a primitive hypertext
document development system. In my multidimensional
book, each scene was a record in the database. You

could perform the query, "Find all the records involving the character Nathan Pilstrom, sort them, and let me read them." Using Dayflo, the first hypertext novel, *David's Sling*, was born.

And it almost died of premature birth. Though written in a multidimensional form, *David's Sling* had to be delivered in a linear form, on paper. And on paper it just was not very good. Jim Baen justifiably complained that the transitions were too sudden, leaving the reader with a jagged-edged series of scenes rather than a book.

Looking back, this was almost inevitable; according to some limited studies of the impact of hypermedia on writing, hyperdocuments tend to be shorter and choppier than linear documents. Why? The writer doesn't put in as much orientation material for hypermedia—instead, he puts in a "button" that lets the reader leap to a more full-blown explanation of a point if he desires it. When I printed the book out on paper, the buttons disappeared, but the choppiness did not.

So the second draft was linearized for paper, smoothed out and polished and prepared for publication. The first hypermedia novel had successfully ended with a linear novel—

And then there came the 1987 CD-ROM conference near Bellevue, sponsored by Microsoft, the fountainhead of software.

And at the CD-ROM conference was Alan Boyd, president of Owl International, with Guide, the first commercial hypermedia tool.

Alan opened a document on-screen and started punching "buttons," icons inside the document. These buttons were references to other documents; suddenly the screen was popping with windows into related information. As the references chained, the topics became more and more distant from the original, yet related through the series of topics linked by those buttons. It was a dizzying experience; I can only describe it as a "flight through Information Space."

Have you ever tried to use the Library of Congress? Every book in the United States is there; entering its gold and marble reading room, one knows that here lies Knowledge, with answers to every question you have ever dreamed . . . but how do you find those answers? The card catalog isn't a box—it is a series of rooms, each larger than most apartments. Just one subject like "advertising" overflows a box of index cards. Once you pick (virtually at random) a book from the set, it takes up to four hours for the librarians to track it down in that vast space of Information. Ultimately you withdraw, defeated; it will be easier to recreate it than to find it.

Hypermedia will change that. In hypermedia the cross-references are built in: the links are as valuable as the data itself. Pick a book on advertising at random: scan to see how relevant it is to your interests. Push the buttons on related books that seem more related to your interest than this one: they open, you scan, and leap onward.

You find one that contains useful data: hold it, continue to scan, now hitting all the buttons associated with that useful data. Two other sources contain information that seems to conflict: open them both up, compare them, reference back to their sources and then to the sources of the sources, until you decide which one is true (or what the underlying difference in assumptions was). This is truly a form of flight, a flight of the intellect.

Guide was the first vehicle designed to help you fly through information space. After five minutes of watching Alan, I knew that this was the way *David's Sling* was meant to be presented. With this, I could do more than tell the story: I could give the reader a universe to roam in. All the notes on the background, the designs of the machines, the biographies of the characters, the extended backgrounds of minor scenes: all could go into that information space to lie at the fingertips of the curious reader.

Returning to work as a software engineer manager, I started to rave about Guide and hypermedia. One of the men who works for me also became intrigued, and told his wife; she promptly went to Owl to see if she could help them shape the future of hypermedia, and soon she was Owl's national sales manager. Suddenly I was negotiating with Owl about publishing *David's Sling* in hypermedia.

And then we hit the rapids on the river. Not all great software advances come out of Bellevue—Silicon Valley is far from dead. Apple announced Hypercard, another hypertext system for the Macintosh. And though Hypercard did not allow multiple windows, thus losing the sensation of flight, it did allow animation, which was missing from early versions of Guide. With Hypercard animation, I could give the reader not only the blueprints of the machines in the book, I could also give him a view of those machines in action.

Hypercard took the computer world by storm. When Bill Atkinson first presented it in public, he received a standing ovation. Suddenly, Guide seemed obsolete. . . .

It's not obsolete, actually—Guide is much better for indexing into massive databases than Hypercard (if you set out to put the Library of Congress on hypermedia, by all means use Guide, not Hypercard). But for *David's Sling*, Hypercard was unquestionably superior. Being a certified Apple developer, I was able to get Hypercard very quickly—

And that's how *David's Sling* found Hypercard.

The world of hypermedia is very new; and both Guide and Hypercard have defects at the time of this writing. But these and other systems will improve rapidly. So what would the ultimate Information Machine look like now, in 1988?

First, there's the computer: a full 32-bit machine, based on a Motorola 68020 (maybe a 68030) or an Intel 80386—the sensation of flight, and the power of animation, only come to life with a *fast* machine.

One megabyte of RAM is marginal—Hypercard takes up 1MB without anything else going on. A 4MB machine would probably be large enough so that there was unused space (in well-written government specifications, the delivered computer must always have 50% unused capacity, because you know that in a year or so you'll need it).

A 40MB hard disk is enough secondary storage (for most of us, for now) but serious information addicts will need a WORM (Write Once, Read Many; you can write on it but not erase and once filled a worm can be written on no more) optical drive with a capacity of 300MB or more. This would be large enough to store about 400 books, if they were just text—but graphics and animation are at least as important as text in well-designed databases, and they take up a lot of space. (Half of the storage for *David's Sling* in Hypercard is for graphics and animation, for example.)

The biggest problem the information addict faces, of course, is getting that data into hypermedia in the first place. He'll have to have a graphics/text scanner that can read images as graphics and characters as text. With such a scanner he'll be able to feed all his magazines into the system; he'll still need to crosslink the articles himself, but he would want to perform many of those links personally anyway because those personal links will be the most valuable ones.

The other straightforward sources of large volumes of raw data are the national electronic networks, such as BIX, Compuserve, GENIE and Usenet. With a properly configured modem, you can program Hypercard to dial up the net of your choice during off-rate hours (say, midnight on Saturday), download all the discussions in conferences of interest to you that have occurred since your last session, pick up your mail, and do a quick search for new conferences that might be useful. With great enthusiasm and greater effort, you could even make Hypercard automatically install buttons, linking messages to their replies and vice versa, allowing you to browse through the conversations within the conferences at hypermedia speed.

Some people would say that the ultimate Information Machine needs a laser printer for beautiful output of the data—but that could be an idea whose time is past. One of the incredible transformations of hypermedia is that, for the first time, it is easier and faster to read things on the *computer* than on *paper*. Why would you deprive yourself of the linkages you have running across your hypermedia information space? The reasons for crippling yourself or others with paper-only reading would have to be strong indeed. Hypermedia is one of the four fundamental improvements needed to achieve the paperless office, which has been talked about for so long that no one quite believes in it any more (and for a longer discussion of the other problems with a paperless office, well, that's another article).

Whew! It's difficult navigating through these rapids here at the beginning of the Information Age, but it will get easier as more and more information appears in hypermedia. As tomorrow's Library of Congress evolves—and indeed comes to sit in our own homes on our own computers, indexed through hypermedia—we will be able to soar ever higher and faster, through a universe of information as important as the universe itself.

*See ad on page 288.*

## Introduction

Sometimes it's easy to trace the inspiration for a story; Evan Sayers knew exactly when the need to write the following story struck:

*It was a visit to the Baltimore & Ohio Railroad Museum that sparked "Turning of the Wheel." I have been interested in the Launch Loop ever since I first read the proposal. When at the B&O Museum, it struck me that the original proposal for the Baltimore & Ohio, the first common carrier railroad in America, was as fantastic for its day as the Launch Loop is today—and possibly as profitable.*

*The Launch Loop was proposed by Keith H. Lofstrom, an engineer living in Portland, Oregon. (The sf community was first introduced to it in a fact article in the December 1983 issue of* Analog. *) The Loop is a continent-spanning magnetic accelerator, designed to send hundreds of tons per day of payload into outer space for the cost of the electrical energy, plus capital costs. For most of its length, the Loop rises out of the atmosphere, but it is driven at each end by ground-based driving motors—the Spools.*

*The Loop motors constantly drive a ribbon of steel faster than orbital velocity, so that the centrifugal force pulling it outward is stronger than the Earth's gravity. This upward lift is used to hold a stabilizing, stationary track.*

*The hardware of the Launch Loop is an extension of a current technology, just as the B&O's steam engines were at their time. This image of the Launch Loop as a "reincarnation" of the first steam engine remained in my mind until it came to me where that reincarnation might be accepted . . .*

# TURNING OF THE WHEEL

*Evan B. Sayers*

There had been a hundred days without rain when the news came from Delhi that Mr. Prabhana's engines had been sold. The telephonist bowed low as he entered Mr. Chatterji's office, for Mr. Chatterji was of a high caste.

"Sahib, Delhi sends a message."

"Repeat it."

The telephonist straightened. His tone changed, to that of one addressing a subordinate. That was his right, as the voice of the Ministry.

"To Mr. Chatterji, Superintendent of Yards and Works. In accordance with the most recent Hard Currency for India campaign declared by Mr. Gandhi, the Ministry of Transport directs that all superfluous engines and rolling stock of the Indian State Railways shall be prepared for transport to the Export Docks at Calcutta within thirty days. There are included under this order and recorded in the records of the Ministry, at Agra, fifteen tank engines numbered . . ."

"Thank you. Is the list written down?"

The telephonist became a servant again. "Yes, sahib."

"Present it to me at once."

"Yes, sahib." The thin paper fluttered to Mr. Chatterji's desk. It was not permitted for subordinates to touch the polished wood. Mr. Chatterji studied the careful writing.

"All seems in order. Inform Mr. Mukala and Mr. Ghotee that the engines are to be prepared."

"Yes, sahib." The telephonist bowed again, but made no move to leave. "Excuse me, sahib, but . . ."

"Yes?"

"What is to be done about Mr. Prabhana?"

No answer came. The telephonist bowed and backed out, closing the door before him. Mr. Chatterji sighed and settled back in his chair. "Yes. What is to be done about Mr. Prabhana?"

Mr. Mukala came to Mr. Chatterji's office first. He was tall and strong, and the odor of semi-coal tar and machine oil clung to him. He still carried a spanner as long as his arm.

"Forgive me, sahib. I came as quickly as I could. There are three diesels still to be repaired . . ."

"Peace, Jaham. How busy will your men be within the next twenty days?"

"As busy as can be expected, sahib. There are three diesels now in the works, and two more to arrive tomorrow. Is there a special job?"

"Delhi requires that the old steam engines be readied for transport."

"To where, sahib?"

"To Calcutta. I believe they are to be exported."

"The connecting rods must be removed, then, and the bearings greased. Each engine must be moved to make sure the wheels are smooth. For some engines, we will require flatcars. Perhaps thirty men, in ten days. More if we must raise them onto flatcars."

"You will make the preparations. Work will commence in five days. This is by the command of Delhi."

"As you command—excuse me, please, as Delhi commands. May I ask one question, sahib?"

"You may."

"Sahib, what is to be done about Mr. Prabhana?"

"Will Mr. Prabhana be in the way when the engines are prepared?"

"Most certainly, sahib, unless he moves away, or is moved. Forgive me, sahib, but I do not want to be the one to move him. He is so close to his turning already."

"I understand. It will be taken care of."

Mr. Mukala bowed low and backed out of the office, turning right as he reached the door to avoid the younger man entering. Mr. Ghotee seemed barely out of school. He made every sign of deference as he shuffled into the door. But he was of Mr. Chatterji's caste, and as soon as Mr. Mukala had departed he took his ease in the leather seat opposite the desk.

"Greetings, Vasani. What is it now?"

"Delhi requires that the old steam engines be prepared for transport."

"So I have heard. So all Agra has heard. But I am the inspector of tracks, not of engines. Surely Mr. Mukala should perform this duty."

"I have already instructed Mr. Mukala. You will send an inspector at once to the north-east corner of the yards, to report on the condition of the tracks under the old steam engines. You will arrange for temporary tracks so that the engines may be transported. It will not sound well in Delhi if Mr. Mukala must lift the engines out of the mud."

"I understand. But a problem remains." Mr. Ghotee paused and raised his eyes boldly. "What is to be done about Mr. Prabhana?"

"This is really becoming most absurd. Mr. Prabhana is no longer a railway employee. Must Delhi wait on Mr. Prabhana's approval?"

"All who work on the railway greatly respect Mr. Prabhana. It will be very hard for my men to certify the tracks as safe, when that will mean the removal of Mr. Prabhana's engines."

Mr. Chatterji almost rose from his seat. Then he relaxed and chuckled, low in his throat. "So, Subchundrum. It seems that Delhi must wait on Mr. Prabhana,

after all. Well, I myself will go and tell him." He
shouted into the next office. "Mayuna, order my railcar!"

A majestic procession crossed the railyards of Agra.
On top of the four-wheeled flatcar, an intricate carpet
was laid. On top of that were woven cushions, and on
top of them sat Mr. Chatterji, cross-legged. One man
stood behind him, holding his parasol; another sat at
the opposite corner, carrying the switchman's key. The
other four laborers ran along the track, pushing the car
ahead of them, singing as they ran. At the end of the
yard the switchman ran ahead to throw the switch, Mr.
Chatterji swiveled as his parasol-carrier stepped nim-
bly around him, and the laborers heaved mightily on
the car's sides to reverse its travel.

There were four such switches before Mr. Chatterji
was obliged to dismount. The switch here was unused,
and rusted closed. They had to lift the car from one
track to the next. Then they were obliged to walk,
slowly, pushing the rattling car down rusted tracks with
weeds that tore against the carpet. The shadow of Mr.
Chatterji's parasol bobbed about his feet.

Mr. Prabhana raised his wrinkled head as they approached. He was seated as usual in the shadow of a
vast freight-engine, with his head against the driving
wheel. The shadow of a driving-rod fell on his face. He
made no movement as Mr. Chatterji dismounted. The
laborers knelt around the two men.

It was absurd, Mr. Chatterji thought. He was the
master here; he should be able to command this frail
old man. But that was not the way. Mr. Chatterji felt
the urge to kneel down among his subordinates, to do
homage to the thin figure supported by the great iron
wheel. Threads of rust wove intricate patterns through
the gray of the driving-wheel, like a red-and-gray version of the Mandala, the Wheel of Life. But Mr. Prabhana
was no red-cheeked dancing Shiva. He was only an old
man, due soon to die and take his next turn on the
Wheel.

"So, the order has come." The voice seemed to come

from the center of the driving-wheel, rather than from a
human being.

"Delhi has ordered that the last remaining steam-
engines be sold. They are to go to Calcutta within a
month." Mr. Chatterji tried not to make it sound brutal, yet not to apologize.

Mr. Prabhana sat motionless. Finally, a soft wheezing
sigh arose from the center of the wheel. "The Wheel
turns slowly, but it turns. Just as the gods dictate our
dharma, so we dictate theirs. It is the way."

"Theirs?"

Mr. Prabhana's hand moved slightly. It was enough.
"Yes. I have lived my whole life with them. When I
was just a boy, I was apprenticed to the hostler. I spent
all my boyhood in the roundhouse, that is but a memory now. I have learned all of their ways and cared for
them faithfully, from that time to this. And now the
Wheel turns for them as well as myself."

"I understand your sentiments, Mr. Prabhana. But I
am surprised to hear you ascribing to them souls, and a
place on the Wheel . . ."

"I know. There is nothing in the Sutras about it. I do
not speak from the teachings of the Sutras. I speak from
my own heart, my own experience. They seem to you
inanimate metal. But I knew them when they were
alive, and each had his own personality.

"Look above me. In your books he is Number 438.
For me, he has always been Gainda, the Rhinoceros.
He makes no sound, you see. He just digs in the
ground, and grunts a little, and pushes, and the task is
done.

"Look to your right. There is Chillahi, the Wailer.
'Oh, my,' he cries, 'my frames are cracking, my boiler
is bursting!' Then he gives one great scream. 'Yiah!' and
pulls a hundred cars five hundred miles.

"I could tell you the same kind of thing about every
one of the engines here. Some have already gone to the
furnaces. They were the difficult ones, the ones that
found it easier to break down than to pull. They were of
no use to the railways, and I let them go. But these—

Sahib, these engines are the most meritorious of all. I have kept them safe for all these years, hoping that the fires may burn once again in their hearts. But now . . ."

"The time comes to all the world." There were murmurings from the laborers but Mr. Chatterji continued. "You must not hold on to your place on the Wheel now. No man can succeed in that."

Mr. Prabhana wearily bowed his head. "Yes . . . no!" His eyes suddenly blazed. "Listen, sahib. I have relatives. When I pass on, they will know what to do with my body. They will place it on the pyre with reverence, and chant the proper prayers, so that my soul may rise up rather than fall. But who is to care for them? When they enter the furnace, what is to become of their souls? Are they to emerge as a thousand cooking pots, or ten miles of sewer pipe? Sahib, I must know the answer to this question. Where are my engines to go?"

"I do not know the answer, Mr. Prabhana. Delhi does not tell me these things. Would you like for me to find out?"

The setting sun gradually lit the iron mandala, turning Mr. Prabhana's robes to orange fire. "Yes, please, sahib. Perhaps I can leave in peace. . . ." He made a gesture of dismissal.

Mr. Chatterji realized that for the last fifteen minutes, he had been kneeling quietly on a disused railroad track. Sharp spurs of gravel insulted his knees. Unsteadily, he rose and returned to his wheeled throne.

It took ten days for the answer to arrive from Delhi. The telephonist brought the news directly to Mr. Chatterji.

"Sahib, Delhi replies to your inquiry. It is most unsatisfactory, sahib."

"Repeat the message."

"The Ministry can inform Mr. Chatterji that the shipment has been consigned to Messerschmitt Proprieties Ltd., Darwin, Western Australia. No further information is available."

"That is unfortunate." Mr. Chatterji permitted the

barriers to drop just that much. "I suppose that Mr. Ghotee will have to give this news to Mr. Prabhana."

"Sahib, Mr. Ghotee will not give the message to Mr. Prabhana. Mr. Prabhana has not been with his engines for the last two days."

"Is he . . . ?" Mr. Chatterji remembered his station just in time. "I regret to hear of this. Have inquiries been made into the reasons for Mr. Prabhana's absence?"

"I have heard that he is ill, sahib." The telephonist dared not go further.

"Then why has Mr. Ghotee not reported progress? The tracks should have been laid by now, if no obstacles remain."

Mr. Chatterji stood. "I will go see for myself. Mayuna, prepare my car!"

As Mr. Chatterji approached the rusted hulks, he became aware of an impropriety. The crane was there, rumbling softly. The gangs of men were there, chanting and bending low—but it was the wrong chant, not a work chant but a lament. Mr. Chatterji's car clanked to a stop behind a circle of praying men.

"Mr. Ghotee, what does this mean?" Then he caught sight of the center of the circle. "When did it happen?"

"This morning, Yardmaster. He came unnoticed. We were taking up the tracks here so that we could lay temporaries. Mr. Armitranjian went around that engine, and saw him. He did not respond when spoken to. That is very unlike Mr. Prabhana."

"That is no longer Mr. Prabhana, Mr. Ghotee. The Wheel has turned for him." Mr. Chatterji stood deep in thought for a moment.

"Mr. Ghotee, this is an official order. You will not disturb Mr. Prabhana in any way until the doctor has arrived and pronounced death. You will return to your task, and finish the removal of this track. This car will remain here. All railway ties on this track are hereby declared unsalvageable."

"I do not understand."

"Any railway ties that you can salvage you will place on this car. When the doctor comes, you will direct him to place Mr. Prabhana on this car. His family lives on the Poona line; take the car there. They are poor people: they will be hard pressed to make him a proper funeral pyre."

"I understand." Mr. Ghotee moved closer to his superior. "Between us, what do you think is Mr. Prabhana's dharma? Up or down?"

"The Wheel turns for him, as it does for us all. But I tell you this, Subchundrum. I will pray at his funeral that the Wheel will carry Mr. Prabhana and his engines together. I think he will be pleased with that."

The roaring filled Sam Frawley's bones. He had felt it as soon as he landed on Melville Island, competing with the Indian Ocean waves. As he had crossed the West Spool, even superconductive sheathing could not keep the roar out of the power coils of his bus. Now at the base of the Loop Control Tower, Sam stood contemplating the graceful sculptured arch on its pedestal, and let the sound he would hear for the next two years seep into his consciousness.

The elevator door opened behind him. "Herr Frawley! Here!" Gunther Weissvogel hurried across the entrance hall. "Admiring our model, I see. Shall I act as the tourist guide for you? We call this 'Gateway to Outer Space.' Appropriate, yes?"

Sam studied the world globe suspended from the top of the arch. "What keeps the globe up, magnets?"

"Ach, from tourists I expect such a question! Our new apprentice operator does not even recognize a model of the Launch Loop when he sees it! Three little sensing supermagnets just like those on the Loop itself, powered by solar cells. And the ribbon drivers are just below. You see?"

Embarrassed, Sam realized that the solid arch subtly shimmered with motion. The steel ribbon was thrown up from the linear motor coils in the base, rose in an arch over the globe and returned to the base in a fraction of a second. It was far too thin to support the globe by its own strength—but its upward momentum, transferred to the globe by the magnets, kept the globe suspended in mid-air. Sam traced the curve with his gaze.

"Let's see . . . it can't be a pure parabola: the weight of the globe has to change it. Do you know . . ."

"How would I know? I am no mathematician, just the head operator."

Sam turned back to study the miniature Loop a bit longer—and the German cried "Collapse!" The unwavering flow of steel wavered and halted. The suspended globe shuddered, spun sharply and crashed to the floor. The roaring around Sam changed to thudding—no, that was his own heart, drowning out the constant background. Sam realized he was sweating.

Gunther chuckled. "If your heart rate did not rise now, we have wasted two years of training. It is your primary job, and that of all operators, to prevent this. You are lucky: there is our best man up there now. Soon you will meet him." The flattened coils of ribbon began to reel back into the base. "It's closing time for the tourists. We put back on the model tomorrow morning; we start the ribbon and insert the globe by hand. It will be not so easy restarting the real thing, eh?" Weissvogel's watch chimed. "Time now. Come, we go up."

"Is the control room up top?"

"Not right at the top. We must save some space for the tourists. But where else would you put it? The controls are all here, where we can see the entire Spool."

The elevator carried only the two operators. The sun had just set when they exited onto the balcony.

"The tourists all leave early; they never see this view. Come, look to the east. . . ."

The sixty-kilometer circle of the Spool surrounded them, sunk into the meadows two hundred meters below. Billions of watts flowed in its superconducting coils, accelerating the kilometers of steel ribbon with the faint, all-encompassing sound of power. Beyond its eastern edge the connecting tunnels formed a distant "V."

The car houses and yards stretched between them en-
meshed in a web of tracks. A cargo ship was busy
unloading fresh-landed cars from the landing-strip in
New Guinea. And beyond that . . .

It looked like a flaming sword, stabbing downwards
out of the starry sky. The barely visible pommel was
the West Station, high above the atmosphere, linked by
its tether to the mountains of Northern Australia. From
it the ribbon stabbed downward, suspended by its own
velocity, toward—but not actually reaching—the super-
magnetic deflector rooted in the island bedrock. It took
a moment before Sam realized the cause of the illusion:
the Loop was in darkness where it touched ground, but
its top, rising out of the atmosphere, was still sunlit. Its
visible tip was tinged with red from the air-dimmed
rays.

It took another moment for Sam to realize that he
was not actually seeing the Loop, but the structure of
vacuum pipes and lift-tracks that carried it through the
atmosphere. The long arc of the Loop that spanned
Australia was invisible: no vacuum pipes were needed
in outer space. As he watched, the sword shortened,
the red flaming tip rising slowly. A tiny red bead passed
down through the tip; intellectually Sam knew that it
was a Loop car headed upward for outer space at half
the speed of sound, but to his eyes it seemed to creep
downward with infinite slowness.

Indeed, the car as he saw it was on the slowest leg of
its journey. When the car reached the West Station, it
would disconnect from its lifting cable and clamp mag-
netically to the exposed ribbon. Then it would draw
power from the ribbon's enormous kinetic energy, moving so fast that an orbiting satellite would be left far
behind.

That speed was the key to the Launch Loop. The
ribbon's speed exceeded the weightlessness of orbit:
the force required to hold it near Earth gave it a negative weight. When the car reached ribbon speed, its—
passengers? cargo?—would feel two Gees of acceleration
*away* from Earth. And when it disconnected at the East

Station, high above the Pacific coast, that force would fling the car upward toward whatever space outpost had been programmed into it. The same force suspended the ribbon itself and its stationary tracks.

"Magnificent, isn't it?" Wiessvogel broke the silence. "Makes you proud of the human race."

"Makes me feel bloody insignificant. To think that a few switches downstairs control all of that . . ."

"Actually, upstairs. This is just the lower gallery. The restaurant and bar are above us. Look behind you: you'll see the windows of the control room. Come on."

The door opened to Weissvogel's fingerprint. "We'll program your prints tomorrow," he promised. A steep flight of steel stairs, lit by a single caged light-tube, led upward. In the observation gallery, the roaring of the Loop had been obvious. Within the center of power, it was a muted whisper.

A carrot-topped youth turned to greet them. "Evening, Gunny. This the new boy?"

Sam Frawley bridled. Gunther stepped in. "Now, Reg, please be nice to him. This is our new night-shift apprentice operator, Sam Frawley."

"Peace be with you." The young man made a sign in the air, then shook Frawley's hand, ignoring the older man's surprise. "Been a quiet day. I think I could make do with a new man." Then he noticed Weissvogel's stare. "All right, Gunny, you want a formal report. Let's show Mr., uh, Sam how we do it by the book."

The German began the catechism. "Good evening, Herr MacArthur. I am your replacement operator for the next shift. What do you have to report?"

"All well. No major or minor problems."

"Power levels."

"Six hundred ninety-four Gwah." Reg MacArthur broke the formal mood. "That's gigawatt-hours, Sam. It's on the high side now; we always speed the ribbon up on Sunday evenings. Darwin and Cooktown buy back peak power on Monday morning."

"Launches." Gunther Weissvogel was following the book.

"Three hundred sixty-two this shift." Reg turned to Sam again. "Bet that surprises you. Straight truth is, the Loop's fair booked up. We're the only cheap road into outer space right now. Until Brazil and France get their cash together, the world's got two ways into orbit: wait six months for a Loop slot, or ride a rocket. Costs us fifteen hundred dollars per half-ton: we charge thirty thousand. Good deal for you Germans, eh?"

"Ribbon status." Gunther made another stab at formality.

"You've got to be joking, Gunny. Ribbon One's up, remember? It's been up since last Friday. We always splice on Friday nights: that's when the ribbon speed is lowest. That's all done at the East Spool, out on the Barrier Reef. The oxygen furnaces are all at the East Spool."

"Anything else?"

"F. A."

"All right then." The German poised himself above MacArthur's chair. "As of 19:15:32, you are RELIEVED." The last word was a shouted cue. As if choreographed, MacArthur slid out of the chair behind Weissvogel's lowering back. The chair was empty for barely a second.

"Good night, all. May the Lord Buddha light your path." MacArthur made the sign again, then dashed down the rattling stairway.

Frawley gazed in amazement after him; then amazement turned to suspicion as Frawley turned to Weissvogel. "Since when has the Loop started hiring Buddha freaks?"

"Since Buddha freaks have been scoring six hundreds on the quals. Get to like MacArthur, Sam. This is an order. He knows more about this Loop than any other operator. He has the feel in his bones, and I do not mean the vibration. I will tell you one time about him and Section Three-Seventy-One. Except for Reg MacArthur, we would have had a collapse that day. Now sit down. Do you have any questions?"

"No . . . oh, yes. What was that about joking about Ribbon One?"

Gunther Weissvogel leaned back and prepared for a

lecture. "You know we have three complete ribbons, each five thousand kilometers long. We spool down and inspect each ribbon once a month. This is the law—after all, the ribbon carries all the Loop's power. So we splice it out at the East End, decelerate it, then use the neutron cameras and ultrasonics to test for flaws. That takes one week. Then we speed it back up, splice it into the working ribbon the next Friday and take that ribbon down. As I say, the law requires that we do all that. Otherwise, we wouldn't bother." He chuckled.

"Ribbon One?"

"Right. You see, there has never been a flaw of any kind in Ribbon One, not even on the ultrasonic microscopes. Two and Three have had half their segments replaced, but not One. We could have run for twenty years on Ribbon One alone."

"Why is Ribbon One so good?"

"It is, you see, a different sort of steel. Ribbons Two and Three were cast in place out of the oxygen furnaces at the East End. But when we started, we had no oxygen furnaces. We had to use scrap. From India, I think. Scrap makes good steel."

Below, on the observation deck, Reg MacArthur gazed out over the darkened town and quietly let the roar seep into his inmost self. Whenever Ribbon One was up, that roar somehow spoke directly to Reg MacArthur's inner self. It spoke of home, and job, and being needed. Within the roar of Ribbon One, with his inner ear, Reg could sometimes hear wheels. Wheels turning endlessly, striving higher but turning always, until and past the world's end.

## Introduction

*One of the big techno-political footballs of the '90s will be the growing prospects for a joint US/USSR Mars mission. Since such a one-shot mission cannot possibly pay for itself in tangible benefits, it will be justified by unquantifiable abstractions: "knowledge to benefit all mankind," "a Peace Dividend," and like that. What it will really do, by soaking up all conceivable space funding, is keep America out of space in a more serious way for another couple of decades.*

*Will that be the intent? Who can really say? In any event, here is an alternative for those who have Mars in their eyes . . .*

# WHICH ROAD TO MARS?

*Donald Frederick Robertson*

One road to Mars.

The first interplanetary transport is a spindly and fragile thing—a folded insect. One month after it rides stacked Orbital Transfer Vehicles out of Earth orbit, a second ship, sans crew, follows.

During the long interplanetary cruise, two Spacelab-derived habitation modules, suspended at the ends of a long tunnel, rotate around the first craft's core. At three revolutions per minute, they simulate a quarter of Earth's gravity for the four-person crew. Near Mars, these modules—along with cruise science and storage modules—fall away, abandoned in heliocentric orbit.

Mars shuts out half the sky as what remains of the vehicle skims the edge of the planet's atmosphere, protected by a huge, cone-shaped aeroshell. Interplanetary speed shed, the ship emerges and thrusters fire to circularize its orbit.

A single Spacelab short module, with attached solar arrays and EVA station, forms a temporary space station to house the single crewmember who will remain in orbit. The other three soon descend to the dusty Martian surface.

After less than four weeks on Mars, our intrepid explorers lift off—with a scant 250 kilograms of samples—to join their companion at the orbiting station. At a pre-determined date, they enter a small "departure vehicle" which accelerates out of Mars orbit, leaving the station behind, its consumables exhausted and orbit decaying.

Meanwhile, that second interplanetary transport, still a month behind the first, has swung by Mars using the planet's gravity to direct it back toward Earth. The departure vehicle docks with the transport in heliocentric orbit, and after crew transfer, is also abandoned.

Upon arrival near Earth, an aerobraked capsule will return the crew to the Space Station, leaving their ship in heliocentric orbit to die.

I have described this Mars mission proposal to make two points: little technology not already in use or being designed as part of the Space Station project is assumed; and with the single exception of the choice of a nuclear power plant for the lander, allowing its use as a source of power by "later missions," not a single part of this mission is reusable. It would at great expense (an estimated 40 billion in 1984 dollars) place three astronauts on Mars for some thirty days while managing to establish essentially no infrastructure for permanent habitation—or even a second mission.

This "throw-away" Mars mission was designed three years ago by Science Applications International Corporation (SAIC) for the Planetary Society. It was designed to put humans on Mars for scientific (and political) purposes, as soon as possible and for the least possible cost.

For the first time in more than fifteen years NASA is funding serious studies of human exploration and utilization of Mars.

The space arena is a very different place today than it was fifteen years ago. Money is far more difficult to come by, despite political and popular support for space expenditures being substantially stronger now than they were at the end of the Apollo program. Due to many years of under-funding and consequent poor planning, more-or-less routine access to space—even to the extent achieved fifteen years ago—is probably at least a decade away; as is a permanent presence in space by any Western nation. The Space Station is in so much technical and financial—and thus political—trouble, that by the time you read this it is more than possible that the program will have been cut back to an entirely automated facility.

Technology, on the other hand, has progressed apace.

NASA and the Los Alamos National Laboratory recently organized a Manned Mars Missions Working Group to, among other things, "examine the impact of new and emerging technologies on Mars mission capabilities."

The Working Group claimed that chemical rocket engines are near their "ultimate theoretical potential . . . in practical application, especially with respect to efficiency and endurance. . . . Chemical propulsion technology as manifested in actual hardware such as the Space Shuttle Main Engine, the RL-10 [Centaur engine], the throttleable Lunar Module Descent Engine, and others are adequate to support Manned Mars Missions today." This means that large amounts of research and development money would not have to be spent on propulsion.

The relatively new idea of aerobraking, at Mars and/or at Earth, could reduce propulsion requirements by as much as thirty to sixty percent over a vehicle propelled entirely by chemical propulsion. Unfortunately, this can also involve a very high acceleration during entry, and it remains to be seen whether, following months of exposure to free fall, the crew can withstand this and remain sufficiently conscious to "fly" their vehicle. Conscious astronauts may be necessary, at least at Mars, because of uncertainties in the thickness and motion of the Martian atmosphere at the point of entry. These uncertainties could result in large errors in the spacecraft's trajectory when it—hopefully—exits into Mars orbit.

Nonetheless, the reentry of United States' Apollo and Soviet Zond spacecraft, falling all the way from lunar orbit, have provided a solid start on this technology. NASA had planned to develop aerobraking for the original Venus Radar Mapper mission, before it was "descoped." Now this technology will have to wait until NASA begins development of an aerobraked Orbital Transfer Vehicle, planned for the period immediately after Space Station funding passes its peak.

Advanced technology such as Nuclear Thermal Propulsion and Nuclear Electric Propulsion have been demonstrated in at least preliminary form. They may be useful in cutting costs but are not considered essential even to a permanent base.

However, the NASA/Los Alamos Working Group said that "if the initial Manned Mars Mission is not planned until the year 2010 or later" anti-proton production is showing sufficient promise to warrant serious consideration as a source of propulsion energy. Matter-antimatter engines could "allow transit times of three to four months each way and would require much less mass in low Earth orbit than that required for chemical propulsion/ aerobraking systems." Anti-protons have been created, stored, and cooled; and major improvements are foreseen for the immediate future. The Group said they believe one of the main requirements for making anti-proton propulsion a reality is adequate "computational ability to calculate anti-proton interactions"!

Propulsion technology may be well in hand, but other kinds of technology are not. The humans on a mission to Mars will be exposed to at least two orders of magnitude more radiation than were Apollo astronauts. The structure of most planned Mars transports may be sufficient to shield against normal solar radiation, with a small heavily shielded "storm shelter" for solar storms. One shelter idea involves wrapping the spaceship's water tanks around a small enclosure, requiring about half of a six hundred day mission's total water supply.

Nonetheless, a major problem remains. Any reasonable shielding mass makes galactic cosmic radiation exposure worse, because the shielding converts each primary cosmic ray particle into multiple secondary particles—which can damage the exposed astronaut. Although apparently not considered by the NASA/Los Alamos Workshop, dynamic, magnetic shielding holds promise in the long term. However, major problems appear to push this technology far into the future. The only near-term answer may be to "weather the storm." If this proves necessary, astronauts on one mission will receive on the order of half the lifetime radiation exposure expected to be allowed for Space Station astronauts, probably limiting each crew to a single flight.

Initial work on closed life support systems is finally accelerating in the United States with the beginnings of the Space Station program, but the Soviets are and will remain far ahead of us. Long-term flight testing of components of such a system have been under way in the Soviet Union for at least two decades and probably longer, as have ground tests of complete systems. System tests are only now beginning in the United States, and it will be near the end of the century—at best—before we can begin serious flight testing on the Space Station.

NASA and Los Alamos came up with an estimated cost for a first Mars mission remarkably close to that estimated by the Planetary Society—on the order of thirty to forty billion dollars. "This amounts to about half the cost of the Apollo program which took place when the United States' Gross National Product was one-third as large as it is now."

Using cost as a measure of difficulty, we might argue that a Mars mission started today would be about half as difficult as was Apollo when President Kennedy first proposed the United States land Americans on Luna. Given that, which of the many possible roads to Mars should we travel?

The first possibility is an entirely automated program

of Mars exploration, perhaps leading to automated industrialization. NASA and Los Alamos dismiss this possibility almost out of hand: "It is unlikely that any of the major scientific issues [of Mars] will be resolved prior to the first human exploration of the planet." They justify this statement by suggesting that even a relatively simple job, "such as effectively positioning seismic stations in noise-free and well-coupled [to the planet] environments, involves choosing the optimum specific location in a general vicinity, drilling and carefully backfilling deep holes, and erecting towers so that telemetry will not be disturbed by the landscape. Furthermore, experience has shown that the ability to check out, calibrate, and repair research instruments *in situ* can make the difference between the success or failure of major costly experiments. In an unexplored environment such as Mars, all this can only be done well by people."

Automating all the different operations necessary for the placement of those seismic stations would not only be difficult, it would also be enormously expensive, requiring large numbers of robots and/or a single robot with a vast number of capabilities. Developing robots with these capabilities, simple for human beings, would involve major research and development expenditures on technologies that are far from understood—in contrast to the well-understood technologies required to place humans on Mars.

For example, let us recall that the Planetary Society and the NASA/Los Alamos study agree that a human Mars mission might cost something on the order of 30-40 billion in 1984 dollars. The Viking project to land two automated probes on Mars, although eminently successful in various secondary roles, utterly failed in its primary mission—to determine the presence or absence of life. A recent NASA publication admitted that Viking's answer to this question amounted to "definitely maybe not?"

For this, humanity paid well over $1 billion—in mid-1970s dollars. But let's be generous and ignore inflation: I think it is clear that even Science Applications' dead-end, one-shot human mission—placing three flexible and intelligent human beings on Mars for a month—would return far more than thirty to forty times the science Viking provided. A successful human mission would, if nothing else, provide a definitive answer to Viking's question.

All this does not mean automated missions could not profitably be flown to Mars, if they were designed for reconnaissance and left creative *science* for later, human missions. Automated "precursor missions" could make a human mission safer and more effective than it would be without them. According to NASA and Los Alamos, "the present understanding of the vertical structure of the Martian atmosphere and its diurnal variation introduces uncertainties in planning aerobraking maneuvers for manned missions. Precursor missions are needed to obtain this information for pre-mission planning, and additional probes may be needed to obtain updates immediately before the manned mission aerobraking activities."

What may turn out to be one of the most important of these precursor missions is already being developed—albeit for entirely scientific reasons.

The Mars Observer is to use a gamma ray spectrometer (GRS), a visual infrared mapping spectrometer, and a thermal emission spectrometer to measure the chemical and mineral composition of Mars' surface. These instruments will map the locations of volatile materials, lava flows, rock types—all of which are poorly known. Mark Adler of the "Mars Underground" has said the GRS will be able to "indicate the amounts of subsurface. . . hydrogen [to tens of centimeters depth] by measuring ratios of fast to slow neutron capture by silicon, as well as by direct neutron capture by hydrogen."

Volatile maps are exceedingly important, because, says Steven W. Squyres of NASA's Ames Theoretical Studies Branch, most of the evidence for currently available water on Mars is poleward of thirty degrees north and south latitude: "Virtually no examples of lobate debris aprons, concentric crater fill, or terrain softening are found equatorward of thirty degrees latitude in either hemisphere. . . . This distribution may mean that the deep regolith [near the equator] has been devolatilized." Since the equatorial regions of Mars contain the areas with the most benign environment, as well as most of the younger, more interesting terrain (from both scientific and resource points of view), Squyres believes studying "the present distribution and transport of water on Mars" is an essential prerequisite to a Mars base.

A second road to Mars might be a human flyby through the Martian system. Such a mission has a number of technical advantages, not the least of which is its simplicity. It was once proposed that a Saturn-V be used to boost an uprated Apollo Command Module with improved ablative reentry shields toward Mars. The Apollo spacecraft would fly by Mars, then be directed back to a direct descent into Earth's atmosphere. Had I been an astronaut, however, I don't think I would have been the first to volunteer to spend the requisite travel times cooped up in an Apollo Command Module.

A more modern plan consists of strapping a Space Station module to two Orbital Transfer Vehicles. The NASA/Los Alamos Working Group is less than enthusiastic about this idea: "Most participants in this study would not consider such a Mars strategy desirable, because of the limited scientific and technological payoff compared to the cost and risk. With a little more effort, the benefits might be significantly advanced."

Such a flyby could, however, be a way to test a developmental transport over interplanetary distances before it was called upon to support a more risky Mars landing. Several observers of the Soviet space program have suggested the Soviets might do something like this as soon as their Saturn-V class booster is operational. I have seen no evidence to support such a contention, but it would be consistent with the Soviets' policy of spending as much as a decade testing automated then piloted versions of prototype spacecraft. The large Cosmos modules for the Mir space station have been tested in just this way, since at least the flight of Cosmos-929, launched on July 17, 1977.

The third road to Mars, a one shot or dead-end program, similar to the Science Applications/Planetary Society proposal or Apollo's limited exploration of Luna, was likewise dismissed by NASA and Los Alamos: "It was generally agreed by the Working Group that the exploration of Mars will require multiple flights and that one of the objectives of a manned Mars program should be the establishment of a permanent scientific base, or 'outpost,' on Mars. Planning and designing for an initial mission should not be so austere or unique that follow-on mission evolution or overall program benefits would be impacted significantly."

This is because the Working Group felt that Mars had such a diverse environment, that any serious attempt to understand it must involve a truly global study of the planet. Anything less would be unlikely to answer the questions scientists want answered—much as Apollo failed to answer the question of Luna's origin, despite five landings. Secondly, the *in situ* production of propellants in the Mars System—requiring at least some sort of permanent facility—would make the overall exploration of Mars far more cost effective.

This, then, suggests the fourth road to Mars. NASA has in fact designed a spacecraft to support a six-person crew on Mars for ten to fifteen months and/or emplace a permanent Mars base in as little as two flights.

The "Trans-Mars Injection stage propellant requirements [for such a vehicle are] very close to the Space Transportation System External Tank capacity. Thus, a ground assembled TMI stage can be designed which could be launched as an STS External Tank to low Earth orbit for the largest single element of the [Mars transport]."

Aerobraking was considered too risky for a first mission, resulting in a mass for the assembled vehicle in

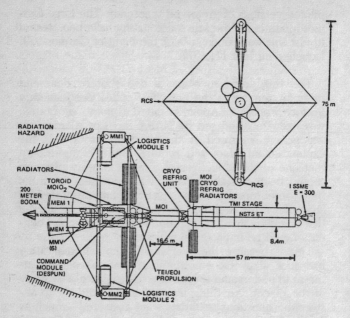

NASA *design for an interplanetary ship capable of placing a six-person crew on Mars for ten to fifteen months, or, in modified form, of emplacing a Mars Base in as little as two missions. The ship is not reusable. NASA drawing.*

Earth orbit of 1,250 metric tons, or more. Transporting this much material to Earth orbit will clearly require a Heavy Lift Launch Vehicle, such as the Advanced Launch System the Air Force has just begun for the Strategic Defense Initiative. Habitation modules, derived from the Space Station, are to rotate on booms to provide one full artificial gravity. Two landing vehicles could land at least two sites on Mars, while four Orbital Transfer Vehicles allow exploration of Phobos and Deimos.

But even an open-ended Mars mission strategy may not by itself be sufficient if the vehicles involved are not reusable. The Congressionally mandated and Presidentially appointed National Commission on Space argued that all future missions should contribute toward a multipurpose infrastructure for travel between the planets. Even automated planetary missions should utilize the same reusable upper stages that will later be used for human missions. The space tugs and aerobraking techniques which make up the Commission's "Bridge Between Worlds" should be built immediately, and used for a Mars Sample Return and other missions. Thus, the cost of Space Tug development could be amortized over a larger number of users, and operational experience could be gained before these vehicles are called on to carry human beings to the planets. This would help answer some of NASA's concerns regarding the risks of using aerobraking on the first Mars missions.

Likewise, although not generally considered necessary for the exploration of Mars, a Lunar Base might provide propellant and radiation shielding for a Mars Mission. Technology and operations in a low-gravity field could be tested on Luna only three days from Earth, before being attempted on distant Mars.

Senator Spark M. Matsunaga has also been thinking about the infrastructure required to get to Mars. At a speech before the National Academy of Science's recent Mars Conference in Washington DC, Matsunaga argued that in the political maneuvering to get it approved, the Space Shuttle became too generalized a vehicle. "Now our Space Station is following the same route. First it expands, then it shrinks, and always it recedes." By the time our Space Station is finally built, "the Soviets will probably be building hotels in orbit, while we, from the ground, sniff disdainfully at the quality of their plumbing."

Matsunaga's solution? Build *two* space stations, one specialized for commercial use and one as an interplanetary transportation node. Since Space Industries, Inc., of Houston, TX, is already building a two-module, human-tended Industrial Space Facility (ISF) for commercial research, development, and production, why should

NASA duplicate the work? Matsunaga believes an uprated ISF can be emplaced by 1992, fully two years before the current earliest Space Station Initial Operational Capability, at a total mixed government and commercial investment of perhaps $2 billion. This is around one-tenth of current estimates for the total cost of NASA's Space Station.

With some of the remaining money, Matsunaga wants to build a relatively simple Space Exploration Complex, which "would consist initially of two, or at the most three, permanently manned modules. Its initial function would be to carry out the complex long-term research activities that must precede meaningful human exploration of space. . . ." It would then support the building of a Mars transportation system.

Meanwhile, while NASA is resisting military and Congressional pressure to make the Space Station a part-time human-tended, or even an entirely automated facility, astronauts have publicly complained that the current "double keel" Station requires of them too much extra-vehicular activity to build. NASA has dutifully simplified the design—and invested still more of the limited Space Station budget in automated construction techniques, to be controlled from Earth.

Spaceflight historian Tim Kyger told me he believes this "creeping automation" is largely the result of continuing use of "soft" pressure suits. These suits cannot operate at the one atmospheric pressure ambient in the Space Shuttle and, to avoid the bends, astronauts must "pre-breathe" pure oxygen for around two to three hours before EVA. Kyger believes that so much of the on-orbit time available with even a four orbiter fleet will be tied up pre-breathing, there may be insufficient total EVA time to construct the Space Station.

Hard suits, which can operate at full pressure and don't require pre-breathing, have been available at NASA Ames for better than a decade. Kyger believes these suits have not been used largely because of "not–invented–here" turf battles between Johnson Space Center and NASA Ames.

Yet if we cannot even learn to live and work in low Earth orbit, how can we hope to get to Mars—six months from a replacement part or the possibility of rescue?

The technology and the plans to get to Mars are either here or very close; the infrastructure is not. But as the Soviets are proving with their relatively primitive Mir Space Station, it is infrastructure that counts, far more than technology. Whatever road we take to Mars— whether we go as a one-shot political gesture, or to stay—the infrastructure and near-term costs are very similar.

All roads to the Solar System lead first to a Space Station.

Another road to Mars.

Two interplanetary vessels, approximately the same size and similar in design to those used in the Science Applications/Planetary Society scenario which begins this article, arrive together at Mars. Larger aerobrakes are used to decelerate both entire spacecraft. One of them docks with the planet's innermost moon, Phobos, where the crew dismantles their spacecraft, burying its habitation and scientific modules in Phobos' regolith for radiation protection. The other ship is used as a permanent rotating space station to give the crew temporary access to a gravity environment.

The money spent in the Science Applications plan to design a Martian lander is used instead to send automated packages of supplies from Earth and to land combined scientific and prospecting rovers on Mars. These are controlled via a communications satellite from the Phobos base to avoid the time-delay of control from Earth—and also reducing the need for expensive artificial intelligence.

Meanwhile, one of the laboratories buried on Phobos uses information obtained in the late 1980s by the Soviet probes of Phobos and Deimos to start pilot production of water from materials mined from Phobos' surface. The dismantled ship's solar arrays provide power to split the water into hydrogen and oxygen. The hydrogen is burned with part of the oxygen as rocket fuel, providing extended transportation within the Martian System, and allowing the return of large samples to Earth. The remainder of the oxygen is breathed by the crew.

To this point, this mission needn't cost one cent more than the Science Applications plan. The risk to the crew is, of course, significantly greater, since no immediate provision is made for their return should something go wrong. Risk, however, is the price of any frontier—and at additional cost, a return option could be provided. The long-term cost, admittedly, is substantially higher, because mission operations would have to continue indefinitely; a Mars landing system would at some point still have to be designed; and more than two interplanetary transports would someday be needed.

In short, because *this* mission has a future.

A few years later, the first freighter arrives from Earth. Soon, it will return to the Earth-orbiting Space Station—and growing space-based industries—with water, oxygen, and hydrogen fuel labeled:

**"Imported From Mars."**

# WILL *YOU* SURVIVE?

In addition to Dean Ing's powerful science fiction novels— *Systemic Shock, Wild Country, Blood of Eagles* and others—he has written cogently and inventively about the art of survival. **The Chernobyl Syndrome** is the result of his research into life after a possible nuclear exchange . . . because as our civilization gets bigger and better, we become more and more dependent on its products. What would *you* do if the machine stops—or blows up?

Some of the topics Dean Ing covers:
* How to *make* a getaway airplane
* Honing your "crisis skills"
* Fleeing the firestorm: escape tactics for city-dwellers
* How to build a homemade fallout meter
* Civil defense, American style
* "Microfarming"—survival in five acres
    *And much, much more.*

Also by Dean Ing, available through Baen Books:

## ANASAZI
Why did the long-vanished Anasazi Indians retreat from their homes and gardens on the green mesa top to precarious cliffside cities? Were they afraid of someone—or *something*? "There's no evidence of warfare in the ruins of their earlier homes . . . but maybe the marauders they feared didn't wage war in the usual way," says Dean Ing. *Anasazi* postulates a race of alien beings who needed human bodies in order to survive on Earth—a race of aliens that *still* exists.

## FIREFIGHT 2000
How do you integrate armies supplied with bayonets and ballistic missiles; citizens enjoying Volkswagens and Ferraris; cities drawing power from windmills and nuclear powerplants? Ing takes a look at these dichotomies, and more. This collection of fact and fiction serves as a metaphor for tomorrow: covering terror and hope, right guesses and wrong, high tech and thatched cottages.

---

*Order Dean Ing's books listed above with this order form. Simply check your choices below and send the combined cover price/s to: Baen Books, Dept. BA, 260 Fifth Avenue, New York, New York 10001.*

THE CHERNOBYL SYNDROME * 65345-8 *
  320 pp. * $3.50                        \_\_\_\_\_
ANASAZI * 65629-5 * 288 pp. * $2.95      \_\_\_\_\_
FIREFIGHT 2000 * 65650-X * 252 pp. * $2.95  \_\_\_\_\_

## Introduction

At first glance, a story set in late medieval Germany might not seem to quite fit with the scientific orientation of this magazine. But "Clash of Arms" really does belong in New Destinies, home to hard–headed sf and serious–minded speculation on the laws governing physical reality. This story illustrates one of the finer points of a pragmatic, rationalist philosophy, and teaches a lesson it would seem can never be taught often enough . . .

# CLASH OF ARMS

*Harry Turtledove*

The tournament held every other year at the castle of
Thunder-ten-tronckh in Westphalia always produced
splendid jousting, luring as it did great knights from all
over Europe. Indeed, one tourney year, the lure proved
too much even for Magister Stephen de Windesore,
who left his comfortable home outside London to travel
to the wilds of Germany.

You must understand at once that Magister Stephen
did not arrive at the castle of Thunder-ten-tronckh to
break a lance himself. Far from it. He was fat and well
past fifty. While that was also true of several of the
knights there, no more need be said than that Magister
Stephen habitually rode a mule.

His sharpest weapon was his tongue, and at the castle
of Thunder-ten-tronckh (or, to be more accurate, in a
tavern just outside the castle), he was having trouble
with that. The Westphalians used a dialect even more bar-
barous than his own English, and his French, I fear, was
more of the variety learned at Stratford-atte-Bowe than
around Paris. On the other hand, he spoke very loudly.

"Me? I don't care a fig for cart horses and arrogant
swaggerers in plate," he declared to anyone who would

listen. To emphasize the point, he gestured with a mug of beer. Some slopped over the edge and splashed the table. He did not miss it; it was thin, bitter stuff next to the smooth English ale he liked.

"You don't like jousts, why did you come?" asked an Italian merchant whose French was hardly better than Magister Stephen's. The Italian was chiefly interested in getting the best price for a load of pepper, cinnamon, and spikenard, but he had an amateur's passion for deeds of dought.

Magister Stephen fixed him with a cold, gray eye. "The arms, man, the arms!"

"Well, of course the arms! *Arma virumque cano*," the merchant said, proving that he owned some smattering of a classical education. He made cut-and-thrust motions.

"Dear God, if You are truly all-wise, why did You make so many dullards?" Magister Stephen murmured, but in English. Returning to French, he explained, "Not weaponry. What I mean is coats-of-arms, heraldry, blazonry—d'you understand me?"

The Italian smote his forehead with the heel of his hand. "Ai, the stupidity of me! Truly, I am seventeen different kinds of the hindquarters of a she-donkey! Heraldry, your honor meant! And I myself an armigerous man!"

"You, sir?" Magister Stephen eyed his chance-met comrade with fresh interest. He certainly did not look as if he came from any knightly or noble line, being small, skinny, excitable, and dressed in mantle, tunic, and tights shabbier than Stephen's own. Still, it could be. The Italians were freer with grants of arms to burgesses than the northern countries.

"Indeed, yes, sir," the merchant replied, paying no attention to Magister Stephen's scrutiny. "I am Niccolo dello Bosco—of the woods, you would say. When I am at home, you see, I am to be found in the forest outside Firenze. It is a truly lovely town, Firenze. Do you know it?"

"Unfortunately, no," Magister Stephen said. He was thinking that it was not unfortunate at all. He had been to Milan once, to watch a tourney, and came away with a low opinion of Italian manners and cookery. That, however, was neither here nor there. "And your arms, sir, if I may ask?"

"But of course. A proud shield, you will agree: Gules a fess or between three frogs proper."

Magister Stephen whipped out quill and ink and a small sketchbook. Rather than carrying a variety of colors around for rough sketches, he used different hatchings to show the tinctures: vertical stripes for the red ground of the shield, with dots for the broad, gold, horizontal band crossing the center of the escutcheon. His frogs were lumpy-looking creatures. He glanced up at dello Bosco, who was watching him in fascination. "Why 'three frogs proper'?" he asked. "Why not simply 'vert'?"

"They are to be shown as spotted."

"Ah." Magister Stephen made the necessary correction. "Most interesting, Master dello Bosco. In England, I know of but one family whose arms bear the frog, or rather the toad: that of Botreaux, whose arms are Argent, three toads erect sable."

The Italian smiled. "From *batracien*, no doubt. A pleasant pun, yes?"

"Hmm?" Magister Stephen owned a remorselessly literal mind. "Why, so it is." His chuckle was a little forced.

The approaching jingle of harness and clop of heavy hooves in the street told of another party of knights on its way to the castle of Thunder-ten-tronckh. Anxious to see their arms, Magister Stephen tossed a coin down on the table top, and waited impatiently for his change. He pocketed the sixth-copper and hurried out of the tavern.

To his annoyance, he was familiar with all but one of the newcomers' shields. He was just finishing his sketch of that one when dello Bosco appeared at his elbow and nudged him. "There's something you won't find often," the Italian said, nodding toward one of the stalls across the road. "A trader who can't give his stock away."

"Oh, yes, him." Magister Stephen had noticed the

bushy-bearded merchant in a caftan the day before. He was a Greek from Thessalonike, come to the castle of Thunder-ten-tronckh with a cartload of fermented fish sauce. To northern noses, though, the stuff smelled long-dead. Now the Greek was reduced to smearing it on heels of bread and offering free samples to people on the street, most of whom took one good whiff and fled.

"*Timeo Danaos et donas ferentis*," dello Bosco laughed, watching yet another passer-by beat a hasty retreat from the stall.

"You know Virgil well," Magister Stephen said.

"Yes, very well," dello Bosco agreed, and Magister Stephen sniffed at the ready vanity of an Italian.

Another party of knights came clattering up the road toward the castle. "It seems our day for surprises," dello Bosco said, pointing at one horseman's arms. "Or have you seen pantheons before?"

Magister Stephen did not answer; he was drawing furiously. He knew of the pantheon from his study of heraldic lore, but he had *not* seen the mythical beast actually depicted on a shield. It had the head of a doe, a body that might have come from the same creature, a fox's tail, and cloven hooves. It was shown in its proper colors: the hooves sable, body gules powdered with golden stars.

"Quite unusual," Magister Stephen said at last, tucking his sketchbook back inside his tunic. Then he turned to dello Bosco, who had been waiting for him to finish. "Sir, you astonish me. Not one in a thousand would have recognized a pantheon at sight."

The merchant drew himself up stiffly; even so, the crown of his head was below the level of Magister Stephen's chin. "I am not one in a thousand—I am myself. And being armigerous, is it not proper for me to know heraldry?"

"Oh, certainly. Only—"

Dello Bosco might have been reading his thoughts, for he divined the exact reason for the hesitation: "You think I am stupid because I am not noble born, eh? Why do I not trash you for this?" He was hopping up and down in fury, his cheeks crimson beneath their Mediterranean swarthiness.

Magister Stephen cocked a massive fist. "I promise you, you would regret the attempt."

"Do I care a fig for your promises, you larded tun?"

"Have a care with your saucy tongue, knave, or I will be the one to thrash you."

"Not only fat, but a fool. In my little finger I know more of heraldy than is in all your empty head."

Magister Stephen's rage ripped free. "Damn me to hell if you do, sir!" he roared, loud enough to make heads turn half a block away.

"Big-talking pile of suet. Go home to mama; I do not waste my time on you." Dello Bosco gave a theatrical Italian gesture of contempt, spun on his heel, and began to stalk away.

Magister Stephen seized him by the shoulder and hauled him back. White around the lips, the Englishman grated, "Dare to prove your boasts, little man, or I will kill you on the spot. Contest with me, and we shall see which of us can put a question the other cannot answer."

"What stake will you put up for this, ah, contest of yours?" dello Bosco said, wriggling free of the other's grip.

Magister Stephen laughed harshly. "Ask what you will if you win—you shall not. As for me, all I intend is to fling you into a dung heap, to serve you as you deserve for insolence to your betters."

"Wind, wind, wind," dello Bosco jeered. "As challenged, I shall ask first—is it agreed?"

"Ask away. The last question counts for all, not the first."

"Very well, then. Tell me, if you will, the difference between a mermaid and a melusine."

"You have a fondness for monsters, it seems," Magister Stephen remarked. "No doubt it suits your character. To your answer: these German heralds have a fondness for melusines, and draw them with two tails to the mermaid's one." Dello Bosco shrugged and spread

his hands. Magister Stephen said, "My turn now—why
is the bar sinister termed a mark of bastardy?"

"Because all English speak French as poorly as you,"
his opponent retorted. "*Barre* is French for 'bend,' and
the bend sinister does show illegitimacy. Any child
knows the bars, like the face, run straight across the
shield, and so cannot be called dexter or sinister."
Magister Stephen did his best to hide his chagrin.

They threw questions there at each other in the
street, and gave back answers as swiftly. Magister Stephen's wrath soon faded, to be replaced by the spirit of
competition. All his wit focused on finding challenges
for dello Bosco, and on meeting the Italian's. Some of
those left him sweating. Wherever he had learned his
heraldry, dello Bosco was a master.

Magister Stephen looked up, amazed, to realize it
was twilight. "A pause for a roast capon and a bottle of
wine?" he suggested. "Then to my chamber and we'll
have this out to the end."

"Still the belly first, is it?" dello Bosco said, but he
followed the Englishman back into the inn from which
they had come several hours before.

Refreshed, Magister Stephen climbed the stairs to
the cubicles over the taproom. He carried a burning
taper in one hand and a fresh bottle in the other. After
lighting a lamp, he stretched out on his straw paillasse
and waved dello Bosco to the rickety footstool that was
the little rented room's only other furniture.

"My turn, is it not?" Magister Stephen asked. At the
Italian's nod, he said, "Give me the one British coat of
arms that has no charge upon the shield."

"A plague on you, and all the British with you," dello
Bosco said. He screwed up his mobile face in thought,
and sat a long time silent. Just as a grinning Magister
Stephen was about to rise, he said, "I have it, I think.
Did not John of Brittany—the earl of Richmond, that
is—bear simply 'ermine'?"

"Damnation!" Magister Stephen exploded, and dello
Bosco slumped in relief.

Then he came back with a sticker of his own: "What beast is it that has both three bodies and three ears?"

Magister Stephen winced. He frantically began reviewing the monsters of blazonry. The lion tricorporate had but one head, with the usual number of ears. The chimaera had—no, it had three heads and only one body. The hydra was drawn in various ways, with seven heads, or three, but again, a single body.

"Having trouble?" dello Bosco asked. In the lamplight his eyes were enormous; they seemed almost a deep crimson rather than black—something that Magister Stephen had not noticed, and that only added to his unease.

The hot, eager gaze made him want to run like a rabbit—like a rabbit! He let out a great chortle of joy. "The coney trijunct on the arms of Harry Well!" he exclaimed. "The bodies are disposed in the dexter and sinister chief points and in base, each joined to the others by a single ear round the fess point."

Dello Bosco sighed and relaxed once more. Still shuddering at his narrow escape, Magister Stephen cudgeled his brain for the fitting revenge. Suddenly, he smiled. "Tell me the formal name of the steps to be depicted under the Cross Calvary."

But dello Bosco answered at once: "Grieces." He came back with a complicated point of blazonry.

Magister Stephen made him repeat it, then waded through. "Two and three, or a cross gules," he finished, panting a bit.

"Had you blazoned the first and fourth 'a barry of six' instead of 'azure, three bars or,' I would have had you," dello Bosco said.

"Yes, I know." Yet even though Magister Stephen had given the correct response, the feel of the contest changed. He was rattled, and asked the first thing that popped into his head; dello Bosco answered easily. Then he asked a question so convoluted as to make the one before elementary by comparison.

Magister Stephen barely survived it, and took a long pull at the wine jar when he had finished. Again, his opponent brushed aside his answering sally; again, he came back with a question of hideous difficulty. The cycle repeated several times; at every query, Magister Stephen's answers came more slowly and with less certainty. Dello Bosco never faltered.

The lamp in the little room was running low on oil. Its dying flickers made dello Bosco seem somehow bigger, as if he was gathering strength from Magister Stephen's distress. Every time he hurled a question now he leaned forward, hands on his knees, waiting for the Englishman's stumbling replies like a hound that has scented blood.

He handled Magister Stephen's next question, on the difference between the English and Continental systems for showing cadency, with such a dazzling display of erudition that the Englishman, desperate as he was, wanted to jot down notes. But there was no time for that. Stretching lazily, dello Bosco said, "I grow weary of the game, I fear. So, then, a last one for you: tell me what arms the devil bears."

"What? Only the devil knows that!" Magister Stephen blurted.

At that moment the lamp went out. Yet the chamber was not dark, for Niccolo dello Bosco's eyes still glowed red, like burning coals. When he spoke again, his voice was deeper, richer, and altogether without Italian accent. "I see that you do not know, in any case, which is a great pity for you. Nor is it wise to bet with strangers— but then, I told you you were a fool."

Dello Bosco chuckled. "And now to settle up the wager. What was that you said? 'Damn me to hell if you do, sir?' Well, that can be arranged." He strode forward and laid hold of Magister Stephen. His grip had claws.

Dello Bosco had not mentioned the Mountain by the Dark Wood outside Firenze, or the Gateway there, or the writing above it. "*Lasciate ogni speranza, voi ch'entrate,*" Magister Stephen read as he was dragged through. Even in such straits he was observant, and cried, "No wonder you said you knew Virgil well!"

"Indeed. After all, he lives with me."

Then the lesser demons took control of their new charge from their master. To show their service, they bore his arms: Gules, a fess or between three frogs proper. Magister Stephen found that very funny—but not for long.

## Introduction

Remember "psionics" and all that? Due to the influence of John Campbell, G. Harry Stine and others, various sorts of "scientific" mentalism became a standard feature of '60s sf. The reason for this was Campbell's reiterated reports in the pages of Astounding (and if you can't believe what you read there what can you believe?) of repeatable psychic experiments with positive results, done in rigorous scientific style.

Turned out that all the smoke and heat concealed nothing more important than badly designed experiments. At least after much excitement psionics just sort of faded, rather like that other Astounding discovery, the Dean Device, a "unidirectional thruster" that was going to open up the Solar System right away, knocking the Laws of Motion into a cocked hat in the process.

Well, psionics is about to make a come-back—if indeed "Fiction This Ain't"—so maybe we ought not count out the Dean Device either . . .

# FICTION THIS AIN'T

*Martin von Strasser Caidin*

On page 2 of *New Destinies* (Fall 1987 issue) the publisher printed the usual disclaimer intended to bulwark him and his organization from crazed people who like nothing better than to sue other people. There are lots of them out there with a long record of bitter complaints and cries of plagiarism and, at times, when they can afford the long green and they've got some sleaze of an ambulance-chasing attorney, it even gets into litigation.

But the disclaimer avoids a lot of this. It states, simply enough: "This is a work of fiction. All the characters and events portrayed in this book are fictional, and any resemblance to real people or incidents is purely coincidental."

That disclaimer is *not* for me. No way, chilluns. I'll stand on everything I say in this—well, *you* can call it an article but I'll flatly consider it to be a statement that made its way to the printed page. And I'll add that this statement is offered in response to request. But because the subject *is* controversial, and the shrinking violet is far removed from one of my favorite flowers (I prefer meat eaters), it's only fair to state in print that I disclaim James Baen and his umpteen enterprises from having responsibility for any part or parcel of this statement.

This is all *my* doing. You want to take dead aim on someone, *you* come at *me*. If ever such responses get to a point of a face-to-face on live television, I also suggest you offer up your soul to God because your ass is going to belong to me. Do I challenge anyone out there? Not at all. I don't much give a rat's ass or a damn what anyone thinks, says, or preaches from whatever pole of prejudice to which they cling.

This statement is on telekinetics. Got that? Telekinetics. TK. What about it?

It is real.

It exists now.

It has been demonstrated under controlled and acceptable conditions almost every day for the past three years. It has been demonstrated *from a distance*—

Through walls so that the TK occurs in another room—

Through mirrored reflections—

With the TK targets in a sealed room—

With all the usual outcries of control of temperature, electrical flow, humidity, houses breathing, shapes, convection, and other factors to be considered, from air pressure to mother's milk and rattling rosary beads.

It's been done by the TK motivator watching a closed-circuit television monitor scanning the targets in a sealed room fifty feet away—

And in a house across the street from where the motivator works the targets—

And a lot more. Including scientists, those from private industry and those from government positions, making certain that everything was the way it was supposed to be for the proof—

And it's been recorded on video tape—

Aha; much crowding forward for immediate response, anything from suddenly straightened posture to a familiarly arched eyebrow. Everything from, "Oh, gee, WOW!" to "Not some more of this psi shit again, man."

You will take note by considering the source of all your conversations on this subject of TK. Your friends and buddies and associates, and what in the name of hell do any of *them* really *know* about telekinetics? Uh-huh, you got it. They don't know elephant elbow hair from whale snot about it, although they may have talked for years about it. Pro or con doesn't matter. Likely, almost positively, *it's been all talk*.

First let's define what we're talking about. Telekinetics. Also called psychokinesis. The Europeans love new phrases and they call it psychotronics.

What is—*our* definition, please—telekinetics? By the by, we'll shorten it to TK and save a lot of space that way. Okay, the question again: *What is TK?*

The sum of many explanations will do. It is the ability of one person or more than one person to influence the spatial position and/or movement of a physical object, or a physical force, from a distance, without any direct or indirect contact or force with that object, and be able to influence—i.e., to alter or change—the spatial positioning or location of that object.

In easier terms, to be able to move a physical target by mind power alone, from a distance, under conditions that totally preclude any physical interference, trickery, sham, fakery or all those other phrases and objections brought up by people who've never seen, witnessed or experienced TK, but appear to know so much about the subject that they talk like experts.

That is a very neat trick. There are many people out there among you who insist that TK does not exist. They are supposed experts on the subject. What they really are, kids, are experts in the fields of psychology, fooling you good folk who are scared to admit out loud that *you* believe. Think about these experts. They claim flatly, absolutely, that such psi phenomena as TK do not exist. *Well, if it doesn't exist then how the hell did they come to be experts on it?*

Ah, but they are superb psychologists. They claim enormous debunking power and they get people to be impressed by this debunkery, and they make pontifical statements, and they're good at cutting up other people, and so the majority of you people out there listen attentively to their malarkey.

They're as much a fake as the seance wizards who brought back Uncle Max's dead dog, Lucifer, to tell the neighborhood cat that the animal kingdom on the "other side" ain't half-bad at all. They just sing a different song.

Hey, hold on. All those voices out there. The outcry of "what kind of people can do this TK stuff?"

Well, that's a good question and it provides immediately the proper podium for the response. Let me tell you what they *ain't*. This will bring no joy to the professional debunkers who know so much about something they profess doesn't exist, but we preclude, eliminate, reject, dismiss, refuse, throw out, eject, reject, bounce, heave and otherwise separate from this discussion anything to do with wizards, lizards, magicians, poltergeists, psychics, witches and warlocks, with the occult or any element of parapsychology past, present or future.

So who are we talking about?

Me.

*You.*

A whole bunch of us.

"Whoa! Hey, wait one! Hold it! Is this guy I'm reading right now claiming he has the ability to move an object by TK?"

*Yep*. Can do. Have been for a couple of years under the various conditions already elucidated.

"Is this guy the only one who can do this?"

Hell, *no*. I've taught other people to do it.

"That is awful damn tough to believe, right?"

Well, first off, what you believe doesn't matter. What the debunkers state doesn't matter.

*What someone can do or cannot do is absolutely not proportional in any way to anyone else's belief or disbelief.*

You may believe your Aunt Harriet, or even myself, can levitate our own bodies. Maybe you believe this implicitly or absolutely, friend. Well, I don't know about the old broad in your family tree and what she can or can't do, but I do know that when it comes to levitation I'm an absolute bust. Me, I need an airplane or some other device like that. I've flown airplanes, seaplanes, balloons, gliders, helicopters, gyrocopters and assorted such devices to assorted heights and that's pretty damned good levitating, but I needed the end product of a vast industry and a lot of energy consumed through engines that either whirled airfoils (called propellers) or slung vast quantities of heated air out the nether end of the jet.

So what *you* believe someone else can or can't do hasn't got beans to do with the doing. Or lack of doing. Just go back through your history books and you'll discover that just about everything you take for granted today in your daily lives *was absolutely impossible not so many years ago*. There's a whole army out there that just loves to debunk, attack, deride, sneer at and piss on what other people can do. Usually it's because *they can't do any of this* and they suck at power by derision instead of accomplishment.

So let's leave that crowd for a moment.

The type of TK we're talking about is simple, straightforward, and about the best shot for accomplishing TK movement. You need a target. The ones we use weigh anywhere from a sixth of a gram way on up to 285 grams. We've moved all those, but the heavier ones have required there be no physical blockage between the TK sender and the target.

So we simplify it. Here's the setup we use. We sealed off one room at the end of the house. Sealed the one window. Closed off the air-conditioning vent. Under stringent test conditions turned off the air-conditioning system. Even turned off all power to the house. Even managed successful TK when all power in the neighborhood was knocked out. What a hell of a way to test. *It still worked.*

In the door we installed a sheet of tempered glass. We sealed the door itself with duct tape. Normally we have about 90 watts of fluorescent lighting in the room.

If you think that's enough to turn objects weighing ten grams, go ahead and set up your lights about eight feet from your targets and try, and be ready for a hernia examination. Takes more than the lights, old buddy.

The targets are placed on vertical points. A needle is inserted in a block of wood, or a block of plastic, or a cork, or an eraser. Don't matter a damn *what*. The needle can be steel, magnetic or nonmagnetic, made of wood or glass or plastic or pewter. That also don't matter a damn. You just want the needle to be basically vertical.

Now, the targets. Most of ours are three inches along the edges. A piece of paper three inches on each side, folded twice so that it can balance pretty well. Piece of glass tape in the center for smoother rotation and greater strength. Now, are we talking pyramid-shaped? Hell, no. The target can be paper, wood, plastic, thin metal, aluminum foil; it don't matter. The shape can be squared, rectangular, round, angled, dart-shaped, star-shaped, or even a paper tube from the center of a roll of toilet paper. Cut a hole through the center of the tube, slap on a plastic cup (like from the screwcap end of a Benzedrex inhaler) and secure it with scotch tape. Drop it onto a needle. That is tougher to turn than others but it does and it has turned.

You place the targets, up to ten inches on each side, on the vertical needles. We now try to get a turning motion. Turning about the horizontal balanced on the vertical point.

We've had these targets in a room sealed off, no one trying to turn anything, and they don't move for a month. Then any one of a half-dozen of us can stand in the hall outside and concentrate *and the targets begin to turn*. They turn clockwise and they turn counterclockwise. Often there's no pattern. It's like a spray effect. There's a residual effect. We've turned these things from out in the hall, left a TV camera running (sorry, you're wrong; no bright lights to cause heat), gone into another room and on the monitor watched the targets turn, stop, reverse direction, start up again.

We wondered about that until we discovered we can turn them with *only* the television screen being observed, and nobody even near the target room.

We now—picture this—are standing in a hallway outside a sealed room, looking through tempered glass, all power to the house cut off, and selecting one or more particular targets, turning them and by selection stopping a turning target and reversing its direction.

That last bit is not always successful. Maybe one time out of four. But if there's only one target on the main table or desk the success rate zooms up, like three times out of four. That's good enough for now.

It doesn't come with a snap of the fingers. It takes practice. Close-up TK movement should be considered only practice because of body movement, breathing, convection—all the factors claimed by the debunkers. But in a sealed room, without heat or artificial light, from a distance, from a TV scanner, *from a photograph?*

How the hell do you manage all that? Well, a good magician can do it if he sets up equipment for it. A deliberate faker can do all sorts of stuff. So we called in some scientists, some from private industry and some from government. We have had four of those scientists—who never believed—doing the actual turning. They're flipped out of their gourds. What they had always insisted was impossible they are doing now by themselves.

What's the TK force? Sorry, friends, *but we do not know.* We've had hundreds of theories, proposals, conclusions, and whatever, but those of us who did it don't know what we're doing except that we can do the TK bit; we're successful. Is it thought waves? I wouldn't know a thought wave if I fell over it.

Have we measured any forces? Not yet; that's coming up now with all kinds of special equipment.

Do things have to be "right" for the TK effect to take place? Well, there have been some moments with hangovers where it wasn't possible to place one foot evenly before the other, let alone "perform" TK. But generally, no. Nothing special.

"Does continuous training and practice make some-one stronger?" You bet it does.

"Can everyone do it?" No. Just like everyone can't be a champion bowler, or a great fighter pilot, or a terrific musician.

"Who can't do it?" You find out when they fail. Almost always they fail because their minds were locked into a "NO!" mode when they were much younger.

"Speaking of young, can the kids do it?" Damn right. The best novice we had was a sixteen-year-old girl, daughter of a church reverend, who believed anything was possible. Bam! She did it right away. Has she continued it? We do not know. Lost touch, so I doubt it. It takes a lot of discipline to do it.

"Any difference between the gents and the ladies?" Well, sure, but not where TK is concerned.

Are those of us who can do this getting stronger? Yes, we are. Slowly but surely. We feel we're close to really starting to understand what's happening. Not yet, not yet; but we're getting closer.

"Would you teach me to do it?" Hey, *who are you?* Where are you? How serious are you? How deter-mined? How disciplined? How open is your mind? You want to know more, you write to Jim Baen who pub-lished this book. Take it up with him.

"Have you been challenged on this TK ability?"

Of course!

But then again, I've been challenged on things all my life. Let me give you a good example of this "It's impossible!" crap that's not nearly as esoteric as TK.

I spent ten years flying a slab-sided, gut-bellied, three-engined German monster of an airplane with cor-rugated metal surfaces and bridge-like wing structure. That's the Junkers Ju-52, famous to German troops in World War II as Iron Annie. This thing first flew back in 1931. Long after World War II we learned of one in Ecuador, in thick jungle growth outside of Quito. That's more than nine-thou feet above sea level. To shorten the long story, we found the battered old wreck, got her flying and brought her to the States. Had all sorts of battles with the Feds on the airplane because of regulations and such, but finally I became the Federal Examiner on this ship. In other words, I was the guy checking out the airline captains on the machine. For you records-keepers her official number was N52JU, and I was the owner.

During this period we heard of some people setting world wingwalk records. They'd pile a whole bunch of people onto the wing and fuselage of an airplane, keep them out there 30 seconds, and claim the record. We insisted the record could be flown with the people *on one wing only*. None of this fuselage stuff. One wing *only*.

Well, some people did fourteen on one wing and hurt a bunch of people. Some other people went more than fourteen and killed some people, the way we heard it. So we decided to go for *nineteen* in the Ju-52. That's nineteen people on one wing; with all their gear weighing four thousand pounds. Someone told the Germans we'd done it with the Ju-52. Flat took the world record.

The Germans, who'd designed and built the airplane, stated it was not possible. It was impossible! We were glory-story tellers who were lying, making it up. Just about all the engineers you ever spoke to said it was impossible.

Well, then, I guess we did the impossible, because we had about sixteen video and movie cameras going aboard five airplanes that day—every kind of verification going. And when we sent a 30-minute tape of the whole thing to Germany, and they reviewed the tape and watched the absolutely impossible, the silence was absolutely deafening.

Now, back to this TK. Sure I've been challenged. Screw those people. They challenge just about everybody. *That's how they make their money*. They can't do it, so they challenge people—

AND THEY SET UP THEIR CHALLENGE IN SUCH A WAY THAT THEY CANNOT LOSE, NO MATTER WHAT YOU'RE CAPABLE OF DOING.

It's a trap, buddy-boy. James Randi is a magician, an author, a performer, a man who loves to do his thing on the Carson show. I understand he's a hell of a magician. He's also a hell of a psychologist. He challenged me.

But he first demanded I sign a piece of paper claiming I was a wizard or a psychic or some other nonsensical stuff designed to have him keep control of the situation. He also demanded the right to send down a representative to test out the situation before he showed up. That's pretty neat; if the situation is dangerous, block it from going any further, because Randi said he'd cough up $120,000 if anyone could show any kind of clearly specified TK movement.

But you couldn't quality for the bread unless you signed all those papers and left yourself wide open for a swift kick where it hurts.

But what the hell. I figured Randi was a sharp cat, I applaud his commercial success (he even sells books on testing your own ESP which, according to him, doesn't exist, but please buy his book *anyway*, right?), and I really didn't have any argument with him. I don't blame him for so much disbelief, because this field is filled with weirdos and nitwits and crazies. So were atomic research and flight and ballooning and skydiving and steamships and submarines, and remember those lunatics who talked about going to the moon, or those idiots who predicted heart transplants? Dumb bastards should have known all that was impossible.

Anyway, I called Randi. Had an interesting talk. He was debunking right from the start and I was blocking the debunking. Told him, "Hey, I don't have a fight with you. I figure I can learn from you, maybe, and that street goes both ways. But I'd like you to get to our place, see what we're doing, check it all out yourself, and then, under those conditions, fella, we'll move by TK. If we can't then we'll pay all your expenses, first class, have you at the best hotels and restaurants, and you can do all the debunking you want to do. You bring your witnesses and I'll have a couple of government scientists and engineers."

Well, he figured he'd be tied up a week or two finishing a book and then, by golly, we could get together and prove just how wrong I was. That week or two has now been a couple of months and no Randi. Maybe it's because of the way the conversation went.

Randi is *very* sharp, intelligent, fast, cunning and all those good things. He asked me if I had particular or favorite TK targets, or did we pick them out at random?

"Sometimes we do that," I agreed. "I have other people stand by the window and select a target and I go after that."

"That's not good enough," he stated. "You've got to have complete mathematical randomness involved."

"Why?" I asked.

"Because the chances of your having success moving a target will be greater if you use a favorite or familiar target—"

Well, thank you kindly, good sir, Mr. Randi, your honor, your worship, your munificence.

*Because if TK ain't possible under any conditions, as Randi has always said, then how the hell can it make any difference WHAT target is used to achieve the TK movement?*

Chew this over. Think about it. Think of what Randi said and how it applies. If he's right it cannot make any difference, so why bring it up at all, because it can't make any difference, right? Then why did he specify the conditions!?

We never have had that meeting. No dinner. The hotel reservations for him have just been pining away. His transportation goes unused. He's never called back and I much doubt if he ever will, and maybe he's got a deal to do some more magic tricks on Carson or even a few stupid pet tricks on Letterman, because Randi *is* a professional showman and he likes public exposure, and hell, man, more power to him and I hope he makes a fortune at what he does.

*But he still stepped in it with his remarks.* We love it.

Will we ask Randi again to show up?

I doubt it. Why bother? We know what we can do no matter *what* he says. I've probably done him a great favor by putting all this out before the public so that if he wants to he can attack me.

Hey, terrific. He'll have to stand in line to do that. Besides, he's a magician, and I don't know any tricks like he does. No fancy footwork. Just drive straight through like a bulldozer. That's my kind of finesse.

Back to you, the reader. I'm not even going to ask what you do or don't believe. *It doesn't change anything.*

But think about something. I don't *need* this stuff. I've published well over a hundred top books, not including many technical ones. I've had several of the biggest TV series in the world ("Six Million Dollar Man" and "The Bionic Woman"), sold about fourteen films to Hollywood, have three pictures now in production, I'm traveling throughout the world, usually flying my own plane, so why would I need any of this grief by leaving myself open as a target?

Well, I could be crazy. But even if I am, IT DOESN'T CHANGE THE FACTS AS THEY ARE WITH THE TK RESEARCH WE'RE DOING, AND THAT'S THE KEY TO ALL THIS.

We don't need, and we don't give a damn for, the approval or blessings or head-noddings of anyone else out there.

Think about that. We don't need them. *They* are the shrill ones. They're the ones crying all sorts of dire warnings.

So we look out the window at all those barking dogs and we shrug and laugh because they don't matter, and it just pisses them off all the more.

Good. Let them holler and shout and bark.

We're moving things.

*So can you.*

# TIMOTHY ZAHN

## *CREATOR OF NEW WORLDS*

"Timothy Zahn's specialty is technological intrigue-international and interstellar," says *The Christian Science Monitor*. Amen! For novels involving hard-edged conflict with alien races, world-building with a strong scientific basis, and storytelling excitement, turn to Hugo Award Winner Timothy Zahn!

---

---

## Introduction

*If you could travel backward in time, would you? And what would you do when you got there? Something, certainly. Everybody would want to change something . . .*

# TIME BOMB

### Timothy Zahn

### I

The bus station was stiflingly hot, despite the light evening breeze drifting in through the open door and windows. In a way the heat was almost comforting to Garwood as he stood at the ticket window; it proved the air conditioning had broken down much earlier in the day, long before he'd come anywhere near the place.

Puffing on a particularly pungent cigar—the smoke of which made Garwood's eyes water—the clerk looked down at the bills in front of him and shook his head. "Costs forty-one sixty to Champaign now," he said around his cigar.

Garwood frowned. "The schedule says thirty-eight," he pointed out.

"You gotta old one, prob'ly." The clerk ran a stubby finger down a list in front of him. "Prices went up 'bout a week ago. Yep—forty-one sixty."

A fresh trickle of sweat ran down the side of Garwood's face. "May I see that?" he asked.

The clerk's cigar shifted to the other side of his mouth and his eyes flicked to Garwood's slightly threadbare sport coat and the considerably classier leather suitcase at his side. "If you got proper ident'fication I can take a check or card," he offered.

"May I see the schedule, please?" Garwood repeated.

The cigar shifted again, and Garwood could almost see the wheels spinning behind the other's eyes as he swiveled the card and pushed it slowly under the old-fashioned grille. Getting suspicious; but there wasn't anything Garwood could do about it. Even if he'd been willing to risk using one, all his credit cards had fallen apart in his wallet nearly a month ago. With the rising interest rates of the past two years and the record number of bankruptcies they had triggered, there were more people than ever roundly damning the American credit system and its excesses. And on top of that, the cards were made of plastic, based on a resource the world was rapidly running out of and still desperately needed. A double whammy. "Okay," he said, scanning the rate listing. "I'll go to Mahomet instead—what's that, about ten miles this side of Champaign?"

"Closer t' seven." The clerk took the card back, eying Garwood through a freshly replenished cloud of smoke. "Be thirty-six seventy-five."

Garwood handed over thirty-seven of his forty dollars, silently cursing his out-of-date schedule. He'd cut things a little too fine, and now he was going to look exactly like what he was: a man on the run. For a moment he debated simply turning around and leaving, trying it again tomorrow on someone else's shift.

But that would mean spending another night in Springfield. And with all the Lincoln memorabilia so close at hand . . .

"Bus's boarding now," the clerk told him, choosing one of the preprinted tickets and pushing it under the grille. "Out that door; be leavin' 'bout five minutes."

Gritting his teeth, Garwood picked up the ticket . . . and as he withdrew his hand, there was a sudden *crack*, as if someone had fired a cap pistol.

"Damn kids," the clerk growled, craning his neck to peer out his side window.

Garwood looked down, his eyes searching the ledge inside the ticket window grille. He'd heard that particular sound before . . . and just inside the grille, near where his hand had twice reached, he saw it.

The clerk's ashtray. An ashtray once made of clear glass . . . now shot through by a thousand hairline fractures.

The clerk was still looking through his window for the kid with the cap pistol as Garwood left, forcing himself to walk.

He half expected the police to show up before the bus could leave, but to his mild surprise the vehicle wheezed leisurely out of the lot on time and headed a few minutes later onto the eastbound interstate. For the first few miles Garwood gave his full attention to his ears, straining tensely for the first faint sound of pursuing sirens. But as the minutes crawled by and no one showed up to pull them over, he was forced to the conclusion that the clerk had decided it wasn't any of his business.

The thought was strangely depressing. To realize that the latest upswing in the "not-me" noninvolvement philosophy had spread its rot from the polarized coasts into America's heartland bothered Garwood far more than it should have. Perhaps it was all the learned opinions he'd read weighing upon him; all the doomsayings about how such a national malaise could foreshadow the end of democracy.

Or perhaps it was simply the realization that even a nation full of selfish people didn't make a shred of difference to the cloud of destruction surrounding him.

*Stop it*! he ordered himself silently. *Self-pity* . . . Taking a deep breath, he looked around him.

He'd chosen his third-row seat carefully—as far from the bus's rear-mounted engine as he could reasonably get without sitting in the driver's lap, and well within the non-smoking section. His seatmate . . . He threw the kid a surreptitious look, confirmed that his first-glance analysis had been correct. Faded denim jeans and an old cotton shirt. That was good; natural fibers held up much better than synthetic ones, for the same reason that plastic had a tendency to disintegrate in his presence. Reaching a hand under his jacket, Garwood checked his own sweat-soaked polyester shirt for new tears. A rip at his right shoulder lengthened as he did so, and he muttered a curse.

"Don't make 'em like they use'ta, do they?"

Startled, Garwood turned to see his seatmate's smile. "What?" he asked.

"Your shirt," the kid explained. "I heard it rip. Guys who make 'em just get away with crapzi, don't they?"

"Um," Garwood grunted, turning away again.

"You headed for Champaign?" the kid persisted.

Garwood sighed. "Mahomet."

"No kidding!— I grew up there. You, too, or are you just visiting?"

"Just visiting."

"You'll like it. Small place, but friendly. Speaking of which—" he stuck out his hand. "Name's Tom Arnold. Tom *Benedict* Arnold, actually."

Automatically, Garwood shook the proffered hand. Somewhere in the back of his head the alarm bells were going off . . . "Not, uh, any relation to . . . ?"

"Benedict Arnold?" The kid grinned widely. "Sure am. Direct descendant, in fact."

An icy shiver ran up Garwood's back, a shiver having nothing to do with the bus's air conditioning. "You mean . . . *really* direct?" he asked, dropping the other's hand. "Not from a cousin or anything?"

"Straight shot line," Arnold nodded, the grin still in place. He was watching Garwood's face closely, and Garwood got the distinct impression the kid liked shocking people this way. "It's nothin' to be 'shamed of, you know—he did America a lot more good than he did bad. Whipped the Brits at Saratoga 'fore goin' over on their side—"

"Yes, I know," Garwood said, interrupting the impromptu history lesson. "Excuse me a second—washroom."

Stepping into the aisle, he went to the small cubicle at the rear of the bus. He waited a few minutes, then emerged and found an empty seat four rows behind the kid. He hoped Arnold wouldn't take it too personally, though he rather thought the other would. But he couldn't afford to take the chance. Benedict Arnold's victory at Saratoga had been a pivotal factor in persuading France to enter the war on the rebels' side, and Garwood had no desire to see if he had the same effect on living beings that he had on history's more inanimate descendants.

The afterglow in the sky behind them slowly faded, and as the sky darkened Garwood drifted in and out of sleep. The thought of the boy four seats ahead troubled his rest, filling his dreams with broken ashtrays and TV sets, half-melted-looking car engines and statues. After a while the bus stopped in Decatur, taking half an hour to trade a handful of passengers for an equally small number of others. Eventually they left; and back out in the dark of the prairie again, with the stars visible above, he again drifted to sleep. . . .

The sound of the bus driver's voice jolted him awake. ". . . and gentlemen, I'm afraid we're having some trouble with the engine. Rather than take a chance on it quitting straight out before we get to Champaign, we're going to ask you to transfer to a bus that's being sent up from Decatur. It ought to be here in just a few minutes."

Blinking in the relative brightness of the overhead lights, Garwood joined the line of grumbling passengers moving down the aisle, a familiar knot wrenching at his stomach. Had it been him? He'd been far enough away from the engine—surely he had. Unless the effective distance was increasing with time. . . . Forcing his jaw to unclench, he stepped carefully down the bus's steps, hoping desperately it was just a coincidence.

Outside, the only light came from a small building the bus had pulled alongside and from one or two dim streetlights. Half blind as his eyes again adjusted, Garwood took two tentative steps forward—

And came to an abrupt halt as strong hands slipped smoothly around each arm.

"Dr. James Garwood?" a shadowy figure before him asked quietly.

Garwood opened his mouth to deny it . . . but even as he did so he knew it would be useless. "Yes," he sighed. "And you?"

"Major Alan Davidson, Combined Services Intelligence. They miss you back at your lab, Doctor."

Garwood glanced past the husky man holding his right arm, saw the line of passengers goggling at him. "So it was all a set-up?" he asked. "The bus is okay?"

Davidson nodded. "A suspicious clerk in Springfield thought you might be a fugitive. From your description and something about a broken ashtray my superiors thought it might be you. Come with me, please."

Garwood didn't have much choice. Propelled gently along by the hands still holding his arms, he followed Davidson toward the lighted building and a long car parked in the shadows there. "Where are you taking me?" he asked, trying to keep his voice steady.

Davidson reached the car and opened the back door, and it wasn't until he and Garwood were in the back seat and the other two soldiers in front that the major answered the question. "Chanute AFB, about fifteen miles north of Champaign," he told Garwood as the car pulled back onto the interstate and headed east. "We'll be transferring you to a special plane there for the trip back to the Project."

Garwood licked his lips. A plane. How many people, he wondered, wished that mankind had never learned to fly? There was only one way to know for sure . . . and that way might wind up killing him. "You put me on that plane and it could be the last anyone ever sees of me," he told Davidson.

"Really?" the major asked politely.

"Did they tell you why I ran out on the Project? That the place was falling down around my ears?"

"They mentioned something about that, yes," Davidson nodded. "I really don't think you have anything to worry about, though. The people in charge of security on this one are all top notch."

Garwood snorted. "You're missing the point, Major. The lab wasn't under any kind of attack from outside agents. It was falling apart because *I* was in it."

Davidson nodded. "And as I said, we're going to have you under complete protection—"

"No!" Garwood snapped. "I'm not talking about someone out there gunning for me or the Project. It's my presence there—my *physical* presence inside Backdrop—that was causing all the destruction."

Davidson's dimly visible expression didn't change. "How do you figure that?"

Garwood hesitated, glancing at the front seat and the two silhouettes there listening in to the conversation. Major Davidson might possibly be cleared for something this sensitive; the others almost certainly weren't. "I can't tell you the details," he said, turning back to Davidson. "I—look, you said your superiors nailed me because of a broken ashtray in Springfield, right? Did they tell you anything more?"

Davidson hesitated, then shook his head. "No."

"It broke because I came too close to it," Garwood told him. "There's a—oh, an aura, I guess you could call it, of destruction surrounding me. Certain types of items are especially susceptible, including internal combustion engines. That's why I don't want to be put on any plane."

"Uh-huh," Davidson nodded. "West, you having any trouble with the car?"

"No, sir," the driver said promptly. "Running real smooth."

Garwood took a deep breath. "It doesn't always happen right away," he said through clenched teeth. "I rode the bus for over an hour without anything happening, remember? But if it *does* happen with a plane, we can't just pull off the road and stop."

Davidson sighed. "Look, Dr. Garwood, just relax, okay? Trust me, the plane will run just fine."

Garwood glared through the gloom at him. "You

want some proof? Is that what it'll take? Fine. Do you
have any cigarettes?"

For a moment Davidson regarded him in silence.
Then, flicking on a dim overhead dome light, he dug a
crumpled pack from his pocket.

"Put a couple in my hand," Garwood instructed him,
extending a palm, "and leave the light on."

Davidson complied with the cautious air of a man at a
magic show. "Now what?"

"Just keep an eye on them. Tell me, do you *like*
smoking?"

The other snorted. "Hell, no. Tried to give the damn
things up at least twenty times. I'm hooked pretty
good, I guess."

"You like being hooked?"

"That's a stupid question."

Garwood nodded. "Sorry. So, now . . . how many
other people, do you suppose, hate being hooked by
tobacco?"

Davidson gave him a look that was half frown, half
glare. "What's your point, Doctor?"

Garwood hesitated. "Consider it as a sort of subconscious democracy. You don't like smoking, and a whole
lot of other people in this country don't like smoking. A
lot of them wish there weren't any cigarettes—wish
*these* cigarettes didn't exist."

"And if wishes were horses, beggers would ride,"
Davidson quoted. He reached over to close his fingers
on the cigarettes in Garwood's palm—

And jerked his hand back as they crumpled into
shreds at his touch.

"What the *hell*?" he snapped, practically in Garwood's
ear. "What did you *do*?"

"I was near them," Garwood said simply. "I was near
them, and a lot of people don't like smoking. That's all
there is to it."

Davidson was still staring at the mess in Garwood's
palm. "It's a trick. You switched cigarettes on me."

"While you watched?" Garwood snorted. "All right,

fine, let's do it again. You can write your initials on them this time."

Slowly, Davidson raised his eyes to Garwood's face. "Why *you*?"

Garwood brushed the bits of paper and tobacco off his hand with a shudder. Even after all these months it still scared him spitless to watch something disintegrate like that. "I know . . . something. I can't tell you just what."

"Okay, you know something. And?"

"No 'ands' about it. It's the knowledge alone that does it."

Davidson's eyes were steady on his face. "Knowledge. Knowledge that shreds cigarettes all by itself."

"That, combined with the way a lot of people feel about smoking. Look, I know it's hard to believe—"

"Skip that point for now," Davidson cut him off. "Assume you're right, that it's pure knowledge that somehow does all this. Is it something connected with the Backdrop Project?"

"Yes."

"They know about it? And know what it does?"

"Yes, to both."

"And they still want you back?"

Garwood thought about Saunders. The long discussions he'd had with the other. The even longer arguments. "Dr. Saunders doesn't really understand."

For a moment Davidson was silent. "What else does this aura affect besides cigarettes?" he asked at last. "You mentioned car engines?"

"Engines, plastics, televisions—modern conveniences of all kinds, mainly, though there are other things in danger as well. Literally *anything* that someone doesn't like can be a target." He thought about the bus and Tom Benedict Arnold. "It might work on people, too," he added, shivering. "That one I haven't had to find out about for sure."

"And all that this . . . destructive wishing . . . needs to come out is for you to be there?"

Garwood licked his lips. "So far, yes. But if Backdrop ever finishes its work—"

"In other words, you're a walking time bomb."

Garwood winced at the harshness in Davidson's voice. "I suppose you could put it that way, yes. That's why I didn't want to risk staying at Backdrop. Why I don't want to risk riding in that plane."

The major nodded. "The second part we can do something about, anyway. We'll scrap the plane and keep you on the ground. You want to tell us where this Backdrop Project is, or would you rather I get the directions through channels?"

Garwood felt a trickle of sweat run between his shoulderblades. "Major, I can't go back there. I'm one man, and it's bad enough that I can wreck things the way I do. But if Backdrop finishes its work, the effect will spread a million-fold."

Davidson eyed him warily. "You mean it's contagious? Like a virus or something?"

"Well . . . not exactly."

"Not exactly," Davidson repeated with a snort. "All right, then try this one: do the people at Backdrop know what it is about you that does this?"

"To some extent," Garwood admitted. "But as I said, they don't grasp all the implications—"

"Then you'd agree that there's no place better equipped to deal with you than Backdrop?"

Garwood took a deep breath. "Major . . . I can't go back to Backdrop. Either the project will disintegrate around me and someone will get killed . . . or else it'll succeed and what happened to your cigarettes will start happening all over the world. Can't you understand that?"

"What I understand isn't the issue here, Doctor," Davidson growled. "My orders were very specific: to deliver you to Chanute AFB and from there to Backdrop. You've convinced me you're dangerous; you *haven't* convinced me it would be safer to keep you anywhere else."

"Major—"

"And you can damn well shut up now, too." He turned his face toward the front of the car.

Garwood took a shuddering breath, let it out in a sigh of defeat as he slumped back into the cushions. It had been a waste of time and energy—he'd known it would be right from the start. Even if he could have told Davidson everything, it wouldn't have made any difference. Davidson was part of the "not-me" generation, and he had his orders, and all the logic and reason in the world wouldn't have moved him into taking such a chance.

And now it was over . . . because logic and reason were the only weapons Garwood had.

Unless . . .

He licked his lips. Maybe he *did* have one other weapon. Closing his eyes, he began to concentrate on his formulae.

Contrary to what he'd told Saunders, there were only four truly fundamental equations, plus a handful of others needed to define the various quantities. One of the equations was given in the notes he hadn't been able to destroy; the other three were still exclusively his. Squeezing his eyelids tightly together, he listened to the hum of the car's engine and tried to visualize the equations exactly as they'd looked in his notebook . . .

But it was no use, and ten minutes later he finally admitted defeat. The engine hadn't even misfired, let alone failed. The first time the curse might actually have been useful, and he was apparently too far away for it to take effect. Too far away, and no way to get closer without crawling into the front seat with the soldiers.

The soldiers . . .

He opened his eyes. Davidson was watching him narrowly; ahead, through the windshield, the lights of a city were throwing a glow onto the low clouds overhead. "Coming up on I-57, Major," the driver said over his shoulder. "You want to take that or the back door to Chanute?"

"Back door," Davidson said, keeping his eyes on Garwood.

"Yessir."

*Back door?* Garwood licked his lips in a mixture of sudden hope and sudden dread. The only reasonable back door was Route 45 north . . . and on the way to that exit they would pass through the northern end of Champaign.

Which meant he had one last chance to escape . . . and one last chance to let the genie so far out of the bottle that he'd never get it back in.

But he had to risk it. "All right, Major," he said through dry lips, making sure he was loud enough to be heard in the front seat as well. "Chi square e to the minus i alpha t to the three-halves, plus i alpha t to the three-halves e to the gamma zero z. Sum over all momentum states and do a rotation transformation of one point five six radians. Energy transfer equation: first tensor is—"

"What the hell are you talking about?" Davidson snarled. But there was a growing note of uneasiness in his voice.

"You wanted proof that what I know was too dangerous to be given to Saunders and Backdrop?" Garwood asked. "Fine; here it is. First tensor is p sub xx e to the gamma—"

Davidson swore suddenly and lunged at him. But Garwood was ready for the move and got there first, throwing his arms around the other in an imprisoning bear hug. "—times p sub y alpha e to the minus i alpha t—"

Davidson threw off the grip, aiming a punch for Garwood's stomach. But the bouncing car ruined his aim and Garwood took the blow on his ribs instead. Again he threw his arms around Davidson. "—plus four pi sigma chi over gamma one z—"

A hand grabbed at Garwood's hair: the soldier in the front seat, leaning over to assist in the fray. Garwood ducked under the hand and kept shouting equations. The lack of space was on his side, hampering the other two as they tried to subdue him. Dimly, Garwood wondered why the driver hadn't stopped, realized that the car *was* now slowing down. There was a bump as they dropped onto the shoulder—

And with a loud staccato crackle from the front, the engine suddenly died.

The driver tried hard, but it was obvious that the car's abrupt failure had taken him completely by surprise. For a handful of heartbeats the vehicle careened wildly, dropping down off the shoulder into the ditch and then up the other side. A pair of close-spaced trees loomed ahead—the driver managed to steer between them—and an instant later the car slammed to a halt against the rear fence of a used car lot.

Garwood was the first to recover. Yanking on the handle, he threw the door open and scrambled out. The car had knocked a section of the fence part way over; climbing onto the hood, he gripped the chain links and pulled himself up and over.

He'd made it nearly halfway across the lot when the voice came from far behind him. "Okay, Garwood, that's far enough," Davidson called sharply. "Freeze or I shoot."

Garwood half turned, to see Davidson's silhouette drop over the fence and bring his arms up into a two-handed marksman's stance. Instinctively, Garwood ducked, trying to speed up a little. Ahead of him, the lines of cars lit up with the reflected flash; behind came the crack of an explosion—

And a yelp of pain.

Garwood braked to a halt and turned. Davidson was on the pavement twenty yards back of him, curled onto his side. A few feet in front of him was his gun. Or, rather, what had once been his gun. . . .

Garwood looked around, eyes trying to pierce the shadows outside the fence. Neither of the other soldiers was anywhere in sight. Still in the car, or moving to flank him? Whichever, the best thing he could do right now was to forget Davidson and get moving.

*The not-me generation.* "Damn," Garwood muttered

to himself. "Davidson?" he called tentatively. "You all right?"

"I'm alive," the other's voice bit back.

"Where did you get hit?"

There was a short pause. "Right calf. Doesn't seem too bad."

"Probably took a chunk of your gun. You shouldn't have tried to shoot me—there are just as many people out there who hate guns as hate smoking." A truck with its brights on swept uncaringly past on the interstate behind Davidson, and Garwood got a glimpse of two figures inside the wrecked car. Moving sluggishly . . . which took at least a little of the load off Garwood's conscience. At least his little stratagem hadn't gotten anyone killed outright. "Are your men okay?"

"Do you care?" the other shot back.

Garwood grimaced. "Look, I'm sorry, Davidson, but I had no choice."

"Sure. What do a few lives matter, anyway?"

"Davidson—"

"Especially when your personal freedom's at stake. You know, I have to say you really did a marvelous job of it. Now, instead of your colleagues hounding *you* for whatever it is those equations are, all they have to do is hound *us*. All that crap about the dangers of this stuff getting out—that's all it was, wasn't it? Just crap."

Garwood gritted his teeth. He knew full well that Davidson was playing a game here, deliberately trying to enmesh him in conversation until reinforcements could arrive. But he might never see this man again . . . "I wasn't trying to saddle you with this mess, Davidson—really I wasn't. I needed to strengthen the effect enough to stop the car, but it wasn't a tradeoff between my freedom and all hell breaking loose. You and your men can't possibly retain the equations I was calling out—you don't have the necessary mathematical background, for one thing. They'll be gone from your mind within minutes, if they aren't already."

"I'm so pleased to hear it," Davidson said, heavily

sarcastic. "Well, *I'm* certainly convinced. How about you?"

To that Garwood had no answer . . . and it was long past time for him to get out of here. "I've got to go, now. Please—tell them to leave me alone. What they want just isn't possible."

Davidson didn't reply. With a sigh, Garwood turned his back and hurried toward the other end of the car lot and the street beyond it. Soon, he knew, the soldiers would be coming.

## II

". . . one . . . two . . . *three*."

Davidson opened his eyes, blinking for a minute as they adjusted to the room's light. He swallowed experimentally, glancing at the clock on the desk to his left. Just after three-thirty in the morning, which meant he'd been under for nearly an hour . . . and from the way his throat felt, he'd apparently been talking for most of that time. "How'd it go?" he asked the man seated beyond the microphone that had been set up in front of him.

Dr. Hamish nodded, the standard medical professional's neutral expression pasted across his face. "Quite well, Major. At least once we got you started."

"Sorry. I *did* warn you I've never been good at being hypnotized." A slight scraping of feet to his right made Davidson turn, to find a distinguished-looking middle-aged man seated just outside his field of view there. On the other's lap was a pad and pencil; beside him on another chair was a tape recorder connected to the microphone. "Dr. Saunders," Davidson nodded in greeting, vaguely surprised to see Backdrop's director looking so alert at such an ungodly hour. "I didn't hear you come in."

"Dr. Hamish was having enough trouble putting you under," Saunders shrugged. "I didn't think it would help for me to be here, too, during the process."

Davidson's eyes flicked to the notepad. "Did you get what you wanted?"

Saunders shrugged again, his neutral expression almost as good as Hamish's. "We'll know soon enough," he said. "It'll take a while to run the equations you gave us past our various experts, of course."

"Of course," Davidson nodded. "I hope whatever you got doesn't make things worse, the way Garwood thought it would."

"Dr. Garwood is a pessimist," Saunders said shortly.

"Maybe," Davidson said, knowing better than to start an argument. "Has there been any word about him?"

"From the searchers, you mean?" Saunders shook his head. "Not yet. Though that's hardly surprising—he had over half an hour to find a hole to hide in, after all."

Davidson winced at the implied accusation in the other's tone. It wasn't *his* fault, after all, that none of the damned "not-me" generation drivers on the interstate had bothered to stop. "Men with mild concussions aren't usually up to using car radios," he said, perhaps more tartly than was called for.

"I know, Major." Saunders sighed. "And I'm sorry we couldn't prepare you better for handling him. But—well, you understand."

"I understand that your security wound up working against you, yes," Davidson said. "If a fugitive is carrying a weapon, we're supposed to know that in advance. If the fugitive *is* a weapon, we ought to know *that*, too."

"Dr. Garwood as walking time bomb?" Saunders's lip twitched. "Yes, you mentioned that characterization of him a few minutes ago, during your debriefing."

Davidson only vaguely remembered calling Garwood that. "You disagree?"

"On the contrary, it's an uncomfortably vivid description of the situation," Saunders said grimly.

"Yeah." Davidson braced himself. "And now my men and I are in the same boat, aren't we?"

"Hardly," Saunders shook his head. The neutral expression, Davidson noted, was back in place. "We're going to keep the three of you here for awhile, just to be on the safe side, but I'm ninety-nine percent certain there's no danger of the same . . . effect . . . developing."

"I hope you're right," Davidson said. Perhaps a gentle probe . . . "Seems to me, though, that if there's even a chance it'll show up, we deserve to know what it is we've got. And how it works."

"Sorry, Major," Saunders said, with a quickness that showed he'd been expecting the question. "Until an updated security check's been done on you, we can't consider telling you anything else. You already know more than I'm really comfortable with."

Which was undoubtedly the *real* reason Saunders was keeping them here. "And if my security comes through clean?" he asked, passing up the cheap-shot reminder of what Saunders's overtight security had already cost him tonight.

"We'll see," Saunders said shortly, getting to his feet and sliding the pad into his pocket. "The guard will escort you to your quarters, Major. Good-night."

He left the room, taking the tape recorder with him, and Davidson turned his attention back to Hamish. "Any post-hypnotic side effects I should watch out for, Doctor?" he asked, reaching down for his crutches and carefully standing up. He winced as he put a shade too much weight on his injured leg.

Hamish shook his head. "No, nothing like that."

"Good." He eyed the other. "I don't suppose *you* could give me any hints as to my prognosis here, could you?"

"You mean as regards the—ah—problem with Dr. Garwood?" Hamish shook his head, too quickly. "I really don't think you're in any danger, Major. Really I don't. The room here didn't suffer any damage while Dr. Saunders was writing down the equations you gave him, which implies you don't know enough to bother you."

Davidson felt the skin on the back of his neck crawl. So Garwood had been telling the truth, after all. It was indeed pure knowledge alone that was behind his walking jinx effect.

He shook his head. No, that was utterly impossible. Much easier to believe that whatever scam Garwood was running, he'd managed to take in Backdrop's heads with it, too.

Either way, of course, it made Garwood one hell of a dangerous man. "I see," he said through stiff lips. "Thank you, Doctor. Good night."

A Marine guard, dressed in one of Backdrop's oddly nonstandard jumpsuit outfits, was waiting outside the door as Davidson emerged. "If you'll follow me, Major," he said, and led the way to an undistinguished door a couple of corridors away. Behind the door, Davidson found a compact dorm-style apartment, minimally furnished with writing desk, chair, and fold-down bed, with a closet and bathroom tucked into opposite corners. Through the open closet door a half dozen orange jumpsuits could be seen hanging; laid out on the bed was a set of underwear and a large paper bag. "You'll need to put your clothing into the bag," the guard explained after showing Davidson around the room. "Your watch and other personal effects, too, if you would."

"Can I keep my cigarettes?"

"No, sir. Cigarettes are especially forbidden."

Davidson thought back to the car ride, and Garwood's disintegrating trick. "Because that effect of Garwood's destroys them?" he hazarded.

The Marine's face might have twitched, but Davidson wouldn't have sworn to it. "I'll wait outside, sir, while you change."

He retired to the hallway, shutting the door behind him. Grimacing, Davidson stripped and put on the underwear, wondering if it would help to tell Saunders that he'd already seen what the Garwood Effect did to cigarettes. The thought of spending however many days or weeks here without nicotine . . . Preoccupied, it was only as he was stuffing his clothes into it that his mind registered the oddity of using a *paper* bag instead of the usual plastic. A minor mystery, to go with all the major ones.

The Marine was waiting to accept the bag when he opened the door a minute later. Tucking it under his arm, he gave Davidson directions to the mess hall, wished him good night, and left. Closing the door and locking it, Davidson limped his way back to the bed and shut off the nightstand light.

Lying there, eyes closed, he tried to think; but it had been a long day, and between fatigue and the medication he'd been given for his leg he found he couldn't hold onto a coherent train of thought, and two minutes after hitting the pillow he gave up the effort. A minute after that, he was fast asleep.

The jumpsuits hanging in the closet were the first surprise of the new day.

Not their color. Davidson hadn't seen any other orange outfits in his brief walk through Backdrop the previous night, but he'd rather expected to be given something distinctive as long as he was effectively on security probation here. But it was something else that caught his attention, some oddity in the feel of the material as he pulled it off its wooden hanger. Examining the label, he quickly found the reason: the jumpsuit was one hundred percent linen.

Davidson frowned, trying to remember what Garwood had said about the potential targets of his strange destructive power. *Engines, plastics, televisions,* had been on the list; *modern conveniences* had also been there. Did synthetic fibers come under the latter heading? Apparently so. He pulled the jumpsuit on, fingers brushing something thin but solid in the left breast pocket as he did so. He finished dressing, then dug the object out.

It was a plastic card.

Frowning, Davidson studied it. It wasn't an ID, at least not a very sophisticated one. His name was impressed into it, but there was no photo, thumbprint, or even a description. It wasn't a digital key, or a radiation dosimeter, or a coded info plate, or anything else he could think of.

Unless . . .

He licked his lips, a sudden chill running up his back. *Engines, plastics, televisions* . . . He'd been wrong; the card *was* a dosimeter. A dosimeter for the Garwood Effect.

Whatever the hell the Garwood Effect was.

He gritted his teeth. *All right, let's take this in a logical manner.* The Garwood Effect destroyed plastics; okay. It also ruined car engines and pistols . . . and cigarettes and ash trays. What did all of those have in common?

He puzzled at it for a few more minutes before giving up the effort. Without more information he wasn't going to get anywhere . . . and besides, a persistent growling in his stomach was reminding him he was overdue for a meal. *No one thinks well on an empty stomach,* he silently quoted his grandfather's favorite admonition. Retrieving his crutches from the floor by his bed, he clumped off to the mess hall.

After the linen jumpsuit, he half expected breakfast to consist of nuts and berries served in coconut shells, but fortunately Backdrop hadn't gone quite that far overboard. The dishware was a somewhat nonstandard heavy ceramic, but the meal itself was all too military standard: nutritious and filling without bothering as much with flavor as one might like. He ate quickly, swearing to himself afterward at the lack of a cigarette to help bury the taste. Manhandling his tray to the conveyer, he headed off to try and find some answers.

And ran immediately into a brick wall.

"Sorry, Major, but you're not authorized for entry," the Marine guard outside the Backdrop garage said apologetically.

"Not even to see my own car?" Davidson growled, waving past the Marine at the double doors behind him. "Come on, now—what kind of secrets does anybody keep in a garage?"

"You might be surprised, sir," the guard said. "I suggest you check with Colonel Bidwell and see if he'll authorize you to get in."

Davidson gritted his teeth. "I suppose I'll have to. Where's his office?"

Colonel Bidwell was a lean, weathered man with gray hair and eyes that seemed to be in a perpetual squint. "Major," he nodded in greeting as Davidson was ushered into his office. "Sit down. Come to apply for a job?"

"More or less, sir," Davidson said, easing gratefully into the proffered chair. "I thought I could lend a hand in hunting down Dr. Garwood. Unless you've already found him, that is."

Bidwell gave him a hard look. "No, not yet. But he's in the Champaign-Urbana area—that's for damn sure— and it's only a matter of time."

Automatically, Davidson reached for a cigarette, dropping his hand to his lap halfway through the motion. "Yes, sir. I'd still like to help."

For a long moment Bidwell eyed him. "Uh-huh," he grunted. "Well, I'll tell you something, Major. Your file came through about an hour ago . . . and there are things there I really don't like."

"I'm sorry to hear that, sir," Davidson said evenly.

Bidwell's expression tightened a bit. "Your record shows a lot of bulldog, Major. You get hold of something and you won't let go until you've torn it apart."

"My superiors generally consider that an asset, sir."

"It usually is. But not if it gets you personally involved with your quarry. Like it might now."

Davidson pursed his lips. "Has the colonel had a chance to look over the rest of my file? Including my success rate?"

Bidwell grimaced. "I have. And I still don't want you. Unfortunately, that decision's been taken away from me. You're already here, and it's been decided that there's no point in letting you just spin your wheels. So. Effective immediately, you're assigned to hunter duty. Long-range duty, of course—we can't let you leave Backdrop until your updated security check is finished. You'll have a desk and computer in Room 138, with access to everything we know about Dr. Garwood."

Davidson nodded. Computer analysis was a highly impersonal way to track down a quarry, but he knew from long experience that it could be as effective as actually getting into the field and beating the bushes. "Understood, sir. Can I also have access to the less secure areas of Backdrop?"

Bidwell frowned. "Why?"

"I'd like to get into the garage to look at my car, for one thing. Garwood may have left a clue there as to where he was headed."

"The car's already been checked over," Bidwell told him. "They didn't find anything."

Davidson remained silent, his eyes holding Bidwell's, and eventually the colonel snorted. "Oh, all right." Reaching into his desk, he withdrew a small card and scribbled on it. "Just to get you off my back. Here—a Level One security pass. And that's it, so don't try to badger me for anything higher."

"Yes, sir." The card, Davidson noted as he took it, was a thickened cardboard instead of standard passcard plastic. Not really surprising. "With your permission, then, I'll get straight to work."

"Be my guest," Bidwell grunted, turning back to his paperwork. "Dismissed."

"What in blazes happened to it?" Davidson asked, frowning into the open engine compartment. After what had happened to his cigarettes and gun, he'd rather expected to find a mess of shattered metal and disintegrated plastic under the hood of his car. But *this*—

"It's what happens to engines," the mechanic across the hood said vaguely, his eyes flicking to Davidson's orange jumpsuit.

Davidson gingerly reached in to touch the mass of metal. "It looks half melted."

"Yeah, it does," the mechanic agreed. "Uh . . . if that's all, Major, I have work to get to."

*All right,* Davidson thought grimly to himself as he

clumped his way back down the corridor. *So this Garwood Effect doesn't affect everything the same way. No big deal—it just means it'll take a little more work to track down whatever the hell is going on here, that's all.*

What it didn't mean was that he was going to toss the towel and give up. Colonel Bidwell had been right on that count, at least; he did indeed have a lot of bulldog in him.

Dr. James Garwood was one of that vanishingly rare breed of scientist who was equally at home with scientific hardware as he was with scientific theory. A triple-threat man with advanced degrees in theoretical physics, applied physics, and electrical engineering, he was a certified genius with a proven knack for visualizing the real-world results of even the most esoteric mathematical theory. He'd been a highly-paid member of a highly respected research group until two years previously, when he'd taken a leave of absence to join the fledgling Backdrop Project. From almost the beginning it seemed he'd disagreed with Saunders's policies and procedures until, three months ago, he'd suddenly disappeared.

And that was the entire synopsis of Garwood's life since coming to Backdrop. Seated before the computer terminal, Davidson permitted himself an annoyed scowl. So much for having access to everything that was known about Dr. Garwood.

Of Garwood since his break there was, of course, nothing; but the files did contain a full report of the efforts to find him. The FBI had been called in early on, after which the National Security Agency had gotten involved and quickly pulled the rest of the country's intelligence services onto the case. In spite of it all, Garwood had managed to remain completely hidden until the report of yesterday's incident at the Springfield bus station had happened to catch the proper eye.

After three months he'd been caught . . . and promptly lost again.

Davidson gritted his teeth, forcing himself not to

dwell on his failure. Bidwell had been right: too much emotional involvement had a bad tendency to cloud the thinking.

But then, there was more than one form of emotional involvement. Leaning back in his seat, stretching his injured leg out beneath the desk, he closed his eyes and tried to become Dr. James Garwood.

For whatever reason, he'd decided to quit Backdrop. Perhaps he and Saunders had argued one too many times; perhaps the presence of the Garwood Effect had finally gotten too much for him to take. Perhaps—as he'd claimed on the ride last night—he truly felt that Backdrop was a danger and that the best thing for him to do was to abandon it.

So all right. He'd left . . . and managed to remain hidden from practically everybody for a solid three months. Which implied money. Which usually implied friends or relatives.

Opening his eyes, Davidson attacked the keyboard again. Family . . .? Negative—all members already interviewed or under quiet surveillance. Ditto for relatives. Ditto for friends.

Fine. Where else, then, could he have gotten money from? His own bank accounts? It was too obvious a possibility to have been missed, but Davidson keyed for it anyway. Sure enough, there was no evidence of large withdrawals in the months previous to his abrupt departure from Backdrop. He went back another year, just to be sure. Nothing.

Behind him, the door squeaked open, and Davidson turned to see a young man with major's oak leaves on his jumpsuit step into the room. "Major Davidson, I presume," the other nodded in greeting. "I'm Major Lyman, date coordinator for Backdrop Security."

"Nice to meet you," Davidson nodded, reaching back to shake hands.

"Colonel Bidwell told me you've been co-opted for the Garwood birdhunt," Lyman continued, glancing over Davidson's shoulder at the computer screen. "How's it going?"

"It might go better if I had more information on Garwood's activities at Backdrop," Davidson told him. "As it is, I've got barely one paragraph to cover two years out of the man's life—the two most important years, yet."

Lyman nodded. "I sympathize, but I'm afraid that's per the colonel's direct order. Apparently he thinks the full records would give you more information about what Backdrop is doing than he wants you to have."

"And Backdrop is doing something he doesn't want anyone to know about?" Davidson asked.

Lyman's face hardened a bit. "I wouldn't make vague inferences like that if I were you, Major," he said darkly. "You wouldn't have been allowed to just waltz into the Manhattan Project and get the whole story, either, and Backdrop is at least as sensitive as that was."

"As destructive, too." Davidson held a hand up before Lyman could reply. "Sorry—didn't mean it that way. Remember that all I know about this whole thing is that Garwood can use it to wreck cars and cigarettes."

"Yeah—the walking time bomb, I hear you dubbed him." Lyman snorted under his breath. "It's hoped that that . . . side effect, as it were . . . can be eliminated. Hoped a *lot*."

"Can't argue with that one," Davidson agreed. So his description of Garwood as a walking time bomb was being circulated around Backdrop. Interesting that what had been essentially a throwaway line would be so widely picked up on. He filed the datum away for possible future reference. "You think Garwood can help get rid of it if we find him?"

Lyman shrugged. "All I know is that my orders are to find him and get him back. What happens after that is someone else's problem. Anyway . . . my office is down the hall in Room One Fifty—let me know if you need anything."

"Thanks."

Lyman turned to go, then paused. "Oh, by the way . . . if your computer seems to go on the blink, don't waste time fiddling with it. Just call Maintenance and they'll take care of it."

Davidson frowned. "Computers go on the blink a lot around here?"

The other hesitated. "Often enough," he said vaguely. "The point is, just tell Maintenance and let them figure out whether to fix or replace."

"Right."

Lyman nodded and left, and Davidson turned back to his terminal. So computers were among the modern conveniences subject to attack by the Garwood Effect . . . and it reminded Davidson of something else he'd planned to try.

It took a few minutes of searching, but eventually he found what he was looking for: a list of maintenance records, going all the way back to Backdrop's inception two years ago. Now, with a little analysis . . .

An hour later he straightened up in his chair, trying to work the cramps out of his fingers and the knot out of his stomach. If ever he'd needed confirmation of Garwood's story, he had it now. The amount of wrecked equipment coming up from the offices and experimental areas to Maintenance was simply staggering: computers, all kinds of electronic equipment, plastic-based items—the list went on and on. Even the physical structure of Backdrop itself was affected; a long report detailed instance after instance of walls that had been replastered and ceilings that had had to be shored up. That it was a result of Backdrop's work was beyond doubt: a simple analysis of the areas where damage had occurred showed steadily increasing frequency the closer to the experimental areas one got. To the experimental areas, and to Garwood's office.

And the analysis had yielded one other fact. The damage had been slowly increasing in frequency over the two years Garwood had been with Backdrop . . . until the point three months back when he'd left. After that, it had dropped nearly to zero.

Which meant that Garwood hadn't been lying. He was indeed at the center of what was happening.

*A walking time bomb.* Davidson felt a shiver run up his back. If Garwood remained at large . . . and if the Garwood Effect continued to increase in strength as it had over the past two years . . .

With a conscious effort he forced the thought from his mind. Worry of that sort would gain him nothing. Somewhere, somehow, Garwood had to have left a trail of some sort. It was up to Davidson to find it.

He fumbled for a cigarette, swore under his breath. Leaning back in his seat again, he closed his eyes. *I am James Garwood,* he told himself, dragging his mind away from the irritations of nicotine withdrawal and willing his thoughts to drift. *I'm in hiding from the whole world. How exactly—exactly—have I pulled it off?*

## III

*. . . times e to the gamma one t.*

Garwood circled the last equation and laid down the pencil, and for a minute he gazed at the set of equations he'd derived. It was progress of a sort, he supposed; he *had* gotten rid of the gamma zero factor this time, and that was the one the computer had been having its latest conniption fits over. Maybe this time the run would yield something useful.

Or maybe this time the damn machine would just find something else to trip over.

Garwood gritted his teeth. *Stop it!* he ordered himself darkly. Self-pity was for children, or for failures. Not for him.

Across the tiny efficiency apartment, the computer terminal was humming patiently as it sat on the floor in the corner. Easing down into a cross-legged sitting position on the floor, Garwood consulted his paper and maneuvered his "remote arm" into position. The arm was pretty crude, as such things went: a long dowel rod reaching across the room to the terminal with a shorter one fastened to it at a right angle for actually hitting the keys, the whole contraption resting on a universal pivot about its center. But crude or not, it enabled him to enter data without getting anywhere near the terminal, with the result that this terminal had already outlasted all the others he'd used since fleeing Backdrop. He only wished he'd thought of this trick sooner.

Entering the equations was a long, painstaking job, made all the more difficult by having to watch what he was doing through a small set of opera glasses. But finally he hit the return key for the last time, keying in the simultaneous-solutions program already loaded. The terminal beeped acknowledgment, and with a grunt Garwood got stiffly back into his chair. His stomach growled as he did so, and with a mild shock he saw that it was ten-thirty. No wonder his stomach had been growling for the past hour or so. Getting up, rubbing at the cramps in his legs, he went over to the kitchen alcove.

To find that he'd once again let his supplies run below acceptable levels. "Blast," he muttered under his breath, and snared his wallet from the top of the dresser. There was a burger place a few blocks away that might still be open . . . but on the other hand, his wad of bills was getting dangerously thin, and when this batch was gone there wouldn't be any more. For a moment he studied the terminal's display with his opera glasses, but the lack of diagnostic messages implied that nothing immediate and obvious had tripped it up. Which meant that it would probably be chugging away happily on the equations for at least another half hour. Which meant there was plenty of time for him to skip the fast food and walk instead to the grocery store.

The overhead lights were humming loudly as Garwood started across the store's parking lot, and for a moment he fantasized that he was out in some exotic wilderness, circled by giant insects made of equal parts firefly and cicada. Out in the wilderness, away from Backdrop and the curse that hounded him.

It might come to that eventually, he knew. Even if he was able to continue eluding the searchers Saunders had scouring the area, he still couldn't stay here. His carefully engineered sublet would last only another five weeks, his dwindling bankroll dropping near zero at about the same time. Leaving him a choice between surrender and finding a job.

Both of which, he knew, really boiled down to the same thing. Any job paying enough for him to live on would leave a trail of paper that would bring Saunders's people down on him in double-quick time. Not to mention the risk he would present to the people he'd be working with.

He grimaced. A walking time bomb, that Intelligence major—Davidson—had dubbed him. A part of Garwood's mind appreciated the unintended irony of such a characterization; the rest of it winced at the truth also there.

The grocery store, not surprisingly, was quiet. Wrestling a cart that seemed determined to veer to the left, he went up and down the aisles, picking out his usual selection of convenience foods and allowing his nerves to relax as much as they could. There were probably some people somewhere who truly disliked supermarkets and the efficient long-term storage of food that made them possible; but if there were, the number must be vanishingly small. As a result, grocery stores were near the top of the short list of places where Garwood could feel fairly safe. As long as he stayed away from the cigarettes and smoking paraphernalia, he could be reasonably certain that nothing would break or crumble around him.

He collected as many packages as he estimated would fit into two bags and headed for the checkout. There, the teen-aged girl manning the register—or possibly she was a college student; they all looked equally young to him these days—gave him a pleasant smile and got to work unloading his cart. Listening to the familiar beep of the laser scanner, Garwood pulled out his wallet and watched the march of prices across the display.

The cart was still half full when a jar of instant coffee failed to register. The girl tried scanning it four times, then gave up and manually keyed the UPC code into her register. The next item, a frozen dinner, was similarly ignored. As was the next item . . . and the next . . . and the next . . .

"Trouble?" Garwood asked, his mouth going dry.

"Scanner seems to have quit," she frowned, tapping the glass slits as if trying to get the machine's attention. "Funny—they're supposed to last longer than this."

"Well, you know how these things are," Garwood said, striving for nonchalance even as his heart began to pound in his ears.

"Yeah, but this one was just replaced Saturday. Oh, well, that's progress for you." She picked up the next item and turned back to her register.

Almost unwillingly, Garwood bent over and peered into the glass. Behind it, the laser scanner was dimly visible. Looking perfectly normal . . . *No*, he told himself firmly. *No, it's just coincidence. It has to be. Nobody hates laser grocery scanners, for God's sake.* But even as he fought to convince himself of that, a horrible thought occurred to him.

Perhaps it was no longer necessary for anyone to hate laser grocery scanners directly. Perhaps all it took now was enough people hating the lasers in self-guided weapons systems.

A dark haze seemed to settle across his vision. It had started, then; the beginning of the end. If a concerted desire to eliminate one incarnation of a given technology could spill over onto another, then there was literally nothing on the face of the earth that could resist Garwood's influence. His eyes fell on the packages of frozen food before him on the counter, and a dimly remembered television program came to mind. A program that had showed how the root invention of refrigeration had led to both frozen foods and ICBMs . . .

The girl finished packing the two paper bags and read off the total for him. Garwood pulled out the requisite number of bills, accepted his change, and left. Outside, the parking lot lights were still humming their cicada/

firefly song. Still beckoning him to the safety of the wilderness.

A wilderness, he knew, which didn't exist.

The bags, light enough at the beginning of the walk, got progressively heavier as the blocks went by, and by the time he reached the door to his apartment house his arms were starting to tremble with the strain. Working the outside door open with his fingertips, he let it close behind him and started up the stairs. A young woman was starting down at the same time, and for an instant, just as they passed, their eyes met. But only for an instant. The woman broke the contact almost at once, her face the neutral inward-looking expression that everyone seemed to be wearing these days.

Garwood continued up the stairs, feeling a dull ache in the center of his chest. The "not-me" generation. Everyone encased in his or her own little bubble of space. *So why should I care, either?* he thought morosely. *Let it all fall apart around me. Why am I killing myself trying to take on decisions like this, anyway? Saunders is the one in charge, and if he says it'll work, then whatever happens is his responsibility. Right?*

The computer had finished its work. Setting the bags down, Garwood dug out his opera glasses again and studied the display. The machine had found three solutions to his coupled equations. The first was the one he'd already come up with, the one that had started this whole mess in the first place; the second was also one he'd seen before, and found to be mathematically correct but non-physical. The third solution . . .

Heart thudding in his ears, Garwood stepped to the table and reached to the ashtray for one of the loose cigarettes lying there. The third solution was new . . . and if it contained the build-in safeguard he was hoping to find . . .

He picked up one of the cigarettes. Squeezing it gently between thumb and fingertips, he gazed at the formula through his opera glasses, letting his eyes and thoughts linger on each symbol as he ticked off the seconds in his mind. At a count of *ten* he thought he felt a softness in the cigarette paper; at *twenty-two*, it crumbled to powder.

Wearily, he brushed the pieces from his hand into the garbage. Twenty-two seconds. The same length of time it had taken the last time . . . which meant that while it wasn't getting any worse, it wasn't getting any better, either.

Which probably implied this was yet another walk down a blind alley.

For a moment he gazed down at the cigarettes. A long time ago he'd believed that this field contained nothing but blind alleys—had believed it, and had done all he could to persuade Saunders of it, too. But Saunders hadn't believed . . . and now, Garwood couldn't afford to, either. Because if there weren't any stable solutions, then this curse would be with him forever.

Gritting his teeth, he stepped over to the counter and began unloading his groceries. Of course there was a stable solution. There *had* to be.

The only trick would be finding it before his time ran out.

## IV

"Well," Davidson said, "at least he's staying put. I suppose that's *something*."

"Maybe," Lyman said, reaching over Davidson's shoulder to drop the report back onto his desk. "A broken laser scanner is hardly conclusive evidence, though."

"Oh, he's there, all right," Davidson growled, glaring at the paper. His fingertips rubbed restlessly at the edge of his desk, itching to be holding a cigarette. Damn Saunders's stupid rule, anyway. "He's there. Somewhere."

Lyman shrugged. "Well, he's not at any hotel or motel in the area—that much is for sure. We've got taps on all his friends around the country, checking for any calls he might make to them, but so far that's come up dry, too."

"Which means either he's somehow getting cash in despite the net, or else he's been holed up for nearly three weeks without any money. How?"

"You got me," Lyman sighed. "Maybe he had a wad of cash buried in a safe deposit box somewhere in town."

"I'd bet a couple of days' salary on that," Davidson agreed. "But any such cash had to *come* from somewhere. I've been over his finances four times. His accounts have long since been frozen, and every cent he's made since coming to Backdrop has been accounted for."

Lyman grimaced. "Yeah, I know—I ran my own check on that a month ago. You think he could be working transient jobs or something? Maybe even at that supermarket where the laser scanner broke?"

Davidson shook his head. "I tend to doubt it—I can't see someone like Garwood taking the kind of underground job that doesn't leave a paper trail. On the other hand . . . do we know if he was ever in Champaign before?"

"Oh, sure." Lyman stepped around to Davidson's terminal, punched some keys. "He was there—yeah, there it is," he said over his shoulder. "A little over two and a half years ago, on a seminar tour."

Davidson frowned at the screen. Princeton, Ohio State, Illinois, Cal Tech—there were over a dozen others on the list. Silently, he cursed the bureaucratic foot-dragging that was still keeping his full security clearance from coming through. If he'd had access to all this data three weeks ago . . . "Did it occur to anyone that Garwood just *might* have made some friends during that trip that he's now turning to for help?

"Of course it did," Lyman said, a bit tartly. "We've spent the last three weeks checking out all the people he met at that particular seminar. So far he hasn't contacted any of them."

"Or so they say." Davidson chewed at his lip. "Why a seminar tour, anyway? I thought that sort of thing was reserved for the really big names."

"Garwood is big enough in his field," Lyman said. "Besides, with him about to drop behind Backdrop's security screen, it was his last chance to get out and around—"

"Wait a second," Davidson interrupted him. "He was already scheduled to come to Backdrop? I thought he came here only two years ago."

Lyman gave him an odd look. "Yes, but Backdrop didn't even exist until his paper got the ball rolling. I thought you knew that."

"No, I did not," Davidson said through clenched teeth. "You mean to tell me Backdrop was *Garwood's* idea?"

"No, the project was Saunders's brainchild. It was simply Garwood's paper on—" he broke off. "On the appropriate subject," he continued more cautiously, "that gave Saunders the idea. And that made Backdrop possible, for that matter."

"So Garwood did the original paper," Davidson said slowly. "Saunders then saw it and convinced someone in the government to create and fund Backdrop. Then . . . what? He went to Garwood and recruited him?"

"More or less. Though I understand Garwood wasn't all that enthusiastic about coming."

"Philosophical conflicts?"

"Or else he thought he knew what would happen when Backdrop got going."

*The Garwood Effect*. Had Garwood really foreseen that fate coming at him? The thought made Davidson shiver. "So what it boiled down to is that Saunders approached Garwood half a year before he actually came to Backdrop?"

"Probably closer to a year. It takes a fair amount of time to build and equip a place like this—"

"Or put another way," Davidson cut him off, "Garwood knew a year in advance that he was coming here . . . and had that same year to quietly siphon enough money out of his salary to live on if he decided to cut and run."

Lyman's face seemed to tighten, his eyes slightly

unfocused. "But we checked his pre-Backdrop finances. I'm sure we did."

"How sure? And how well?"

Lyman swore under his breath. "Hang on. I'll go get another chair."

It took them six hours; but by the end of that time they'd found it.

"I'll be damned," Lyman growled, shutting off the microfiche record of Garwood's checking account and calling up the last set of numbers on the computer. "Fifteen thousand dollars. Enough for a year of running if he was careful with it."

Davidson nodded grimly. "And don't forget the per diem he would have gotten while he was on that seminar tour," he reminded the other. "If he skimped on meals he could have put away another couple of thousand."

Lyman stood up. "I'm going to go talk to the colonel," he said, moving toward the door. "At least we know now how he's doing it. We can start hitting all the local landlords again and see which of them has a new tenant who paid in cash."

He left. *Great idea*, Davidson thought after him. *It assumes, of course, that Garwood didn't find a sublet that he could get into totally independently of the landlords. In a college town like Champaign that would be easy enough to do.*

The financial data was still on the display, and Davidson reached over to cancel it. The screen blanked; and for a long moment he just stared at the flashing cursor. "All right," he said out loud. "But why pick Champaign as a hideout in the first place?"

Because his seminar tour had taken him through there, giving him the chance to rent a safety deposit box? But the same tour had also taken him to universities in Chicago and Seattle, and either one of those metro areas would have provided him a far bigger haystack to hide in.

So why Champaign?

Garwood was running—that much was clear. But was he running *away* from something, or running *toward* something? Away from his problems at Backdrop, or toward—

Or toward a solution to those problems?

His fingers wanted a cigarette. Instead, he reached back to the keyboard. Everything about the Champaign area had, not surprisingly, been loaded into the computer's main database in the past three weeks. Now if he could just find the right question to ask the machine.

Five minutes later, on his second try, he found it.

There were men, Davidson had long ago learned, who could be put at a psychological disadvantage simply by standing over them while they sat. Colonel Bidwell, clearly, wasn't one of them. "Yes, I just got finished talking to Major Lyman," he said, looking up at Davidson from behind his desk. "Nice bit of work, if a little late in the day. You here to make sure you get proper credit?"

"No, sir," Davidson said. "I'm here to ask for permission to go back to Champaign to pick up Dr. Garwood."

Bidwell's eyebrows raised politely. "Isn't that a little premature, Major? We haven't even really gotten a handle on him yet."

"And we may not, either, sir, at least not the way Major Lyman thinks we will. There are at least two ways Garwood could have covered his trail well enough for us not to find it without tipping him off. But I think I know another way to track him down."

"Which is . . .?"

Davidson hesitated. "I'd like to be there at the arrest, sir."

"You bargaining with me, Major?" Bidwell's voice remained glacially calm, but there was an unpleasant fire kindling in his eyes.

"No, sir, not really," Davidson said, mentally bracing himself against the force of the other's will. "But I submit to you that Garwood's arrest is unfinished business, and that I deserve the chance to rectify my earlier failure."

Bidwell snorted. "As I said when you first came in, Major, you have a bad tendency to get personally involved with your cases."

"And if I've really found the way to track Garwood down?"

Bidwell shook his head. "Worth a commendation in my report. Not worth letting you gad about central Illinois."

Davidson took a deep breath. "All right, then, sir, try this: if you don't let *me* go get him, someone else will have to do it. Someone who doesn't already know about the Garwood Effect . . . but who'll have to be told."

Bidwell glared up at him, a faintly disgusted expression on his face. Clearly, he was a man who hated being maneuvered . . . but just as clearly, he was also a man who knew better than to let emotional reactions cloud his logic.

And for once, the logic was on Davidson's side. Eventually, Bidwell gave in.

He stood at the door for a minute, listening. No voices; nothing but the occasional creaking of floorboards. Taking a deep breath, preparing himself for possible action, he knocked.

For a moment there was no answer. Then more creaking, and a set of footsteps approached the door. "Who is it?" a familiar voice called.

"It's Major Davidson. Please open the door, Dr. Garwood."

He rather expected Garwood to refuse; but the other was intelligent enough not to bother with useless gestures. There was the click of a lock, the more elongated tinkle of a chain being removed, and the door swung slowly open.

Garwood looked about the same as the last time Davidson had seen him, though perhaps a bit wearier. Hardly surprising, under the circumstances. "I'm impressed," he said.

"That I found you?" Davidson shrugged. "Finding people on the run is largely a matter of learning to think the way they do. I seem to have that knack. May I come in?"

Garwood's lip twisted. "Do I have a choice?" he asked, taking a step backwards.

"Not really." Davidson walked inside, eyes automatically sweeping for possible danger. Across the room a computer terminal was sitting on the floor, humming to itself. "Rented?" he asked, nodding toward it.

"Purchased. They're not that expensive, really, and renting them usually requires a major credit card and more scrutiny than I could afford. Is that how you traced me?"

"Indirectly. It struck me that this was a pretty unlikely town for someone to try and hide out in . . . unless there was something here that you needed. The Beckman Institute's fancy computer system was the obvious candidate. Once we had that figured out, all we had to do was backtrack all the incoming modem links. Something of a risk for you, wasn't it?"

Garwood shook his head. "I didn't have any choice. I needed the use of a Cray Y-MP, and there aren't a lot of them around that the average citizen can get access to."

"Besides the ones at Stanford and Minneapolis, that is?"

Garwood grimaced. "I don't seem to have any secrets left, do I? I'd hoped I'd covered my trail a little better than that."

"Oh, we only got the high points," Davidson assured him. "And only after the fact. Once we knew you were here for the Beckman supercomputer it was just a matter of checking on which others around the country had had more than their share of breakdowns since you left Backdrop."

Garwood's lips compressed into a tight line, and something like pain flitted across his eyes. "My fault?"

"I don't know. Saunders said he'd look into it, see if

there might have been other causes. He may have something by the time we get you back."

Garwood snorted. "So Saunders in his infinite wisdom is determined to keep going with it," he said bitterly. "He hasn't learned anything at all in the past four months, has he?"

"I guess not." Davidson nodded again at the terminal. "Have *you*?" he asked pointedly.

Garwood shook his head. "Only that the universe is full of blind alleys."

"Um." Stepping past Garwood, Davidson sat down at the table. "Well, I guess we can make that unanimous," he told the other. "I haven't learned much lately, either. Certainly not as much as I'd like."

He looked up, to find Garwood frowning at him with surprise. Surprise, and a suddenly nervous indecision . . . "No, don't try it, Doctor," Davidson told him. "Running won't help; I have men covering all the exits. Sit down, please."

Slowly, Garwood stepped forward to sink into the chair across from Davidson. "What do you want?" he asked carefully, resting his hands in front of him on the table.

"I want you to tell me what's going on," Davidson said bluntly. He glanced down at the table, noting both the equation-filled papers and the loose cigarettes scattered about. "I want to know what Backdrop's purpose is, why you left it—" he raised his eyes again— "and how this voodoo effect of yours works."

Garwood licked his lips, a quick slash of the tongue tip. "Major . . . if you had the proper clearance—"

"Then Saunders would have told me everything?" Davidson shrugged. "Maybe. But he's had three weeks, and I'm not sure he's ever going to."

"So why should I?"

Davidson let his face harden just a bit. "Because if Backdrop is a danger to my country, I want to know about it."

Garwood matched his gaze for a second, then dropped his eyes to the table, his fingers interlacing themselves into a tight double fist there. Then he took a deep breath. "You don't play fair, Major," he sighed. "But I suppose it doesn't really matter anymore. Besides, what's Saunders going to do? Lock me up? He plans to do that anyway."

"So what is it you know that has them so nervous?" Davidson prompted.

Garwood visibly braced himself. "I know how to make a time machine."

For a long moment the only sound in the room was the hum of the terminal in the corner . . . and the hazy buzzing of Garwood's words spinning over and over in Davidson's brain. "You *what?*" he whispered at last.

Garwood's shoulders heaved fractionally. "Sounds impossible, doesn't it? But it's true. And it's because of that . . ." he broke off, reached over to flick one of the loose cigarettes a few inches further away from him.

"Dr. Garwood—" Davidson licked dry lips, tried again. "Doctor, that doesn't make any sense. Why should a . . . a time machine—?" He faltered, his tongue balking at even suggesting such a ridiculous thing.

"Make things disintegrate?" Garwood sighed. "Saunders didn't believe it, either, not even after I explained what my paper really said."

The shock was slowly fading from Davidson's brain. "So what *did* it say?" he demanded.

"That the uncertainty factor in quantum mechanics didn't necessarily arise from the observer/universe interaction," Garwood said. "At least not in the usual sense. What I found was a set of self-consistent equations that showed the same effect would arise from the universe allowing for the possibility of time travel."

"And these equations of yours are the ones you recited to me when you wrecked my car and gun?"

Garwood shook his head. "No, those came later. Those were the equations that actually show how time travel is possible." His fingers moved restlessly, worrying at another of the cigarettes. "You know, Major, it would be almost funny if it weren't so deadly serious.

Even after Backdrop started to fall apart around us Saunders refused to admit the possibility that it was our research that was causing it. That trying to build a time machine from my equations was by its very nature a self-defeating exercise."

"A long time ago," Davidson said slowly, "on that car ride from Springfield, you called it subconscious democracy. That cigarettes disintegrated in your hand because some people didn't like smoking."

Garward nodded. "It happens to cigarettes, plastics—"

"How? How can people's opinions affect the universe that way?"

Garwood sighed. "Look. Quantum mechanics says that everything around us is made up of atoms, each of which is a sort of cloudy particle with a very high mathematical probability of staying where it's supposed to. In particular, it's the atom's electron cloud that shows the most mathematical fuzziness; and it's the electron clouds that interact with each other to form molecules."

Davidson nodded; that much he remembered from college physics.

"Okay. Now, you told me once that you hated being hooked by cigarettes, right? Suppose you had the chance—right now—to wipe out the tobacco industry and force yourself out of that addiction? Would you do it?"

"With North Carolina's economy on the line?" Davidson retorted. "Of course not."

Garwood lips compressed. "You're more ethical than most," he acknowledged. "A lot of the 'not-me' generation wouldn't even bother to consider that particular consequence. Of course, it's a moot question anyway— we both know the industry is too well established for anyone to get rid of it now.

"But what if you could wipe it out in, say, 1750?"

Davidson opened his mouth . . . closed it again. Slowly, it was starting to become clear. . . . "All right," he said at last. "Let's say I'd like to do that. What then?"

Garwood picked up one of the cigarettes. "Remember what I said about atoms—the atoms in this cigarette are only *probably* there. Think of it as a given atom being in its proper place ninety-nine point nine nine nine nine percent of the time and somewhere else the rest of it. Of course, it's never gone long enough to really affect the atomic bonds, which is why the whole cigarette normally holds together.

"But now *I* know how to make a time machine; and *you* want to eliminate the tobacco industry in 1750. *If* I build my machine, and *if* you get hold of it, and *if* you succeed in stamping out smoking, then this cigarette would never have been made and all of its atoms *would* be somewhere else."

Davidson's mouth seemed abnormally dry. "That's a lot of *ifs*," he managed.

"True, and that's probably why the cigarette doesn't simply disappear. But if enough of the electron clouds are affected—if they start being *gone* long enough to strain their bonds with the other atoms—then eventually the cigarette will fall apart." He held out his palm toward Davidson.

Davidson looked at the cigarette, kept his hands where they were. "I've seen the demo before, thanks."

Garwood nodded soberly. "It's scary, isn't it?"

"Yeah," Davidson admitted. "And all because I don't like smoking?"

"Oh, it's not just you," Garwood sighed. He turned his hand over, dropping the cigarette onto the table, where it burst into a little puddle of powder. "You could be president of Philip Morris and the same thing would happen. Remember that if a time machine is built from my equations, literally *everyone* from now until the end of time has access to the 1750 tobacco crop. And to the start of the computer age; and the inception of the credit card; and the invention of plastic." He rubbed his forehead wearily. "The list goes on and on. Maybe forever."

Davidson nodded, his stomach feeling strangely hollow. *A walking time bomb*, he'd called Garwood. *A time bomb*. No wonder everyone at Backdrop had been so quick to latch onto that particular epithet. "What about my car?" he asked. "Surely no one seriously wants to go back to the horse and buggy."

"Probably not," Garwood shook his head. "But the internal combustion engine is both more complicated and less efficient than several alternatives that were stamped out early in the century. If you could go back and nurture the steam engine, for instance—"

"Which is why the engine seemed to be trying to flow into a new shape, instead of just falling apart?" Davidson frowned. "It was starting to change into a steam engine?"

Garwood shrugged. "Possibly. I really don't know for sure why engines behave the way they do."

Almost unwillingly, Davidson reached out to touch what was left of the cigarette. "Why you?" he asked. "If your time machine is built, then everything in the world ought to be equally fair game. So why don't things disintegrate in *my* hands, too?"

"Again, I don't know for sure. I suspect the probability shifts cluster around me because I'm the only one who knows how to make the machine." Garwood seemed to brace himself. "But you're right. If the machine is actually made, then it's all out of my hands . . . and I can't see any reason why the effect wouldn't then mushroom into something worldwide."

A brief mental image flashed through Davidson's mind: a black vision of the whole of advanced technology falling to pieces, rapidly followed by society itself. If a superpower war of suspicion didn't end things even quicker. . . . "My God," he murmured. "You can't let that happen, Doctor."

Garwood locked eyes with him. "I agree. At the moment, though, you have more power over that than I do."

For a long minute Davidson returned the other's gaze, torn by indecision. He could do it—he *could* simply let Garwood walk. It would mean his career, possibly, but the stakes here made such considerations trivial. Another possibility occurred briefly to him. . . . "Why did you need the computer?" he asked Garwood. "What were you trying to do?"

"Find a solution to my equations that would allow for a safer form of time travel," Garwood said. "Something that would allow us to observe events, perhaps, without interacting with them."

"Did you have any luck?"

"No. But I'm not ready to give up the search, either. If you let me go, I'll keep at it."

Davidson clenched his jaw tightly enough to hurt. "I know that, Doctor," he said quietly. "But you'll have to continue your search at Backdrop."

Garwood sighed. "I should have known you wouldn't buck your orders," he said bitterly.

"And leave you out here, threatening a community of innocent bystanders?" Davidson retorted, feeling oddly stung by the accusation. "I have a working conscience, Doctor, but I also have a working brain. Backdrop is still the safest place for you to be, and you're going back there. End of argument." Abruptly, he got to his feet. "Come on. I'll have some of my people pack up your stuff and bring it to Backdrop behind us."

Reluctantly, Garwood also stood up. "Can I at least ask a favor?"

"Shoot."

"Can we drive instead of flying? I'm still afraid of what influence I might have on a plane's engines."

"If you can sit this close to that terminal without killing it, the engines should be perfectly safe," Davidson told him.

"Under the circumstances, 'should' is hardly adequate—"

"You're arguing in circles," Davidson pointed out. "If you get killed in a plane crash, how is anyone going to use your equations to build a time machine?"

Garwood blinked, then frowned. "Well . . . maybe I wouldn't actually die in the wreck."

"All right, fine," Davidson snapped, suddenly tired

of the whole debate. "We'll put an impact bomb under your seat to make sure you'll die if we crash. Okay?"

Garwood's face reddened, and for a second Davidson thought he would explode with anger of his own. But he didn't. "I see," he said stiffly. "Very well, then, let's find a phone booth and see what Saunders says. You *will* accept suggestions from Saunders, won't you?"

Davidson gritted his teeth. "Never mind. You want to sit in a car for fourteen hours, fine. Let's go; we'll radio Chanute from the car and have them call in the change of schedule to Backdrop. And arrange for a quiet escort."

## V

"I hope you realize," Garwood said heavily, "that by bringing me back you're putting everyone in Backdrop at risk."

Saunders raised polite eyebrows. Polite, stupidly unconcerned eyebrows. "Perhaps," he said. "But at least here we understand what's going on and can take the appropriate precautions. Unlike the nation at large, I may add, which you're just spent nearly four months putting at similar risk. Under the circumstances, I'm sure you'd agree that one of our concerns now has to be to keep you as isolated from the rest of the country as possible." He shrugged. "And as long as you have to be here anyway, you might as well keep busy."

"Oh, of course," Garwood snorted. "I might as well help Backdrop to fall apart that much soo—"

He broke off as a muffled cracking sound drifted into the room. "More of the plaster going," Saunders identified it off-handedly. "Nice to hear again after so long."

Garwood felt like hitting the man. "Damn it all, Saunders," he snarled. "Why won't you listen to reason? A working time machine *cannot be made*. The very fact that Backdrop is falling apart around me—"

"Proves that the machine *can* be made," Saunders cut him off. "If you'd stop thinking emotionally for a minute and track through the logic you'd realize that."

Abruptly, all the vaguely amused patience vanished from his face, and his eyes hardened as they bored into Garwood's with an unexpected intensity. "Don't you understand?" he continued quietly. "When you left, the probability-shift damage to Backdrop dropped off to near zero. Now that you're back, the destruction is on the increase again."

"Which is my point—"

"No; which is *my* point," Saunders snapped. "The probability-shift effect cannot exist if a working time machine isn't possible."

"And yet that same effect precludes the manufacture of any such machine," Garwood pointed out. "As I've explained to you at least a hundred times."

"Perhaps. But perhaps not. Even given that the concept of time-travel generates circular arguments in the first place, has it occurred to you that a working time machine might actually prove to be a *stabilizing* factor?"

Garwood frowned. "You mean that if we have the theoretical capability of going back and correcting all these alterations of history then the wild fluctuations will subside of their own accord?"

"Something like that," Saunders nodded. "I did some preliminary mathematics on that question while you were gone and it looks promising. Of course, we won't know for sure until I have all the equations to work with."

"And what if you're wrong?" Garwood countered. "What if a working time machine would simply destabilize things further?"

A flicker of Saunders's old innocent expression crossed the man's face. "Why, then, we won't be able to make one, will we? The components will fall apart faster than we can replace them."

"In which event, we're back to the probability-shift effect being a circular paradox," Garwood sighed. "If it prevents us from building a time machine, there's no time travel. If there's no time travel, there's no change in probabilities and hence no probability-shift effect."

"As I said, time travel tends to generate paradoxes

like that." Saunders pursed his lips. "There's one other possibility that's occurred to me, though. The man who brought you back from Champaign—Major Davidson—said in his report that you'd been trying to find an alternative solution to the time travel equations. Any luck?"

Garwood shook his head. "All I found was blind alleys."

"Maybe you just didn't get to look long enough."

Garwood eyed him. "Meaning . . .?"

"Meaning that one other possible explanation of the probability-shift effect is that there is indeed another set of solutions. A set that will let us build the machine and still be able to go back and change things."

Garwood sighed. "Saunders . . .don't you see that all you're doing is just making things worse? Isn't it bad enough that things fall apart around me? Do you want to see it happening on a global scale? Stabilization be damned: a time machine—a real, functional time machine—would be the worst instrument of destruction ever created. *Ever* created."

"All I know," Saunders said softly, "is that anything the universe allows us to do *will* eventually be done. If *we* don't build the machine, someone else will. Someone who might not hesitate to use it for the mass destruction you're so worried about."

Garwood shook his head tiredly. The discussion was finally turning, as he'd known it eventually would, onto all too familiar territory: the question of whether or not the fruits of Backdrop's labor would would be used responsibly by the politicians who would inherit it. "We've gone round and round on this one," he sighed, getting to his feet. "Neither of us is likely to change the other's mind this time, either. So if you don't mind, it's been a long drive and I'd like to get some rest."

"Fine." Saunders stood, too. "Tomorrow is soon enough to get back to work."

In the distance, the sound of more cracking plaster underlined his last word. "And if I refuse?" Garwood asked.

"You won't."

"Suppose I do?" Garwood persisted.

Saunders smiled lopsidedly and waved a hand in an all-encompassing gesture. "You talk too contemptuously about the 'not-me' generation to adopt their philosophy. You won't turn your back on a problem this serious . . . especially given that it's a problem partially of your own creation."

For a long moment Garwood considered arguing the latter point. It had been Saunders, after all, who'd pushed Backdrop into existence and then dragged him into it.

But on the other hand, it wasn't Saunders who knew how to build the damn time machine.

Wordlessly, he turned his back on the other and headed for the door. "Rest well," Saunders called after him.

His office, when he arrived there the next morning, was almost unrecognizable.

Two pieces of brand-new equipment had been shoe-horned into the already cramped space, for starters: a terminal with what turned out to be a direct line to the Minneapolis Cray III supercomputer lab, and an expensive optical scanner that seemed set up to read typewritten equations directly onto the line. *So Saunders is capable of learning,* Garwood thought sardonically, careful not to touch either instrument as he gave them a brief examination. The electronic blackboard that had fallen apart shortly before he left Backdrop was gone, replaced by an old-fashioned chalk-on-slate type, and his steel-and-plastic chair had been replaced by a steel-and-wood one. Even his desk looked somehow different, though it took him a long minute to realize why.

All the piles of papers had been changed.

Silently, he mouthed a curse. He hadn't expected the papers to remain untouched—Saunders would certainly have ransacked his desk in hopes of finding the rest of his time-travel equations—but he hadn't expected everything to get so thoroughly shuffled in the process.

Clearly, Saunders had gone about his task with a will and to hell with neatness; just as clearly, it was going to take most of the day to put things back where he could find them again. With a sigh, he sank gingerly into his new chair and started restacking.

It was two hours later, and he was not quite halfway through the task, when there was a knock on the door. "Come in, Saunders," he called.

It wasn't Saunders. "Hello, Dr. Garwood," Major Davidson nodded, throwing a glance around the room. "You busy?"

"Not especially." Garwood looked up at him. "Checking to make sure I'm still here?"

Davidson shrugged fractionally, his gaze steady on Garwood. "Not really. I believe Colonel Bidwell has been able to plug the hole you got out by the last time."

"I'm not surprised." The look in Davidson's eyes was becoming just the least bit unnerving. "May I ask why you're here, then?"

Davidson pursed his lips. "The random destruction has started up again since we got in last night."

"This surprises you?"

Davidson opened his mouth; closed it. Tried again. "I'd . . . rather hoped you weren't so clearly the pivotal point of the effect."

"I thought we'd discussed all that back in Champaign," Garwood reminded him. "I'm the only one who knows how to build the machine, so of course the probability-shift effect centers around me."

Davidson's eyes flicked to the computer terminal/ optical scanner setup. "And Saunders wants you to let him in on the secret."

"Naturally. I don't intend to, of course."

"And if he doesn't give you that choice?"

"Meaning . . .?"

"Meaning he tried once to use hypnosis to get your equations out of me. With you, the method would probably work."

Garwood's mouth felt dry. "He knows better than to

try something that blatant," he said. Even to himself the words didn't sound very convincing.

"I hope so. But if he doesn't . . . I trust you'll always remember that there's at least one other person in Backdrop who recognizes the danger your knowledge poses."

Garwood nodded, wishing he knew exactly what the man was saying. Was he offering to help Garwood escape again should that become necessary? "I'll remember," he promised. "You're going to be here for a while, then?"

Davidson smiled wryly. "They let me out on a tight rein to go after you, Doctor. That doesn't mean they want me running around loose with what I know about Backdrop. I'll be on temporary duty with the security office, at least for the foreseeable future." He paused halfway through the act of turning back toward the door. "Though I don't suppose the term 'foreseeable future' has quite the same meaning as it used to, does it?"

Without waiting for an answer, he nodded and left. *No, it doesn't*, Garwood agreed silently at the closed door. *It really doesn't*.

He thought about it for a long minute. Then, with a shiver, he turned back to his papers.

One by one, the leads faded into blind alleys . . . and two months later, Garwood finally admitted defeat.

"Damn you," he muttered aloud, slouching wearily in his chair as far away from his terminal as space permitted. "Damn you." An impotent curse hurled at the terminal, at the program, at the universe itself. "There has to be a way. There *has* to be."

His only answer was the vague and distant crash of something heavy, the sound muffled and unidentifiable. A piece of I-beam from the ceiling, he rather thought— the basic infrastructure of Backdrop had started to go the way of the more fragile plaster and electronics over the past couple of weeks. Saunders had spent much of that time trying to invent correlations between the increase in the destruction with some supposed progress in Garwood's mathematical work, and he'd come up with some highly imaginative ones.

But imaginative was all they were . . . because Garwood knew what was really happening.

Perversely, even as it blocked his attempts to find a safe method of time travel, the universe had been busily showing him exactly how to transform his original equations into actual real-world hardware.

It was, on one level, maddening. He would be sitting at his typewriter, preparing a new set of equations for the optical scanner to feed into the computer, when suddenly he would have a flash of insight as to how a properly tuned set of asynchronous drivers could handle the multiple timing pulses. Or he'd be waiting for the computer to chew through a tensor calculation and suddenly recognize that an extra coil winding superimposed on a standard transformer system could create both the power and the odd voltage patterns his equations implied. Or he'd even be trying to fall asleep at night, head throbbing with the day's frustrations, and practically see a vision of the mu-metal molding that would distort a pulsed magnetic field by just the right amount to create the necessary envelope for radiating plasma bursts.

And as the insights came more and more frequently— as a working time machine came closer and closer to reality—the environment inside Backdrop came to look more and more like a war zone.

Across the room the terminal emitted a raucous beep, signaling the possibility of parity error in its buffer memory. "Damn," Garwood muttered again and dragged himself to his feet. Eventually he would have to tell Saunders that his last attempts had gone up in the same black smoke as all the previous ones, and there was nothing to be gained by putting it off. Picking up his hardhat, he put it on and stepped out of his office.

The corridor outside had changed dramatically in the past weeks, its soothing pastel walls giving way to the stark metallic glitter of steel shoring columns. Senses alert for new ripples in the floor beneath him as well as for falling objects from above, he set off toward Saunders's office.

Luck was with him. The passages were relatively clear, with only the minor challenge of maneuvering past shoring and other travelers to require his attention. He was nearly to Saunders's office, in fact, before he hit the first real roadblock.

And it was a good one. He'd been right about the sound earlier; one of the steel I-beams from the ceiling had indeed broken free, creating a somewhat bowed diagonal across the hallway. A team of men armed with acetylene torches were cutting carefully across the beam, trying to free it without bringing more down.

"Dr. Garwood?"

Garwood focused on the burly man stepping toward him, an engineer's insignia glittering amid the plaster dust on his jumpsuit collar. "Yes, Captain?"

"If you don't mind, sir," the other said in a gravelly voice, "we'd appreciate it if you wouldn't hang around here any longer than necessary. There may be more waiting to come down."

Garwood glanced at the ceiling, stomach tightening within him as he recognized the all-too-familiar message beneath the other's words. It wasn't so much interest in Garwood's safety as it was concern that the cloud of destruction around him might wind up killing one of the workers. Briefly, bitterly, Garwood wondered if this was how Jonah had felt during the shipboard storm. Before he'd been thrown overboard to the whale . . . "I understand," he sighed. "Would you mind passing a message on to Dr. Saunders when you have the chance, then, asking him to meet me at my office? My phone's gone out again."

"A lot of 'em have, Doctor," the engineer nodded. "I'll give him the message."

Garwood nodded back and turned to go—

And nearly bumped into Major Davidson, standing quietly behind him.

"Major," Garwood managed, feeling his heart settle down again. "You startled me."

Davidson nodded, a simple acknowledgment of Garwood's statement. "Haven't seen you in a while, Dr. Garwood," he said, his voice the same neutral as his face. "How's it going?"

Garwood's usual vague deflection to that question came to his lips . . . "I have to get back to my office," he said instead. "The workmen are worried about another collapse."

"I'll walk with you," Davidson offered, falling into step beside him.

Davidson waited until they were out of sight of the workers before speaking again. "I've been keeping an eye on the damage reports," he commented in that same neutral tone. "You been following them?"

"Not really," Garwood replied through dry lips. Suddenly there was something about Davidson that frightened him. "Though I can usually see the most immediate consequences in and around my office."

"Been some extra problems cropping up in the various machine and electronic fabrication shops, too," Davidson told him, almost off-handedly. "As if there's been some work going on there that's particularly susceptible to the Garwood Effect."

Garwood gritted his teeth. The Garwood Effect. An appropriate, if painful, name for it. "Saunders has had some people trying to translate what little he and the rest of the team know into practical hardware terms," he told Davidson.

"But they don't yet know how to build a time machine?"

"No. They don't."

"Do you?"

Again, Garwood's reflex was to lie. "I think so," he admitted instead. "I'm pretty close, anyway."

They walked on in silence for a few more paces. "I'm sure you realize," Davidson said at last, "the implications of what you're saying."

Garwood sighed. "Do try to remember, Major, that I was worrying about all this long before you were even on the scene."

"Perhaps. But my experience with scientists has been that you often have a tendency toward tunnel vision, so it never hurts to check. Have you told anyone yet? Or left any hard copies of the technique?"

"No, to both."

"Well, that's a start." Davidson threw him a sideways look. "Unfortunately, it won't hold anyone for long. If *I'm* smart enough to figure out what the increase in the Garwood Effect implies, Saunders is certainly smart enough to do the same."

Garwood looked over at Davidson's face, and the knot in his stomach tightened further as he remembered what the other had once said about Saunders using hypnosis against him. "Then I have to get away again before that happens," he said in a quiet voice.

Davidson shook his head. "That won't be easy to do a second time."

"Then I'll need help, won't I?"

Davidson didn't reply for several seconds. "Perhaps," he said at last. "But bear in mind that above everything else I have my duty to consider."

"I understand," Garwood nodded.

Davidson eyed him. "Do you, Doctor? Do you really?"

Garwood met his eyes . . . and at long last, he really *did* understand.

Davidson wasn't offering him safe passage to that mythical wilderness Garwood had so often longed for. He was offering only to help Garwood keep the secret of time travel out of Saunders's grasp. To keep it away from a world that such a secret would surely destroy.

Offering the only way out that was guaranteed to be permanent.

Garwood's heart was thudding in his ears, and he could feel sweat gathering on his upper lip. "And when," he heard himself say, "would your duty require you to take that action?"

"When it was clear there was no longer any choice," Davidson said evenly. "When you finally proved safe time travel was impossible, for instance. Or perhaps when you showed a working time machine could be built."

They'd reached the door to Garwood's office now. "But if I instead proved that the probability-shift effect would in fact keep a working time machine from actually being built?" Garwood asked, turning to face the other. "What then?"

"Then it's not a working time machine, is it?" Davidson countered.

Garwood took a deep breath. "Major . . . I want a working time machine built even less than you do. Believe me."

"I hope so," Davidson nodded, his eyes steady on Garwood's. "Because you and I may be the only ones here who feel that way . . . and speaking for myself, I know only one way to keep your equations from bringing chaos onto the world. I hope I won't have to use it."

A violent shiver ran up Garwood's back. "I do, too," he managed. Turning the doorknob with a shaking hand, he fled from Davidson's eyes to the safety of his office.

To the relative safely, anyway, of his office.

For several minutes he paced the room, his pounding heart only gradually calming down. A long time ago, before his break from Backdrop, he'd contemplated suicide as the only sure way to escape the cloud of destruction around him. But it had never been a serious consideration, and he'd turned instead to his escape-and-research plan.

A plan which had eventually ended in failure. And now, with the stakes even higher than they'd been back then, death was once again being presented to him as the only sure way to keep the genie in the bottle.

Only this time the decision wasn't necessarily going to be his. And to add irony to the whole thing, Davidson's presence here was ultimately his own fault. If he hadn't skipped out of Backdrop six months ago, the major would never even have come onto the scene.

Or maybe he would have. With the contorted circular logic that seemed to drive the probability-shift effect nothing could be taken for granted. Besides, if Davidson hadn't caught him, perhaps someone less intelligent would have. Someone who might have brushed aside his fears and forced him onto that airplane at Chanute AFB. If that had happened—if the effect had then precipitated a crash—

He shook his head to clear it. It was, he thought bitterly, like the old college bull sessions about free will versus predestination. There were no answers, ever; and you could go around in circles all night chasing after them. On one hand, the probability-shift effect could destroy engines; on the other, as Davidson himself had pointed out, it logically shouldn't be able to crash a plane that Garwood himself was on. . . .

Garwood frowned, train of throught breaking as a wisp of something brushed past his mind. *Davidson . . . airplane . . .?*

And with a sudden flood of adrenaline, the answer came to him.

Maybe.

Deep in thought, he barely noticed the knock at the door. "Who is it?" he called mechanically.

"Saunders," the other's familiar voice came through the panel.

Garwood licked his lips, shifting his mind as best he could back to the real world. The next few minutes could be crucial ones indeed . . . . "Come in," he called.

"I got a message that you wanted to see me," Saunders said, glancing toward the terminal as he came into the room. "More equipment trouble?"

"Always," Garwood nodded, waving him to a chair. "But that's not why I called you here. I think I may have some good news."

Saunders's eyes probed Garwood's face as he sank into the proffered seat. "Oh? What kind?"

Garwood hesitated. "It'll depend, of course, on just what kind of latitude you're willing to allow me—how much control I'll have on this—and I'll tell you up front that if you buck me you'll wind up with nothing. Understand?"

"It would be hard not to," Saunders said dryly, "con-

sidering that you've been making these same demands
since you got here. What am I promising not to interfere
with this time?"

Garwood took a deep breath. "I'm ready," he said, "to
build you a time machine."

## VI

Within a few days the Garwood Effect damage that had
been occurring sporadically throughout Backdrop's several fabrication areas jumped nearly eight hundred percent. A few days after that, repair and replacement
equipment began to be shipped into the complex at a
correspondingly increased rate, almost—but not quite—
masking the even more dramatic flood of non-damage-
control shipping also entering Backdrop. The invoice
lists for the latter made for interesting reading: esoteric
electronic and mechanical equipment, exotic metals,
specialized machine tools for both macro and micro
work, odd power supplies—it ran the entire gamut.

And for Davidson, the invoices combined with the
damage reports were all the proof he needed.

Garwood had figured out how to build his time machine. And was building it.

*Damn him.* Hissing between his teeth, Davidson
leaned wearily back into his chair and blanked the last
of the invoices from his terminal screen. So Garwood
had been lying through his teeth all along. Lying about
his fears concerning time travel; lying about his dis-
agreements with Dr. Saunders; lying about how noble
and self-sacrificing he was willing to be to keep the
world safe from the wildfire Garwood Effect a time
machine would create.

And Davidson, that supposedly expert reader of people, had fallen for the whole act like a novice investigator.

Firmly, he shook the thought away. Bruised pride
was far and away the least of his considerations at the
moment. If Garwood was building a time machine . . .

But *could* he in fact build it?

Davidson gnawed at the inside of his cheek, listening

to the logic spin in circles in his head. Garwood had suggested more than once that the Garwood Effect would destroy a time machine piecemeal before it could even be assembled. Had he been lying about that, too? It had seemed reasonable enough at the time . . . but then why would he and Saunders even bother trying? No, there had to be something else happening, something Garwood had managed to leave out of his argument and which Davidson hadn't caught on his own.

But whatever it was he'd missed, circumstances still left him no choice. Garwood had to be stopped.

Taking a deep breath, Davidson leaned forward to the terminal again and called up Backdrop's cafeteria records. If Garwood was working around the clock, as Davidson certainly would be doing in his place . . . and after a few tries he found what he was looking for: the records of the meals delivered to the main assembly area at the end of Backdrop's security tunnel. Scanning them, he found there had been between three and twelve meals going into the tunnel each mealtime since two days before the dramatic upsurge in Garwood Effect damage.

And Garwood's ordering number was on each one of the order lists.

Davidson swore again, under his breath. Of course Garwood would be spending all his time down the tunnel—after their last conversation a couple of weeks ago the man would be crazy to stay anywhere that Davidson's security clearance would let him get to. And he'd chosen his sanctuary well. Down the security tunnel, buried beneath the assembly area's artificial hill, it would take either a company of Marines or a medium-sized tactical nuke to get to him now.

Or maybe—just maybe—all it would take would be a single man with a computer terminal. A man with some knowledge of security systems, some patience, and some time.

Davidson gritted his teeth. The terminal he had; and the knowledge, and the patience. But as for the time . . . he would know in a few days.

If the world still existed by then.

## VII

The five techs were still going strong as the clocks reached midnight, but Garwood called a halt anyway. "We'll be doing the final wiring assembly and checkout tomorrow," he reminded them. "I don't want people falling asleep over their voltmeters while they're doing that."

"You really expect any of us to *sleep?*" one of the techs grumbled half-seriously.

"Well, *I* sure will," Garwood told him lightly, hooking a thumb toward the door. "Come on, everybody out. See you at eight tomorrow morning. Pleasant dreams."

The tech had been right, Garwood realized as he watched them empty their tool pouches onto an already cluttered work table: with the project so close to completion they *were* going to be too wired up for easy sleep. But fortunately they were as obedient as they were competent, and they filed out without any real protest.

And Garwood was alone.

Exhaling tiredly, he locked the double doors and made his way back to the center of the huge shored-up fabrication dome and the lopsided monstrosity looming there. Beyond it across the dome was his cot, beckoning him temptingly. . . . Stepping instead to the cluttered work table, he picked up a screwdriver set and climbed up through the tangle of equipment into the seat at its center. Fifteen minutes later, the final connections were complete.

It was finished.

For a long minute he just sat there, eyes gazing unseeingly at the simple control/indicator panel before him. It was finished. After all the blood, sweat, and tears—after all the arguments with Saunders—after the total disruption of his life . . . it was done.

He had created a time machine.

Sighing, he climbed stiffly down from the seat and returned the screwdrivers to their place on the work table. The next table over was covered with various papers; snaring a wastebasket, he began pushing the papers into it, tamping them down as necessary until the table was clear. A length of electrical cable secured the wastebasket to a protruding metal plate at the back of the time machine's seat, leaving enough room for the suitcase and survival pack he retrieved from beneath his cot. Two more lengths of cable to secure them . . . and there was just one more chore to do. A set of three video cameras stood spaced around the room, silent on their tripods; stepping to each in turn, he turned all of them on.

He was just starting back to the time machine when there was a faint sound from the double doors.

He turned, stomach tightening into a knot. It could only be Saunders, here for a late-night briefing on the day's progress. If he noticed that the cameras were running—realized what that meant—

The doors swung open, and Major Davidson stepped in.

Garwood felt an instantaneous burst of relief . . . followed by an equally instantaneous burst of fear. He'd specifically requested that Davidson not be cleared for this part of Backdrop. . . . "Major," he managed to say between suddenly dry lips. "Up—ah, rather late, aren't you?"

Davidson closed the doors, his eyes never leaving Garwood's face. "I only hope I'm *not* here too late," he said in a quiet voice. "You've done it, haven't you?"

Garwood licked his lips, nodded his head fractionally toward the machine beside him. "Here it is."

For a long moment neither man spoke. "I misjudged you," Davidson said at last, and to Garwood's ears there was more sorrow than anger in the words. "You talked a lot about responsibility to the world; but in the end you backed down and did what they told you to do."

"And you?" Garwood asked softly, the tightness in his stomach beginning to unknot. If Davidson was willing to talk first . . . to talk, and to listen. . . . "Have you thought through the consequences of *your* actions? You went to a lot of illegal trouble to get in here. If you kill me on top of that, your own life's effectively over."

A muscle in Davidson's cheek twitched. "Unlike you, Doctor, I don't just talk about responsibility. And there *are* things worth dying for."

Unbidden, a smile twitched at Garwood's lips. "You know, Major, I'm glad you came. It gives me a certain measure of hope to know that even in the midst of the 'not-me' generation there are still people willing to look beyond their own selfish interests."

Davidson snorted. "Doctor, I'll remind you that I've seen this nobility act of yours before. I'm not buying it this time."

"Good. Then just listen."

Davidson frowned. "To what?"

"To the silence."

"The—?" Davidson stopped abruptly; and all at once he seemed to get it. "It's *quiet*," he almost whispered, eyes darting around the room, coming to rest eventually on the machine beside Garwood. "But—the Garwood Effect—you've found a way to stop it?"

Garwood shook his head. "No, not really. Though I think I may understand it a bit better now." He waved a hand around the room. "In a sense, the trouble is merely that I was born at the wrong time. If I'd lived a hundred years earlier the culture wouldn't have had the technological base to do anything with my equations; if I'd been born a hundred years later, perhaps I'd have had the time and necessary mathematics to work out a safe method of time travel, leaving my current equations as nothing more than useless curiosities to be forgotten."

"I'd hardly call them useless," Davidson interjected.

"Oh, but they are. Or didn't you notice how much trouble the various fabrication shops had in constructing the modules for this machine?"

"Of course I did," Davidson nodded, a frown still hovering across his eyes. "But if the modules themselves were falling apart . . .?"

"How was I able to assemble a working machine?" Garwood reached up to touch one of the machine's supports. "To be blunt, I cheated. And as it happens, *you* were the one who showed me how to do it."

Davidson's eyes locked with his. "Me?"

"You," Garwood nodded. "With a simple, rather sarcastic remark you made to me back in my Champaign apartment. Tell me, what's the underlying force that drives the Garwood Effect?"

Davidson hesitated, as if looking for a verbal trap. "You told me it was the possibility that someone would use time travel to change the past—" He broke off, head jerking with sudden insight. "Are you saying . . .?"

"Exactly," Garwood nodded. "There's no possibility of changing the past *if my machine can only take me into the future.*"

Davidson looked up at the machine. "How did you manage that?"

"As I said, it was your idea. Remember when I balked at flying back here and you suggested putting a bomb under my seat to make sure a crash would be fatal?" Garwood pointed upwards. "If you'll look under the seat you'll see three full tanks of acetylene, rigged to incinerate both the rider and the machine if the 'reverse' setting is connected and used."

Davidson looked at the machine for a long moment, eyes flicking across the tanks and the mechanism for igniting them. "And that was really all it took?" he asked.

"That's all. Before I installed the system we couldn't even load the modules into their racks without them coming apart in our hands. Afterwards, they were still touchy to make, but once they were in place they were completely stable. Though if I disconnected the suicide system they'd probably fall apart en masse."

Slowly, Davidson nodded. "All right. So that covers the machine. It still doesn't explain what's happened to your own personal Garwood Effect."

"Do you really need an explanation for that?" Garwood asked.

Davidson's eyes searched his. "But you don't even know how well it'll work," he reminded Garwood. "Or if there are any dangerous side effects."

That thought had occurred to Garwood, too. "Ultimately, it doesn't matter. One way or another, this is my final ticket out of Backdrop. My equations go with me, of course—" he pointed at the secured wastebasket— "and all the evidence to date indicates Saunders and his team could work till Doomsday without being able to reproduce them."

"They know how to make the modules for this machine," Davidson pointed out.

"Only some of them. None of the really vital ones—I made those myself, and I'm taking all the documentation with me. And even if they somehow reconstructed them, I'm still convinced that assembling a fully operational machine based on my equations will be impossible." He paused, focused his attention on the cameras silently recording the scene. "You hear that, Saunders? Drop it. Drop it, unless and until you can find equations that lead to a safer means of time travel. You'll just be wasting your own time and the taxpayers' money if you don't."

Turning his back on the cameras, he climbed once again up into the seat. "Well, Major," he said, looking down, "I guess this is good-bye. I've . . . enjoyed knowing you."

"That's crap, Doctor," Davidson said softly. "But good luck anyway."

"Thanks." There were a handful of switches to be thrown—a dozen strokes on each of three keypads—and amid the quiet hum and vibration of the machine he reached for the trigger lever—

"Doctor?"

He paused. "Yes, Major?"

"Thanks," Davidson said, a faint smile on his lips, "for helping me quit smoking."

Garwood smiled back. "You're welcome."

Grasping the trigger lever, he pulled it.

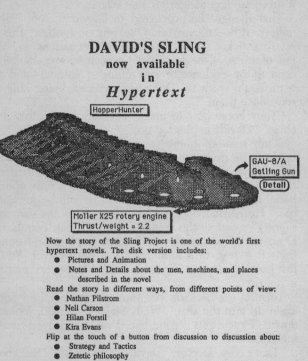